Choosing Forever

A CHERRY PEAK NOVEL

HANNAH COWAN

Also By Hannah

Swift Hat Trick trilogy

Lucky Hit

Between Periods

Blissful Hook

Overtime

Vital Blindside

Greatest Love series

Her Greatest Mistake

Her Greatest Adventure

His Greatest Muse

His Greatest Treasure

Their Greatest Strength

Cherry Peak series

Strung Along

Catching Sparks

Chasing Home

Stealing Sunshine

Choosing Forever

Amateurs In Love duet

Craving The Player

Taming The Player

Snowbell ridge

Snow Harm, No Foul

Till Cupid Do Us Part

Fake A Chance On Me

Harbour Of Hope

Power Shift

Anna's House
School
Bryce's house
Delaney's house
Darren's house
Town Hall
Bridal Shop
Rustic Ridge
Firestation
Shop
Brody and Anna's house
Peak Side
Guest house
Main House
CHERRY PEAK
STEELE RANCH
Steele Ranch

Loved By You - Chelsea Cutler	2:58
Penthouse - Kelsea Ballerini	3:03
The Last Time - Taylor Swift, Gary Lightbody	4:59
How Do We Stay In Love? - Blake Rose	2:40
20-20 - Ella Langley	3:15
Tastes Like You - Brett Young	3:21
All I Forgot - Ashley Cooke, Joe Jonas	2:58
This Town's Yours - Canaan Cox	2:56
I Almost Do - Taylor Swift	4:05
Done It By Now - Restless Road	3:24
Siren Sounds - Tate McRae	3:04
Take On The World - You Me At Six	4:31
Stranger - Stellar	2:12
Love In Letting Go - Warren Zeigers	3:20
Want This Beer - Josh Ross, Julia Michaels	2:40

For those of us who have made a mistake that we would have done anything to take back. This book is about second chances, because sometimes, that's all we need to make things right again.

PROLOGUE

FOURTEEN YEARS AGO

"You need a shower."

I snort a laugh and tug Delaney closer. The old bleachers are hard under my ass as I adjust myself, trying to get her on my lap already. There's nobody here anymore but us, and any minute now, the floodlights are going to turn off, drowning the field in darkness.

My girl never risks it, though. No matter how many times I get her alone up here after a game, she keeps me on my best behaviour.

"Yeah, I do," I reply.

She leans her head against my shoulder and whispers, "Not yet."

"No, not yet. I've still got you for a while. Your grandma loves me too much to give me hell for bringing you home a few minutes late."

"She'd love you even more if you followed her rules to a T."

"You know that's not true."

Her giggle strikes the softest parts of me. "Alright, fine."

"Did you see that the land behind the drive-in is still up for sale?"

"No. Have you been reading the newspaper again?" she teases.

I shrug, pushing forward. "I've just gotta keep an eye on things. We're going to be graduating high school soon, and once we're finished with university, I want to know where we'll live."

"And you think that land will still be for sale? In five years from now?"

"A guy can hope, Elle. I mean, it would be perfect for us. We could walk to the drive-in every weekend, and I bet we could hear the movies on the nights we wanted to just sit out on the porch. If you squint, you can see it from here. It's behind the goalpost."

"As long as we stay in this town and somehow convince our friends to stay here with us, I don't care where we live."

"Including the shack on Steele Ranch that Wade's been trying to tear down?"

"If you put a water line in and fixed up the bathroom so I could have a hot shower every day, yeah, I'd move there with you."

"I'm spoiled," I mumble softly.

Delaney runs her hand up and down my thigh, her lips ghosting across my jaw. "Have I told you that I love you recently? Like, in the last fifteen minutes?"

"You have, but I could hear it again. Especially since I just won yet *another* game for you."

"For me," she echoes, squeezing my knee. "You're sucking up for something."

"I'm not sucking up. I'm being sweet," I clarify with a smirk.

"You're always sweet. It's why I've kept you around so long."

I laugh, the sound low and rough. "You're my goddamn girl, Elle. You know that?"

"I think I've got a bit of a clue," she murmurs, twisting on the bleachers to gaze up at me.

Cupping her cheek, I thread my fingers through her long, soft hair and bring her in for a kiss. Her eyes flutter closed, and then the floodlights click off. The dark rolls in, creating a shield between us and the rest of Cherry Peak.

I've never needed to keep her hidden in the dark, though.

Delaney's my lifetime girl, and I'm looking forward to showing her off in the light for the rest of my life.

1

Delaney

PRESENT

IF I KNEW HOW DRASTICALLY ONE STAFFING CHANGE WOULD unravel my carefully constructed peace, I'd have stayed home this morning.

Instead, here I am, balancing one-legged on a child-sized chair with a chunk of hair in my mouth while my boss tells me the worst news in the history of bad news. I spit the hair out and wobble, my two palms smacking hard against the whiteboard.

"I think I misheard you," I croak.

The principal of Cherry Peak Elementary School almost appears flustered when she replies, "I'm sorry, Delaney. But I hope you understand why I chose to swap the classes this way. Daisy needs a chance to teach an older class."

"Can't she swap with Kimmy instead? The fourth graders are incredibly bright," I argue weakly.

I'd know, considering I taught them last year. I've taught every third-grade class for the last four years. In my eight years of teaching at this school, I've never been told only a week before classes start that I'm being switched to teach another grade. It's incredibly last-minute, and I've never liked sudden changes.

"Kimmy already shifted two years ago."

My throat is sticky when I carefully lower my feet to the ground and debate begging my boss to change her mind.

"I've already finished my lesson plan, and the classroom is nearly done, Penny."

Penny—Mrs. Ashford—tweaks the corners of her mouth into a small smile that looks too much like pity to give me any relief. It's the same type of smile that I saw for too long when I moved back to Cherry Peak. Plenty has changed since that day eight years ago, but still, too many things are the same.

"I know, and I wish I could change how last-minute this is. That's completely on me, but when I spoke to Daisy on my way here, she did offer to swap plans with you to help the transition."

"You already spoke with her?"

"I did. She's alright with the swap if you are. I would appreciate your acceptance with this, Delaney."

Ouch, that bites. Daisy is the newest teacher at the school and someone I consider a close friend. Because of that, she should have known I wouldn't want to make this change.

"Will I need to switch classrooms, or do I get to keep this one?" I ask, defeated.

This morning, I was up at dawn with a smoothie I made from the last of my orchard strawberries and an excitement to get the final touches done to my classroom. I've made improvements since last year and even picked up custom name tags for all the desks from a custom printer up in Calgary yesterday. It's bright and colourful in here but, most importantly, welcoming.

I learned early on in my teaching career that I didn't want the starched rainbows on the walls and sleek, beige chairs that nobody wanted to risk getting a sore bottom sitting on. The only acceptable decorations in my eyes were neon colours and fun, cheesy sayings scribbled all over the whiteboard and printed on poster paper. But then again, maybe that's just how I was raised.

Sneaking a look around me now, I can admit that I'll be

disappointed if the work I've done so far to liven this place up further this year was wasted.

"It would be easier if you swapped. Emails and letters have already gone out to parents letting them know classroom numbers. Of course, if that's going to be an issue . . ." She trails off, and from the quirk of her brow as she waits for an answer, I know better than to argue with her despite my frustration.

"No issue."

Her teeth gleam in the fluorescent lighting. "Wonderful! Thank you, Delaney. I'll leave you to get moved around, then."

Before I can worry about schooling my expression, she's spinning on the heels of her pumps and clip-clapping her way out of the classroom. I stare at the door once she's gone, afraid that if I move now, I'll wind up slamming it shut like an angry adolescent.

I readjust my metaphorical cap and, like I've done a million times already, push past my emotions and get to work. It's not the end of the world, and I refuse to treat it as such.

Darren Huntsly won't ruin my love for teaching the way he ruined Cherry Peak for me.

"I'm so sorry, Della. Penny totally railroaded me this morning. I assumed she'd talked to you about it first! Gosh, I should have known better and just turned her down."

I snap my eyes up from the tiny packets of sugar on the diner table, finding Daisy. She's out of breath as she grips the back of the booth and dives behind the table, her cheeks a bright pink.

My friend of only a year grabs my hands tightly, refusing to let them go again. "Are you mad at me? Please tell me you're not mad at me. I'm going to tell Penny I changed my mind and refuse to swap classes."

"Take a breath, Daisy. I'm not mad at you," I reassure her.

Mad isn't the way I would describe how I'm feeling right now. I knew realistically that Daisy wouldn't have done this to upset me. She knows why teaching the second graders this year is the *worst*-case scenario, and out of every woman I know in this town, Daisy Mitchell is the one I trust to watch my back the most.

"Okay, you're not mad. But you're upset. I'd be worried if you weren't. Tell me what I can do to help," she rushes out.

The gold band on her ring finger digs into my palm as she continues holding my hands. Bryce, her fiancée, has a matching one. They're simple placeholders until they get married and can give each other tattooed ones.

Saying Bryce Mitchell is going to take a while to get used to. For Daisy as well, I think.

"It feels like a terrible joke from the universe, doesn't it?" I ask.

Daisy smiles apologetically and puffs out a breath. When she releases my hands, it's so that she can wave down a waitress.

"What did you do recently to have karma snapping at your heels like this?"

"Your guess is as good as mine."

She tightens the clear elastic at the end of her over-the-shoulder braid and leans her elbows on the table. "I'm serious, Della. I'll call Penny right now and tell her that I'm not teaching your grade."

"It's not my grade. Not any more than the second was yours."

The waitress joins us in a blur of navy and the scent of fresh coffee. I turn away the coffee and a potential meal while Daisy does the opposite. She immediately takes a sip of the black coffee when we're alone again.

Before her plain white mug has been clunked down onto the table, she's asking, "Do you think you can do it? And don't just tell me what you think I want to hear. Tell me the truth."

"That depends on what you're asking about specifically."

I'm stalling. It's as obvious to her as it would be to a stranger on the street. The moment I accept that I don't know if I *can* do this, it becomes real. And that thought is enough to make nausea churn in my stomach.

Daisy blinks twice at me, her head tipping to the side. "Are you really going to try that? You know it won't work with me."

I wring my hands together, a clump of fear clogging my airway. The empty diner grows hotter until I'm positive I'm sweating through my blouse.

"Hey, talk to me, sweetie. Tell me that you're going to be okay, or I'm calling Penny right now and demanding she put things back the way they were," Daisy adds as gently as she can with her concern.

"No, don't do that," I mumble before clearing my throat. "I'm a grown woman and a professional. I've got this."

"I didn't ask you if you could handle it. I asked if you were going to be okay with it."

"While I appreciate you being so open to speaking up for me, I'm not going to get special treatment. And especially not because of this. I'm a fantastic teacher, and I love what I do. I love the kids and being a part of their journey in life. That's what matters, right?"

Daisy focuses on me, her eyes a bright blue that I swear I can see my reflection in. While they're usually full of life and excitement, right now, they're so pitifully sad that I have to fight to keep myself bunkered down in this booth.

"Two things can be true at once," she murmurs.

"And what two things are those?"

I regret my question immediately. There's no time to take it back before Daisy's reply comes.

"You can be all of those things and still not want to teach his daughter."

The way I flinch is ridiculous. My chest shrinks, growing too tight and confined.

"Please don't, Daisy."

"Tell Penny no, Delaney. Don't do this to yourself," she pleads, reaching across the table for my hands.

They're too slicked with sweat, so I tuck them into my lap with a brief shake of my head. That only makes Daisy's frown deeper, her eyes sadder. Everything about that grates on me. It isn't pity as much as it is pain for me and my jagged past in Cherry Peak. I'm not sure which would be worse at this point.

"I'm not saying no. But I appreciate you looking out for me, though."

"I'll always look out for you. We all will. Which is why I just don't think this is a good idea. If this is about wanting to prove something—"

I cut her off, my voice tight. "I don't need to prove anything to *anyone* in this town."

Just myself.

"No, you don't. And that's why I wish you'd turn this down."

"It was only a matter of time," I say, as if that helps stall the cracking in my chest.

After seven years of watching the only man I've ever loved raise his little girl, I thought I had at least one more year before I was forced to get to know her. To call her name every day, grade her tests, and help answer questions she doesn't know the answers to.

I've run out of time already. And despite the burn in the backs of my eyes at the mere thought of it, I know there isn't any escaping it now. There's no more escaping him and the pain of our past.

Darren Huntsly broke me eight years ago, and now . . . now, he's going to try and do it again. Only this time, it will be the little girl with her daddy's eyes who finishes me off.

2

Darren

I'M ONLY BACK IN CHERRY PEAK FOR FIVE MINUTES BEFORE I WANT to leave again.

The back seat of the car is whipped open the moment I park on the driveway. Abbie's hardly had a chance to finish her yawn and wake up from her sleep before her mother's diving in to unbuckle her.

"You were supposed to be home an hour ago!" Sasha scolds, a fiery glare aimed my way.

I ignore her evil eye, pretending I didn't see it in the rear-view before climbing out. My ex-wife is already bundling our daughter into her arms and pulling her out of my car by the time I reach them.

"There was an accident on the highway," I say shortly.

One that I worried we wouldn't make it past without running out of gas. We were at a standstill for four hours before they got the semi out of the way and could open one of the two lanes of traffic back up. What a phone call that would have been to her.

As expected, Sasha doesn't give a shit about my reasoning. "I wasn't expecting to be here waiting this long. Clearly, you could have given me a bit more clarity on the situation."

I take a moment to sort myself before replying, the long drive and current time taking its toll on my already dwindling patience. After riding such a high this past weekend, showing Abbie my favourite hidden camping spots in the mountains, I knew I'd be slapped by reality the moment we pulled back into Cherry Peak.

I've lived here my entire life, but the older I get, the more I've contemplated leaving. If I didn't have Abbie . . . I can't say if I wouldn't have already.

"You didn't need to pick her up tonight. She's tired, Sasha."

Abbie yawns again, loud enough to slice through the tension that's grown. "I just want to go to bed here, Dad."

"Let's go inside, then, sweetheart. You'll see your mom in the morning."

Sasha's fingers flex on Abbie's shoulders before falling away. If I thought I was getting the evil eye before, now it's downright murderous. It's almost more relaxing to see her be this pissed off at me than whatever the alternative is. This is the constant mood between us. It's familiar. Worse now that I'm changing plans on her without asking first.

With a huff, she butts me to the side and crouches in front of Abbie, smoothing her hands up and down her arms. The crinkle of her nose as she takes in the dirty fabric of our daughter's fall jacket makes me proud.

"Alright. I'll be back as soon as you're up tomorrow morning. We'll go out for breakfast to catch up, okay?"

"Okay, Mom," Abbie whispers.

"I love you. Go right to bed. You need to be getting back on your regular sleep schedule. I'm sure you were up far too late the last few nights."

Abbie blinks, recognizing the firm tone of Sasha's voice as a partial scolding.

"It's still summer break. Dad didn't let me stay up *that* late."

"We'll see you in the morning, Sasha," I say, inserting myself before she can continue with her backhanded comments.

She stands, pinning me with a narrowed gaze. "I'm serious."

"I know you are. And she still has a week to get back on a routine."

"You won't be feeling as casual about this come the first day of school. In case you forgot, this is your first year having to worry about it."

I dig my tongue into my cheek. Abbie snags my hand, and my attention snaps down to her. She yawns again, and I know without having to look at the time that we're well past her *bedtime*. Her obvious exhaustion is enough to have me cutting this conversation short.

"Good night, Sasha. I'll text you when we're up in the morning," I grit out before guiding Abbie away from the car. Without looking at my ex-wife again, I reach into the back seat and grab our two bags. "Have a great rest of your night."

"Well then, give me a hug, Abs. I'll see you tomorrow bright and early," she tells Abbie.

"'Night, Mom. Thanks for letting me stay here tonight."

"I'll have you all week. I suppose I shouldn't hog you."

I spin back around and join them before locking the car. "You heard her. Let's head in."

My daughter doesn't even attempt to take her bag from me, knowing I'd just tell her that I'll carry it. I'd laugh at that if it wasn't for the woman still looming like a storm cloud hovering above my head.

The instant Abbie turns her back to us and slumps her way up to the front door, Sasha's jabbing her finger into my chest. The shade of red on her cheeks is shocking, considering the lack of evening light.

"Don't argue with me in front of her like that, Darren! I swear, I knew you were going to do this when I agreed to let you take her for the weekend. Every time she comes back from one of your trips, she's got an attitude that I have to work through. You spoil her too much," she whisper-hisses.

I shake my head a single time and swallow my immediate

laugh. If there's one thing I've learned while co-parenting with a woman who only ever wants to see the worst in me is to learn when to keep my mouth shut and when to argue. Right now, arguing with Sasha is the last thing I want to do. It won't do anything but escalate the situation.

She might use giving me permission to take Abbie for the weekend as some form of leverage, but that's easy to shrug off. Our custody agreement is simple. It rotates every week with shared alternating holidays. If I want to take our daughter on a weekend trip to the mountains three hours away, I can do that without her permission, the same way she can take her to her new fiancé's parents' house without mine. I choose to ask for it because despite our disagreements, I still appreciate and respect her as Abbie's mother.

There's no leverage there for her to use.

With a blank expression, I gently push her finger away and nod to where her SUV is parked along the curb. "Go home, Sasha. I've got Abbie, and you'll see her in the morning."

Some of the ire dulls in her eyes. "Text me the minute she wakes up, Darren. I'm serious."

"I took a ton of photos of her while we were gone. I'll send those tonight."

It's as close to a peace offering as I've got in me tonight.

"Thank you. I'd appreciate that."

"Dad! Unlock the door, please," Abbie calls.

I back off Sasha and leave her on the driveway without another word. Once I'm coming up behind Abbie, she's the only thing on my mind.

"Don't start, Poppy."

"I haven't even said anything."

"You didn't need to. Your face says enough."

"So, then there's no point in me keeping my words to myself."

"We're not talking about this right now. I can handle Sasha."

The rough noise Poppy replies with is spot-on, really. I've been "handling" Sasha for years now, and I don't think I'm getting any better at it. If anything, it's the opposite.

I lean on my back foot and grimace when the heel of my boot sinks into the ground. The field I'm in is huge, empty, and fucking wet after the endless rain today. We're two hours north of Cherry Peak and a few gravel roads from the main highway on a plot of land my younger sister and her soon-to-be-husband have just purchased.

The woman herself is standing ankle-deep in mud and glaring at me with a fierceness that I've had to bear witness to for the last twenty-nine years. We're only one year apart, but fuck, she acts like she was born at least another five before I was.

Garrison, her fiancé, watches me from her side, his usual asshole expression set in place. I can't help but stare at his outfit, a laugh bubbling in my throat. Since the guy notices everything, he cocks a brow at me.

"Yes?"

"What the fuck are you wearing out here?"

"Don't tease him to try and distract us. We're talking about Sasha right now, D," Poppy pushes.

I leave that alone and drop my focus to the once-shining black shoes now sunken into the mud. "If you want to build a house out here, you can't be wearing those fancy shoes. The ground holds moisture. I thought you'd moved past the whole city boy thing."

"I came straight from the office," he grunts, lifting his foot and shaking it off. "My boots are at home."

"And what about you? There's no excuse for your fancy little booties," Poppy returns, toeing my boots with hers.

The pink cowboy boots she's had for years now are old and worn down, but still very her. I gave up wearing boots like that when I was a teen. If I wanted my toes to be squashed all the time, I'd buy cheap shoes a size too small. Cowboy boots are too damn expensive to be as uncomfortable as they are.

And my *"fancy little booties"* are dark brown work boots. The kind that are halfway between clunky and fashionable. Or so Bryce tells me. They were a gift from my closest girlfriend last Christmas.

"I carved four hours out of my day to be here today instead of heading back to work. Be nice to me," I tell her.

"The least you could have done is brought my niece with you so I'd have someone to giggle with while you boys talk."

I scoff a laugh. "We all know you wouldn't be standing around giggling with or without Abbie. You have more to say about the house than Garrison does."

"She has an entire notebook full of ideas for you," Garrison says.

"Did you bring it with you?"

Poppy nods and reaches into her purse to pull it out. "Of course I did. I need this to be perfect. After the house is finished, I'll never be moving again."

"This will be forever, then?" I ask, already knowing the answer.

It's been forever for Poppy and Garrison since he arrived in Cherry Peak and sent my sister into a tailspin. Now, they're finally ready to put down permanent roots somewhere a bit closer to home. In a perfect world, those roots would be in Cherry Peak itself, but my sister has always been too big for our hometown. She has dreams that would be smothered there. The grumpy billionaire in front of me right now gave her the push to make them a reality instead.

Poppy leans into his side, gazing up at him softly while saying, "Yeah, it's forever."

I look away, unable to keep watching that all-consuming love pulse between them. A gnawing sensation grows in my stomach, and I take a step back, eyeing the open field. It's easy enough to distract myself with the possibilities this generous amount of land offers for their potential house. I've never designed anything for family before, but this is what I love. It's my bread and butter and the entire fucking Thanksgiving dinner.

Between drowning in architecture, volunteering at the fire station, and spending time with Abbie, I've worked hard to keep myself busy these last few years.

Busy is good. It leaves me less time to sit and think.

"Good. I've already given you the warning, but I know how to burn a body. Bet I'd be pretty good at it too," I say.

Poppy rolls her eyes, sighing. "Hasn't it gotten old threatening him by now?"

"No."

"Death by fire isn't appealing to me," Garrison states, deadpan.

I tip my chin. "Glad we have an understanding. Now, back to the house. Show me your designs."

Poppy's quick to hand the book over, and I peel the front page open to an explosion of pink and purple pen. The heart at the top corner with a P+G scribbled inside has me forcing back a laugh before I scroll my eyes down the rest of the page.

"Obviously, I don't need all of these things," she says, watching me as I read.

I flip to the second page. "If you're building a forever home, you should have everything you want. Doesn't matter if it's a need or not."

"That's so mature of you," Poppy teases, flicking me in the jaw.

Swatting her away, I fix my gaze on Garrison. "I'm assuming the budget covers everything in this notebook?"

"There is no budget."

Show-off. I'm pretty sure my sister just shivered, and now I'm grossed out.

"Alright. I've never worked with family before, but I'm going to keep my process the same if that's fine with you. I'm assuming I'll just have you constantly calling me for updates."

Poppy flicks me again. "Don't make it sound like such a bad thing. I call you twice a week already."

"That's for Abbie, and you know it."

"Only every two weeks it is." She uses a long, manicured nail to tap at one of the points on the second page. "This one is really important to me. I know I didn't initially mention it, but Wade mentioned Kip getting old . . ."

Garrison steps in to finish. "He's not riding him enough. Old man's got bad hips now, and Eliza gave him too much shit about hopping up on Kip all the time. Johnny's been working him still, but it isn't the same. Kip's not himself."

Wade and Eliza Steele run the biggest cattle ranch in Alberta right out of Cherry Peak. Johnny, being Wade's officially unofficial protégé, has been floating around our friend group for a while now, but this is the first I'm hearing of Wade finally feeling his age. For a full-blooded rancher to not be able to ride his horse has got to be more painful than his hips. And knowing that Garrison's built a bond almost as tight with the black beast of a horse as Wade has makes it easier to understand why he'd be so worried.

"So, you want a stable for him on your land," I say, piecing it together.

"I know you don't do ranch projects, but I was hoping you'd say yes because I'm your sister. Special family privileges, right?"

"It's not that I don't do ranch projects, Pops."

"Okay, so you just don't like them. Either way, I'm really hoping you'll say yes to this one. It would need to be big enough for both Kip and Honey," she says.

It's not all that surprising that she'd want to have the horse she's taken to bonding with too. Not to mention that I've heard Kip and Honey are attached at the hip now. The last time I was on Steele Ranch was for Brody Steele's wedding, and even then, I didn't pay much attention to the horses in the pastures.

"The Steeles are letting you take them both?" I ask.

Poppy smirks. "Of course they are. All I had to do was ask nicely."

"Right. I'm sure that was it."

"Well? Will you do it?" She grips my arm and widens her eyes, begging me with fluttering lashes and a pout that she still pulls off as well as back when we were kids.

"I'll do it. But only if you don't give me a hard time about it. The reason I don't do ranch work is because I can't take the barked orders and blunt answers from grumpy, stubborn old men." I stare at Garrison, and he huffs a low laugh in response.

Knowing he's got the point of my words, I carry on. "Before the blueprints are finalized, you'll need to put me in contact with the builder you're going to use. Do you have zoning markers for the property already?"

"I've got everything in the car. If you need anything else, I'll get it for you," Garrison answers.

"Thanks. Is it okay if I take this notebook home with me? I'll go through it this week and start brainstorming."

"Sure. Make sure to show my ideas to Abbie so she knows she can design her own room at Aunt Poppy's."

"You let her do that and she'll beg me to add a waterslide and a heated pool in it."

"My little water bug," Poppy sings, smoothing her hand out on my arm before dropping it. "I love her."

"She's very loveable," I poke.

The clouds above us break, and thunder claps above the mountains behind us before the first pelt of rain hits my nose. I stifle a groan and adjust the cap on my head, pulling the brim down to shield my face.

"Great. I'm so done with this goddamn rain," Poppy snaps, using her arm to cover her face.

Garrison's quick to shrug out of his suit jacket and hold it above her head. The fawning look she gives him encourages me to get us moving.

"We can finish talking about this when you're in Cherry Peak this weekend."

Poppy nods, and the three of us rush toward the road. The ground is already flooding with pools of water, and by the time we make it out of the mess, the legs of my jeans are covered in mud. I stomp my feet on the gravel to dislodge the mud in the soles of my boots, but there's not much use trying to clean off here.

I wipe a hand down my face and wait until Garrison's grabbed a thick black folder from their car before saying, "I'll let you know when I'm home."

"Yes, you will. And don't think that I've forgotten about what we were talking about before you got all architect on me. You can't keep taking shit from Sasha. It's called co-parenting for a reason. If you want to spoil your daughter during her last weekend of pre-school freedom, you do that. It's what makes you a good dad," Poppy snips.

"I'll keep that in mind, Pops."

Garrison opens the door of his Mercedes-Benz and places an encouraging hand on Poppy's back. I nod at her, waving for her to get in.

She hesitates with a hand on the door. "I love you, D. If you ever need anything—"

"I'll call."

Garrison helps her into the car before turning to me. "Thank you for taking this on, Darren. I appreciate it."

"Keep treating my sister the way you are, and you won't have to thank me for anything."

He lingers for a beat later, like maybe he wants to say something else, but eventually slips into the passenger side without another word. I watch their headlights fan out on the road and the smoke of the exhaust puff into the rain before tugging my car door open and finally slipping inside.

My clothes weigh a thousand pounds as I crank the heat and drop my head back against the seat. The silence pricks at my skin, growing worse with every second it takes to crank the radio and yank my hat off. I drop it onto the passenger seat and use the hem of my shirt to dry my face.

The loud buzzing coming from the cup holder draws my attention. My phone dances around as three texts come in one after the other. I try to dry my hands as best as I can before grabbing it.

Now, seeing my best friend's name on the screen wouldn't usually send me into a spiral, but today seems to be truly one of a kind because suddenly, I want to throw up.

> Bryce: You didn't hear it from me, but shit, Darren. Don't lose your mind on me, okay?
>
> Bryce: Daisy isn't Abbie's teacher anymore.
>
> Bryce: Delaney is.

I drop the phone and lose it somewhere beneath my seat. *What?*

3

Delaney

THE THING ABOUT PISSING OFF THE UNIVERSE IS THAT YOU NEVER actually know when it's going to strike back at you.

For me, that day is now. The first one of the brand-new school year.

My fingers slip from the corner of my desk when I push to a proper stand and force myself to smile at the first few students who come barrelling into my classroom. The tension in my muscles causes me to stand like I have a wedgie, and that quite possibly is one of the worst looks I could have right now.

I won't let my terrible morning snowball into a terrible day. There are too many left in the school year to already start on the wrong foot. Sure, yeah, I poured rotten milk into my cereal this morning and made a toaster waffle that was freezer burnt. Then ripped the back of the skirt I'd initially squeezed myself into when I bent over to put my shoes on before quickly changing into the only clean backup I had, which is both frumpy and the colour of mustard on a hot dog bun that's been left in the sun for hours. But who cares?

Certainly, not me.

I love dressing like someone's grandmother on the first day

of school when twenty students and a few sets of parents are going to be getting their first impressions of me.

Heat caresses my thighs as I rub my sweaty palms down my skirt, hating the way the material scratches against my skin.

It's fine. *It's. Fine.*

The little boy who comes storming my way first has the energy of someone who's chugged a pot of coffee before leaving his house this morning. I don't allow myself to flinch back the way I want to and instead offer my hand for him to shake.

"Hi! I'm Ms. Delaney. Or Ms. Dell, whichever you want to call me. What's your name?"

"Zachary! My mom's outside. Can I sit anywhere?"

"It's nice to meet you, Zachary. Do you go by Zach for short?"

He pushes his blond hair back dramatically, grinning. "My friends call me Zach."

"Well, I hope to be your friend by the end of the school year. For now, you can find your desk down this first row here," I say, pointing to my left.

I was here for hours, writing out names on makeshift tags and sticking them onto the desks. If I hadn't been moved from my original classroom, there would be no need for this quick effort because all their names would be stuck nice and pretty to their desks with custom tags.

Again, it's fine.

"Okay!" Zachary runs down the aisle, searching for his name.

The next few students who arrive are followed by their parents, and with every hand I shake and person I greet, I pray they can't tell how sweaty my palms are. I glance up at the clock above the door and pluck at the top button of my blouse, debating going to the window and opening it so I can cool down.

In a town as small as Cherry Peak, the whole *everyone knows everyone* saying is completely true. It's the worst part about living here. Nearly every set of parents I speak to, I already know. Apart from the families living in the surrounding munici-palities—mainly ranches—it's impossible to meet anyone new here.

It's not necessary for every student's parent to come and meet me on the first day, but plenty do regardless. I think it gives them some peace of mind. A reminder that the person they're putting in charge of their children's well-being for eight hours in the day is someone they know outside of these walls.

That's why once I've checked off every student's name but one, I feel a hot flush of anger course through me. The little girl I've been dreading seeing over the last week is the only one not here yet, and I know better than anyone to put that blame on her father.

If he wanted to make a fool out of me again, he didn't have to involve his daughter. All he'd have to do is bring Sasha with him to my classroom, and if that were the case, they'd have been the first ones here. Darren's had a habit of not watching the clock for the majority of his life.

The chatter in the room is nothing but static in my ears as I adjust the waistband of my skirt and swallow the bile clawing up my throat.

I tell myself that I'll give them one more minute. Anything longer than that and they'll miss the first bell. God, I don't know if this is the usual for them or an anomaly. I've never stayed in the hallway this late to see because I didn't want to risk seeing them. All I have to go on is what I knew ten years ago.

For the last eight of those years, this is how I've lived my life. Never lingering anywhere, whether that's the grocery store or the sidewalks downtown. If there's a chance of seeing Darren or Abbie, I'm rushing through my tasks with my head down. I haven't been lucky every time, but at least he seems to want to avoid me as much as I want to avoid him.

That's the thing about heartbreak in a small town. There's nowhere to hide from the person who broke you.

"Alright," I start, turning to face the class. Screw Darren and his mind games. "Please make sure you've all found your assigned seats, and if you need any help—"

The sound of shoes clapping against the floor in the hallway shuts me up. I snap my head in the direction of the noise.

The little girl who pops up in the doorway grins wide while trying to catch her breath. "Hi! I'm Abbie!"

It's nearly impossible to school my features in a way that I trust hides the devastation I feel at the cheery, high-pitched voice. I swallow, pressing a hand against my middle and hoping it looks like I'm brushing off my blouse instead of like I'm trying to hold my guts from spilling out through reopened wounds.

Abbie's just as beautiful as she was when I saw her last. Her hazel hair is up in two braided pigtails, and her excited brown eyes . . . I avoid looking at them for longer than a second. There's no backpack with her, and her pretty yellow dress isn't smothered with a jacket, so she must have found her locker well enough. But once I force myself to look up and behind her, it's made clear that she's alone.

My hand falls to my side when I force a smile. "Hi, Abbie. I'm Ms. Delaney."

"Or Ms. Dell!" Zach shouts.

I release a breath. "Yes, or Ms. Dell."

"I'm sorry for being late. Am I in trouble?" she asks plainly, eyes held on me.

Lifting a hand, I point at the last empty desk. Hopefully, the shakiness isn't obvious to anyone but me. "No. No, you're not in trouble. The bell is about to ring, though, so if you can take the empty seat behind Rosie, we'll wait for it before taking attendance."

When I was going through my student list, I'm ashamed to admit that I debated putting Abbie at the back of the class. It would have been completely selfish and pitiful, but for one second, I did consider it. If only to create more distance between us.

She's not to blame for the past, though. And putting her at

the back of the classroom wouldn't do anything but punish her. That's not who I am. Regardless of my past with her father, Abbie's innocent.

"Thanks!" she says before scurrying into the room and slipping between the desks to the only empty one.

The bell rings while she's sliding into her seat. I glance at the open classroom door and give it a subtle roll of my eyes. Not every parent comes to meet their child's teacher on the first day anymore, but my gut tells me that he chose not to for a reason.

And that reason is me.

Darren

FUCK.

I don't care how long we've been apart; there isn't anyone who knows Delaney Brooks the way I do. Eight years change a lot about a person, but it will never be long enough to touch the things engrained in you. And the Delaney I knew hated nothing more than being late for something.

I heard the first bell ring two minutes ago, and shit, I should not still be searching for a parking spot in this crowded lot. Instead, I *should* be taking the opportunity handed to me and getting the hell away from this place. She's already going to be pissed at me, and interrupting her class is only going to make matters worse.

So why am I whipping into the only open spot I can see and clunking the gearshift into Park?

The silence is startling when I get out of the car and palm the door, wishing it were colder against my hot palm. I shove it closed and start toward the school.

There's something fundamentally wrong with me. Not just mentally, but emotionally. Because there's no reason for me to be going inside the school. Not a single one.

Delaney hates me. Rightfully so. And Abbie doesn't need me to hold her hand with these things anymore. The last time I tried, she shook me off to appear grown-up, only to crawl into my arms afterward and tell me she still loves me because apparently, I looked *that* broken by it.

I can tell myself that I'm going for her and so that I can make a good impression on her teacher, but she'll be the only one to believe that lie.

Sasha certainly won't once she learns that Daisy's no longer her teacher, if she doesn't already.

Squeezing the brim of my ball cap, I walk faster across the wet pavement. I curse myself a little harder once I've gotten into the school and take the path I've had memorized since I was a student here.

Every classroom is the same, and the hallway is painted with the school colours the way they were back then, only refreshed after years of wear. You could blindfold me and I'd be able to locate each bathroom and make my way to the locker rooms.

I try to think about my time here as little as I can. Every year after I turned fifteen is splashed with the reminder of what I lost and can never get back.

With a too-familiar pang in my stomach, I head straight for Daisy's old classroom. It was only last year that I was inside of it helping her and Bryce fix up the mess left from a bunch of shit teenagers with nothing better to do than mess with the school.

Now, I'm here for utterly selfish reasons.

The door is closed, but I can hear her voice through it. My chest grows so tight I push at it with my palm out of fear of my lungs popping. There's nothing I can do to ignore the effects of that twinkling falsetto and the memories it dredges up like a net full of ghosts. I lean a shoulder against the wall and steal a look down the hallway to make sure nobody's watching before heaving in a breath.

Leave, Darren.

But I can't. I want to see her. Even if it only lasts long enough for her to slam the door back in my face.

It's been so long . . . and shit. I only need a second to confirm she actually is still in town despite never seeing her anymore. Regardless of how many corners I look around or shops I wander into with no purpose other than to see if she's there, she never is.

There was a time when that was a relief. Back when Abbie was just a baby and my marriage was so new I couldn't handle seeing her everywhere I turned without falling into the same pit of regret that I once let suffocate me.

I rap my knuckles against the door before I can back out.

One minute. One look. One second, even. That's it.

Yeah fucking right.

4

Delaney

"Okay, we're going to start with attendance, and then I'd love to get to know all of you a little bit if that's alright?" I ask once the final bell finishes ringing.

For a group of seven- to eight-year-olds, they're incredibly tuned in to me so far. Maybe it's just first-day magic, or maybe I got lucky and a well-behaved class is my reward for being swapped so last minute. Either way, I'm going to take advantage of their attention for as long as they offer it to me.

I don't remember the last time that I didn't have to use one of many attention-grabbing exercises to get through a morning attendance. It's a relief and maybe even a sign that this could be my best year yet. If I haven't just jinxed it, of course.

The list of student names rests on my desk as I stare down at the first one and clear my throat. Despite feeling excited about being gifted a potentially well-behaved class, I can't pretend that it's going to be all that easy getting through this year. Maybe it's because I didn't move out of Cherry Peak when I had the chance, back before I had integrated my adult life here, but the universe has a funny way of giving me something good with a side of struggle.

It would have been so easy to stay away, but . . .

"Abbie," I call out.

The little girl with her daddy's brown eyes shoots her arm into the air and wiggles her fingers in response. Her toothy grin is a dulled blade digging into my spine. My next breath sears my throat.

Still, I carry on down the list. Each name I read burns a little less.

I get halfway through the list when three knocks against my classroom door make me jump. My knee bangs against the corner of my desk before I hop up and swallow a curse.

"Give me one second and we'll continue with attendance," I say through a wince.

I toss an easy glance at the class and half stroll, half limp to the door. There's a tall shadow behind the glazed window in the door that causes a cool dread to pool in my belly. It doesn't take seeing the face of the person on the other side to know who it is.

I know better than anyone what being close to Darren feels like, and right now, the weird clunking sensation in my chest is exactly that. Because if there's one thing Darren Huntsly always succeeds at, it's twisting me up so tightly that it takes weeks, sometimes years, for the knots to unravel.

Back when we were teenagers, I didn't bother untying them. The constant tug and pinch of them felt like a reminder of us. Of what we were and the life we promised each other we'd have. But now? They ache with a ferocity that terrifies me after how long we've been apart.

Suddenly, I hate him again.

It takes everything in me to haul the door open and bring myself within arm's length of him. There's nowhere near enough space between us. I'm throttled with the need to create more, but I can't get myself to move back. As easy as blinking, I grow lost in his closeness and the scent of familiar cologne. Memories spear into my mind, but I shove up my walls, refusing to replay them right now.

I stare at the mustache that now lives above his top lip

instead of the eyes that I know are the same exact shade as melted milk chocolate. It's criminally attractive yet not at all what I expected to see from the man who used to shave his face every single morning because he hated the scratchy feeling of stubble on his jaw.

Darren parts his lips, and I ignore the soft pink shade of them before looking at the curling hair behind the ear with the closed, empty piercing in its lobe. The dark curls are the longest I've ever seen them, and I know that if he took off the ratty old baseball cap flattening them, they'd be messy too.

His skin is still smooth and clear, and his eyebrows are large and a tad bushy without being too much for his face. The Steele Ranch–branded cap he's wearing is one I've seen a million times, but I know it isn't the same one he wore when we were teenagers. It's missing the bleaching on the left side of the brown brim from when he left it out in the sun for the entire month of July.

By the time he speaks, I've latched my gaze onto his chin and offered him a sickly fake smile that even a stranger wouldn't believe to be real.

"Hi."

"Hi. What do you need?"

A heavy, tense pause. "The parking lot is full."

"Okay. Is this about Abbie?"

Those peachy lips stay parted, but no words escape them. With every second we spend in this awkward, strained silence, the more tense I get. I'm glad I didn't open the window now because one strong breeze is all it would take to have me barrelling over.

Darren clears his throat not once, not twice, but three times before finally speaking.

"Yeah. She won't be late again. It was my fault."

My eyes move upward without my consent, greedy to get their first look at him in months. The heat of that first glance knocks the breath out of me, leaving me gasping to replenish my empty lungs.

"Right," I push out, gripping my hip to keep my hand busy. "An in-person apology wasn't necessary. You're not my student, and Abbie wasn't too late."

His eyes may still be that rich chocolate brown, but that's where the similarities end. I fell in love watching the dreams trapped within them dance, and as I focus on them now, I can't find a single one left.

Has he achieved them all? Or simply given up on them? I shouldn't care to know which option is the right one.

"I know. I just want Abbie to have a good first day. It's already awkward with you—"

I step outside the room and pull the door closed behind me before the kids can pick up on anything we're saying. Lifting my hand, I cut him off. "I don't let outside regrets dictate what I do inside my classroom. Your daughter is not going to bear the weight of what happened with us."

His flinch is obvious, my choice of words striking true. I swallow the apology that slithers up my throat before it can escape.

"Right. Great, then," he says, nodding as his back foot moves.

"If that was all you wanted, I have to finish attendance."

"Yeah, that's all."

I tip my chin. "Have a great day, then."

His nostrils flare as he takes a full step back and then stops, palming the wall of the little alcove we're in. I freeze, trapped beneath the weight of his sharp gaze. He taps his fingers against the cement wall, and I can't help but steal a look at the one that used to wear a simple gold band.

Emotion burns the backs of my eyes. I release a tight breath and meet his stare again.

"Do you still live in town?" he blurts.

My brain runs a mile a minute, trying to make sense of that

question. Not only is it inappropriate for this setting, but it's not his place to ask at all, regardless of where we are.

I tighten my hold on the doorknob, reassuring myself of the escape route. "That isn't any of your business."

"Fuck if it isn't, Elle. You're a ghost in this town."

"My name is Delaney, Darren. Not Elle," I hiss, the air growing too thin.

He leans forward, the brim of his cap shading the bottom half of his face. "You'll always be Elle to me."

"It's a good thing I'm nothing to you anymore, then. Me being your daughter's teacher doesn't change that. Nothing will. So, you can leave now. If you need to speak with me again, you can send an email or call the front office and leave a message. You can find all of that information in the welcome package that will be in Abbie's backpack this afternoon."

I'm proud that my voice doesn't crack the way my chest is.

Darren's muscles coil like he's preparing to move closer to me, but I step back before he can, shaking my head. It's like he came here planning to confuse me. Maybe even confuse himself, too, if his pained expression is anything to go by.

"Hold on, Delaney. I want to be cordial, at least. We can't ignore each other forever."

"Is that what we've been doing? Ignoring each other?" I ask, huffing in disbelief at his gall.

So what if I've been ignoring him? What else did he expect?

"Yeah, I'd say so. The last time I saw you was Bryce's opening night at Into The Shade."

I look past him at the empty hall before replying, "This isn't the time to be talking about anything other than your daughter's education."

"So meet me another time to talk about something other than that."

"No. No, I won't *meet you another time*. You need to leave now," I say, pushing the last sentence out a bit harder as I try and wrap my head around that.

Bryce's opening at the tattoo studio was like . . . eight months ago. My relationship with Daisy had me unable to turn her invitation down the way I wanted to when it was first brought up. The group of women in their circle have been too welcoming for me to reject such an important moment. Especially because of Darren.

Poppy might be his brother, but she was good to me before we broke up, and now, she's back in my life. Even if she kept her distance from me the same way I did her brother for far too many years.

Him bringing that day up now, as if he has any damn right to, isn't helping his case in the slightest.

"At least think about it," he pleads.

"I don't need to. It won't be happening. And even if it were, the moment we're spotted in public together, it will be Sasha standing in front of me right here. I won't be the subject of her abuse again."

He sucks in a breath before ripping his hat off and threading fingers through his hair. The dark locks gleam, healthy and thick, before they're trapped beneath the cap again.

"She has no say in who I speak with," he argues tensely.

I roll my lips and push the door open behind me just a crack. "Have a great day, Mr. Huntsly. I'm very excited to get to teach Abbie this year."

"Delaney," he tries a final time.

"Hopefully, she enjoys her time in my class."

Turning around, I give him my back and lift my chin. When I step back into the classroom, my smile is not only faker than before, but the pain in my chest is ten times stronger.

I'm not certain of many things, but one thing I'll never be able to question is whether it'll get easier to see Darren. If time has proven anything, it's that no, if anything, it'll get harder.

5

Darren

"Are you sure you didn't want to go to the party? They're celebrating you, after all."

"They're celebrating the team, Elle. I'm good doing that with you right here."

Delaney rolls her eyes at me, but I know she likes when I say shit like that. The way she crinkles her nose and rolls her bottom lip between her teeth gives her away. Well, that or her instant blushing. Either-or.

She flicks the back of my hand. "That's not a very quarterback thing of you to say."

I let loose a gruff laugh. "And what exactly is a 'very quarterback' thing to say?"

"You don't even like this movie," she mutters, changing direction.

I drop my legs from where they were cupping her sides and lean back, creating enough distance between us that I can gently spin her around to face me. Sitting in the bed of Brody's truck at the drive-in, the same way we do every Friday night—football game or not—Delaney's in her usual place between my legs.

Usually, she'll use this position to say things she knows I won't like, just so she doesn't have to see my reaction to them. Tonight, she's spent more time looking back at me than at the movie playing on the giant projection screen.

It would worry me if I didn't already have a gut feeling as to why she's so antsy tonight.

"I don't. But you do. And I think we both know that I'd watch paint dry as long as you were sitting right here."

Squeezing my thighs, I keep her locked in place, trapped in my hold. Pink explodes on her cheeks, making the generous splatter of light brown freckles harder to see. I run the pad of my thumb down the bridge of her nose, over my favourite patch of them. I've never met another girl who has the same number of freckles as my Delaney does, and I hope I never do. One day, I'll force her to sit with me while I count each one.

"Next time, you can choose the movie," she offers.

"We'll have to break into the projection room, then, so they don't keep replaying the same five."

"Oh, is good boy Darren going to do something reckless? For me?" she teases, raising a hand to knock my hat off my head.

She plunks it onto hers, squishing the pretty curls she did for the game tonight. I gather the ends and pull them over her shoulder before cupping the back of her neck. The purple tinsel threaded through her bright blonde hair matches the jacket I tried to set over her shoulders when we first got here. Now, it's abandoned on the truck bed.

Her long cardigan and straight-legged jeans have her pretty covered already, but I've always loved the sight of her in my letterman. I won't deny that it's a possessive thing. Fuck, I'd have her wearing my clothes every single day if I thought she'd go for it. No, Delaney likes her comfortable jeans, long skirts, and cardigans.

"I'm not that good of a boy, Elle."

The corner of her mouth curls. "No? Not according to your perfect attendance and test scores."

"I'm intelligent beyond my years and motivated. Not *good*."

"What if I like you a little good? *And* intelligent *and* motivated?"

I curl my fingers in the soft hairs at her nape and guide her close. "If that were the case, I'd tell you that I'm all of those things because of you."

"Well, then, how lucky am I?"

I've asked myself how I got lucky enough to have Delaney Brooks in my life ever since I met her in the third grade. She was reading a book far too advanced for our grade, but I asked her to explain it to me anyway. Then, I begged my parents to get me the rest of the series for Christmas that year and gave them to her. I still remember the fat, wet kiss she laid on my cheek as a thanks.

"I'm going to give you everything, Elle. There isn't anything I'm not ready to do to make sure you get the life you've always dreamed of. Football is just another way for me to get us there."

Delaney pushes off the truck bed and shoves my thighs flat before crawling on top of them. When she sits again, we're so close she can easily press her forehead to mine as she asks, "What about your dreams? You need to make sure you're leaving room for those too."

"The only dream I have is you."

I lift my chin and kiss her. Her skin is hot in my hand as I guide her closer and palm her hip, getting a handful of thick wool. My girl smiles against my lips and leans forward, using her soft lips to drive me wild. When I open my eyes, hers are the first thing I see.

"I love you, Darren."

"And I love you, Delaney."

Slowly, I release her hip and pluck at the chain I've been wearing around my neck for a few days now. She watches as I pull it out from beneath my shirt and tug it hard enough for the clasp to break. It was cheap and simple, anyway. Just something I needed to carry the real reason why I insisted we spend our night here when she nearly wavered and encouraged us to head to the party with our friends.

The ring dangling from the chain snags her attention. She squeezes my shoulder and tucks that lip back between her teeth.

"I knew it," she whispers.

"Your dad would kill me if I asked you to marry me already, so this is the closest I can get right now. One day, when we're both finished school and we're back in this town, I'll give you the real thing. Then, you'll be my wife," I declare, trying not to grin.

Her hand is warm in mine when I pull it from my shoulder and hold it between us. She flicks her eyes up to hold mine, even as I slip the silver ring from the broken chain and slide it onto her finger. The full weight of her attention makes my heart soar the way it does every day I get to spend with her.

"What do you think?" I ask softly, stroking the band.

Without looking at the ring, she says, "I love it. I love you."

"You don't think it's too simple?"

She steals a look at the ring for half a second before staring at me again, shaking her head. "A piece of string would have been enough to make me happy."

"And are you happy, Elle?"

Pressing her lips to mine, she gives me the answer I need. I guide her hand to my chest, over the thin material of my tee and the thrashing heart beneath it. She spreads her fingers and leans into the touch, her kiss growing fiercer.

"Yes. I've never been happier," she declares against my lips. "You're my forever man."

I lean back an inch and dart my eyes between each of hers. "When did you first see the ring, you beautiful little snoop?"

"You had it on when you were running laps on the field yesterday."

"I knew you weren't on the bleachers just to study. Did you even get any work done with your creeping?"

"I'm surprised you noticed me amongst all your admirers.

You should have heard the things the girls were saying about you."

I take my hat off her head and put it on mine backward before running my fingers through the full length of her silky hair. "I hope you told them to fuck off."

"And ruin their day? No, I don't mind it, really. Not anymore."

"Good. The only girl I've ever noticed is you. On and off the field," I say.

Delaney rubs her nose against mine. "Besides, they don't know that you won't be pursuing football as a career. It sounded like they were interested in finding a pro."

"They don't know me at all, baby."

"Your sister said something along those lines to me the other day, you know? She's going to freak out when she sees the ring."

"Oh? She's playing matchmaker again, then. I was threatened that if I messed up and lost you, she'd disown me."

Poppy's a spitfire. Yeah, she's only fifteen, but she's got the spirit of a grown woman. My sister isn't afraid to speak her mind to anyone about anything. I've always loved that about her, but shit, good luck to the man she marries. He's going to need a spine of steel to avoid being railroaded by her.

"I believe that. She's my girl," Delaney sings.

"I never thought I'd need to fight off my sister when it comes to my girlfriend."

Her smile is soft as she drags two fingers along my jaw. "Don't be jealous. I like how it looks on you too much."

She yelps when I grab her by the waist and lean us back until I'm hovering above her and the letterman jacket she snubbed tonight is squished beneath her. The thick blanket I laid out keeps the bed of Brody's truck from getting her cardigan dirty.

"I can be more jealous if you want," I offer, voice dipping as I brush my lips against hers.

She smooths a hand up my back. "Do it at your own risk."

"You make it sound so good, how am I supposed to ignore that?"

"In that case, I was considering asking Jayden if he could lend me his jacket for a few days. It's been quite cold, you know, with fall coming and all," she drawls, naming one of my teammates.

"His football jacket?"

"Mm, that's the one."

I narrow my eyes and nip at her jaw. "The only jacket you need to be wearing is the one beneath you."

Slipping a hand underneath her, I give the jacket a yank and free it. The heavy material is purple and beige, with a big number seventeen on the arm and back. *My* number.

"Well then, what are you waiting for? Put it on me," she teases.

We move back until we're sitting nearly on top of each other, and then she extends her arm for me. I guide it into the first sleeve before doing the same to the other. Once both of her arms are inside of it, I whistle, giving my head a rough shake.

"Fucking beautiful, Elle."

She waggles her brows and shimmies both shoulders. "Yeah? I don't look like I'm wearing a sack?"

"Nah, but even if you did, you'd still be hot as fuck."

"Yeah, I guess I could settle for this one," she says with a sigh, shrugging.

"Settle," I echo, wetting my lips. "That's one word for it."

"Do you have one more fitting?"

"I've got three. Meant to be."

"You're a cheeseball tonight, babe."

"Well, it's a good fucking thing you aren't lactose intolerant," I joke, scooping her into my lap.

She chokes on a laugh. "Stop it before I get the ick."

"The ick? Fuck out of here with that, Elle. There's no such thing as ick between us."

"Oh, I'm not too sure about that. Maybe ten years down the road, you'll be singing a different tune."

My pulse skips. "Ten years down the road, I plan on already knowing everything you do that could ick me out. And I'm completely sure that I'll still love you."

Her expression softens, the teasing gleam in her eyes quickly replaced with a warmth that I can feel brushing my skin. She holds her hand up between us and wiggles her ring finger.

"I'd hope so. I mean, look at this ring."

"It's a pretty nice placeholder, right?"

She nods and snuggles into my hold like there's nowhere else she'd rather be, and I know that right here, right now, there isn't anywhere better for her.

For either of us.

6

Delaney

Blaring sirens wake me.

I lurch up from the . . . couch? My heart pounds as I take in the room, realizing that I must have fallen asleep working again. When I turn my head to the front window, the pain in my neck zaps down my spine, and the papers in my lap fall to the floor. Massaging the knot growing beneath my skin, I push to my feet and feel my stomach drop at the red lights flashing down the street.

It's loud, almost to the point my eardrums ache as I stand in front of the window and gawk out at the street. My neighbours are doing the same, some outright standing on their front porches and on the sidewalk. There's no such thing as discretion in Cherry Peak.

Inhaling, I snap my eyes to the crack I left open in the window. The fire is close enough that the scent of it is floating inside, thick and strong.

The heavy cardigan and fluffy slippers I'm still wearing are warm enough, so I go outside to the front step, joining my nosey neighbours. Smoke burns the back of my throat when I breathe in, glancing down the street in the direction of the flashing red lights. The two Cherry Peak fire engines are barely visible, but there's no mistaking where they're heading. Giant plumes of black smoke fill the sky above the flickers of orange flames in the direction of the town sign.

Where the drive-in sits.

Panic sets in as I grip the thin metal railing, my fingers going numb. The older couple across the street from me have the sides of their robes clenched tightly in their hands as they stare at the smoke. In a blink, I'm rushing back into the house.

I grab my car keys and don't waste time searching for proper shoes before heading back outside and toward my car. The engine cranks, and then I'm tearing down the street. Silence makes my anxiety worse, but I keep the radio off, my focus set on the road ahead of me.

The drive-in isn't popular anymore. Nobody goes there but teenagers looking for a spot to smoke weed and drink before they're eighteen. That wasn't always the case, though. Not for me.

I can't—*it* can't disappear. Not yet.

The end of the road is closed off ahead of me. Not only is it the easiest way out of town, but it's also the only way to access the drive-in. It's impossible to get a proper breath when I make it past the last of the buildings in town and get my first real view of the fire. Of the roaring flames and thick smoke filling the sky.

I tighten my hold on the steering wheel and slow down, a piece of my soul chipping off and floating away at the scene that unfolds up ahead.

The projection room is crumbling, half of the building already collapsed while the rest of it burns the brightest. The few RCMP officers we have in town are managing the road blockage, and I swallow thickly when I park behind the first cruiser blocking my lane of the road.

Moving slowly, I park my car and step outside without bothering to turn it off. One of the officers is already headed my way by the time I get my bearings. The wall of smoke is so close now that I cough to clear my throat.

"You can't be here, Ms. Brooks. Especially not outside with this smoke," he says, already lifting an arm to usher me back into the car.

I take a closer look at him, trying to figure out where we must have met before. The name stitched onto his uniform doesn't ring a bell, so I let it go, knowing I won't be able to focus on that right now.

"What happened?" I ask, glancing over his shoulder at the scene behind him.

The fire engine parked sideways between the drive-in and the police cruiser blocks off a lot of my view, and that only makes me more frustrated. This place isn't mine, but it feels like it is. Too many of my core memories were made here.

Watching it burn . . .

"We're not sure yet. The fire started small, but the structure was already old and weak. For now, we need everyone to stay back. We've got the station working to contain as much of the fire as they can before it spreads to the woods."

My chest lurches. It's instinct to look for him.

From the moment I learned Darren had already started volunteering at the station, I began worrying with every blare of fire engine sirens despite knowing it was no longer my place to care. The thought of him running into fires has never felt right, and right now, it feels the worst it ever has.

Panic makes it hard to speak. "Is the entire station here?"

"Every available firefighter in Cherry Peak, and they've made a call for additional stations," the officer says.

"Are you sure? Even volunteers?" I ramble, pivoting to the side.

"Yes, even volunteers. Now, I really need you to get back into your car. This is an uncontrolled area. It isn't safe."

I nod on instinct, even if I don't mean to. My fingers are cold as I lift them to pull my hair back. It already stinks like smoke.

Or that could just be the air. Everything smells like fire and gleams with orange and red. The snap of the wooden structure gets swallowed by a sudden cracking noise.

I stumble back a step when the last standing leg of the projection building gives. In the blink of an eye, the remaining piece of the drive-in collapses, sending the closest group of firefighters falling back with shouts of warning.

Embers float into the cloudless sky, joining the stars as the fire roars with a vengeance. I palm my throat and blink back the burn in my eyes as they wander the field, searching. A sea of identical brown jackets decorated with stripes of bright yellow and helmets hiding hair makes it harder to find him. With each name I read, my fear doubles in size until it's so big I can taste it.

My vision blurs when I finally find the man I'm looking for. The name on his back causes me to shake from head to toe with relief.

Huntsly.

"Please, Delaney, you need to get in your car and go home. There will be an update in the morning," the officer shouts over the screaming fire.

I'm already close enough to the car that I can lean against the door for balance. I suck in huge breaths as he opens it and helps me into the driver's seat. This time when I look at the name on his uniform, I recognize it.

"We went to high school together, right?" I blurt out.

He blinks, surprised. "Yes. We were in the same twelfth-grade French class."

Johnson . . . "Sam Johnson?"

"That's me. I wear contacts now, so I don't blame you for not recognizing me without the big round glasses I used to wear. Especially in a situation like this. Which, speaking of . . ." He leans back and hovers at the door, a hand gripping the top. "Go home and try and get some sleep."

"I won't be able to sleep," I admit weakly.

It doesn't matter if he hears me or not. The sound of another car crawling up behind mine snags his attention long enough for me to safely sniffle without him noticing. The swell of emotions inside of me is all-consuming, and I know I need to leave, but what if this is the last time I ever see this place?

I don't want my last memory of this place to be of it up in flames, crumbling piece by piece.

It doesn't seem like I have a choice, though.

With a grimace, Sam pats my window. "Good night, Delaney."

I let him shut the door without another word. The stink of smoke stains the upholstery and lingers in the vents. I turn off the air conditioning to avoid sucking in any more tainted air and wait for Sam to guide the car behind me into a U-turn before I start to do the same.

The back of my neck tingles, an invisible finger stroking it. I dart my stare from the rear-view mirror to the windshield, where across the field, two dark eyes pierce into me.

Darren stands in front of the fire, his brown jacket heavy on his shoulders and a mask strapped around his face that would hide his features enough to keep his identity a secret from anyone else.

I freeze as we stare at one another, a silent devastation passing between us. It makes it impossible to so much as release a breath of relief, knowing that he's okay. Not emotionally, but physically. We're the same that way.

The hose in his hands looks like it weighs a million pounds, and I don't blame him for the way his arms sag. I want to scream at him to run back to the fire and save the drive-in before it's too late. To not let our place burn to the ground after I've avoided it for the last eight years. But it isn't our place anymore, and even if they did manage to get the fire out right now, I'd just continue to avoid it the way I avoided him after school yesterday.

So instead of disobeying Sam's orders and running across the field to beg Darren to save this place, I bring my gaze back to the mirror and leave.

Some places aren't meant to be saved, and the memories we made here are better off as ashes.

"I KNEW YOU'D BE AWAKE," Poppy says, eyeing me from the porch.

Her auburn hair is piled up into a messy bun on the top of her head, and she's wearing a bright pink sweatsuit with fluffy brown slippers. There's not a fleck of makeup on her face or the usual diamonds in her ears. She's the Poppy from the past tonight. A fitting reminder, considering.

My shoulders droop as I use the doorframe to support my weight. "It's four in the morning, Poppy."

"So why are you still awake?"

"Why are you?"

The youngest of the Huntsly siblings snorts a laugh and lifts a bag in the air. "Fair enough. Can I come in despite the ungodly hour?"

"That depends. What's in the bag?"

"Licorice and cherry Coke. I'm hoping they're still your favourites."

There's a sharp twist in my chest. "You remembered that?"

"As if I could forget. You didn't use to go anywhere without both."

She rubs her lips together, stopping herself from saying more. I'm grateful for that hesitation tonight. I'm too exhausted to think about the past much more than I already have.

"Yeah, you can come in. Sorry for the smell."

With a small smile, she nods and slips inside. "The smoke? I don't think that's coming from in here."

"It's both. I haven't been able to shower." I shut the door before joining her in the cramped living room, still full to the brim of my grandmother's furniture.

"You went to see the fire, didn't you?"

Dropping my eyes to the threadbare carpet, I whisper, "I had to."

"I'm sorry, Delaney. I figured you wouldn't have stayed inside and watched the flames."

"Don't be. It was only a matter of time before something happened to the drive-in. Time just ran out," I ramble, blinking quickly. Gripping my hips, I glance away at the staircase and breathe in through my nose. "You can sit. I'm sorry it's such a mess."

She shrugs it off, flashing a grin and taking a seat on the loveseat. "I like it. Everything feels very homey."

"My grandma liked collecting things, including furniture. One of these days, I'll have a chance to finally get everything packed up and put in storage."

"I've been meaning to ask how you're doing after, you know. I would have been here sooner if I hadn't been . . ."

I swallow thickly and wipe a palm down my thigh. "Don't apologize. You've been great. I don't need coddling."

The loss of my grandmother last year wasn't sudden by any means. She'd been sick for years, slowly getting worse with every birthday. Still, I struggled with her absence once she was gone. She's the main reason I stayed in Cherry Peak, and this house—her house —is a constant reminder of her. Living here after she passed wasn't my plan, but this town isn't really bursting with open real estate.

"I could have been better. Stopped by sooner or forced you out of the house more often. Daisy's been keeping us all updated, though."

"You're fine, Poppy. I'm doing good now. And yeah, that's nice of her. I figured she was doing that," I say tightly.

Has Darren been around while she's been giving everyone updates on me? *Who am I kidding?* He probably gets up and leaves the moment my name is brought up.

I'm aware of Saturday nights at Peakside, the only bar in

town, and how every member of their close-knit group is invited. It's tradition for them. While I've been invited to a few by both Daisy and Poppy, I've never joined them. Out of every main location in Cherry Peak, Peakside is the one place I haven't stepped foot into since the moment I moved back.

I don't belong there with them.

"If you ever need help going through her things, I'm only a call away," Poppy offers.

Sitting in the oversized armchair, I try to smile at her. "I wouldn't bother you for that. It's too long of a drive."

"Not for long. Garrison and I are moving closer."

"What? When?"

She frowns slightly. "Not soon enough. But we're building a house only two hours away. Close enough to Calgary for work and at least a half hour closer to everyone here."

"That's exciting, Poppy. Good for you guys."

"Thank you. We're hoping to have it finished before the wedding, but Darren's certain that won't happen—" She cuts herself off and winces.

I shake my head, playing off my discomfort. "You can say his name around me. He's not the boogeyman."

"He's not *always* the boogeyman," she corrects me. "But honestly, we don't need to talk about him. Even if I know you can handle it, we have more than enough to talk about without involving my brother. He's not why I came to see you at four in the morning, anyway."

"You came to check on me. I know," I assure her. "But we both know why the drive-in means so much to me."

The sadness in her eyes forces me to dart my eyes away from her. "Memories haunt the places we thought we'd outgrown, Della. You're allowed to feel the pain of losing one as important to you as the drive-in."

My throat strains around my next words. "I can't."

Not without grieving Darren too. And I've done that one too

many times already. I can't grieve the loss of one without the other when they're so tightly intertwined.

"Maybe they'll rebuild it," she murmurs, reaching up to tighten her bun.

"I'm not sure it would be worth the cost."

"It's a shame they stopped taking care of it. If they rebuilt it now, I wonder if we could all band together to help keep it running."

My smile feels heavy as doubt wiggles in my gut. "Maybe."

Noticing my reaction, she lets it drop and starts digging in the bag beside her. "I'm sorry. Let's snack and forget about it for now, yeah?"

I catch the bag of licorice when she tosses it across the room. "That sounds great."

The licorice is sweet, but the ache in my heart doesn't budge. Still, I chew and pretend it's enough while Poppy keeps me company.

7

The bitter churn of nausea in my stomach sends me straight to the bathroom. I hit my knees on the tile in front of the toilet and throw up. The smoke clinging to my clothes and hair makes everything worse. I squeeze my eyes shut and grip the back of the toilet. It's so cool against my hot palms.

By the time I'm finished, it's hard to swallow past the burn in my throat. I struggle to my feet and use a sweaty hold on the vanity to haul myself to the sink. The water I splash on my face doesn't get colder, no matter how long I leave the right tap running.

I turn it off and heave over the sink, refusing to look into the mirror. What I'd find in my reflection would ruin me. Fray the last of my resolve and leave me broken on the floor.

Delaney shouldn't have been there. Fuck, I'd have preferred her anywhere else.

She's avoided me like the plague for months since the last time we saw each other, but there she was, watching me fail to save the only place that hadn't erased the story of us. Decades' worth of memories gone up in flames. Just like that.

"Want a beer?"

Lifting my head, I look at where Bryce is standing in the hall, watching me.

"I thought you'd be asleep by now," I say, voice shot to hell.

"Unlikely. Abbie went back to bed after you left, and I haven't heard her move since."

"Thank you for coming. I know it's late."

That's an understatement. Abbie's going to be up for school soon, the sun already cresting over the horizon.

She shifts to give me room to exit the bathroom and follows me into the kitchen. I go right for the coffee machine. It's already full and ready.

"Don't apologize for that. It was bad, right?" she asks.

I pour myself a cup of the fresh coffee and leave it black. "It's gone, B. All of it."

"Shit."

"Caleb's got the station there for a few more hours, cleaning up the debris. I couldn't stay."

My best friend steps in front of me and takes my mug of coffee away to set it on the counter. She confirms how messed up I look when she wraps her arms around me and gives me a rare hug.

I tense my jaw as a wave of emotion rolls over me. Returning the hug, I cling to her a bit tighter than I would have normally.

"Do you have any Baileys to put in that coffee?" she mutters into my shoulder.

"I doubt I'd keep it down."

With a heavy exhale, Bryce pulls back and stares up at me with blue eyes focused enough they can dissect my every thought.

"Should I ask?"

"Ask what?"

She scowls, handing me back my coffee. "Don't play dumb. You know exactly what I'm talking about. I remember you asking me these same questions when it came to Daisy."

"That was different. The two of you were always different."

"Fuck that. I can still stand here and ask you how you're feeling and what you're thinking. The drive-in was *your* place, D. It belonged to you two. The rest of us were always just visitors."

I pull away from her and leave the kitchen. She doesn't let me get away. When I sit on the couch, she joins me, keeping a further distance now.

"She was there," I say, dropping the words into the silence.

"There . . . at the drive-in?"

"At the drive-in. Watching as it burned and we failed to save it."

That haunted look in her eyes as she stared at me followed me home. It reminded me of the last time I saw her before Abbie was born.

"By the time we got there, it was already up in flames. The projection room went first, then it just collapsed. There's nothing left, Bryce. Nothing."

She remains silent for a second, hands fidgeting with her long black hair. "Can it be rebuilt?"

I don't mean to laugh, but it comes out anyway. Bitter and dark. "With what money?"

"I could talk to my dad. Tell him how important the drive-in was to the town," she offers.

"No offense to your dad, but he never gave a shit about that place. It didn't go up in flames on its own. Our guess is someone tossed a blunt, and it caught on the old wood. The town let it get to that point, B."

The mayor saw it as a waste of space and money. Most of the town did. Hell, even I'd written it off for too long.

"I know. That doesn't mean I couldn't try and convince him to change his mind."

"And if you did? Then what?"

She stretches her legs out and lets her head fall back against the couch. "I don't know. You could help me instead of pissing all over my parade."

"How?"

Her brow lifts when she looks at me. "That depends on how badly you want it fixed."

"What would be the point?"

"Darren," she says pointedly. 'I'm going to give you the benefit of the doubt because you've been up all night, but are you being serious?"

I scrub a hand down my face. "You're not talking about the drive-in."

"Thanks, genius."

"There's no fixing what happened with Delaney. She hates me, and I don't blame her for it."

Bryce reaches over and shoves at my arm, scowling. "I never took you for a quitter."

"I'm not. I'm just realistic. Yesterday was the first time I've spoken to her since your opening day at the shop, and it was just as awkward. She would have slammed her classroom door in my face if we were alone."

I leave out the part about me begging her to see me outside of school. That was just way too desperate. I don't know what we would have even spoken about.

"I never knew you spoke at the shop."

I stiffen.

"It was brief."

She eliminates the empty cushion between us, tucking a leg beneath her as she leans over. "Spill it."

"Since when are you a gossiper?"

"Since now. Don't turn this on me."

If Bryce is one thing, it's stubborn. Too damn stubborn for her or anyone else's good. Once she sets her mind on something, that's the end of it. It's suddenly my least favourite quality about her.

I play it safe with my explanation. If she knew everything that was said or the way those words left me feeling, she'd never let this go.

I still haven't.

"I told her I was sorry to hear about her grandmother. She thanked me."

There's a subtle fall of her lips before she asks, "That's it?"

"Sorry to disappoint."

"Fuck off. That doesn't change anything."

"There isn't anything to change, Bryce. We're the past."

"You can still fix the drive-in. If you won't do it for yourself, do it for Abbie. Don't you want her to be able to grow up watching movies there like we did?"

I glare at her. "Don't bring my daughter into this."

"Isn't she already in this? I'd say that she's the most important part in what happened—"

"Leave it alone. There's no point in entertaining the thought of rebuilding the drive-in unless there's some sort of approval from your father."

"Okay, so once I have it?"

"Why is this so important to you?" I ask, startling myself with the question.

Bryce absorbs it, not letting my shitty attitude affect her. "If there was even the smallest chance that she'd forgive you, would you want it?"

There's no question. Even after all this time.

"You know I would."

"Then I'll talk to my dad, and when I get a yes, you need to promise me that you'll do whatever it takes to get the drive-in rebuilt."

I hate how skeptical I am, but there's no fighting it off yet. "Fixing the drive-in won't make her forgive me, Bryce."

"No, but the process could help show her why she should."

"You want me to use this as a way to get back in her good graces?"

"We both know an approval from my dad won't do much more than kick-start the permit process for a renovation. So, we'll need the town to help build it. Volunteer or some shit like that. The fire station could help, right?"

"I'd have to talk to Caleb before answering that. But still, I don't know if the town cares enough to try."

"They will."

"She's not coming back to me, Bryce."

"Don't."

I shake my head, the constant throb behind my ribs growing in intensity. "It's been eight years."

"And you're still lost without her."

Sucking in a sharp breath, I glance up at the ceiling. "It doesn't matter how many times I tell myself that she's gone, I still want to bring her home to me."

"It's not too late to try."

"It was too late the moment I let her go."

"I don't believe that."

"You're supposed to be the doom-and-gloom one of us. Go back to that," I mutter.

"That's the way I prefer things, but you've decided to steal my entire personality today. Give it back and we'll see."

"Can we just talk about this more later?"

"If that's what you want," she relents, albeit reluctantly.

"I need to shower before Abbie gets up."

Nodding, she glances at the time on her phone. "Yeah, Daisy's already awake."

"Go have breakfast with her before she heads to work," I tell her, pushing off the couch. "And thank you. For coming to watch Abbie and for this. I'm sorry that I couldn't . . . I can't talk about it all right now."

"Don't apologize. You dealt with a lot tonight already."

"Yeah. It was a night."

"I love you," she says, startling me.

Bryce has said that to me plenty of times over the years, but ever since she's fallen in love with Daisy, it's been more often. The sunshine woman she now calls her fiancée has brought my icy best friend out of her shell in the best ways.

I offer her a hand and tug her up before stealing another hug. "I love you too."

"I'll keep you posted. Don't ignore me when I text, or I'll come back over here and kick your ass."

"I believe you."

"Good." She shoves out of my arms and gives my cheek a pat. "The mustache looks good, by the way."

"Garrison told me it looked like a rat on my lip."

"Garrison lacks taste."

I snort. "Have you told him that?"

"Too many times to count. So, don't take his criticisms to heart. It looks good on you. Daisy was gushing about it the other day."

"Oh, good. Were you jealous?"

"Of you? Not a chance."

"Ouch."

"Didn't you already get enough compliments from me?"

"I figured you were changing into the warm and fuzzy type, that's all," I tease, some of the pain in my chest easing for the time being.

"Now I'm leaving. Walk me out?"

I do so without hesitation. She shoves her feet and the hems of her long PJ pants into the black boots she wore over. I hide a laugh behind a cough.

"Drive safe, Ice," I say.

She gives me a long look, checking me over before nodding. "I'll text you."

"I'll be on the lookout."

And I am. The text that comes in exactly five hours later sends a zap of fear through me from head to toe.

Bryce: Drive-in is a go. Time to talk to Caleb.

8

"Hi, Della!" Daisy sings.

I pause halfway through shutting my classroom door and glance down the hall. The twin buns on the top of her head don't move an inch as she bounces my way. Space buns and yellow overalls are hard to pull off, but Daisy Mitchell can pull off anything with ease. I've seen it happen on more than one occasion.

"Hi, Daisy."

"Gosh, when's the last time we even had a staff meeting? Any bets on what this one's about?"

"Nothing good, most likely."

The email was sent out halfway through the day with no warning or explanation, just the order for every staff member to attend if possible. It's the last thing I want to do today.

Last night was one of the worst nights I've had in a long time. Poppy stayed for a couple of hours before I kicked her out, demanding she go home to her man and catch up on as much sleep as possible. It was probably pointless, considering they're staying at Steele Ranch while their new house gets built, and from what I've heard, it's impossible to sleep past sunrise out there.

The only thing I could hope for was that one of us would get a couple of hours of sleep. I knew it wasn't going to be me.

"I'm hoping for a raise," Daisy says.

I finally close the classroom door the rest of the way before joining her in the hall. "That's the only way I wouldn't be annoyed spending my evening here."

"If they have food, I'll keep my complaints inside."

"That's fair. I'll even settle for a hot coffee."

Daisy laughs and adjusts the strap of her massive book bag where it rests on her shoulder. That thing could knock someone out with one swing.

"Speaking of coffee, have you noticed that the pot in the staff room is *always* empty recently?"

I shake my head, picking up my walking speed when she starts getting a bit ahead of me. "I've stopped drinking the stuff in there. It's always burnt."

"Okay, right? I thought that they'd just stopped making it because it always tasted like ass. But no, I think someone's just emptying the entire pot into a big mug or something and not making another one after."

"And you're really bothered by that," I note, a laugh teasing my throat.

She whips her head so fast in my direction I'm shocked when it doesn't fly off. "Yes! It's common decency to start another pot after emptying it. That's like using all the toilet paper and not replacing the roll."

I pinch my lips together, staring straight ahead.

"Don't tell me you do that, Della," she groans.

"I live alone! If I don't replace the roll, it's me who has to grab another one."

"And what if you had company? A *man*?"

Sobering slightly, I roll my eyes at her. "That hasn't happened in a long time, so I think I'm safe."

"Until you aren't. Then, you'll be calling me and apologizing."

"Apologizing? Not a chance."

"Yup. You will be."

"You know, maybe it's been me stealing all the coffee," I say, shrugging a shoulder.

Her finger jabs into my arm. "Don't even joke about that. I've had to start buying coffee every morning on my way here, and while I love the café, I'd love to not have to spend five bucks on something I could be having for free here."

"Have you ever, I don't know, tried making coffee at home?" I tease, eyeing the three teachers slipping into the conference room ahead of us.

"Okay, well, you see, I love Bryce, but she makes *the* worst coffee. I'm talking worse than the burnt stuff here. And I don't have it in me to tell her that and take over the job. It's safer if I just don't go anywhere near it at all."

"That's acceptable, then. You're just being a good girlfriend."

"Exactly! You get me, Della."

"I'll see what I can find out about the coffee, alright? Put my sleuthing hat on."

She grips my arm, giving it a thankful squeeze. "You're the best."

I flash a smile and follow her into the conference room. We've got to be close to the last ones here with how crowded it is. Several sets of eyes fall on us as we find a couple of seats near the back of the room. It smells like burnt coffee in here, and I swallow a giggle when Daisy stares in disgust at the carafe on the table.

It's safe to say that we stay seated while we wait for Penny to get here. Once she does, the energy in the room stays the same, relaxed but curious. Nobody seems worried about what this is about, but we're clearly all antsy to get home.

"Hi, everyone. Thank you for staying back for this today. I know it was last-minute, and I promise it won't take too long."

I glance at Daisy and find her doing the same to me. Her lips twitch in a humoured smile before we look back at Penny together.

"As I'm sure you all know, the drive-in caught fire last night."

My throat tightens as I listen, discomfort making me shift on my chair.

Penny frowns, tucking a curl behind her ear. "I can imagine that it was a bit of a shock to hear the sirens so late, but there is good news amongst the bad. Mayor Lemieux has set forward a plan to rebuild it. That's why I've asked you all to join me here this afternoon. In addition to putting forward this rebuild, he's asked for some help from the community, including the school."

"I'm sorry, Penny, are you saying that the mayor wants the drive-in fixed?" I ask, surprising myself.

The attention of the entire room falls on me, and I immediately want to make a run for it.

"Yes, he does, and I have a volunteer form for everyone to fill out on your way out. So, if you're interested in helping, please consider adding your name," Penny says, glancing around the room.

It doesn't make sense. How have they figured this out in less than twenty-four hours when the drive-in has been abandoned for almost ten years? And to create such an elaborate plan?

"What exactly are we volunteering for?" Daisy asks.

There are a few hums in agreement with her question before Penny answers. "The mayor can only allocate enough funds from the town's budget to cover a little over half of the rebuild. For the remainder, there will be a series of fundraisers and community events with the goal of collecting enough to cover the rest. The volunteers will include as many people from town as possible."

"So, we'll be volunteering to host a few fundraisers?" Claira, the fifth-grade teacher, asks.

"Amongst other tasks. I don't have all of the information quite yet, but once enough volunteers have been gathered, there will be a meeting at town hall to further explain. For now, what I can share is that there will be basic cleanup groups and others in charge of organizing fundraisers and reporting to the mayor's team."

It's the most unusual thing I've heard in a long time. Don't get me wrong, Bryce's father isn't the worst mayor we could have been given for Cherry Peak. While he's done great things for the town, he's also let us down. I could write a list of things he could be choosing to focus on right now instead of the drive-in nobody cared about.

"If you're interested in signing up to help, you can do that on your way out. Starting tomorrow, I'll have the form in the staff room for a week," Penny explains.

The clipboard in her hands is set on the table at the front of the room, right beside the carafe of coffee. Daisy leans into my side, eyeing the table.

"Do you think she put that there on purpose?" she whispers.

"Maybe it's been her stealing all the coffee."

Her gasp is so loud Penny turns to us, not saying anything. I struggle to hold back a laugh while Daisy pops off her seat.

"If nobody else is going to write their name first, I guess I will."

I look up at her. "Adding Bryce's name too?"

"And yours," she announces with a sly wink.

Without waiting for me to reply, she slips through the chairs and, like she said, is the first to sign the form. I watch closely as she writes one name, then another, and *another*. Mine, no doubt about it.

Another two staff members join her once she's finished and spun around. The rest of the teachers stand, until nobody is left sitting but me.

Feeling awkward as hell, I get off my seat and adjust my jeans, pulling them up despite them already sitting perfectly on my hips. Nobody's watching me, but I feel like they are. Watching, judging, analyzing why I wasn't up at the table with Daisy, excited about this project.

Too many of my peers remember me from high school, and those who don't have been reminded by gossip. Time doesn't really do much to make people forget about the mistakes you've made or the drama you caused when you live in a small town. Everything lingers in Cherry Peak, and right now, there are too many faces in here that remember who I was when I left for university and refuse to let that woman go.

At one time, that was Darren's girlfriend. Now, it's the girl he tossed aside.

They've never cared about Delaney the person. The woman who hadn't spoken to Darren for the entirety of his marriage. Hell, I ignored his entire family because I was too afraid to see them, let alone interfere in a marriage that broke my heart savagely in half.

"Ready to go, Della?"

I blink, clearing my head. Daisy's standing in front of me now, trying and failing to hide a frown.

"Yeah. Did you sign us both up?"

"Of course. But I can scratch it off if you don't want to volunteer. I've gone and pushed you into something again, haven't I?"

I shake my head, rubbing her arm. "No. It could be fun."

"You're sure?"

"I'm sure."

Her eyes glow, telling me how she's feeling before her words do. "Then I'm excited. I wonder how long we'll have to wait before the town meeting."

"Considering how fast the mayor got things rolling here, I doubt very long at all."

"You sound suspicious."

I tap her arm and encourage her to leave the room with me before saying anything else. Others have already started to filter out, and I'd feel bad about spacing out long enough to miss Penny's final statements if I wasn't a bit grateful for that.

Once we're back in the hall and on our way outside, I say, "I'm not suspicious, just . . . surprised. It seems really out of place, doesn't it? All things considered."

"Maybe it was always the plan and we just didn't know it? The fire could have sped things up."

"Yeah, I guess."

"I think we should at least give it a fair shot. I'd love to be able to go to the drive-in again. Especially with Bryce."

My heart warms and aches at the same time. "It was always a good date night spot."

"Exactly! I was too young when it was open that I never got a chance to go at all, really. Let alone with a date."

Our age gap is hard to notice most of the time, yet it's also why it's sometimes easier to talk to Daisy than it is to Poppy or even Bryce.

Daisy wasn't around to see me and Darren together. Everything she knows now, she was told after getting with Bryce, and that means she doesn't know the ins and outs of our history. To her, the drive-in was just a fun date spot. But to me and everyone else in their group, it's the place I fell in love with Darren and where he slid a ring on my finger that I didn't take off for four years.

"It was a great spot, Daisy. You're right. A reno might be what it takes to bring the place back to the front of everyone's minds," I tell her.

She beams at me and pushes the school door open. "This is going to be really, really fun. I can feel it in my bones."

I don't have the heart to tell her that she probably just jinxed it.

9

Darren

I palm my beer while staring at the photo Sasha sent me. The chatter happening around me at the table in Peakside is muffled, ignored again.

Abbie's sitting on an oversized reclining chair in a home theatre. She's grinning for the camera while her five fingers are deep in a bucket of popcorn. I love seeing her smile like that, but the bite of envy appears the way it always does when I see her at Brad's place.

Sasha's fiancé is loaded after a long, successful career in real estate, and he doesn't have a shortage of toys or luxuries to make sure everyone knows it. Bryce loves to say that Sasha clearly grew to have a type over the years we were together. I know better than to think she chose Brad because he was anything like me.

She hates me. Has for a long time now.

Really, she probably chose him because he's a more successful version of me. That's if it had anything to do with me at all, which, when it comes to her, things usually do. It's become tradition.

"Is that my beautiful niece?" Poppy asks, sneaking a look at my phone.

Sandwiched between me and Garrison, she's been very snoopy all night. I've lost count of how many times she's heard my phone buzz and asked who I was texting.

I tilt the screen so she can see the photo properly. "It is."

"Oh. She's at Brad's."

"Geez, Pops. Don't make it sound any more disappointing," Anna teases.

The wife of Cherry Peak's homegrown country star smiles at my sister, the corners of her eyes crinkling with humour. I glance over at Brody, her husband, and find him taking a sip of beer while staring boldly at her. It's almost too intimate of a look, so I dart my eyes to the end of the table, where Bryce and Daisy have taken up only one chair beside Johnny and Rory.

My best friend already has her eyes on me despite the hands she has roaming over Daisy's thighs. I cock a brow. Bryce does the same. I scowl. Bryce copies.

"It is repulsive," Bryce says, brow still lifted and lips flat.

Daisy shakes her head. "You can't say that about Abbie's stepdad, Frosty."

"I can and I will. He's a turd. The only time he's ever around Darren is to rub something in his face. Why else is he always sending Abbie home with upgraded versions of everything she already has?"

Swallowing, I soothe my dry throat with foamy beer.

"Because he's making a show of his wealth," Garrison mutters, knowing better than any of us what that looks like.

"Do you think they'll be helping with the drive-in reno?" Johnny asks.

I eye the long-haired cowboy and get hit with the startling realization that he somehow looks even older than he did last Saturday. Daisy's twin brother isn't all that much younger than the rest of us, but where Daisy's always had this maturity in her eyes, Johnny's were always full of a bright sense of life and freedom that intimidated me for a while.

He's the guy who kept up a façade that he didn't take much

of anything seriously and was just in search of a fun time. The group of us learned quickly that wasn't all he was interested in, and when Aurora—Rory—came to town, it became clear as day that I'd misjudged him. Our friendship has grown steadily over the last few years and took a huge leap the past couple as I've dealt with Sasha's engagement. I trust Johnny with as much as I do Brody and fuck, even Garrison. That says enough.

Brody barks a laugh. "Not a fuckin' chance. I doubt even Garry here will be offerin' to help pick up trash."

"I'm quite capable of filling a garbage bag, Brody," Garrison grates.

Poppy kisses his cheek, smoothing a hand down his arm. "Don't bully my man, guys. You'd be surprised how handy he's gotten recently."

"Not interested in learning about that," I quip, expression twisting with disgust.

Johnny adjusts Rory on his lap and sets his chin on her shoulder as she meets my gaze and says, "Are you planning on helping, Darren? I heard that the entire station was."

"Yeah, Caleb signed us all up. Is everyone else?"

"Yep! I got every business downtown to fill out the volunteer form too," Anna says.

Brody stretches his arm along the back of the booth, draping it over Anna's shoulders. "I heard a rumour that Wanda's back. She sign up too?"

"I can neither confirm nor deny that yet," Rory answers.

Being half-sisters with Wanda Rose, the daughter of one of the biggest names in country music outside of Brody, Rory knows more about her whereabouts than the rest of us do. She left a few years back to head out to Toronto and hasn't been back since. Not until now, supposedly.

Cherry Peak loves gossip, and the unexpected return of Wanda Rose is no exception to that.

"Well, then there should be enough help. I'm just surprised the mayor decided to care about it," Brody says.

Anna tips her chin in agreement before looking at Bryce. "Did you speak with him about it, Ice?"

Bryce doesn't so much as blink before replying, "Briefly."

"Briefly? And that was enough to convince him to care?" Johnny asks, not buying it.

"Yep."

I hide my every reaction to their questions and Bryce's very obvious lie. We both know he only agreed because he's still trying to buy back his daughter's love after letting his wife trample all over her for years. She used it to our advantage, but it still wasn't easy by any means.

And I know she did it for me.

"Right. We'll just have to choose to believe you there," Johnny says.

Bryce flips him off. "It's sounding a lot like you want to be put to work the hardest."

"Never been afraid of hard work, Ice," he retorts with a quick wink.

"I personally think that this is going to be really fun. Like one last hurrah before we all get married and start popping out a thousand babies," Daisy gushes.

Bryce's arm tightens around her, a glimmer of awe there and gone in her eyes. "You heard her."

"How about we focus on gettin' Darren out on a date before talkin' about babies? He's got some catchin' up to do," Brody says, the pointedness of his voice reminding me of the brief conversation we had at Bryce's Into The Shade opening.

"Who pissed in your coffee this mornin'?"

"Life," I mutter.

"Tell it to fuck off, then. She's alone. Go talk to her."

I don't pretend to not know who he's talking about. I've been staring at her since the moment she got here exactly fifty-four minutes ago.

"It's better if I don't."

"Why? Because you don't want to put yourself out there?" he asks.

"This day is about Bryce. Not me."

"Bryce isn't even over here. She's been doing flash tattoos for the last hour."

I know. She threatened to give me one on the tip of my nose if I didn't stop hovering around her.

From the moment Delaney walked in the door, none of the pre-rehearsed lines I'd repeated to myself mattered. They'd disappeared into nothingness, leaving me with an empty brain. So, yeah, I was unapologetically using Bryce as a shield.

That didn't stop me from looking at her, though. I just couldn't stop myself. After going so long without catching a glimpse of her freckles or platinum hair, one unexpected glance had me desperate for more. It was like the Earth had been off course and finally realigned. Like I've been living in a windowless room and finally got to see the sun again.

"One day, she's goin' to stop comin' to things alone," Brody says, voice low.

My muscles lock as I force my words up through the sudden nausea. "She will."

"And by then, you won't have the power to do anythin' about it," he adds.

"It would be fair. I was with Sasha."

"And miserable the entire time. I don't think you've ever accepted just how bad you were doin' back then or how obvious it was to everyone who knew you."

"It's in the past now. Why does it matter? You're wanting me to go up to my ex-girlfriend and what, Brody? Ask her if she's okay after losing her grandmother? The one person she had left in this town? I didn't do it two weeks ago when I should have."

"I'm sure she'd still appreciate hearin' it from you. Especially from you."

My stomach rolls, heat flushing up my throat. "She came here alone, surrounded by my friends and our families. She did that for Bryce and the women in our lives because they simply asked her to. I have no place ruining that kindness and making it about me."

Brody lays a hand on my shoulder, firmly tugging me. "So make it *about her. That's all. Then let it go. It's clearly been upsettin' you that you haven't reached out to her since we all heard about her grandma."*

"Fine. Yeah. Then you'll let it go," I demand.

He keeps his expression unreadable. "For now."

I adjust the brim of my cap and glance past him at where Delaney still stands. As I push past the guilt and fear sizzling in my gut like wet Pop Rocks, I duck around Brody and head in her direction.

Every step is heavy and feels like there's fresh cement in my shoes. I pass a few groups of people who look from me to my destination before spinning to whisper to someone. I grit my teeth and ignore them all. If Bryce or Poppy were with me, they'd make a show of telling them to fuck off. It's what they've been doing on my behalf for the past decade, even if I don't need them to defend me at every turn. It's second nature at this point to ignore the voices of those who don't really know shit about me.

Deep green eyes snap toward me. I slow my pace, struggling beneath the weight of emotions in that simple stare. My ribs pierce into my heart when Delaney straightens in her spot beside the bathroom door and closes off her expression. The flowy burnt-orange skirt she's wearing brushes her calves when she twists and shifts enough that she's no longer facing me directly.

I should have taken that as sign enough that this conversation wasn't going to go well.

Instead of listening to my gut, I stayed, and the words that followed broke my heart all over again. I don't think I can have it happen again. Not when I haven't healed from the very first break. Agreeing to go along with Bryce's drive-in rebuild idea was reckless. Yet, I haven't been able to bail out yet.

Delaney Brooks might have been my first, last, and only heartbreak, but I still refuse to believe that that's all she'll be.

"Last I remembered, I was the first one of us to fall in love," I say.

Bryce's surprise matches Brody's. It's Poppy who speaks first.

"Well, how about that? You're not trying to forget about your great love anymore, then?"

"I didn't say that."

"Didn't have to. We all know what or *who* you're talking about," Johnny teases.

Daisy's the one I look to now, knowing better than anyone that it's her who's grown closest to Delaney.

She meets my waiting eyes and smiles knowingly. "So, back to the rebuild."

10

Delaney

"Darren's going to drop dead when he sees you," Poppy squeals.

I flush, eyeing myself in the vanity mirror. "Do you think so? It isn't too much? Should I put back on the dress from earlier?"

"Are you kidding? You're going to be the most beautiful girl at prom. If I look half as good as you for mine next year, I won't have any issues with finding a date."

"You're already gorgeous, Poppy."

Darren's sister flashes me a soft smile. "I know. I've really started to love my body again the last few weeks. It's beautiful."

"It is. You are."

"Anyway, this isn't about me and my good looks. It's about you," she says.

I laugh, popping the lid off my favourite nude lipstick. "And Darren."

"Prom isn't about my brother. If it weren't for us, he wouldn't have even known that corsages were a thing."

"Isn't that a very typical teen guy issue?" I ask, running the smooth edge of the lipstick over my bottom lip. "Grayson didn't know about them either."

My younger brother couldn't have cared less when I brought it up and asked him. He was too busy with his nose in his game controller.

"Probably. Teen boys suck. I'm pretty sure Bryce is going to avoid taking one to prom at all. You honestly got lucky with my brother."

"Don't let him hear you say that," I joke. With a final look at my reflection, I pull in a long breath. "I hardly recognize myself, Pops. You killed the hair and makeup."

She gives her deep red hair a flip over her shoulder. "Thank you, thank you. I'm a natural talent."

"Do you really think Darren will like it?"

I've tried telling myself that it's only one night out of the hundreds we've already spent together, but my heartbeat still refuses to stop racing. I enlisted Poppy's help not only because I knew she could do a better job than I could, but because I wanted her friendship tonight. While she's a year and a half younger than me, she's still the best friend I have in town.

Not only is she honest and kind, but she's gotten to know me like a sister over the years I've been with Darren. We're our true selves around each other, and I'm almost as grateful for her as I am her brother.

"He'd tell you you're the most beautiful girl in the world, even if you showed up wearing a cardboard box," Poppy declares.

My hair is curled and pulled back into a half updo with a few pieces left out to frame my face. I pluck at one and say, "I know he would. That doesn't mean he'd be telling the truth, though."

"Nah, it absolutely does. He's so stupidly in love with you. Now, get up and do a spin so I can see the full look."

I roll my eyes and grin before doing as I'm told. My heels are a bit wobbly despite my attempts to break them in as I lift my arms and do a wonky twirl. My deep green, sequined dress is form-fitting enough for my boobs to stay tucked in tight as I move, a laugh erupting as Poppy starts cheering.

Our laughter mixes and carries out the open window as I lose my balance and grab her, using her arms to steady myself. Poppy takes the chance to pull me in for a hug. We clutch each other tight.

"Oh, I missed all the fun, didn't I?"

I glance up over Poppy's shoulder and find my grandma's eyes watching us. My grin spreads wider somehow.

"You made it," I say while Poppy lets me go.

My grandma clucks her tongue. "Did you doubt me?"

"No. But I know how hard—"

She gives her head one firm shake and pulls me close. Her lips meet my cheek before I'm being held at arm's length and she's giving me an up-and-down look.

"You're a vision, Laney. A dream for that boy of yours."

I swallow past the ball in my throat. "Thank you."

"When's he getting here?"

Poppy waves her phone in the air, drawing our attention. "He's outside! This isn't a drill. He's outside!"

"You better get down there to greet him, then," Grandma says.

"Or you could stay up here, and I'll go down and greet him. We could record you going down the stairs, and you could keep it to play at your wedding one day. Oh, I just gave myself the shivers," Poppy rambles, hearts in her eyes.

I roll my lips. "Isn't that a little cliché?"

"Cliché? You're going to prom with the same guy you've been dating since you were fifteen. There's a literal promise ring on your finger, Delaney. No offense, but can it get more cliché than all of that?"

"She has a point," Grandma interjects, smoothing a hand down my crown.

I exhale, automatically reaching to twirl the thin band on my left finger. "Alright. But at least tell him that I'm not trying to back out of going."

"Deal," Poppy says at the same time the doorbell rings. "I'll call you down when we're ready!"

I let her go without another argument, and Grandma wraps an arm around my shoulders. The soothing motion of her rubbing my bicep has me relaxing slightly.

"Your parents wish they were here to see you today. You know that, right?"

"I do. There's nothing they could have done to make it work."

Grandma sighs and holds me tighter than a frail old woman should be able to. "You're my girl, Laney. I'm so proud of you, and so are they. One day, we'll all be here together to celebrate you and the beautiful life you're going to have."

"I know. I'm pretty sure the entire hall could hear them cheering over video during the grad ceremony."

"Good."

I wouldn't have chosen for my parents to both work jobs that have taken them all over the world, but it's what's given me the childhood I've had. Them being in London this week instead of here to watch me graduate and attend my one and only prom hurt at first before I reminded myself that they'd be here if they could.

And I've got my grandma and Grayson with me. Not to mention Darren, Poppy, and the entire Huntsly family.

"Let's get you down to see Darren now, hmm?"

A swarm of butterflies fills my stomach. I can't stop the climb of my smile.

"Yeah, it's time," she adds, taking in my reaction.

We leave my bedroom, and I grip her arm a bit tighter the closer we get to the staircase. Darren's voice travels toward me.

"If you're trying to build anticipation, Poppy, I don't think I can handle any more."

"It'll be worth it."

"I know. She's worth everything."

There's no making me wait any longer after hearing that. I release my grandma's arm and rush down the hall. I'm still as wobbly as earlier when I clack a heel to the first stair and draw my favourite pair of brown eyes.

Darren's lips part as he stares at me, the hand that was fiddling with his tie dropping to smack his thigh. Time stills as if it's giving us a moment to just . . . stare at one another while slowly closing the distance. We linger in place once we're only one stair apart, our eyes roaming and exposing the words still held inside.

The corner of my mouth tips up when I lower my gaze to see him pinching his thigh. His throat bobs, colour crawling up his neck and ears. In a flash, he's taking my hand in his.

I step off the final stair and lean up on my toes when he cups my cheek in his hand. He glides his fingers down past my throbbing pulse and settles them on the back of my neck, holding me there.

"Let me marry you, Delaney Marie Brooks."

I clutch the waist of his suit jacket and flutter my heavy lashes. "You know that we have to wait four years."

"Four years is too fucking long, Elle."

"It's the only way I'll know you mean it."

He blows out a breath that fans over my nose and leans down to kiss me.

It's hungry, desperate, yet nothing that I worry will scar my grandmother for life. I respond in kind, hoping he can feel the confidence I have in us. The promise I've been giving him since the day he asked me to be his girlfriend three years ago, when nobody, not even us, thought it would be much more than an infatuation meant to burn off quickly. That's all love is expected to be with fifteen-year-olds, but it was the opposite.

I knew from the moment he found a nine-year-old Delaney nursing a grass-stained, skinned knee on the football field with a book in her hand that he was meant to be something far more than an infatuation. Unlike all of the other boys our age, he saw me and rushed into the school before coming back out with a giant wad of wet paper towels in his hands. He plopped himself on the ground in front of me and began cleaning the smeared blood and grass from my skin while telling me about how many times he'd done the same thing while learning to play football. My books caught his eye, and suddenly, I was gifted the rest of the series from him the following Christmas.

I didn't say much of anything to him then, but from that day on, we were attached at the hip.

"Four years," he relents, the words lingering on my lips.

I press my thumb over the smear of nude lipstick left on his mouth and laugh when he tries to lick it. "Let's focus on tonight. Not tomorrow or four years from now. Just tonight."

"Anything you want, baby."

"Anything?"

Fire flares in his eyes. His massages the back of my head, teasing the delicate mess of curls and bobby pins that Poppy created earlier. I lean into his teasing touch and run my fingers over the gelled swoop of his hair.

"I'm still here, in case you forgot. And so is Grandma B. Do you really want to scar such a sweet old lady with your love talk?" Poppy interjects.

Grandma's laugh is croaky but kind, the way it always is. "I'm not a prude, Poppy. Let them love on each other. One day, you'll find yourself doing the same thing with someone of your choice."

Darren stares at me, content despite the teasing. Like he'd be okay with doing just this for the rest of forever.

"You look incredible, Elle. I don't know what I did to deserve you or to find you so early on in my life, but I feel really fucking grateful that I did."

I trace the strong length of his nose with a freshly manicured nail. "You can show me just how grateful you are when I force you to dance with me tonight."

"And if I already want to dance with you?"

"Then I'd say I love you," I muse, giving him a peck while he takes hold of my waist and tugs me in close.

"Did you remember the corsage?" Poppy asks.

I look away from Darren and to his sister, noticing the phone she has lifted in front of her face. Darren releases me and spins to the entrance table. When he faces me again, it's with a giant white flower in his hands.

"You reminded me ten thousand times today to pick it up, Pops," he says.

I extend my hand for him, and he slips the flower and its black band onto my wrist. His eyes fix themselves to the ring on my finger before flashing back up at me. With a smirk, I wiggle my fingers at Poppy.

"Did you help him pick this out?"

"She did *not*," Darren answers for her. "In case she tries to take credit."

Poppy scoffs. "I would never."

I laugh, knowing just as well as Darren that teasing her brother about something like this is absolutely something Poppy would do.

"Let's do pictures. Your mom keeps asking for some," Grandma says with a hand on my arm.

Excitement flows through me. "Okay, but no lame poses, okay?"

Grandma ignores me and gets to work. Darren traces the low cut back of my dress, and I shiver while wrapping my arm around his front, my hand tucked beneath his jacket.

"The lame poses age the best," he murmurs, lips to my ear.

"Fine. But we have to love them enough to hang one up in our new house once you've built it."

"You have a deal, Elle."

11

Darren

Abbie snaps the beaded bracelet on her wrist and leans forward between the seats to snag the bag of licorice I keep in the console. Her hair flies in the wind from the open window when she flops back in her seat. I watch her in the rear-view mirror long enough to witness her chomp the end of a licorice and focus on the empty fields outside of town.

"What if I were saving those?" I ask, brow raised.

"You don't like them. Why are they always in the car?"

"How do you know that I don't like them?"

She juts her chin and rips another chunk off the licorice. "'Cause you never eat them."

"Maybe I do when I'm alone so you can't steal them like you are right now," I throw back, turning off the main road.

Gravel crunches beneath the tires as I slow the car to a crawl. Suddenly, the last thing I want to do is joke around about candy. There's no chance I can let my nonchalant mask slip without spooking my daughter, though.

As far as she knows, the drive in was just a fun place to hang out when I was a teenager. We're here today to fulfill the volunteer demands Caleb placed on all of us at the station. I had *nothing* to do with this idea because if Sasha heard a different story . . . that's simply not a situation I'd like to focus on right now.

"It's busy here," Abbie notes.

"Most of the town is taking part in the rebuild."

"Do we get to come here and watch movies after it's fixed?"

My stomach tightens, an immediate dismissal on my tongue. I swallow it. "Sure."

"Cool!"

So easily settled, my daughter pushes up a bit higher in her seat and sticks her head as far out the window as it'll reach. The rows of vehicles already in the parking lot take me a bit by surprise. Bryce told me there were going to be a lot of people here, but I guess I didn't fully believe her.

I spot Brody's pickup beside Johnny's, and Bryce's car a few spots down. My palms become slick with sweat as I search for the same silver car that I see in the school parking lot every morning I drop Abbie off, because that's all I've convinced myself I can do for now.

Continue to watch Delaney like a fucking stalker.

Pulling into the closest empty space I can find, I rein in my nerves and tuck them away for now.

"Alright, remember not to run off on me today. The station did a good job of clearing debris, but there could still be anything hanging around," I say.

"Like a nail?"

I hesitate briefly, running that terrible possibility through my head. "I was thinking something a little less dangerous happening than you stepping on a nail, but yes, I guess just like a nail."

"I'll be careful," she swears, finished with her candy now.

I tug the keys out of the ignition and unlock the doors. "You mean it?"

"I swear it," she vows with a grin.

"I'll be counting on it, then. Let's go."

We step out at the same time, and she doesn't take off like she would have three years ago. Instead, she pats her thighs and looks up at me for direction.

"Let's look for your aunts."

She hums in agreement. "I didn't see Auntie Pops' car."

"I wouldn't be surprised if Garrison didn't want it to get dirty on these roads."

"He let me use washable markers on the windows last time I was at their house."

Pausing, I glance down at her. "He did?"

"Yep. And he helped me wash them after."

"I guess I stand corrected, then."

Abbie's grin sparkles. "Can we get a Slurpee after we're done?"

"Sure, sweetheart. Let's just focus on finding out what we're here to do today for now."

I drop a steady hand to the back of her head and pat her hair. She huffs and reaches up to swat me away, her smile still locked in place.

"I'm not a kid anymore," she says pointedly.

"You'll always be a kid to me. My little girl, more like."

"Yeah, yeah."

"There you are. You're almost late," Bryce chides.

Pivoting, I offer her a forced smile. Abbie abandons me completely for my best friend. She joins Bryce a few paces away and gives her a usual hug.

"Hi!"

Bryce relaxes the immediate tightness in her shoulders at the affection and slowly lowers her arms around the little girl. She meets my gaze over Abbie's head and cocks a brow.

"How hard did your dad try to delay leaving the house, Abs?" she asks.

The question's meant for me instead, but I hold back, letting my daughter answer.

Abbie pops back a step and glances at my chest. "He changed shirts three times."

"Wrong." It was actually four times.

"Don't call your daughter a liar," Bryce drawls.

Abbie pouts. "Yeah, Dad. Don't call me a liar."

"Don't turn her against me, Bryce. Or it'll be you she's spending every night making bracelets with."

Bryce pales, blue eyes wide. "Fu—screw off."

"It's okay. I know 'fuck' is a bad word," Abbie says, placating Bryce with a hand on her arm.

I choke back a laugh. "Abbie. Don't say that."

"Say what? Fuck?" she asks, head cocked.

"Yes! Don't say fuck, or your mother will be taking your new vocabulary up with me."

"Eh, you can just blame me," Bryce says.

I meet her stare. "That might be worse."

"I won't tell Mom," Abbie offers.

With a long exhale, I say, "How about we just abandon the conversation and move on. Where do we go now, Bryce? Is there some sort of check-in?"

"My dad's making a speech in a few minutes, and I already know what your assignment is."

"You organized everyone?"

She rolls her eyes. "Your surprise is hurtful."

Bryce and social events don't always add up, let alone ones like this. She knows better than I do that my surprise is warranted.

"What do we get to do, Auntie?" Abbie asks.

Bryce peels her attention from me, making sure to do it slowly so I know I'm not off the hook yet. "You're going to make some posters to promote the drive-in with the other students from the school."

"Really? Cool! Is Dad helping?" She turns her head to look up at me. "Are you going to help me?"

"Your dad is going to be working on a different team, kiddo," Bryce answers.

"I am?"

She narrows her eyes, almost as if she can't believe I'd ask her that. "Yes."

"Great," I say.

"Can I go help now?" Abbie asks, bouncing in place as she looks over the field for the other kids.

"We can bring you there. Then, I'll get your dad over with his group."

"Sweet."

A car door closes from somewhere in the open lot, and my stomach jumps. I haven't spotted Delaney yet. She's not beside the lingering pile of wood in the field or by the bright orange tent set up on the left of it. While Cherry Peak is small, I'd be able to pick her out in a crowd a hundred times this size. Not only that, but I'd have felt her presence the moment I stepped onto the gravel road. Like a tickle in the back of my mind or between my ribs, I'd have felt it.

That's why I know that it was her closing that door.

Instead of turning around to confirm it with sight rather than feeling, I meet Bryce's waiting stare and freeze. She's far more confident than I am. Not only about this whole rebuild idea, but about Delaney and me too. Maybe it's the whole best friend thing we've had going on forever, but she's always been vocal about her disappointment in the decisions I made all those years ago with Delaney.

Between her and Poppy, I've lost track of the number of chastising speeches I've been forced to endure. I've deserved each one.

"It's Ms. Delaney!" Abbie cheers.

I can't look back yet. Bryce sighs.

"Can I say hi, Dad?"

My voice sounds weird when I say, "You don't want to go see the group you'll be working with first?"

"Not yet. I want to say hi to my teacher."

Bryce breaks eye contact and glances over my shoulder. "Hey, Delaney."

It's habit to reach up and touch the brim of my hat. The tear in the corner of it reminds me of which one it is. My stomach becomes so tense it's painful. *Of course.*

"Hi, Bryce. And hello, Abbie. I love your shorts."

Her voice is a punch to the gut. Drawing air into my lungs is stressful.

"Darren," she adds, my name weighed down like it's strenuous for her to speak it.

I suck back a pained hiss when Bryce steps close to me and kicks the back of my ankle. With a wince, I shift and turn around. The toe of a cowboy boot runs back and forth in the dirt, creating a deep groove as I keep my eyes lowered.

Bryce kicks me again. I look up and immediately wish I'd just let her do it for a third time instead.

"Delaney," I breathe out.

Nobody should look this fucking beautiful just to volunteer cleaning up a mess of burnt wood on scorched land. Her eyes are cool despite her attempt at a smile as she stares at my hat. They've always been the one part of her that she could never control. Angry, sad, happy, her eyes always gave her away. And right now, it's killing me that she so obviously wants to be anywhere but here.

"Thank you. I put the gems on by myself," Abbie announces, pride thick in her words.

"That's incredible. I used to bedazzle my clothes when I was your age too, but my mom always found them loose in the dryer after the first wash or stuck inside my brother's T-shirts."

Abbie giggles. "They get stuck to my dad's clothes."

"Sometimes a bit of sparkle makes an outfit."

I struggle to swallow. "Haven't found any in our dryer, though."

"When's the last time you checked, D?" Bryce asks, watching me a bit too closely.

"Never!" Abbie erupts, laughing harder now.

It's impossible not to stare at Delaney. Not because I want to see her reaction to my daughter's laughter, but because I simply can't help but steal another glance. In the late-morning sun, her hair is brighter, almost a shade too light that it's white. It drapes her shoulders in loose waves that rustle in the wind but never fly into her face.

Her short frame is hugged by a plain, blush-pink long-sleeve she's tucked into the band of a pair of high-waisted blue jeans. There's a plaid shirt tied around her waist that hangs behind her thighs, and with the addition of the cowboy boots that remind me a bit too much of the same pair I used to hide under my bed when we were too young to be seeing each other . . . Fuck.

I'm transported back in time too easily, and it's damn hard to keep fighting off the memories that follow any amount of time near her. My first instinct is to forget about all the mess and pain between us and take her in my arms. It's been almost a decade since I've had her there, and I crave it more than anything else.

"Thank you for organizing this, Bryce. I should go find out where I'm supposed to go, I suppose," she says, avoiding looking at me now.

I take that on the chin. "You could stick around until the mayor starts speaking."

A long pause, and then the full weight of her stare rocks me back onto my heels. Delaney keeps a neutral expression, but fuck, I see through it.

"I want to say hi to a few other people before then."

"Like who?"

The question's out before I can stop it, and now there's no stopping the reaction to it. I wait for Bryce to kick me again, but instead, she blows out a long breath that's fucking worse.

Delaney narrows her stare and tightens the tie at her middle. Then, in the blink of an eye, she's focused on my daughter with a strained yet warm smile, making it obvious that I've been dismissed.

"Enjoy the weekend, Abbie. I'll see you Monday morning."

My daughter holds her hands against her middle the way she does when she's stopping herself from hugging someone. "Okay. See you, Ms. Delaney."

"See you, Abbie. Bye, Bryce. Darren."

"Try not to get a sliver during cleanup," Bryce replies.

Delaney huffs a laugh. "You too."

She ignores my heavy gaze as I watch her, not speaking. For some reason, that's what strikes me the deepest. Her lack of acknowledgement. And here I go, sounding like a goddamn selfish asshole again.

"Did you remember sunscreen?" I ask.

She snaps her eyes in my direction. I see the surprise appear for a moment before she washes it out with annoyance.

"Yes. I always do."

Not always. She used to forget it every other time we stepped outside and would come inside with pink skin.

I nod and let it go. Some things—too many things—have changed, but some never will. And I think I'm about done with trying to pretend otherwise. Not when I've finally got her closer than I have for way too many years.

I've yearned for her since the moment I let her go but have shoved it down deep enough that I convinced myself it had disappeared. That changed at Into The Shade, and now, it's time to remind her of who I am and who we used to be together.

This might be my last chance.

12

Delaney

"T HERE ARE MORE IMPORTANT THINGS IN THIS TOWN THAN THE drive-in. The playground at the school hasn't been upgraded in nearly ten years. It's borderline unsafe to have the kids playing on it. Pulling slivers out of fingers wasn't on the curriculum."

"We can vote Lemieux out soon. He doesn't seem to have any clue how to run this town."

"You don't think this has anything to do with his running for re-election?"

"Why would it? Nobody wants this place rebuilt, so he's not gaining much."

"Well, not *nobody*."

The pointed silence that follows that weighted sentence pulls me from where I've fallen into my thoughts. It's been twenty minutes since I got here, and the mayor only finished speaking a second ago. It took half that time for the gossiping to commence.

There was nothing of importance shared besides a blanket statement about how the drive-in has played an important part in our town's history and that we need to band together to make sure the younger generation of Cherry Peakers can share similar experiences. The only useful piece of information was that not only are we responsible for getting the land ready for another structure to be built, but to do the actual building, we need to raise money. All of us together need to come up with enough successful fundraisers to raise tens, if not hundreds, of thousands of dollars.

It feels unlikely.

"For the majority of the town, then. And last time I checked, she was also a teacher at our school. Shouldn't the playground be more important to her?"

My skin tightens over my bones at the realization that they're talking about me. That I have to be the *she* in their conversation. A conversation that I was not invited to join.

Standing a few feet over from the group of teachers I've spent the last few years working alongside, I debate inserting myself in the conversation just to see what they do. Would they backtrack, pretend that they were talking about someone else, or be straightforward?

I watch the sixth-grade teacher lean closer to the new football coach and say something too quiet for me to catch this time around. I'm stuck in place, a bit mortified and a lot annoyed.

Some things will never change about a small town.

"I never took teachers for gossips," a friendly voice muses.

Sam Johnson, the RCMP officer from the night I watched this place burn to the ground, appears beside me. He keeps a generous distance between us, holding himself away almost shyly.

I clear my throat, hoping my cheeks aren't as pink as I fear they are. "You'd be surprised."

"The station's just as bad sometimes. One thing Cherry Peak doesn't lack is opinions from people who know nothing about a situation."

"It's tiring, right?"

Dressed in his uniform, he nods and holds his hip. "Very. But that's what we get for living here, I guess. There are other towns we could disappear into where we wouldn't have this issue."

That's exactly what my brother did. Leaving Cherry Peak was an easy decision for him, and now he lives a few hours away in Snowbell Ridge, working some stuffy job all alone. The only way to get him back here is to beg, and we're not the type of siblings to do that for some face time.

"That doesn't make it fair, though. Privacy and respect should be the bare minimum regardless of where you live."

"I won't argue with you there. We'd have a hell of a lot less disputes if we could all just get along."

Lifting my brows, I take a breath and let them fall again. "I sound naïve, don't I?"

"Not naïve. Maybe just a bit too wishful," he says lightly.

I chuff a laugh. "Too wishful. What a personality trait."

"I could think of worse ones."

My slight smile falls as I register the flirtatious tone of his voice. I hate how wrong it feels to have a man show interest in me, even as innocently as Sam. Shit, I'm broken. So incredibly broken.

He's a good-looking guy too. Tall and bulky enough to make it clear that he works out often and avoids the majority of my favourite foods. There's no hint of hair anywhere on his face, and his eyes are a shade of green similar to mine. Maybe it's a mix of all those things that explains why I'm not interested.

I hate that I know I'm right.

Sam isn't interesting to me because his hair is blond, he doesn't have a mustache, and his eyes aren't brown.

Frustration heats my chest as I shake that off, refusing to believe that I'm still holding out for a man who doesn't want me. I'm done with that. Way, way done.

"I'm sorry. That came off too strong," Sam rambles, face flushed. "I came on too strong."

Shaking my head, I reach out and touch his elbow. The immediate discomfort irritates me enough that I put more pressure behind my touch as if to tell myself off.

"No, no. You didn't. I'm sorry. I was up late last night."

It's not completely a lie. I was up late flirting with the idea of a stomach ulcer because of how stressed I got just thinking about today.

Sam's tense features relax as he glances down at my hand. "Alright. I'm glad to hear it. Well, not about you being up late."

"I know what you meant," I say, offering a smile.

"I'm not usually so messy with my words. I guess that's a Delaney effect."

Unsure of what to say to that, I just laugh. Thankfully, it doesn't sound awkward.

Sam is quick to fill the silence before it can stick around too long. "Anyway, do you know what group you've been assigned to?"

"No. I think they're posting groups right now."

He looks around and slips his hands into the pockets of his jacket. "It's like waiting to see which team you're on in gym class all over again."

"You've got a point. I'm just hoping I wasn't chosen last."

"You? I remember you being chosen early for every sport back then."

"I don't. But maybe I just blocked a lot of that time out of my memory," I joke to hide the bite in my side.

"I think most of us have probably done that."

Pushing past the urge to let the conversation die, I ask, "Is there a job you're hoping you're assigned to?"

"Not really. I'm just hoping not to have to work on any fundraisers."

"You're not a fan of them?"

"I don't mind the fundraising part, but the planning isn't for me. I'm not a very organized person. Are you?"

"I think so. It's the teacher in me."

Sam chuckles, and slowly, the space he left between is cut in half. "Maybe I could get some tips sometime. If I'm lucky, we'll be teamed up together."

"If you're lucky? You want to be lectured on how to be more organized?"

"By you? Any day," he says boldly.

I swallow and laugh stiffly. "We'll have to see, then."

His eyes flick down to my mouth before he clears his throat and lifts them again. "You know, even if we aren't put on the same team, I'd love to—"

"Hey, Elle. The groups are posted. We're on the same one."

Darren's voice startles me hard enough that I gasp. Loudly. For both him and Sam to hear. My cheeks burn as I whip around to face Darren and glare up at him.

"It's Delaney."

He isn't fazed by my snappy comment. Instead, he smirks in response, one brow tugging up. "Okay, *Delaney*. You're in my group."

Sam hasn't shifted an inch. He watches Darren curiously, almost like he's trying to figure out what he's thinking. My first instinct is to wish him luck. Darren isn't one to let just anyone into his mind. At least, he never used to be. But then again, it's not my place to interfere. I hardly know Sam, and right now, I could say the same about Darren.

"And what group is that? I think I'll go and look for myself," I say.

Darren shrugs. "Go for it. But I'm telling the truth."

"Your truth doesn't matter to me."

"It should, considering I've always been a man of my word."

A laugh bubbles out of me. It's low, dark, a cruel noise that for a brief moment, I hope digs into him as deep as it does me. Darren flinches, but as much as he deserves it, I don't get any satisfaction from his pain.

"I'm not sure you know what that means," I bite out.

He reaches up to touch that damn hat again, and my eyes follow the movement. Seeing it once was enough, but again? It's starting to chafe.

"Enlighten me."

"You're old enough to run an internet search."

A puff of air escapes him. "Fair enough. We're on the first round of cleanup."

"Sam isn't with us?" I ask.

Apparently, hearing his name is enough to remind the officer that he's still here and not just watching from afar. He blinks a few times and focuses on me, offering an uncomfortable smile.

Darren ignores him. "No. Just you, me, and a few of the guys from the fire station."

"Oh, how did I get so lucky? Who put me there?"

I'm snippy, but seriously? Out of all the groups, I'm on the one with my ex-boyfriend and all of his friends? This is bad karma for something.

"No idea. But I figured we could walk over together."

"I'm capable of walking over on my own. I was in the middle of a conversation, actually," I toss back.

There's a break in his mask as the corner of his eye twitches. "You're more than welcome to finish it."

"But I thought it was time to go?"

Sam clears his throat. "I should go find my group, actually. We'll catch up later, Delaney."

"Oh, alright. Yeah. We can talk later," I agree weakly.

It's obvious that I don't want him to stay for anything other than to be a buffer between me and Darren. Shit. I refuse to use anyone just to get a rise out of a ghost from the past. Nope. *Not* happening.

Sam takes a wide step back, his gaze lingering before shifting to Darren. "Have fun, guys."

"You too," I croak.

He's hardly two feet away when Darren speaks again. "How well do you know that guy?"

"What?"

"Sam, was it? How well do you know him?"

I stare at him in surprise, my arms crossing over my chest as I grapple for an appropriate response.

What he really deserves is a very colourful *screw you.*

"Why does it matter to you?"

The tick of his jaw is almost satisfying to witness. "It doesn't. I just think you should be careful with who you're letting into your life."

"And why's that? Because you're so concerned? Cry me a river, Darren."

His reply doesn't matter enough to keep me standing here. The audacity of this man to think he can ask any sort of question about my personal life is astounding. I'd rather have this discussion with Banana, Anna's fluffy cow, than with Darren.

"You wouldn't believe me even if I admitted that I was concerned," he says, following after me.

I spin right back around and jab a finger in the air. "If anyone here was going to be a danger to me, it wouldn't be Sam."

Darren presses his lips together while he lurches to a stop. "What are you insinuating?"

"I don't know. What *am* I insinuating?"

"I'd never hurt you."

"Not physically. But there are plenty of ways to hurt someone without lifting a hand. Now, if you'll excuse me, I'm going to take a look at group assignments myself. Stop following me."

"I want to talk to you, Delaney. Have a real conversation. I wasn't putting that out there at the school for shits and giggles. I meant it."

My heart tries to jump out of my chest and into his arms as I struggle with the lingering pull to him that won't just disappear once and for all. It's never mattered how many nights I stayed up begging the universe to suck the memory of him out of my head. There's always been Darren's face in my mind, reminding me of what could have been.

I stare him straight in the eyes and speak slowly, concisely. "Prove it."

His single step forward steals my breath. "Fine."

"Fine."

"And when I do? Then what?"

My shoulders go loose, a façade of ease transforming me.

"Then I'll listen."

13

Darren

I figured she'd be pissed off.

I'd have been concerned if she was at all agreeable to my nose suddenly being in her personal life. Only it's not all that sudden. Not to me or anyone who's had to listen to my endless whining over the years. I've known more about her life than I'd ever admit to, and I'm still trying to figure out if that makes me as much of a creep as I think it does.

While there were rumours of her heading onto her first date since coming back home, I was staying up all night drinking myself into a stupor while listening to Sasha ream me out for not picking up the right design of diapers that morning. When she was coming home from a week-long trip to Greece for her parents' vow renewal ceremony, I was on my front porch, staring at the road to town searching for her headlights to pull in.

I always thought that just meant I cared enough despite everything to at least make sure she was taken care of. That it was my duty as someone who loved her in the past to keep tabs on her in the present in case anything bad happened.

It wasn't until I spoke to her for the first time in years that I realized how pathetic it was believing those lies. I've never searched for her in a crowded room or stayed up too late scrolling social media for a sign of life because I was just looking out. *Doing my due diligence.*

I did those things because I missed her and have regretted letting her go every single day since our last goodbye.

That's my burden to bear, though. I'm the one who made the mistakes I did, even if they led me to my daughter. Abbie is the light that I needed at the darkest point of my life, and I owe her everything for pulling me back into half the man I was before I lost Delaney.

Watching Delaney move around the old drive-in grounds with a slight scowl and an annoyance that has her boots kicking up dirt with every fierce step, it's even harder to deny how badly I still want her.

Because I do. I want the anger she's been shoving down and the heat from the flames she's just itching to spit at me. Then, I want her honesty. The secrets she's hidden in the deepest parts of her subconscious that I know are there because they're in mine too. The truth will set us free, even if it ravages me in the process.

"You're staring at her like a weirdo, Darren," Poppy whispers pointedly.

Brushing up beside me, my sister flicks a look to Delaney and sighs when I don't reply instantly.

"Why don't you just go and try to talk to her? Isn't that the whole point of getting her put in your group?"

I lift a finger to my mouth and make a shh noise. "Can you not expose me already?"

"As if she didn't put that together instantly."

"Even if she has, it hasn't changed her desire for us to speak."

She blinks at me, deadpan. "Did you expect differently?"

"I didn't expect anything."

"But you hoped."

"Apparently, it was misplaced."

Her fingers curl around my wrist before she tugs, forcing me to face her, unable to shy away from her demanding stare. "Be honest with me for a second here, D."

"About what?"

"I've been avoiding asking you directly because I didn't want to upset you, but you've lost that privilege now. What happened at Into The Shade? Because I know that day changed something for you. You went from avoiding all things related to Delaney to asking about her in ways that you think won't give away your interest. But news flash, I'm your sister, and I know you better than anyone else does. Other than Della."

I search the grounds for the rest of the station, not finding them close enough to have heard Poppy's rant. Only then do I suck in a long breath and let my walls down. I rub my sternum, needing some sort of calm.

"Talking about it here won't do anything to help. I don't know how to go up and talk to her without apologizing so many times she tells me to shut up," I admit.

Sympathy bleeds into her eyes. "Talk to her like you used to. Even if she doesn't talk back. I don't know what it's like to lose someone I loved so young and still want them years later, but I do know what it feels like to lose someone I love and wish they would come back to me."

"Garrison," I say, not bothering to ask.

She nods. "Time and distance might work for some people, but it never has for me, and it never did for you and Delaney. I won't continue to tell you that you made a mistake because you know it as well as I do. But maybe it's time to stop letting the past hold so much power over you. Everyone makes mistakes. Messing things up with a woman you love doesn't make you special. The way you earn back her forgiveness is what will."

"And if it's impossible to earn her forgiveness?"

She drapes her arm behind me and squeezes tight. "Then you need to move on completely."

My pulse thrashes as I immediately reject the idea. "So, forgiveness it is, then."

"I'd say that's the best bet for the both of you," she agrees, her tone light and almost teasing.

"You don't think if I go up to her right now, she'll punch me in the face?"

She lets loose a small laugh. "I knew you already managed to piss her off. What did you do?"

"Might have butted into her business. There's a guy sniffing around."

"Sniffing around? Is he a dog?"

I run two fingers over my mustache, fidgeting. "You know what I meant. Fuck, I should have kept my mouth shut. It was too much, too soon."

"Maybe she just doesn't like your mustache."

Stilling, I glare at my sister. "Are you trying to make me self-conscious?"

"Is that possible?"

"Last I checked, yup."

"Damn, you learn something new every day," she sings, eyes twinkling.

"I'm going now before I wind up shedding tears."

With a slight smile, she nudges her chin to where Delaney's moved on to chucking chunks of wood into a pile. "Good luck."

"Yeah, I'll need it."

Every step I take toward the woman fearlessly whipping pieces of charred wood still full of nails has me feeling a bit queasier. It would be incredibly easy for her to spin around and use my face as a target instead.

Maybe that would help break the ice. We could get even a bit that way.

Fuck. *No,* that would be the opposite of helpful.

"Do you want a pair of gloves?"

I wince at how awkward I sound. And when Elle snaps up from her crouched position, she picks up on it too. Before she can say anything back, I speak again despite knowing better.

"For your hands. Gloves. Because of the nails. Slivers."

Holy shit.

"Do you have gloves, or are you asking just to ask?"

Am I sweating? "I can find you some."

"I can find my own gloves," she says, turning me down instantly.

"Alright. I'll help you another way, then."

Brows flying up, Delaney uses the toe of her boot to kick another piece of wood aside. "There are plenty of other areas to clear. Plus, I thought the fire station was already supposed to have done all of this?"

"We've been working on it."

She hums and drops back down to her haunches to pick up a cracked four-by-four. Flipping it over, she taps a fingernail to a missing chunk of it.

"Are you upset that it's gone?"

"The drive-in?"

Delaney nods and tosses the wood.

"Seeing it up in flames hurt more than I expected it to," I reveal.

"I always expected it to be here, guarding the town. I guess I waited too long to come back."

"It won't be gone forever."

She turns away from me and stares out at the now empty field. The hunch of her shoulders is a dagger to the chest. "It won't ever be the same as it was."

"Is that such a bad thing? Maybe this is what we all needed," I offer, dragging my foot through the dead grass.

"We needed to lose a key structure from our past? For what? To be punished?"

My other foot moves through the grass. "It's hard to move on when our ankles are tied to something anchoring us in place."

"Don't make this about us."

"Isn't it, though? Nobody gives a shit about this place but us, Elle. We're the only ones standing here with an ache in our chests because the one place still calling to us is gone. Nothing but fucking ashes in the scorched grass."

Eyes burning with the hottest flames I've ever seen, she whips around, her head shaking. "It's. *Delaney*."

"You're angry with me. Good, you should be. I want you to be pissed off and honest about it. We can't continue to ignore each other and pretend that it's fine," I say, knowing damn well that I'm right back to being too much, too soon.

She could turn and run any second, and fuck, that's scary. But if I'm not honest, we won't get anywhere. We'll be stuck in this cycle that's tearing me up inside for the rest of our lives.

"You want me to be angry so that you can justify the hatred you hold for yourself and the choices you made! This isn't about me or us, Darren," she snaps.

"We can't go back in time. I can't change the things I did, but I also can't keep pretending that I don't hate what we've been doing since. You were more than my girlfriend. You were my best friend, and I miss you. Have been missing you for years."

She sucks in a sharp breath, eyes wide and full of disbelief. My hope rises, then quickly falls at the sight of her obvious step backward. "It's going to take a lot more than that to change anything. You don't get to just say those types of things and expect change."

"But there's a chance."

"For friendship?"

For now. "Yes."

"You deserve an outright denial."

My heart leaps. "So give me one."

"I can't do this right now."

She's going to leave. I can see it flashing in her eyes and in the firm twist at the corner of her pursed lips. There's fear tangled in the panic, painting a portrait that singes my gut.

"Then when?" I ask, more breathless than if I'd just run laps around this charred field.

"I don't have that answer."

"Think about it, then. Please."

"I need space." She lifts her hands and waves them between us. "Put things back to how they were."

That's the last thing I want. Still, I nod. "Okay. Whatever you want."

"Bye, Darren."

She spins and walks off as a cruel sense of déjà vu washes over me. This isn't the first time I've heard those words, afraid they'd be the last she'd say to me. The only difference is this time, I'm dead set on there being a different outcome than all those times before.

Goodbye for now, not forever.

14

Delaney

DAISY AND BRYCE ASKED ME TO BE HERE. DAISY AND BRYCE ASKED me to be here. Daisy and Bryce asked me to be here.

They're my friends, and friends don't ditch on important celebrations because the atmosphere is uncomfortable. I need to suck it up before I make tonight awkward. Who cares if everyone is looking at me and wondering why on earth I'm here. They can eat shit if they think I shouldn't be here to celebrate a friend's accomplishment.

Oof. Okay, so I'm clearly feeling a bit stabby tonight.

At least Brody's singing is enough to hide the harrowing silence that's followed my every move. If I had to walk past one more group of people who stopped talking the moment they sensed me, I'd have impaled someone's arm with an inky tattoo needle. It's better with something in the background, even if it's the same country song that I've heard playing a million times on the local radio station.

Leaning against the furthest wall from the busier half of the shop, I watch as Bryce finishes up what must be her tenth flash tattoo. The recipient of the frog wearing a matching rain boot and jacket set grins down at her wrist and thanks Bryce before hopping out of the chair.

I've never gotten a tattoo. Not during a drunken night out in college or amid a complete breakdown. There's nothing I want permanently inked on my body yet. Bryce is the opposite and has more colour on her skin than anyone else I've ever known. Every day I see her, I think she's gotten something new done. She's halfway through her second sleeve now and has added a daisy to the patch of skin behind her ear.

"Stay out of the sun for a few days and wash it with soap when you shower. Lotion up after," she instructs while snapping her black gloves off.

"Got it! Thanks, Bryce."

The dark-haired ice queen gives a shrug of acknowledgement before falling into her cleaning of the station she's at. I move my attention to the opposite side of the shop, where Shade, the huge, burly owner of this shop, is wearing a heavy black hoodie and jeans to match and flirting with a woman who is at least double his age, if I remember her correctly.

We're not in Cherry Peak, but everyone at the shop tonight ventured from that direction. Oak Point is a blink-and-you'll-miss-it little town nestled up against the Rocky Mountains with a population half the size of CP. I'd move here myself if I could fool myself into believing that the incredible view would be worth the aches and pains of small-town living that I've already dealt with for decades.

Shade shakes out his thick back hair before dragging his tattooed fingers through it and glancing in my general vicinity. The music that's been filling the studio comes to an end as my stomach sinks. Shade winks and grins wide enough for a dimple to appear.

"Little Devil!" he calls out, eyes bright. "You look hot."

"Don't flirt with my girlfriend," Bryce groans.

I blink, settling when Daisy floats by me, her dress flying up around her knees. She wiggles her finger at him. "You're going to get kicked in the nuts, Shade."

"Worth it."

My friend gets swallowed in his arms and, like the hugger she is, squeezes him tight enough to make him wince. "We'll see about that."

They jump into conversation as I dart my eyes elsewhere and hold in a sigh. I'm being a buzzkill. I'm shocked Poppy hasn't already come to find me with one of the Jell-O shots we made last night in her hands. I've seen more of her in the last few months than in the last seven years.

Losing my grandmother has only just started getting easier to accept. I still hear her voice calling from upstairs, asking me to watch every new episode of her favourite telenovela and feel the ghost of her hands on my cheeks. Her presence is heavy at home, and maybe that's why I've spent so many nights at Bryce and Daisy's.

I'm hiding from the reality of what's happened and the loneliness that hangs around me, growing thicker every day.

The air shifts, that fog thinning enough for me to see the tall figure cutting through it. Pain expands in my chest as my ribs constrict. Darren got here before I did, but I've managed to avoid him the way I always do.

While that means I haven't gaped at him all night or followed him through the crowds, I still felt it every time he's looked my way. Even a simple, fleeting glance sent prickles up and down my spine.

He wasn't supposed to come to see me, though. Communication between us is rightly non-existent. That's the way I needed it to be.

So why is he still walking my way and not turning somewhere—*anywhere*—else?

Holding my breath, I shift and turn away. My skirt gets bunched in my fists as I grip the soft fabric and release a forced exhale.

"Can I join you over here?"

"I don't own this wall."

Silence.

I inwardly cringe and force myself to release my skirt. "Yeah, sure. You can join me."

"Alright," he says lowly.

His shoulder comes into view before the side of his neck does. The ball of his Adam's apple strains upward when he swallows and turns his head, staring down at me. I cross my arms and take half a step backward before meeting his gaze.

Immediately, I wish I'd just walked away instead.

"How are you?" he asks, so much sympathy in his eyes that I feel it in my bones.

There's no point in wasting my time lying. "Been better."

Nodding, he slips a hand into the pocket of his jeans. "I've been wanting to stop by. Bring you something to eat in case you weren't feeling up to cooking."

"I'm glad you didn't."

Hurt flashes across his face before he tucks it into a box. "That's fair. I'm still sorry. Your grandmother was a great woman, and she should have had more years here with us."

"Do you even know how old she was when she died?" I ask, the question whipping between us like. It leaves the air split, singed with a fire so hot nothing can cool it. The fresh wound in my heart oozes poison as it widens. "Or when it happened?"

Darren's eyes blow wide, exposing the truth quicker than words. "I—"

"You don't. So please don't try and say shit like that to me. Not here, not right now."

"You haven't spoken with anyone about it. Not Poppy or Bryce and sure as shit not me, Delancy. But you can tell me the details. Do it right now if you want. I'll listen to whatever you need to say," he offers, somehow balancing on the border between whispering and being loud enough for the entire room to hear us.

I wet my dry lips. "This isn't the place for a conversation like this. Tonight is about Bryce."

"It will still be about her even if you talk about your grandmother."

"What makes you think that you're who I want to be speaking about her with?" I attack, skin growing too warm.

Darren reaches a hand out. I freeze the moment the tips of his fingers make contact with my bare arm. The skin of my elbow comes to life, buzzing like a beehive as I part my lips on a silent whimper. I snap my head back, our eyes connecting and holding despite every voice in my head hissing in warning.

"I just want to listen. Let me do that for you right now," he begs softly.

A burn begins in my nose before spidering outward. My eyes tingle with the threat of tears while I retreat mentally.

It makes no sense why his fleeting offer can affect me so badly. A decade of growing distance between us, and I'm so easily yanked back as if it was never there to begin with. I don't know anything more dangerous than that. Than being *so* vulnerable when it comes to just one person. Nobody deserves that much power over someone else.

I move quickly, only half caring if he follows and the repercussions that would bring.

It's dark in the bathroom. Still, I bypass the light switch and stand in front of the sink, ignoring the mirror until Darren appears. The door shuts with a click of the latch behind him.

"Talk to me," he mutters, voice steady as he flicks on the light.

Leaning against the door in this tiny room, his wide frame is more pronounced, impossible to deny. With shoulders that stretch the fabric of his shirt, thighs thick enough to test the seams of his dark-wash jeans, and hair hidden beneath a baseball cap on the "correct way," he looks so incredibly different from the Darren I used to know, yet still the same.

Boyish was never a word I'd use to describe him, even when

we were young. There was always a manly aspect to him that he used to intimidate men double his age. Sure, his love of football and exercise helped keep him in shape in high school, but he was at least two inches shorter and fifty pounds lighter back then.

I can't pinpoint when the change hit him hardest, but it wasn't until after Abbie was born, and I stopped being able to look at him without crying so hard I'd nearly puke.

"She was sick. Her body just . . . gave out. The fight was long," I croak.

"She'll be remembered forever. Not just by you, but by the whole town. Everyone who knew your grandmother loved her."

Heat slicks up my spine. "Is that why you weren't at the funeral? Because she was so loved by everyone?"

He pauses. "I didn't know if you'd be okay with me there."

"That's bullshit. She deserved to have you there. You were like another grandchild to her, and you know it. She loved you right till the end," I snap, chest heaving with pained breaths.

Darren flinches, an invisible handprint blooming on his cheek from the force of my words. "I didn't know that. How could I? She cut me out the moment you did."

"She cut you out because I was heartbroken. Worse than that. I was—" I cut myself off, biting my tongue. "Just because she stopped speaking to you doesn't mean she forgot about you. That woman cared about you so much she demanded watching that fucking grainy video of us on her deathbed. Too many of her last words included you, and where were you when she was being lowered into the ground?"

Stricken by my blows, Darren deflates against the door. His skin is pale, forehead damp as he lets loose a breath.

"She had this idea in her head that we'd . . . that we'd somehow find our way back together. There was more romance in that woman than common sense, but that's just who she was. A hopeless, lovesick woman too fixated on a broken relationship to see that there isn't enough glue in the world to fix it. But it didn't matter that I thought that. I still sat beside her and listened to her reminisce on me and you despite the pain it caused me because I knew she was going to die. I knew she was going to *die*, Darren, and I thought that at least you'd be there after she was gone to show her even half the respect she continued to grant you long after what happened between us. Turns out I was wrong. We both were."

"I'm sorry, Delaney. I didn't know," he chokes, the apology catching in his throat.

"You shouldn't have had to know all of that to show up for her."

And for *me*. That day fucking destroyed what little of me I had left and had been struggling to regrow.

"You're right," he agrees.

I know I should leave. One shove from me and he'd be jumping out of the way for me to escape this hell of a room. But I stay rooted in place instead, feeling as though I'm sinking into the tile. "Do you even remember the video?"

Darren's eyes are such a dull shade of brown as he stares at me. "Which one?"

"Prom. She made me watch the old, grainy thing with her all the time."

"Why? I figured . . . I assumed it was deleted a long time ago."

I snort. "Yeah, I tried to do that a million times. Grandma refused. She believed I'd regret losing it."

His brows knit together, discomfort twisting his expression. "She was stubborn."

"That's a nice word for it."

"I'm sorry you had to watch that video."

"I don't want your apologies. You can't staunch heavy bleeding with a single piece of gauze."

"What if I use something thicker? What if you just let me try?" he offers, leaning away from the door.

His right hand falls to the round edge of the sink as he

spreads his fingers over the smooth porcelain. I focus on his blunt nails and then the strain in the back of his hand, veins flexing.

"I'm not interested in building a bridge," I say, unsure if that's the full truth or a lie I'm telling myself.

His grip on the sink loosens. His voice betrays a heavy sense of defeat. "Okay, Delaney."

"I want to leave now, please."

Like I knew he would, he steps aside without needing to be asked again. I wait until he's a safe distance from it before passing him. Sucking in a breath at our sudden closeness, I try to make myself smaller to avoid touching him even briefly. That can't happen again. Especially not in a bathroom where there's nowhere to hide from my reaction to it.

"I really am sorry for your loss and for not being there to support you at the funeral. Both of you deserved that from me."

My throat is clogged. I only manage a nod, my attention fixed on the doorknob.

Maybe I linger because I'm hoping he says something else. A declaration that could fix everything that's happened between us. Except I know nothing like that exists because there isn't any *fixing* this. Not through apologies or declarations or any of my grandmother's wishes to the universe.

I have to remember that before I wind up in a situation that's bound to leave me shattered once again. Without replying, I open the door and slip out of the bathroom, leaving him behind me the way I did the day I returned to Cherry Peak.

15

Darren

Downtown at noon. Don't be late. Oh, and wear
swim trunks.

Caleb's text came at midnight. It interrupted my long night of
being hunched over the desk in my bedroom, squinting at my
computer screen. I'm three days behind on delivering a rough
rendering to one of my boss's favourite clients, a hotel mogul
expanding his reach from Calgary to Vancouver.

I've worked on my fair share of hotels over the last couple of
years, but this one is . . . a lot. Twenty stories fit with a rooftop
pool, two gyms, three ballrooms, a conference room, a high-end
bar / restaurant, and a deadline of only three months has me a *bit*
stressed. Toss in being single-handedly in charge of creating my
sister's dream house, and I'm one more broken pencil from
losing my mind.

My brain screams with overuse as I rub my eyes and get out
of the car. The feeling of swim trunks at the beginning of October
isn't my favourite, but I know better than to ignore my captain's

orders, a volunteer at the station or not. I just wish I'd been able to find my good pair.

I'll be teased about how short these ones are the moment my friends spot me. I don't blame them either. Fuck, they're an inch above my knees and a peach colour that, depending on the light, makes it seem like I'm naked from the waist down.

I lock my car and start toward the cluster of people at the end of the street. The shops on this side of downtown are blocked off by the same cement barriers herding what appears to be the entirety of Cherry Peak's population. It smells like mini donuts and fresh lemonade, almost like the fire station decided on a fair instead of a few mini games as their fundraiser.

Whatever they planned was fine with me, considering I didn't have the chance to help. The past week has been quiet without Abbie, but with the silence comes a heavier work schedule. When I'm with my daughter, she's the centre of my attention, and often, my work falls to the back burner so I can spend as much time with her as possible. Working from home is a blessing when she's with me but a curse when she's gone with Sasha.

"There he is! The star of our dunk show," Caleb drawls, coming at me from the side.

I brace for impact when he lifts a fist and brings it near my armpit. "Star of the what?"

"The dunk show. Well, technically, it's one of those toss 'n dunk tanks. You know, like from a good ol'-fashioned carnival?"

"I was wondering what the trunks were for, considering the current temperature."

He gives my legs an inspecting look before pursing his lips. "Yeah, what's with those?"

"What's wrong with them?" I ask, already knowing the answer.

"They look like they'd fit Abbie."

"Fuck off. It's October. All of my good pairs are already tucked away for next year," I grunt.

"That's what you get for being so goddamn organized."

"Just say you're jealous and move on, Cap."

"Nothing to be jealous of besides the hair on your legs. Mine's so thin now."

I scoff a laugh and shake my head. "Are we gonna start talking leg hair tips now?"

"Not a chance.

"Sounds good to me."

"Did you bring a towel with you?" he asks, eyeing my car behind us as we head for the fair.

"No. If you'd told me what I was doing today, I'd have been better prepared."

"Oh well. I'll make sure to give you plenty of time to air-dry before sending you home."

"What would I do without your generosity?" I ask blandly.

"Live a boring, boring life."

I don't bother telling him that I'm already there.

"How long am I stuck here being dunked into what I assume is freezing water?"

"Oh, not that long."

I lift a brow. "Right. Now, be honest this time."

"Three hours, give or take one. We're hoping for a turnout big enough to bite off a chunk of the funds needed for the drive-in. Put on a good show, and I'll buy you a celebratory drink at Peakside tonight."

Shit, it's going to be a long day. The only thing—or *person*—that could make this worth it is a visit from Delaney. I'll take being dunked by her instead of another day of going without a glimpse of her. It's been a week since we spoke at the drive-in grounds, and without taking Abbie to school as an excuse to show up and talk to her, I've had to let go of any hope I had of a reunion.

Instead, thoughts of her have kept me up to the point that I'd rather be staring at a computer instead of lying in bed. At least if

I'm going to stay up all night in front of my computer, I'll get some work done.

"My shoulders already hurt from the weight of your expectations," I joke.

"Yeah, I bet, asshole," he returns before we reach the barriers.

A few people turn to look at us as we step through the gap between the cement blocks and join them. Of course, I'm the only person here in shorts. Even the woman manning the burger grill across the street is wearing jeans.

"Don't forget to smile, D. It's dazzling when you decide to use it," he adds.

The dunk tanks are red and blue and have been placed smack in the middle of the section of downtown they've blocked off for today. Surrounded by a rounded, short silver fence and a small table and two chairs at the entrance gate, it's clear the dunking is the main event.

I wasn't expecting to see two dunk tanks, and I bite my cheek to stifle a laugh at who's sitting on the seat above the second tank of water. It was an evil move on Caleb's part for Brody Steele to be dunked repeatedly in front of his wife's hair salon, but a move fitting for his best friend to pull.

The country music star glowers at Caleb when he stops beside his tank and moves a hand to hover over the huge red button I assume leads to our wet demise.

"Push it and I'll be draggin' you in with me," Brody threatens beneath the disguise of a friendly smile.

Caleb smirks. "Do you have that much trust in your reflexes, pop star?"

"Give it a try. I'm interested to find out," I say, leaning back on my left foot.

Brody points at my seat and clucks his tongue. "Up you go, Darren. I'm not in this alone."

With a jostle of my shoulder, I tug my shirt off. The cool temperature bites at my bare chest as I carry myself over to the stairs at the back of the tank. It's not only Brody and Caleb watching me, but they're the only ones I pay attention to. I slip my shoes off and climb onto the red seat, wiggling when the flat wood presses against my ass.

"Can I hop off quick and be the first to dunk him?" Brody asks Caleb.

Caleb debates that too long before replying, "Are you paying?"

"Fuck no he isn't. He's not dunking me right now," I say, raising my voice just enough I know they can't miss it amongst the growing chatter around us.

Brody huffs and shoves back his hair with his fingers. Without a cowboy hat on, he looks . . . not like himself. I'm sure he's missing it more than a shirt and jeans right now.

"Buzzkill."

"Pop star."

"Okay, children, stop fighting, or you'll be in time outs," Caleb threatens teasingly.

I roll my eyes. "Can he go first, Dad? I'm sure everyone here wants to dunk Brody Steele."

"I think I'll let the crowd choose who goes first, actually. It's time to let the dunking begin!" Caleb announces, spinning and walking away from us.

Suddenly, he's slipping out of the gate and parking his ass on the chair at the table. A line quickly forms in front of him, and he cackles like a hyena while dropping a locked cash box in front of him. Eliza Steele, Brody's grandmother, joins him a moment later and takes hold of the box, safeguarding it.

I look down at the water beneath me and shift on the seat. There's a nipping breeze forcing goosebumps to pebble my skin as I drop my hands to my knees and wait. The first person who Caleb lets into the gate heads directly for Brody, and I relax slightly at the confirmation that I might actually survive here without too many dunks.

Despite Brody's scowling demeanour, I know he doesn't mind doing this. He's used his name to help this town more than once since he made it big time, and we appreciate him for it while still respecting that he shouldn't have to. Him agreeing to this today means a lot to me, even if it wasn't my idea. This drive-in rebuild is for me, and he knows that as well as I do.

"There are red balls right here," Caleb explains, leaning over the fence. "You get three tries to hit the target, and once you do, it'll be a splash zone."

"Sick!" the kid yells, looking no older than twelve.

He's quick to grab the three balls in his arms and start launching them at the target. Brody's eyes grow wide as he grips his knees and glances at me for help. I sigh and lift my hands in a half-assed, *there's nothing I can do* type of way.

Fucker, he mouths.

I laugh and squint when the sun flashes in my eyes. Lifting a hand to shield myself from the bright light, I stare in Brody's direction, waiting for him to go swimming. Ball three gives me my wish.

Brody's curse gets muffled by the water that swooshes into his mouth when he drops into the tank. The boy hollers victoriously while those watching cheer along with him. I clap and wait for Brody to pop out of the water to discreetly give him the finger.

His blond hair is soaked, rivulets of water trickling down his face before he whips his head back and sends the strands flying. It's like watching a fucking hair commercial, and from the wolf whistle coming from Anna's salon, she's got to be thinking the same thing. I steal a glance in that direction and am met with Anna herself standing in the doorway with heart eyes as she stares at her husband putting on a show.

"Again!" she shouts, using her hands to carry her voice.

Brody shifts to look at her and grins, light filling his entire demeanour. He starts twisting the gold band on his finger before I look away, giving them as much privacy as they're going to get.

"Who's next?" Caleb asks.

An array of different voices replies, and I settle on my seat, preparing myself for the next few very long hours of this. *It'll be worth it.* If I get the chance to be there when we finish the drive-in and Delaney gets to see—

My skin prickles with awareness before I hear her voice cut through dozens of other ones.

"Oh, thank you, but I'm not . . . No, I'm not. Let someone else go, Caleb."

"You're next in line. Sorry, Delaney, but I don't make the rules."

"You heard him, Della. How about we both go at the same time. I've been wanting to dunk Brody for years now. Plus, it's for the drive-in!" Poppy encourages.

I swallow and look past Caleb at the group of women hanging out at the gate. Bryce is already looking at me, a silent knowing written all over her as she darts her eyes between Delaney and me. I nod, hoping she can see my appreciation—not for forcing Elle into participating in this, but for coming at all without me bringing it up and begging her to do it. She did it solely because she knew I'd want her here.

"My aim is terrible," Delaney argues.

My sister grins. "Perfect. So is mine."

"Bryce and I will go after the two of you do!" Daisy says.

As if my attention has started to chafe, Delaney peeks at me from the corner of her eyes. It's subtle, quick, nothing more than a question answered, but I feel that single look all the way down to my toes. The warmth that ripples through me battles the chill of the wind, keeping me heated as I sit in place, unable to move a muscle.

Yeah, I think I owe Caleb a thank you for volunteering me for this.

16

Delaney

I'VE PICTURED THROWING SOMETHING AT DARREN MORE TIMES THAN I can count, but I never thought I'd actually get the chance to.

The balls in my hands feel like they're getting heavier by the second as I lightly toss them into the air and pretend I'm alone instead of in front of several curious bystanders. Darren's eyes remain locked on my face, his focus sharp. I meet his stare and tighten my grip on the balls.

He looks far too good up there today with his tan skin and rippling biceps on display. I didn't think it was mandatory to be shirtless for this. I almost wish it was mandatory to *not* be. I don't remember him being so muscled back in high school. No, instead of his thickly packed abdominal muscles, there was a softness to him. Now, I know one press of my palm to his stomach would prove just how firm he's become.

Firm and warm and— No.

I swallow the excess moisture in my mouth and grip the balls tight. There's no reason to be attracted to him anymore. Maybe if I tell myself that I'm not enough times, I'll believe it.

Okay. I don't think his wide chest and the bulge of his biceps when he reaches up to rake fingers through his hair are attractive at all. And I really, really don't like when he runs his fingers over his mustache and smirks like he knows he's been caught doing it. *It's so, so tacky.* Who likes mustaches, anyway? Certainly *not* me.

"You ready?"

I jump, a curse exploding free as Daisy's face appears in front of me, blocking my view of Darren. "Shit!"

"Oops." She hides a smile behind her hand.

Bryce smirks and eyes me curiously before pulling Daisy back into her side. When she smacks a kiss to Daisy's cheek, I force myself to look back at where Darren's sitting. He's leaning forward now, his back slightly arched as he slips his gaze between my group of girls, then plop his eyes back onto me.

Daisy's perfume wafts up my nose as she leans close to my shoulder and whispers, "I don't think anyone would report you to the authorities if your aim was bad enough you sacked him instead of the target."

"I'd prefer to use my knee for that," I admit bluntly.

Her giggle rings in the air. "You know what? Hell yeah. You go, girl."

"I'm going to pretend I didn't hear that," Poppy says.

Bryce snorts a laugh. "As if you haven't debated giving your brother a swift kick to the dick a few times."

"Not everyone has the same fascination with inflicting pain on male genitals the way you do, Ice," Poppy pokes.

With a shake of my head, I ignore the rest of their banter and dig my eyes into Darren's, hoping for a second that I'm making him uncomfortable. As good as it should feel to stare so openly at him like this after so long, it's unease that swims in my belly instead of happiness.

He's watching me like he has the right to, and that pisses me off as much as it hurts me.

I launch the first of three balls too hard at the target. It bounces off the side and rolls onto the pavement before smacking into the cement blockade. My tongue grows heavy in my mouth as I squeeze the second and shift my feet until I feel steadier.

Now that Brody's out of the water and back on his seat, Poppy follows my lead and lets go of her first ball. It doesn't even brush the target, and Brody howls in triumph.

"Don't get cocky now, Brody!" she shouts.

He sticks his tongue out and says, "Bring it on."

She winds her arm back and, with one eye squinted in concentration, throws the second ball. It comes closer but still misses. Her groan is subtle enough I hardly pick it up.

Darren's voice dances on the breeze. "Show her how it's done, Elle."

My breath dissipates. Curious looks stab at my back as I follow the sound of his voice. He either called me that to anger me enough that I'll whip the ball as hard as humanly possible or to try and spark some sort of moment between us.

He'll get the first option.

With Poppy concentrated on sending Brody into the water tank, I pull my arm back and hurl the ball at Darren's button. It clips the edge of it, and he doesn't so much as flinch before his seat gives out. His eyes hold mine as he falls, only disappearing once his head sinks under the water.

Blinking, I force myself backward as a weird, slimy feeling fills me. My shoulder butts into Bryce's as I stumble. She catches me with a hand on my arm and cautiously turns me until I'm forced to look at her.

"You good?"

"Mission accomplished," I say, putting on my best attempt at not sounding freaked out.

"Right. Want to get some mini donuts?"

"You don't want to try dunking Darren?"

She shakes her head, letting her hand drop. We both ignore the sound of water splashing. "I prepare other torture methods."

"That doesn't surprise me."

"Good."

"Mini donuts sound good," I relent.

She leans into Daisy and whispers something that draws her fiancée's attention. I smile at her, and she returns it before nodding and cheering Poppy on with her last ball.

"My treat," Bryce tells me before leading the way out of the fenced-in area.

Caleb offers me a high-five as we pass him. "You should join the station's softball team, Delaney. That was one hell of a throw."

I flash a half-smile. "I'm going to pass on that. But thank you."

"Worth a shot. Darren refuses to join us, too."

"He's never been one for sports outside of football."

"Alright, we're leaving now. Make lots of money for the town today, or you'll answer to me, Caleb," Bryce threatens.

He salutes her and hands a few balls to Eliza when she drops money into the cash box. "You got it, boss."

"Leave the women alone," Eliza scolds him before handing the balls off to the next person and grinning at Bryce and me. "You go enjoy yourselves! I've got a few sourdough loaves for sale in the market. Tell them I sent you, and pick which one you'd like most. Don't let them try and trick you into paying!"

"We're not robbing you of sourdough, Eliza," I say lightly, reaching behind Caleb to pat her back. "I've watched a few sourdough videos online, and it looks complicated. You deserve your money's worth for the effort."

"Oh, it's not that hard. Starter, flour, salt, and water, darling. You're more than welcome to join me the next time I bake a few loaves."

"I'll take you up on that sometime," I say before stepping back to Bryce's side and waving. "We'll see you later."

"Enjoy the day, ladies."

"Bye, Eliza," Bryce says.

"She's the nicest person in town," I declare once we've made it away from the line of people.

"That's why everyone loves her."

"I worry about her getting taken advantage of sometimes."

"She's tough as shit. I wouldn't put too much thought into that."

"I'm sure Brody would bubble wrap her if he could," I joke.

"She and Anna would have matching bubble suits."

The sweater I slipped on before leaving the house this morning is thick enough to block the wind from chilling me to the bone as we wander down the blocked-off street. We pass the Beautifully Bold studio, then the Thistle and Thorn hair salon. Poppy and Anna best friended so hard that even their businesses are side by side.

Bryce gives the handmade lemonade stand a side-eye. I roll my lips to hide my smile when I see her ex's mother handing out overpriced lemon juice and sugar drinks from behind it. The scent of mini donuts slaps me in the face, and then my stomach is growling.

"Dunking your ex into an ice bath must work up an appetite," she notes bluntly.

"Amongst other things."

"Donuts or sourdough? Your choice."

Both would be a good start. "Donuts."

Without another word, Bryce butts her way into the line, not leaving room for me to join. I watch her suspiciously enough that she clarifies, not giving a shit about anyone overhearing.

"I'll buy them. Daisy loves the sugar, so it's a safer bet to get the biggest fucking bucket there is. I'm sure the guys could use something, too, after their cold baths."

Drawn by her voice, the teen boy in front of her turns back and gazes up at her with wide, lovesick eyes. When she looks forward again, she jerks her head in surprise.

"Can you back up?"

"You're beautiful. Single?" he asks, the corner of his mouth curled into a smirk.

It's impossible not to laugh out loud at the visceral unease that explodes on Bryce's face. The poor kid clearly doesn't realize that he's dangling himself above the open mouth of a venomous snake because he doesn't turn to leave like he should.

"You're a child."

"I'm sixteen. Pretty much an adult, babe."

"Go get your donuts before your mom comes looking for you," Bryce says, tone as flat as the brim of his snapback hat.

He closes his lips, cheeks growing red. I almost feel bad for him as he spins around on his heels and, in a flash, is at the window of the donut truck without so much as speaking another word. Bryce glances back at me with a disturbed expression that makes me laugh.

At least he knows what to look for to tell if a girl isn't interested now.

For the next five minutes, I hang back and wait for Bryce to order the donuts. When she rejoins me by the curb, it's with a yellow, plastic bucket in her hand. She swings it dramatically once she notices I'm watching.

"Hope you're as hungry as your stomach made you out to be."

"I'm starving," I confirm.

"Want me to pop the top before we get back? I can't guarantee Daisy will share once we do."

Laughing, I look back in the direction of the fundraiser set up. The line's still as long as it was when we left, but now . . .

"Was Darren only staying for a few minutes?" I ask, stomach tightening.

"Don't worry about him. I can tell him to get his own."

My breath slows. "He's not there."

"What?"

Bryce grows alert as she sneaks around someone walking in front of us to get a better look at where only Brody's sitting above a tank of water. Caleb's still there guarding the gate and money box, and there's a red ball rolling along the pavement beside Brody.

I catch the tilt of Caleb's head as he leans to the side and steals a quick look through the crowd to the left of him before doing the same to the right.

"Did he have other plans?"

And why does it matter so much to me? The sooner he's gone, the better. That's the way I should be feeling. Knowing that I'd see him today had me nervous pacing all morning. Yet here I am, searching this crowded makeshift fair for any sign of him the way I did the halls at school this week.

There are kids blowing bubbles, a dog hopping beside them that's snapping its teeth, trying to pop each one, and an elderly couple watching them with warm eyes, all a few feet from us. Too many conversations are happening at once to try and pick apart a specific one, and even though I'm close to Bryce, I worry I'll lose her amongst the crowd beside and behind us.

It's obvious that there are more people here than usual. The town's population isn't this impressive. I'd bet all of Oak Ridge is here in addition to some Calgarians who've come down to participate in dunking *the* Brody Steele. It's good publicity for him and fantastic help for the whole fundraising thing. But the number of people clogging the street makes it harder to find Darren. Not one voice sounds like his.

That used to comfort me. Right now, it makes me want to climb the back of one of these downtown shops to get a better view into the street. Maybe I'd be able to find him that way.

"He doesn't have Abbie this week, so I doubt it," Bryce says, her voice drawing me back through the door I've opened in my mind.

"Maybe he went to the bathroom."

Bryce's grunt is noncommittal. "Maybe."

"Do you know where he is?" I ask, picking up the pace when the gap between us grows.

"No. But I have a feeling in my gut."

"A bad one?"

"One I always get when Sasha's involved."

Just hearing her name hurts. It's a sucker punch to the chest, winding me as I strain with the urge to shut down and run away.

As if sensing that, Bryce slows back to a regular pace and softens her voice slightly. "Take the donuts to Daisy. She'll be chomping at the bit for them by now."

I straighten, sending her a sharp look. "Where are you going?"

"I'm going to see if I'm right."

"About . . . Sasha doing something?" I ask, hating the way her name sounds.

"What I feel for her isn't very pro-woman, Delaney. She's a happiness-sucking leech who I have no doubt showed up here and started something with Darren just because she wanted to be an asshole to him in front of his friends. Maybe I'm wrong and Darren just skipped off to take a piss, but I want to check for myself before joining everyone again."

"I can always hit her over the head with the donut bucket," I blurt out.

My eyes flare wide as Bryce whips to the side, her mouth parting around a shocked laugh.

"I think I forgot how fun you can be, Della."

It's an innocent comment that sparks something in me that I've yet to distinguish. Something that nearly tugs loose a version of myself that I thought I'd lost. I've felt hints of it over the last year, starting when Daisy moved back to town and all but held my hand as I was invited into the group of her, Bryce, Anna, and Poppy. It's grown over the months and is now almost encouraging me to open up further.

"I think I did too," I admit on a weighted breath.

Bryce's eyes lower to the bucket of donuts before rising. "I'm offering you an out because we care about you. Today's about fun. Not drama."

I should ask her to clarify who she means by "we," but instead, I pop the lid off the bucket and get us each a donut.

Bringing mine to my mouth, I say, "You're not going alone. I'll risk it."

17

Darren

TWELVE YEARS AGO

"ARE YOU JUST GOING TO STAND THERE, OR ARE YOU GOING TO HELP me pack?"

Elle stands at the end of her bed, staring down at me. With the firm mattress beneath my back, I hang my head off the edge and palm the back of her knee, ushering her closer. She lurches forward, knees bracketing my face.

I grin and turn my neck to kiss her soft skin. "I much prefer lying right here."

"Darren," she groans, nose twitching with the effort to hide her amusement. "Help me."

"Well, when you ask me so sweetly . . ."

"How are you so relaxed right now? I leave in two weeks."

The energy shifts, my stomach souring. I grip her a little tighter, like I'm trying to keep her from slipping away. It's a natural reaction made worse by our upcoming break.

Fuck that break. It's a mistake, but we're already too far into it now to change our minds.

"I'm not relaxed, baby. I'm just trying not to waste my time with you worrying about what's coming. Two weeks are going to fly by," I explain.

Her expression drops, sadness leaking into her eyes. She pulls back only to drop onto the mattress beside me. The moment her fingers find my hair, pushing it back from my forehead, I shut my eyes.

"I'm scared, Darren."

I open my eyes again and twist onto my side so I can peer up at her. Her small hand is soft and smooth in mine when I take it and link our fingers on her lap.

"Talk to me," I murmur.

She chews on her lip, her mind running a mile a minute. "Maybe I should have just gone to school with you and saved us from all of this drama. We could have been packing to move into our first apartment together or our dorms on campus. Instead, we're going to be in different provinces, hours away from each other at different schools."

And single. Both of us for the first time in three years.

"Don't go there, Elle. I'd never have let you choose a school based on me. That's the whole point of this. You need to get away from this town. Experience life in a different place with different people. Live your life without feeling like you owe me all of your time and attention."

"I'm sure I could learn how to do that without breaking up," she states stubbornly.

"We're not breaking up."

Her eyes roll into the back of her head. The hand in mine grows warmer, slicker. "You can call a donkey an ass, but it's still a donkey."

I laugh and bring our hands toward my body. With them pressed against my sternum, I say, "I see your point, but it's a bit off the mark."

"A break is the same as breaking up. We won't be boyfriend and girlfriend, Darren. The freedom to grow and expand my horizons comes at the cost of losing you."

"You're not losing me. I'll still be here, calling and texting and bugging you every chance I have."

"So what's the point of taking a break, then?" she asks, frustrated.

When her fingers slip from mine and curl back in her lap, I know I'm losing her.

"The point is that I'm not taking anything from you. You told me we needed four years after high school to know marriage was the right next step. And when I put that ring on your finger, that was me promising that I'm willing and ready to give you that. Four years and you'll know that I'm serious about making you my wife for the rest of my life. So, let me prove myself to you, even if it kills us to be apart."

She snaps her hand back out and yanks on mine. Her strong grip betrays her fear. "The risk might not be worth it."

"It will be, Elle. Because I know once you come back here to me, we'll both be ready to start the rest of our lives together. What's four years when we have decades to be together?"

I pull our hands to my lips and kiss her knuckles, keeping them there. My beautiful Delaney releases a pained breath and sniffles. Frowning, I bring my free hand to her cheek and stroke the round curve of it. A tear cascades down to pool against my finger.

"I'm just going to miss you. I don't want to realize two years down the road that we made a mistake that we can't ever come back from. A lot can happen in four years, Darren."

"What's bothering you the most? Tell me everything you're thinking so I can help put your mind at ease."

She blinks, her bare lashes growing wet. "What if you fall in love with someone else? I could come home to see you with a new life and no space left in it for me. That's . . . that's my worst fear."

"That isn't going to happen. It isn't even a possibility. It's you, Elle. It's only ever been you," I swear.

"And if it does? It would kill me to see you with anyone else. I'd leave Cherry Peak for the last time."

"Then it's a good thing it won't. I can't imagine myself with anyone but you. This break is going to be hard, baby. It's going to kill us both, but I have to believe it'll be worth it. You'll come back knowing what else is out there so you won't doubt us in the future. I won't ever be the person who holds you back and risks you resenting me years down the road for it."

"And what about you? You don't think you'd grow to resent me if I kept you tied to me without letting you experience life as a single guy? I don't want this to only be for my benefit, Darren."

"I don't want to experience being single for that reason, and neither do you. I could give a shit about being a single guy."

"So then just tell me that it was ridiculous of me to bring this up so we can stay together instead. I don't want to find myself without you."

I release her and push into a sitting position. It's easy to lift her onto my thighs, and she instantly wraps her legs around my back and her arms behind my neck.

Dropping my forehead to hers, I inhale, memorizing the smell of her perfume. "I love you, Delaney. I love you enough to let you go see what's out there outside of this town and the woman you are with me. And when you've learned all there is for you to learn, I'll be here waiting for you with my arms open as the man I've learned I am too. I'm going to give you the best version of myself."

"It feels wrong," she whispers, hiding her face in my chest.

"It'll never feel right to be away from you."

I miss her already, and she's right here in my arms. There's a reason she's started doing her homework on the old bleachers at the football field, and it isn't because it's the easiest place for her to think. I'm so goddamn needy that the only time I can concentrate properly is when she's around me, even twenty feet away on the sidelines.

Nobody warned me about how clingy I'd be or how deeply I'd fall in love so young. Yet here I am. Delaney is my soulmate, and I consider myself the luckiest guy in the world to have found her so early on in my life. Any longer and I'd risk missing out on her entirely.

The thought of that scares the shit out of me and makes me think that we might be making the right choice here, even though it fucking hurts. If we wait any longer, we won't be able to pry ourselves apart at all.

Delaney pulls her head out from where she's tucked it into my neck. The red ring around her eyes creates an ache deep in my chest.

"Can you just promise that you won't forget about me while we're doing this? You're my best friend before anything else. I don't know what I'd do without you in my life at all."

"That's never going to happen. *Ever*," I swear.

The corners of her mouth tip up slightly as she nods, sniffling again. "Then fine. But I'll never forgive you if you break your promise."

"Luckily, we'll never have to worry about that."

18

Darren

PRESENT

Usually, I always have an inkling when Sasha's going to appear out of nowhere to ream my ass out for something, but I'm so off-kilter today that she managed to take me by surprise.

Her voice is cruel as she snaps at me, uncaring about the volume of her voice. The only privacy I could find close to the dunk tanks was behind the back of the burger stand. It's sure as shit not far enough away to muffle her words.

"And when did we agree to that? I've said it a million times. You need to keep your sister and her friends in check."

The heat radiating from the grills beside us blasts into my side as I try to keep a relaxed posture in front of my ex-wife. "I'm sorry if Abbie heard about it, but that wasn't my intention. It wasn't Poppy's or Bryce's either."

My ex-wife uses both of her hands to pull her red hair behind her shoulder and tightens her glare. "What a coincidence."

"Drop the attitude, Sasha. If you want to ream me out over a misunderstanding, then maybe you can do it later when we're in a more private setting."

"And give you a chance to avoid the conversation? Not happening. We'll get to the bottom of it right here, right now."

Dread poisons the tip of the knife in my side. It's a miracle I managed to convince Sasha to take our conversation away from the dunk tanks at all. A pissed Sasha doesn't care where we are or who's around. She'll let her feelings fly for all to see and hear, consequences be damned.

I'd be more understanding of that right now if I didn't think her argument was ridiculous. She was looking for something to be mad at me for these last few weeks, and she's finally got one. That's all this is. Bringing this up in front of my friends at an event supposed to be for families doesn't sit well with me.

"I don't have plans to take her away from Cherry Peak anytime soon. Not for one day or a month. Poppy only mentioned a trip to BC as a spitballed idea for some time in the future. I'm sorry that Abbie heard her and took it as something it wasn't."

It was nothing more than a random thought dropped into a conversation the last time Abbie and I were over at my sister's house for dinner. It happened over a month ago, and this is the first I'm hearing of it.

"And on this hypothetical trip, would Delaney be joining you?" Sasha asks, her voice sly but expression bursting with anger.

I grow stiff, mind starting to run wild. "Why would you ask that?"

"I'm not an idiot! I've heard all about Ms. Delaney, our daughter's new *teacher*."

"Okay, but that doesn't explain why she would be coming on a trip with my family," I say slowly, taking too much care forming each word.

Fuck my life. I'm an idiot for not realizing this is why she came here today. It had nothing to do with a theoretical trip and all to do with my ex-girlfriend. Maybe I should be more surprised that it took her this long to approach me about her being Abbie's new teacher.

It wouldn't surprise me if she were waiting for a moment like this, though. This is a perfect opportunity to make me look bad in public.

Sasha shakes her head, sneering, "Don't treat me like I'm being dramatic. I saw you interacting earlier!"

Glancing behind her, I wince at the same people who have been lingering close to the burger truck for a while now, pretending like they have no interest in the conversation but not moving on. My spine steels as discomfort grows thick in my muscles.

"This isn't the place for this conversation, Sasha," I say, dropping my voice.

"Yes it is! At least you have nowhere to hide right now. I need an answer, Darren. Are you seeing her again?"

"No."

"No? That's all you're going to give me?"

"No, I'm not. And if I were, I wouldn't be going to you for permission."

She sucks in a breath, eyes flaming. "Yes, you will. You're not a teenager anymore. Abbie is involved now."

"Don't talk down to me. I'm *more* than aware that Abbie's involved." I heave a breath and swipe a hand over my head. "I'm not having this conversation here. Where's Abbie?"

"She's with Brad at the market. I figured I would keep her away from us while we talked. Discussions about her father and schoolteacher aren't good for her to hear," Sasha snaps.

I scowl, losing my patience quicker than I can recoup it. "You know that I'm still on the fence about him being alone with her."

Sasha lifts both of her brows, lips firming. "Well, it looks like we're both making missteps, then."

"Sasha," I warn.

"Yes? What's wrong, Darren?"

"You clearly came here to get a rise out of me, and I'm not dealing with it. Please go back to Abbie and respect that I don't trust your fiancé to be the sole caretaker of our daughter yet. I'm trying to get there."

"Okay, and what about me?"

"What about you?"

"Am I not allowed to have doubts about who's watching Abbie as well?"

I blink slowly. "I'm the only one watching her when she's with me, other than my parents or sister. Don't tell me you have a problem with my family now. I've never once put up a stink about yours."

"They're only watching her outside of school."

"Spit it out, Sasha," I demand, exhausted.

"Do you really expect me to allow your ex-girlfriend to watch our daughter at school without either one of us there but be sympathetic to you not wanting my soon-to-be husband watching her on his own?"

There isn't a word for how dumbfounded I am by that. My expression exposes my thoughts, encouraging a frustrated scoff from Sasha.

"Are you really trying to compare my not wanting Abbie alone with Brad because I don't know him enough to trust him yet to her being in a classroom with her . . . schoolteacher?"

She grips her waist and juts her chin, eyes cruel. It's the same stance she had the day I watched Delaney walk away from me for the last time, my heart torn to shreds and bleeding. My breath grows thready at the reminder.

"Yes. I am."

All at once, I'm hit with memories and emotions that I've been ignoring for so long. My shoulders threaten to curve forward beneath the weight that slams atop them.

Swallowing, I turn away from her and glance at the sky. I'm still half-naked with my trunks dripping water down my thighs and pooling beneath my feet. The chill helps keep me from feeling like I'm going to ignite into flames, even as my cheeks thump with heat.

I turn at the waist the moment Bryce's voice reaches us. "It seems we missed the invitation for this little rendezvous."

Sasha's immediate reaction to my best friend's appearance is to fake a smile that Bryce doesn't buy. The smile is gone in a flash. She stares at the woman standing slightly behind Bryce and huffs a breath.

"Unbelievable."

Delaney's gaze is soft and almost apologetic when I let Sasha's comment go and look at her. Embarrassment plows through me at the realization that she quite possibly heard some of Sasha's and my conversation. The one centred around her.

"We were just about done, actually," Sasha says.

Bryce's voice is ice-cold. "Yeah, I'd hope so."

"We'll talk later, Darren."

I nod, the ball in my throat too big for me to speak.

The downward twitch of Delaney's lips draws my attention. I zero in on her frown, hating that it's there because of me. I'd take any other expression after this long of being away from her besides that one.

Dropping my stare, I step around Sasha and leave.

The last thing I want to do is make things more awkward, and with the ache behind my ribs, I know there isn't any point in me sticking around. If I do, I'll wind up saying something I shouldn't. There won't be any hope of getting so much as a moment of time with Delaney to try and convince her to give me another shot if I make a fool of myself. She's seen me do that too many times in the past already.

I move quickly through the crowds and pop out on the opposite side of the street. The water squishes between the soles of my feet and my slip on sandals as I keep my pace steady and slip through the gap between the station and Beautifully Bold. Suddenly, it's quiet, nobody wandering this way.

My inhale is deep, but nowhere near as soothing as I hoped.

With my back to the street, the only tell that I'm not alone anymore is the slight scuffing of feet on pavement. I tense, sensing who it is before she speaks.

"Are you okay?"

I drop my head and laugh, letting the rough noise of disbelief carry through the silence. "I figured if anyone would follow me, it would be Bryce."

"She tried to. I . . . I figured she could cover for you with Caleb instead."

"You didn't want to talk to him? Eliza's with him. I'm sure she'd love to talk with you."

"It didn't really have anything to do with Caleb."

"Oh."

Swiping a hand over my mouth, I risk turning around. Glittering green eyes nearly knock me to my knees, especially this close up. The gold flecks are there, bright and demanding. Like they're jealous of the green to the point they're trying to outshine it.

Delaney fidgets with a loose string on the sleeve of her purple sweater, her lips rolling before she says, "I never meant to cause any issues between you and Sasha. Daisy was supposed to be Abbie's teacher this year, and I was only told the week before school started that she'd be in my class. But I promise you that I'm not treating her any differently than her classmates because of our history. She's taken care of."

"I know," I reassure her quickly, not liking that she's second-guessing that. "I had no doubt. Abbie likes you."

She nods once, glancing away in what looks like an attempt to hide a wince. "Okay. Good."

"I'm sorry that I called you Elle again."

Her brow jolts upward. "That's a first."

"A first what?"

"You've never apologized for that before. It's weird."

"I mean, I can continue using it, then," I offer loosely.

"Don't get ahead of yourself."

"Fair enough."

"I'm not going to apologize for dunking you," she says, her stubbornness peeking through.

I fight off a smile. "I would hope not. I deserved it."

"You deserve quite a few dunks."

"I'll have Caleb close off my line and give you unlimited shots."

The freckles across her nose are starting to lighten the way they always do in the fall. Fuck, she's gotten more beautiful as the years have gone on. How is that possible? Am I going to drop dead at the sight of her in another ten years?

I suck in a long, deep breath and flex my fingers at my sides, unable to stand still this close to her.

She watches my every move, and I almost puff my chest when her gaze snags on my exposed abdomen, glossing over slightly. It feels damn good to know that I'm not alone in the attraction that I feel for her. Sure, I'm not the same guy I was when we were together, but I think I look better. Not as scrawny. Beefier, I guess.

I'm proud of my dad bod.

"That's not necessary," she mumbles.

"Have dinner with me tonight instead, then."

Suddenly, she flicks her wide eyes up to meet mine. "What?"

"Dinner, Delaney. The kind where you eat," I tease gently, testing her reaction.

She doesn't immediately shut me down, although she doesn't look all that interested either.

"It's Saturday."

"Do Saturdays not work for you?"

"It's Peakside night," she says, like that's an obvious reason for doubt.

"Are you . . . going to Peakside tonight?"

Her expression twists. "No. No, I mean, aren't you? It's *Saturday*."

Okay, either she really thinks I can't survive without one

Saturday night with my friends, or she wants to reject me but doesn't know which approach to take.

"I can miss one. I'd rather have dinner with you," I state.

"Darren," she says on a sigh, her eyes darting to stare off behind me.

"It's just dinner. We can spend it planning a fundraiser of our own. One better than dunk tanks," I suggest, acting on impulse.

"We don't have to plan anything on our own to begin with."

"But don't you want to? I want to have had something to do with the drive-in being rebuilt that isn't getting my ass wet. This is our chance," I push, taking a few steps toward her.

She watches my feet. "It's more than your ass that's gotten wet."

"That's exactly why we need to do something better. Just meet me for an hour. Let me buy you something to eat while we run through some ideas."

I'm close to getting on my knees at this point. Should I be ashamed of that? Who cares. I'd beg for a million hour-long dinners with her if it meant I could be near her again, hearing her talk about anything. If I have to organize something to make that happen, then I'm happy to do that. I'll make the time.

I can tell I'm close to convincing her. She's stopped pulling that loose string in her sleeve and is now twisting it around her finger, ready to snap it off. There's a tongue indent in her cheek as she thinks, eyes still wandering.

"You're not going to buy me dinner."

My confidence deflates like a leaky balloon. Have I really grown so out of tune with her body language?

"I'll buy my own. And you have one hour," she adds, discarding her sleeve.

I let loose an exhale. "Deal."

"I'm not promising that I'll end up helping with your fundraiser either."

"That's fine."

"Then okay. We'll have dinner."

And there's my opening.

It's the chance I've been needing for a year now, and there's no fucking chance I'm going to screw it up.

19

Delaney

Dinner? Really, Delaney?

Why on earth did I decide that agreeing was the right move? Oh, right, because the moment I heard Sasha speak to him with that same snotty, know-it-all tone that I did all throughout middle and high school, I wanted nothing more than to rip her away from him again.

I haven't just been avoiding Darren. I've been avoiding Sasha too. At least with Darren, I knew he would have respected the distance I had put between us. Whether out of fear of what would transpire between us or just not wanting to talk and risk a blowout.

But knowing Sasha as well as I do, I had no doubt she'd say or do something that would hurt me deeper to prove a point. She's always been that way. Marrying Darren and having Abbie only made her worse. The divorce didn't do a thing to change that.

"Tell me that I have something to do at home, Daisy," I plead into the phone.

My closest friend hums. "You're too organized for that. If I had to guess, I'd say . . . you've already planned for the entire school year."

"I should have said no to this."

"Maybe. But you didn't."

"That's not helping, you know? Why can't you just tell me to get back into my PJs and go to bed? Where's the support?"

I stare at my front door, waiting for the storm in my head to manifest into reality and tear it off the hinges. All I have to do is take three steps forward and open it myself, but I can't seem to move.

"Because that's not actually what you want me to say, Della. It's okay if you want to go out with him."

"I don't."

"Are you sure? Not even just to talk? There have to be things you want to get off your chest. It's been a long, long time since you've had that chance."

"We talked at Into The Shade," I mutter.

"Okay, and how was that?"

I groan and wiggle my toes in my wedges to bring some blood back into them. "Are you trying to convince me to go or stay?"

Her laugh is a twinkle in my ear. "That bad, huh?"

"It went exactly the way you'd expect with two people who've avoided speaking for eight years. I can't think about it without cringing."

"Okay, well, you could always just avoid those tough conversations tonight. What was it that he said you were going to do? Brainstorm fundraising ideas?" She sounds as disbelieving as I've felt about it.

"Supposedly."

"And do you have any ideas?"

"It doesn't matter if I do. I doubt whatever we come up with tonight will ever see the light of day. It was all a ruse; I just don't know for what."

"Come on, Della. Yes, you do. He wanted to take you to dinner."

"I don't trust it. Why would he want to do that all of a sudden? There's been almost a decade for him to try."

"You tell me. Clearly, something's changed. The divorce, maybe?"

"It's been finalized for years now."

Daisy takes a few beats to reply. "Maybe something or someone kicked him in the ass, then. Gave him the push he needed to do what he's been wanting to since the ink dried on the divorce papers."

I shake my head, flinging that idea right into space before it can implant into my brain. "I'm going to go now."

"To dinner, right? Not to hide in your bed for the rest of the night?"

"Yes, to dinner. I promise."

"And you said he wasn't picking you up?"

"No. I told Bryce to tell him that he could meet me at Rustic Ridge instead."

Of all the places we could do this tonight, I jumped at the chance for it to be at the diner. I'm not a fan of the people who will no doubt be watching us, but at least it's public.

"You told . . . Bryce to tell him?" she asks, the words strained like she's trying not to laugh.

"He doesn't have my number anymore." I made sure to change it the first chance I could.

She chokes on a laugh before letting another fly free. "Oh, he's in for a ride, isn't he?"

"What? I wasn't going to offer it to him already!"

"Okay, sweetie. Fair enough. Make him work for those digits."

"I'm going to hang up now," I threaten, shuffling in place as my feet begin to ache already.

"Yes, you do that so you're not late. Especially since you're *walking*."

It's impossible not to crack a smile at her attitude. "Goodbye, Daisy."

"Goodbye!" she sings.

I hang up before she has the chance to add anything else. My purse falls down my arm to

my elbow as I slowly approach the door. It's now or never—or maybe I should change my shoes. Or my outfit. Actually, maybe I should just stay home after all. Palming my phone, I chew on the inside of my lip and slowly move one foot behind me.

Three gentle knocks on the front door have my phone flying into the air before clunking against the wall and falling to the floor. I trip over the rug lining the hall and gawk at the door. My heart pounds in my ears when I smack a hand against the old table I've taken to using as a coat rack to catch my balance.

"Holy shit," I mumble before gulping down a mouthful of air.

Another three knocks come. With wide eyes, I stare at the solid wood door and keep completely still. There would have to be an actual window in the door for someone to see me right now, but that doesn't help me relax.

Nobody's knocked on my door in . . . a long time. Months before my grandma passed at least.

"Delaney?"

I double blink. I've got to be going crazy. Right? I've stood here so long that I've started to hallucinate.

"I know you said not to pick you up. But I had a feeling that you still don't like walking alone once the sun's begun to set, and I figured you wouldn't want to drive such a short distance."

My hold on the table grows heavier, tighter as I use it to support my weight. There's a jab in my chest, straight through the ribs and piercing deep.

Slowly, I move to the door and unlock the deadbolt. I stall with a hand on the handle, confused and with my mind racing. He shouldn't be here, but he is.

Maybe it's against my better judgment to open the door. Still,

I do it if only to get an answer to the question flashing behind my eyes.

"You remembered that?"

Darren's standing right in front of the door. So close I immediately smell his cologne and aftershave on the breeze. He's dressed up tonight. It's almost jarring to see him having put so much effort into his appearance after standing witness to the opposite for so many years.

With the well-fitted, dark jeans, a slightly wrinkled, mossy-green long-sleeve, shaved jaw that makes his mustache stand out all the more, and no baseball cap, he looks like my Darren from the past.

I lower my eyes to his throat, unable to keep staring at him right now.

His Adam's apple bobs when he says, "It's one of the thousand things that I remember."

"When did you decide you wanted to grow a real mustache?" I ask, immediately wishing I had stayed silent instead.

What the hell kind of question is that? *And right now?* There's no hope for me.

He doesn't miss a beat with his reply. "I'm not sure. I tried the whole beard thing, and suddenly, I looked like I should have a mug shot on a wanted poster."

"It was a bit . . . much," I agree.

"A mustache is cleaner. If I have no facial hair, I look twelve, though. It's a good compromise."

I tongue my cheek and raise my eyes. Two deep pools of brown welcome me, strong and steady. "Right."

"You look beautiful tonight—always. You always do, not just tonight."

With a pathetic, needy noise trapped in my chest, I keep a straight face. "This isn't a date."

"You should be complimented regardless. Date or not."

"Not by you," I argue weakly.

"Okay, Elle. Not by me. How about we just go?"

"Delaney," I correct him. "But yes, let's go."

He retreats slightly, opening a small gap for me to slip out and shut the door behind me. I linger with my back to him for a second longer before joining him on the chipped porch stairs.

The way he's eyeing my feet has me blurting out, "What's wrong with my shoes?"

"What?"

"My shoes. You're looking at them funny."

He steps off the last stair and slides his hands into the pockets of his jeans, glancing away. There's a hint of a smirk on his lips that he's trying to hide. "Are you sure you don't want to change them before we leave?"

"Oh, sorry, do I not look like a wedged-heel kind of woman to you?"

His smirk grows to an unabashed level when his eyes roam up my body to snare mine. "I didn't say that."

"Then what are you saying?"

"I'm just thinking back to the last time you wore shoes like that."

Dropping a hand to palm my waist, I lean to the side. "I don't know what you're talking about."

But I do.

It was prom, and Darren wound up carrying me from his car to my bedroom at one o'clock in the morning because my feet were throbbing so badly that I couldn't walk on my own. It was also the first time he'd been given approval to spend the night with me at my parents' house while they were away. He'd been sneaking in through my window before then. Which, to this day, I'm positive my grandma knew about but never once told my parents.

"I can drive us to where we're going instead of walking if you're adamant about wearing the shoes. They look good on you either way," Darren says, the compliment obvious amongst the nonchalant offer.

"I'm sure I can survive the five-minute walk to the diner."

"You could. If that's where we were going."

"Darren."

"Delaney," he drawls.

"This isn't a date."

"You keep reminding me of that."

"Because you need to be reminded." I start walking, hearing him follow a beat later.

"Rustic Ridge is where teenagers go to meet up or friends get together for Sunday brunch."

"Don't try to justify breaking the rules, Darren."

"I didn't break any rules."

A snort escapes me. "You broke two."

"One."

"Two."

"The only one I broke was picking you up. I never said this is a date. That's all on you."

"Bullshit," I mutter.

He shifts closer, the heat from his arm teasing mine. "It can be a date if you want to let the rule go."

"You're not winning this battle."

"It kind of feels like it."

"Where are we having dinner if it's not the diner?" I ask, ignoring his last comment.

"You'll see."

I come to an abrupt stop. Darren gets a few steps ahead before realizing I've stopped moving. There's an obvious patience in his body language as he slowly turns around and leaves room for me to speak.

"No more surprises. I hate them."

A muscle twitches above his brow. "When did that start?"

"Around the same time I came home from university."

The air changes. I shiver at the chill while Darren slams his mouth shut and nods, something dark passing through the eyes now avoiding me.

"I thought you'd be interested in seeing what the drive-in grounds look like now. Considering we're going to be talking about another fundraiser idea tonight, it felt fitting. The walk is short, but I doubt it will feel like it when you're in uncomfortable shoes," he says.

"Oh."

A large hand runs over the top of his head before rubbing at his nape. "I should have gotten your number from Bryce and given you a warning earlier."

I knew I shouldn't have worn these shoes. It was pointless to put them on. I'll never admit it, but I did solely so I'd feel extra good about myself in Darren's presence. I've spent so long doubting myself that I guess I wanted an extra bump of confidence. Look what it got me.

"We can just drive," he offers, focused on me again.

"Fine. But don't get any ideas. You're only driving me so I don't have to change my shoes."

He tips his chin. "Of course. That's it."

"Fine," I repeat.

"I'm parked behind us."

"Right. The fancy car."

He chuckles under his breath, and we start back the way we came.

20

Delaney

THE ONLY THING DARREN'S NEW CAR HAS IN COMMON WITH HIS OLD one is the scent of cheeseburgers and over-salted fries.

The white bag with the logo for Rustic Ridge stamped onto the side crinkles in the back seat when we hit the dirt road leading to the drive-in grounds. The scene is so familiar that I can feel the tingle of nostalgia trying to make a guest appearance. Lucky for me, I'm too stressed and nervous to make room for yet another unwanted emotion tonight.

Instead, I keep my eyes on the road and pat my knees as the silence in the car dips further into awkwardness. The sunset is pretty, at least. There's nothing but highway, empty fields, and the snow-tipped mountains in the distance out this way. The sun paints the sky a myriad of pastel colours, stealing my attention. In another world, I'm sitting on a wraparound porch in the middle of nowhere, staring out at this view with—

"Do you still like banana pudding milkshakes?"

I swallow too loudly. "What?"

"Do you still like banana pudding milkshakes? Or have you finally outgrown them?"

"What does that mean?"

"They're gross to everyone but you."

My cheeks warm as I stop my patting and outright grip my knees instead. Then, I twist to face him, ignoring the way the seat belt digs into my collarbone.

"If that were true, they wouldn't have made banana pudding a flavour of milkshake to begin with, nor kept it all these years," I argue.

I've been ordering that same milkshake at Rustic Ridge for the last fifteen years. Surely if it were that unpopular, they'd have discontinued it by now. Even if it would have devastated me to have to order anything else.

Darren adjusts his posture in the driver's seat. *Fidgeting.* "You underestimate the power you have."

"I highly doubt I have enough of this mystery power to single-handedly keep an item on a menu that I only order from once every few weeks."

"Why that little?"

"Why do I only order it every few weeks?"

He tips his chin. "Yes."

"Why are you so curious about my milkshake order all of a sudden?"

"I'm just curious, Delaney. About you and what you've been doing all these years. How you've been doing."

"You have a funny way of showing it," I mutter, immediately turning forward again, closing myself off.

"Alright, that's fair."

"Thank you for the feeling validation," I toss out sarcastically.

He blows out a low breath. "That's not what I—that's not how I meant that to sound. We're nearly at the drive-in, so we can either get the blows out right now, right here, or out in the field. It's your choice."

"I don't want to deal any blows, Darren," I relent, exhaustion already creeping in.

It's not the kind that makes me want to go to sleep but rather the type that has me debating surrendering just so I don't have to keep up the effort it's taking to freeze him out. God, it would be so easy to just let my walls fall and welcome him back into my life. Sitting here beside him right now could feel as easy as breathing if I did. Maybe I'd feel relaxed again for the first time in a decade.

It all sounds too good to be true, which means it definitely is.

"Alright. But the option is there. I'd say we're a bit overdue for a blowout, don't you?" he asks.

"What would be the point of that? To clear your conscience?"

"My conscience hasn't been clear in a long time. I doubt it will be now, even if given the chance. My encouraging you to open up to me isn't to heal my regret or guilt. I'm trying to get us to start over, Delaney."

I let his words settle, keeping my lips sealed shut.

He said regret. Is that how he feels when he thinks back to what happened with us? With a stomach bubbling with regret? Because that would be a right fucking delight.

"What do you regret, exactly? Which part?" I snap, heat blasting from my belly up to the tips of my ears. In a motion quick enough to make the ends of my hair fly up and the edge of the seat belt rip at my skin, I twist. "The fighting between us every day or the way you put a concrete end to us because you got someone else pregnant? Or am I wrong? Maybe you didn't hook up with her until after you broke things off. I don't know! All I do know is that I offered to remove the distance between us hundreds of times and had to find out after two years of torturous silence that you were engaged and having a baby with someone else."

"Delaney, that's not—"

The tightness in my chest is painful. It's hard to breathe in here. Like the air's thinned out and too hot.

I pull my hair behind my shoulders and realize my fingers are shaking and cold. Suddenly, I can't be here anymore. Panic blares an alarm in the front of my skull, driving me to clutch at the door handle, finding it locked.

"Let me out," I demand, voice ghostly.

Clicking from the blinker soothes me slightly. The gentling of Darren's voice worsens the tightness in my chest.

"Okay. Let me pull over."

I tighten my hold, ignoring the way it slips the slicker my palm grows. One second, I'm buckled into the seat and shoving the door open, and the next, a hand that doesn't belong to me is releasing the buckle, and I'm diving into the fresh air.

My back is smushed against the door once I shut it behind me and palm my throat. The sunset is fading as the dark is moving in, swift and cruel. There are no frogs out this way, only the occasional *moo* from a cattle farm or cricket in the long grass along the dirt road. Rocks crunch under my stupid, ridiculous wedges with every step I take toward the ditch, counting each thump of my pulse beneath my fingers.

There was a part of me that knew this was where I'd be right now. It's the smart section of my brain. The realist that I listen to nine times out of ten. Tonight was the exception.

I shouldn't be here. Not in that car or on this road, and most importantly, not with Darren. Date or not, this was always how tonight was going to go. We've avoided confrontation for a long damn time, and the clock was ticking down to the inevitable blow-up.

That doesn't make it any easier to handle, though.

My wounds haven't healed. They're a long ways from it. How could they be any other way with the both of us in this town? Every unexpected sighting or whisper of his name on the wind has ripped off every scab I've managed to grow. We've been co-existing in Cherry Peak like friends whose friendship has had a natural die-out rather than exes with a painful past.

I flinch when a door closes behind me. Slowly, I drop my hand from my neck and wrap it around my front instead. It's boots disturbing the gravel, and a second later, it's woodsy cologne that floats on the breeze.

"Losing you is the biggest regret of my life, past, present, and future. I've made peace with the reality that I ruined the best thing I've ever had and won't be able to change what happened while still feeling guilty for being grateful for the little girl I get to call my daughter."

My eyes close on their own, the weight of his words too much. "You should be grateful for Abbie."

"That doesn't change that it should have been . . ." He trails off, cutting himself off. "If I could go back and change things, I would in a heartbeat. I'd never have been naïve enough to believe that a break would work for people like us or let us lose ourselves afterward. You wouldn't have spent even two hours without a call or text from me, let alone ten years of silence. I wouldn't have spent every one of those days missing the fuck out of you, Elle, because you would have still been my girl. I don't deserve your forgiveness, and I don't need it to try and make up for what I did and the way I hurt you. I'm just asking for us to talk about everything together the way we should have back then. I only need one night."

"Is this some sort of healing thing for you? Were you tasked with clearing out your unfinished business or something?" I ask weakly, shivering as the temperature seems to drop with no warning.

He's moved closer. I can feel his . . . his energy behind me. The maturity and strength that I find more staggering than his outrageous good looks or the confidence with which he carries himself now. Fuck, the knowledge and experience that he lacked all those years ago. It's like he's seen everything he's ever needed to see and learned every lesson in the book.

"I don't need a therapist to tell me to do this," he states, low voice unwavering.

Unlike me.

How lucky he is not to have needed a stranger to help pick

him up off the floor when his world splintered. To not have needed instructions on how to find my way back to the land of the living when everything around me was so dark and exhausting.

I shut down those thoughts and bite out, "What, then? Who's responsible for this sudden desire to make things right?"

"You. It was you. It *is* you."

"I don't understand."

"Can we get back in the car and talk about this while we eat? Your milkshake is going to be just flavoured milk if we stand out here any longer."

With a ball in my throat, I force myself to turn around, taking in his sudden closeness. There's a tug somewhere deep in my chest that demands I crumple against him and allow him the opportunity to carry the weight of some of the pain I've been carrying. I deny it again, kicking it into a cage with a heavy, keyless lock.

"Showing up with my favourite milkshake wasn't going to win you forgiveness," I say.

A dull flame of humour sparks in the depths of his eyes. "Worth a shot."

"What kind of cheeseburger did you bring me?"

He answers immediately. "A double with extra cheese and pickles and no mustard or onion."

Shit. Of course he remembers the way I like my burgers. Screw it all to hell, but all of this remembering is starting to pick at me. It's one thing for him to claim that he remembers everything about me and another to prove it over and over again.

When I told him he had to earn the chance to talk about things the first time he showed at the school, I wasn't expecting him to do it this way, nor for it to actually work. Maybe I'm just lonely. Way lonelier than I thought I'd been. That seems like an explanation I can live with. Especially when the alternative is me still being so weak for this man that I'm giving in because of a double cheeseburger and milkshake.

"You can have one hour. I mean it. No longer than that," I say.

"Deal."

"And there better be extra-salty fries in that bag too."

His grin is instant, unabashed. *Almost downright cocky.*

My stomach tumbles, and I know I'm in trouble.

21

Delaney

I STARE ACROSS THE ROOM AT WHERE MY NEW ROOMMATE IS STARING back at me, her face flat.

We've been sitting like this since I got all of my things brought in and began to unpack. The dorm room is small for two people, but it could always be worse. Or that's what I thought before this girl appeared.

In all honesty, I'm just assuming she's my roommate. She sat on the bed confidently, like she owned it, so I figured that this was the Brooklyn whose name was written on the whiteboard on the door. If she's not, then I probably shouldn't move, anyway. Best not to spook her . . .

"Your name is Delaney?" she asks bluntly, the deep blue of her eyes lacking any sort of emotion.

My head snaps back in surprise. "Yes. Are you Brooklyn?"

"Yes."

"Okay."

"I don't like people in my space. Would you like me to draw a line between our beds?"

"Uh, no, I don't plan on touching your bed."

She squints at me, unimpressed. "I'll draw a line."

"Alright. Go for it," I relent.

"Rules."

Lifting my brows, I move my head forward, urging her to continue. "Rules?"

"What's your major?"

"Education."

"Do you have any friends?"

"I just got here."

"So, no friends," she mutters, nodding.

"Not yet."

She ignores that and stands, peering down at me curiously. "Boyfriend?"

"Why do you need to know that?" I ask, starting to ramble.

I haven't prepared an answer for that question yet. What is the correct answer to that, even? Technically, I don't have a boyfriend anymore, but it's only been two days since Darren left for Calgary and I came, well, here. I'm not ready to say no to that question.

"You don't," Brooklyn states dully, already busying herself with something in one of her boxes, her interest gone.

"What? You don't know that. I didn't answer the question."

"It's yes or no. You said something else."

"Okay, I wasn't aware this was a test," I snap, growing frustrated.

"I'm merely asking so I know if we need to create a signal of some sort. A sort of sock on the doorknob scenario."

Blinking, I stare at her. "I used to have a boyfriend. We're taking a break. So, I guess he's still kind of my boyfriend."

"So, you're single."

"Not exactly—"

Brooklyn stares at me over her shoulder, deadpan. "You're single."

"Okay, fine. I'm single!" I throw my hands up and gather my phone and sweater from the bed. "I'm going out now."

"Rules, Delaney. Don't touch my stuff, and if you're going to have people over, leave a note. My side of the room is off limits."

"I have to go on your side to go to the bathroom."

She huffs and looks up at the ceiling, as if she's over having to deal with me already. "I'll include a path when I draw on the floor."

"I'm leaving now," I say instead of responding to that.

Grunting, she waves me off. "Bye."

Well then. I leave the room quickly and make it out of the building before pulling my phone out. Without thinking better of it, I send off a text.

My roommate is going to knife me in my sleep. How's yours?

Nerves swarm when I read it back and curse. So much for space.

Darren answers instantly, putting my fear to rest. *He's been high since I got here. Pretty sure I'm being hotboxed as we speak.*

Finding a spot in the courtyard, I hunker down and send him another message, a smile warming my face.

Tell me everything.

Brooklyn glares at me when she gets into the room, already reaching into her pocket for her earphones. My music isn't loud by any means, but she hates it. That's one of the first things I learned about her this year.

"I didn't know you were still here," I say in defense of myself breaking one of her thousand rules.

"Clearly. I just forgot something. Carry on."

"Weirdly, I think I'm going to miss you this summer."

"Weirdly?"

I laugh and tug my final pillowcase off before dropping it in my laundry basket. "Yeah. All year, we've avoided becoming friends, but I still got used to having you as a roommate."

"Who's to say we won't be stuck together next year too."

"Awe, are you a bit hopeful, Brooke?"

She rolls her eyes and lifts her mattress, revealing a tiny hunting knife. I choke on a surprised inhale.

"What? It's not like I ever stabbed you with it."

"Yeah, lucky me."

"I'll see you around, Delaney. Good luck with that guy."

I flush, nodding. "Yeah, see you."

She disappears, leaving me alone again. Her side of the room is empty, and mine is still overflowing with stuff I'm behind on packing. I blame that on Darren. He's kept my mind occupied these last few days as I tried not to be too upset with him bailing on going home for the summer.

Sure, I knew it was a long shot, but I just thought with how often we were talking that he'd want to see me. It was a ridiculous thought. This break was my idea, and he's only making sure we don't cross any more lines since we've jumped right over the no texting or calling one.

It's just been hard only being able to see his words or hear his voice every few days. I want to see him . . . touch him. My heart yearns for him, wondering why I ever thought of doing this in the first place. This year was a complete waste. The only thing I've learned about myself is that I'm a total hermit and hate college parties.

Maybe things will change when I go home. A summer by myself . . . I don't remember the last time I had one of those.

I check my phone again. No messages.

The last one I sent says it was delivered, but there's no indication that he saw it. Grandma waves at me from the front steps, her silver hair ruffling in the August breeze. I set my phone down, abandoning any hope of Darren texting me back before I head back to school for another year.

"Drive safe, Laney! And call me when you stop for dinner."

With the front windows down, I shout, "I will. Love you, Grandma. Don't forget to call the pharmacy tomorrow!"

"Stop worrying about me and hit the road. You have a long trip ahead of you!"

Impossible. With the cold she had these last two months, I've become used to driving her to and from the hospital and making sure she was taken care of. The version of myself that's going back to Vancouver this year is tired and more worried than I was the first time I left town. Other than several hours spent in the kitchen teaching myself how to cook, the entire summer was just . . . hard.

Two months flew by. One blink, and I'm back in my car, my heart heavier than the last time.

"You're really here?" I ask, tears pricking my eyes.

Darren's chuckle sends a shiver down my entire body. "Yeah, Elle. My cab's pulling up right now."

Without a second thought, I drop the call and run down the sidewalk to where I can see the yellow cab stopping along the curb. My pulse races as I run straight to him, not giving him a chance to get his bag out of the car before I'm jumping.

He catches me, his strong arms coiling around me as I cling onto him, legs curled at his hips. Burying my face into his throat, I breathe him in.

"I'm taking this as you're happy to see me?" he rasps.

It's been seven months since I've seen him. A Halloween party in Calgary wasn't my ideal idea for spending time together, but I didn't complain. I couldn't when that was my only chance.

But now, he's mine for this spring weekend, and we can do whatever we want.

"I can't believe you're really here."

"I'm sorry it took me so long to come."

"It's okay. I have the entire weekend planned. Starting with a tour of campus."

He nods and turns his head, bringing our mouths close. I stare into the same brown eyes I've ached to see again and wait, seeing what he's comfortable doing. The lines are growing blurrier between us, but surely he's not going to let them actually matter this weekend. Not after this long of being apart.

Throat pulling with a swallow, he smooths a hand down my back but doesn't kiss me like I was hoping. "Sounds good, Elle."

I slide off him and settle on the ground again. Smiling, I pretend I'm not disappointed and wave at the cab driver.

"Thanks for getting him here okay."

Darren snaps into motion and pays the guy before grabbing his bag and tossing it over his shoulder. I tap my thighs and nod in the direction of my building.

"Uh, we should drop your bag off first."

"Good point. Do I get to meet the infamous Brooklyn?"

I huff a laugh, punting the awkwardness behind us. "She'll probably show up once or twice. When I told her you were coming, she packed a bag."

"What are the odds that she asked to be roomed with you again this year?"

"Honestly, I think pretty high. She acts tough, but she's got a soft spot for me."

"Can't say I'm surprised. You're pretty easy to love," he says, the words flowing easily, as if it's still second nature for him to speak like that.

My heart clunks in my chest, words evading me. A foreign feeling of hope appears, and I grab onto it tight.

"That's something we both have in common," I reply.

Warmth covers my hand when he takes it and threads our

fingers. My throat burns with emotion that I choke down. Right now isn't for that.

The only thing I want to focus on is having him here with me and finally starting to feel like he'll do what I've been wanting him to do since we started this break and put an end to it.

THE LACK of air conditioning in Darren's dorm is suffocating as I lean against the kitchen counter and take another long sip of overly foamy beer. It's July, and I'd hoped that his roommate would be gone by now, but of course, he's not.

The all-year-living building is a blessing and a curse. Having to put up with his party freak of a roommate is a definite curse.

"You look warm," Darren says, appearing in front of me.

He's started growing a mustache this year, and it looks way too good on him. I'm pretty sure twenty-year-olds aren't supposed to be able to grow mustaches, but there's no denying his. With the new facial hair in addition to the muscles he's bulked up during his time here, I'm quickly losing my composure.

It's been two years since we've been . . . intimate, and I'm slowly losing my mind. After he left Vancouver in the spring, I've been slowly giving up hope of him putting an end to this break and finally sweeping me off my feet and into his bed.

Instead of doing that, he's opted back to putting us in the best friend category. I've never hated one of my decisions as much as the one that started this mess.

"It's a sauna in here," I reply, fanning my face with my hand.

"You're overdressed."

Glancing down at myself, I frown. "What? I didn't think this was against the dress code."

"That's not what I meant. You're in pants and a long-sleeve. It's thirty-five degrees outside."

He pinches my sleeve and pushes it up to my elbow before doing the same to the other. "Come with me."

I follow without argument. He pushes his bedroom door open and brings me inside.

"I can't fix your pants, but you can wear a T-shirt," he says.

The small dresser against the wall opposite his double bed is cluttered with schoolbooks, empty boxes of pencils, a calculator, and a familiar picture frame. I roll my lips, staring at the photo of us at our high school graduation.

"I didn't mean to take this one with me. It's yours."

Blinking, I take the shirt he's offering me and hold it close. The dark grey fabric is soft, and I know without looking at the design on the front which one it is.

"You could always keep it here. For when I come visit," I suggest, almost shyly.

"Is that a good idea? That feels pretty permanent."

"Is permanent a bad thing? I thought that's what this has always been."

He frowns. "Of course it's permanent. I just meant that we still have two years of this."

"Two years," I repeat, letting that sink in. "Or we could have two years of something else, Darren. What if this wasn't the right decision?"

"You can't know that yet."

"Don't you? Do you think this is right?"

He shakes his head, turning to sort through his messy textbooks. "It was your choice."

Desperation claws at me. His words are right, but they sound so wrong.

"Tell me to put an end to it, then."

"I'm not going to do that. Especially tonight."

I stare down at the shirt in my hands and grip it tighter. "Don't you want me?"

The question plops onto the floor. Darren doesn't speak, letting the silence start to crawl down my throat, suffocating me.

There's a crack in my chest. Then, I'm swallowing my pride and pulling my shirt off. It slips from my fingers, falling to the ground at my feet. The pulse from the music in the living room is wrong, and so is the heat in this place. Everything around me is wrong.

Darren's the only right thing. He's always been the right one.

"Darren," I whisper, taking one small step toward him. "Answer me."

The pain in his eyes throttles me when he turns around, gazing at me in a way I haven't seen him look in too long. I hold my breath when he looks at my bare chest and then flicks back up, a muscle ticking in his jaw.

"I've always wanted you, Delaney. But you said four years. You've been saying four years since we were teenagers, and when I put that ring on your finger, you made me agree again. I'd have married you already if I knew that's what you wanted and were ready for. But you need these four years. Not two, but four. Don't ask me to break that agreement right now and risk you resenting me for it later."

He flicks a look at the shirt in my hand, and I use shaking hands to put it on.

"We've let the lines blur, and now, things are all messed up. We can't keep doing this to each other."

"We're fine, Darren. I'm sorry. Just, don't leave me—I'll be fine with the boundaries. I can't cut you off completely. Please, don't do that," I plead, my voice breaking.

Suddenly, he's in front of me, gathering me into his arms. "I'm not doing that. We're not, Elle. Don't go there."

"I can't lose you."

His exhale is weighted, like he's just as scared as I am.

"I won't lose you."

22

Darren

Tonight, in the driver's seat of my car, I'm fifteen all over again.

My mustache is saving me from having to swipe at a sweaty upper lip as Delaney examines the fry pinched between her fingers, most likely deciding if I was lying or not about the extra salt. For the record, I wasn't. The waitress at the diner who took my order was new, and I could tell she was slightly disturbed by the contents of it, but that was the last thing I cared about. There was only one person's opinion on my mind, and she's sitting beside me.

I miss her. Present tense, never past. There hasn't been a single day where I haven't wished she were right beside me. Even without speaking to one another, I feel a rush of contentment and comfort that not a single other person on this earth has given me.

I'll never be able to take back the mistakes I've made. I was too young and stupid to recognize them as they were happening in real time, but I'm older now. Much older. I've got everything I've ever wanted but her. My Elle.

"Do they pass inspection?" I ask, attempting to keep my tone as smooth as possible.

Delaney pinches the fry harder before nipping at the end of it. A beat later, she swallows and then says, "They'll do."

"The waitress will be glad to hear that."

That draws her attention. No longer evading my eyes, she blinks at me pointedly. "Oh?"

"She was new and absolutely thought I was high with a serious case of the munchies."

She snorts in disbelief. "You? High? She must have just moved here."

"Is it so out of pocket to think I'd ever get high? Weed is legalized, you know?" I tease, chomping two fries into my mouth.

Her pale pink nails tap at the edge of her Styrofoam milkshake cup. "You hardly drank, let alone smoked. Unless that's changed?"

"I drink beer."

"Sixteen-year-old girls drink beer too."

I grin, unable to help myself. "For someone who claims they don't want to take any shots at each other today, you came prepared with a few."

"That one was low-hanging fruit. I'm sorry."

"Don't be sorry." Bringing my straw to my lips, I spread out more comfortably in my seat and eye her drink. "Does your shake taste the same as it used to?"

She follows my stare. "It does."

"Good."

"Yeah."

The threat of awkward silence lingers, testing me. I take a few gulps of my strawberry shake before setting it in the cup holder and turning enough to stare straight at Delaney. She's reluctant to look at me, and I'm desperate enough for her attention that it's easy to convince myself it's because she's nervous. Not that she just doesn't actually want to be here with me.

Fuck, that thought could break my heart if I let it.

"I'm sorry. For everything, yes, but mostly for how I handled what happened that night. I shouldn't have forced you away like that. I should have realized the mistake I made and chased you down the highway before you could get on your plane."

Delaney stops breathing. I hold mine too.

"So why didn't you?" she asks, voice thready.

"I thought we were better off. All of the fighting and the things we said that we didn't mean . . . The distance that felt much farther than it really was. It seemed like the right idea at the time, but by the time I realized it wasn't, it was too late. I couldn't just call you up and ask for you to give me another chance."

"You could have, actually. I waited for you for two years to do exactly that. In case you forgot, I actually waited so long that I had convinced myself that when I came home for the final time, it would be to you still waiting for me, regardless of our breakup. You know what I found instead."

I shut my eyes, pain ricocheting through every inch of my chest. "I should have. I know, I should have. I've thought about it more times than you'd believe."

"We can't change the past."

"We can make up for it, though. I can. If you give me a chance to, I can. *I will*," I swear, desperate.

She shakes her head softly, eyes on her lap. "Tell me what happened."

"With . . ."

"Sasha. Tell me everything."

I adjust the temperature in the car, dipping the A/C lower than normal. "Okay. I'll tell you anything you want to know."

"Were you with her when I was coming to visit you? Before then?" She fires the question like a bullet.

"No! Fuck, Elle. I wasn't with anyone during that time but you. There was never anyone but you. You had a lock on every inch of my body, inside and out."

"So when did it start? Did she play any part in why you put an end to everything? I knew things were hard, and we were obviously drifting apart, but for you to just end it like that? So completely? I think I convinced myself she was the reason for the breakup, even if the timing of Abbie didn't really line up."

"No, she didn't have anything to do with my terrible decision that night," I say, putting emphasis on every word. "Not at all. I hardly remember meeting her again after high school. She wasn't ever around on campus when I was, or if she had been, I never saw her. Sasha was just . . . there that night."

The ball in my throat makes it hard to breathe. I couldn't sound more like a piece of shit. Regardless of my self-loathing, I force myself to continue, knowing she deserves to know every bit of truth.

"That last year of school was miserable for me. I didn't eat or sleep, and I sure as shit never went back home. The only thing being back in Cherry Peak did was remind me of you. So, I stayed in Calgary and went to class, and when I wasn't in class, I was locked in my dorm, drinking until I forgot why you weren't there beside me and could just be without regret. Blue held party after party in that place, and I let him without complaint."

Too curious to avoid seeing her reaction, I look across the cab. Delaney's staring out the window, the inside of her cheek hollowed as if she's biting down on it. My fingers shake when I tug at the collar of my shirt to try and clear my airway.

"You took everything from me, Darren," she whispers, hurt and betrayal thick in her voice.

Oh, baby.

I choke, "I'm sorry, Delaney."

"My hometown, my friends, your family, who I saw as an extension of mine. I was alone."

"I never meant to take everything. I didn't even mean to take myself. Every choice I made was a mistake. The worst ones I could have ever made that snowballed into a million more. It was *always* supposed to be you. I was young and stupid and didn't know the repercussions of what I was doing. I was beyond naïve and thought that it would all be fine in the end. We'd take that time apart for real, and once we graduated and went back home, we could pick up where we left off without all of the painful things that were happening. I thought it was easier than the constant fighting and the short phone calls or missed flights. We were meant to be together, and I assumed nothing would get in the way after we were ready for the commitment we knew was coming. I was *so* fucking wrong, and I learned that the hard way."

"You *were* wrong. And it wasn't me, Darren. You chose someone else," she says, the words turning colder than the air blowing through the vents. "You can regret what happened and wish things were different, but they can't ever be the way they were going to be back then. Sasha got the life I wanted with you. She got to watch you become who you are now. Without me."

My stomach turns. Scrubbing a hand down my face, I let out a wavered exhale. "I would take it back. I'd back every single thing but my daughter. She's the only connection I have to Sasha now, but she's my little girl. Abbie was the only light I had in the darkest moments of my life. She put me back together when I thought I was too lost to find myself again."

"I'd never want you to regret that little girl. She's your daughter."

"She is."

"And Sasha was your wife," she says, tripping over the last word. "You married her."

I can hardly speak. Every word sounds hollow, unfamiliar. "It was the right thing for me to do. She was pregnant with my daughter. I grew up in a household with both parents. That's what I wanted for her, even if it wasn't the right thing for me."

"Why did you sleep with her? If you were so broken up about me, why her when you could have waited for me the way you claim you wanted to."

"I don't know," I mutter with a raw wince.

Delaney tucks her hair behind her ear, still avoiding looking at me. "Yes you do."

"She was . . . there. She was just there, Delaney, and I know how pathetic that sounds. When I hit rock bottom, she was there, and the morning after, I found my true bottom hidden far beneath that one."

Silence is her only reply. For long enough that we both finish our milkshakes and avoid reaching into the diner bag for food that we can't stomach now. The clock runs toward the end of my hour, a cruel reminder that I might not ever get another one.

"Did you . . . date her? Before that night?"

I whip my head toward her. Finally, she's looking at me. Our eyes clash, and I breathe deeply, filling my lungs in a way I haven't been able to since we started speaking about this. She presses her lips together and blinks, the slightest crinkle between her brows. A tell that I recognize immediately.

"No," I blurt out. "I hadn't dated anyone after you. It was always you."

"It doesn't surprise me that you married her, Darren. She was pregnant."

"I owed Abbie two parents."

"You weren't happy, though, were you? I saw you during those few years you had a ring on your finger. What did marrying her cost you?"

I almost laugh. It's not the time for me to answer that question. Not when tonight has already been hard enough. If she ever gives me another chance to sit and talk like this, maybe I'll tell her then.

"I survived," I say instead.

Almost reluctantly, her chin dips before she darts her stare to the bag of food. "What fundraiser ideas do you have?"

"What?"

"We need to talk about the fundraiser you wanted to do," she explains, as if I simply missed what she said.

I try to keep my expression neutral despite my confusion. "Right now?"

"You have fifteen more minutes tonight. We can save the rest of the conversation for next time."

"Next time," I echo, heart racing.

She reaches into the paper bag and pulls out her burger while cocking a brow at me. "Eat, Darren. Yes, we can have a next time. One more night."

I don't make her say it again. Not when I could risk waking up from this dream to find myself alone again.

23

Delaney

"Stop staring at me like that, Poppy," I mutter around the rim of my coffee cup.

"I'm not looking at you like anything."

"Yes you are."

"How am I looking at you, then?"

With a roll of my eyes, I set my coffee on the table and relax into my chair. For a coffee shop, the ambience is top-notch. The recent renovation brought with it low lighting, plush chairs, and the disposal of the bar-height tables that always killed my back. There's even a small stage at the front of the place that has yet to be used. If it ever will be.

"Like you're itching to ask me a million questions. I'm shocked you've lasted this long, honestly. It happened days ago."

Poppy bundles her red hair behind her shoulders and leans forward until her arms drape over the tabletop. "Start talking. *Please*. I'll die if you don't. I'm dying already!"

"I blame Daisy for this. She's the one who told you, right?"

"It was Darren, actually, but now I'm offended that you told Daisy and not me? Who next? Bryce?" She pouts, her glossy bottom lip wavering.

"Darren told you?"

"Duh. He loves me too much to keep something like this a secret."

I cross my legs beneath the table and lean back against the chair, worrying my lip. Is it really that big of a deal that he told his sister about us meeting up? Surely, he just knew she'd like to be kept in the loop. That's sibling responsibility. Yeah, that's it.

"If he was the one who told you in the first place, why haven't you just asked him for answers the morning after?"

She blinks slowly at me, deadpan, before her lashes pick up speed. "Sorry, was that a serious question?"

"Okay, sassy. Forget I asked."

"If my options are you or Darren, I'm going to choose you for real answers. He'll give me a dumb guy rundown, and I need *more*. The juicy details."

"I'm sorry to be the bearer of bad news, then, but there are no juicy details. All we did was eat cold burgers in his car."

She clucks her tongue and flicks my wrist. "Nuh-uh. Don't try it with me, Della."

"Try what? I'm being serious. We talked and ate. That's it. I can tell you about the fundraiser we're putting on next weekend if you want."

"I'm going to pinch you really, really hard," she warns.

I let loose a laugh and scoot closer to the table. "Fine. But when you realize there truly aren't any juicy details, you can take it up with your brother."

"Deal. Now, start talking."

The dramatics . . . "Did he ask you anything about me recently?"

"Like what?"

"Just anything specific. Like, my food orders or whether I still like banana milkshakes?"

Poppy's hands fly to her neck before travelling to cover her mouth. The hearts in her eyes could rival those in a cartoon.

"He really does remember everything about you," she whispers in awe.

"Don't start crying, Poppy. My fast-food order is hardly everything."

"But it's a good sign toward it. I bet if you made a list of questions for him, he'd have all the answers."

She could be right, but I'm not in the position to be thinking about that. All we did was talk for an hour, and while it was an important talk, there's still a lot of work to be done between us if we want any sort of friendship.

"You're probably right," I agree lamely.

"Well? What else? Come on, Della, don't hold out on me. Let it out into the world."

"I asked about Sasha. She's mostly who we talked about."

Poppy's expression droops slightly, her enthusiasm drifting away. "It's good you asked about her."

"It didn't feel good, Poppy. It felt draining. Like I was trudging back through every bad memory of that time that I have."

"And what about now? How do you feel?"

"I'm confused. I thought I should be relieved or even just somewhat at peace, you know? After all these years, I finally asked the questions I've been dying to know the answers to, but they didn't feel good to hear. All they did was remind me of how we got here in the first place."

"I'm sorry, honey," Poppy murmurs, soothing the pink mark on my wrist from her flick with a soft touch. "Maybe it was too soon."

"No, that's not it. It's been the better part of a decade. That's long enough to miserably kick this around. I can't keep going on like this. Looking over my shoulder for him . . . Wishing that I'd decided to leave instead of staying."

"Don't say that, Delaney. Don't even joke about it. You leaving would have devastated me."

I press my lips together in a weak smile and shrug. "We

didn't speak for years. Not until Daisy started at the school and we were kind of pushed back together. Would you have even noticed if I hadn't stayed?"

The crack that moves through her is almost audible as she pushes away from the table and as far into her chair as possible. Her face crumbles, eyes falling to her lap instead of where she's held my stare for the last half hour.

"I'd have noticed," she starts, teeth sinking into her lip repeatedly before she finally releases it. "Would you think I was making excuses if I said that I was trying to protect my brother's feelings? In hindsight, I know that isn't enough. Not when you and I were as close as we were. Your feelings should have mattered as much as his did. And they did—please believe me. I just . . . he's my brother."

My hand shoots across the table before my brain catches up. I lay it palm up in front of her and focus on keeping my expression clear, open.

"It's okay. I knew when I flew back to school that night that the odds of losing you were high. It's what I expected because of how close you two were. I've never resented you for that."

"You should have. Abandoning you wasn't right. You were so far away, all alone, and I should have been there for you."

"Hey, you're here now," I say.

She cracks a smile at that, some light returning to her face. "I am. To stay. Even if my brother shows his ass again and doesn't do what he's supposed to, I'll be here. That's a promise."

"Alright, Pops. I'd really like that."

Her hand clutches mine. "Sisters, Della. With or without my brother."

It sounds perfect. I'd be an idiot not to take the declaration seriously. Yet, I can't believe it just yet. Not so quickly.

With her hand in mine, I take in a slow breath and then say, "Do you believe in second chances, Poppy?"

"Yes," she answers without even half a second of hesitation.

"I want to."

"But you don't yet."

"I just don't know if it's possible to get over what happened completely. Everything is so different now compared to then. We're not the same people, and there's a part of me that knows that what happened won't repeat itself. We're too grown now to repeat the same mistakes, but there's still that wiggle of doubt. And fear too. I mean, he has a daughter, Poppy. And an ex-wife. Darren and I can become friends again, sure, but what about his family? I can't pretend they don't exist, and I don't want to. It's just that I don't know if I can handle that hurt," I ramble, clinging to her tighter. "And friends? Shit, how am I supposed to be friends with him after—"

"After you were in love? The kind of love that others yearn for their whole lives?" she asks, sighing knowingly. "I don't know. Is that all you want to be? Friends? Is that the line you're drawing between the two of you? Because if it is, then Sasha doesn't matter. She'll have no involvement in your friendship. And Abbie loves everyone she meets. You're already in her life because of your teacher status, so being friends with her father won't bother her. Unless that's not what you're worried about. Is it?"

It's not. The real reason is worse than that. It's selfish and cruel, and I'm ashamed of ever thinking it. Of ever wishing Abbie were mine instead. That I'd been the one to bring Darren's baby girl into the world. Our world.

The thought has kept me up into the night too many times. I've cried a million tears into the drain of my shower, reminiscing about a life that I'll never have until finally, I moved on, and I could see the sweet girl in public without drowning in pain. Or I thought I'd gotten over it. I went out on dates and let other men replace the image of him in my mind. Only they never lasted.

"Shit, Poppy. I don't know. I've avoided thinking about that for way too long. The possibility of ever being more than friends with him died the day I came back home. I've spent years working to kick him from my heart, and all it takes is one damn day to throw me back into the mess I was. What am I supposed to take from that?"

"I think you already know what you're supposed to take from that. How was it when you were together? Did it feel good at all?"

I reach for my coffee and take a long swig of it. "I missed him. Being so close to him but having to keep a distance was overwhelming. He left an imprint on me that won't ever leave."

"Are you going to do it again?"

"Eat with him in his car?" I ask, sounding far more at ease than I am on the inside.

"Sure. Or, you know, going out with him to do something that doesn't involve you hunkering down in his car and talking about all of the miserable moments in your lives."

"I agreed to another meeting. Only one for now."

Poppy's eyes bulge. She reaches for her drink and pounds it back before slowly setting it back down and clearing her throat. When she speaks, it's with an overly calm tone that draws a laugh up my throat.

"That sounds promising."

"Yeah, I can tell that's what you took from what I said," I joke.

She huffs and releases my hand long enough to wiggle a finger at me across the table. "Don't pretend like this isn't a big deal to you too. You're willing to go out with him *again*. That's huge."

"We haven't decided on anything yet. If Darren had it his way, he'd make it another date."

"A date?" she squeals, unable to help herself this time. Too bad she forgot to reach for her coffee.

"Only in your brother's eyes. I'm still trying to figure out what he's trying to accomplish here."

"I mean, from that, I'm sure I could piece it together."

"You say that as if it's easy to understand, though. I mean, why now? After all these years? It doesn't make sense."

Poppy keeps smiling, not sharing my confusion. "Let him explain himself, then. Knowing my brother, he has a plan. You could throw a curveball into it and demand answers if you really wanted. He never could keep a secret when it came to you."

"I'll think about it. I need a few more days to just process all of this," I say.

"Understandable. Let him wait, Della. He deserves it."

I return her smile and let myself relax again in her company.

"I'm going to get something to eat. I think they have the cherry turnovers again; do you want me to snag you one?" I ask, already pushing away from the table.

"Please."

"Got it. Be right back."

I move through the shop at a slow pace, content with enjoying the lack of line in front of the counter. It's quite empty in here for a Saturday morning. I wouldn't be surprised if everyone was still sleeping after last night's rave of a farmer's market. Apparently, Eliza Steele brought the moonshine that Johnny's started making in his back shed, and it was a huge hit.

That would explain the hollering and terrible singing I heard on the street at two in the morning.

I'm eyeing the case of pastries on the counter when the bell above the door rings. The barista slides in front of the till at the same second I check to see who's walked in. Bryce's signature scowl greets me before I drop my gaze to the little girl standing beside her.

Abbie Huntsly waves at Poppy, instantly spotting her and heading right for the table.

Our table.

24

Delaney

Darren's daughter plops into the seat between Poppy's and mine and beams at her aunt. Bryce follows close behind, a silent guardian who everyone in this town knows not to mess with.

Abbie's quite literally a bundle of joy. With her typical braided pigtails, a floofy dress that looks like it could have been snagged right off the rack at a beauty pageant, and scuffless white flats, she's nothing short of a princess. The natural blush to her cheeks enhances the slight dimple in her left cheek that she got from her dad. It's not all she got from Darren, but for some reason I refuse to pinpoint, it's the one that I always seem to focus on.

Bryce pushes the back of Abbie's chair in and examines the coffee I've abandoned before glancing directly at me. I lift my hand to wave, knowing she's already noticed me creeping on the table. She quirks a corner of her mouth and wiggles her fingers.

"Delaney? Did you want to order something?"

I jump at the voice, whipping my head back around to look at the barista, who apparently knows my name. "I'm sorry. Yes, please. I'll do two cherry turnovers."

"You got it," she says, luckily not pointing out my brain lag.

"Actually, could you make that three? And a sprinkle donut?"

She nods and adds the extra pastries to my order before telling me the total. I'm on autopilot as I pay for the food and take a step back to wait for her to slip them into a paper bag.

"You look like a real-life princess, Abs. Where did you get your dress?" Poppy asks, the café too empty not to hear every word of their conversation.

Abbie's high-pitched, sweet-as-icing voice hides the crinkle of the pastry bag. "Dad ordered it on the computer! He let me pick it."

"Oh, trust me, we can tell it wasn't him who chose it," Bryce says.

Poppy laughs. "Be nice, Ice. Darren's fashion sense isn't that terrible. At least not anymore."

"Has your dad been watching fashion shows on TV again, Abbie?" Bryce asks.

"Mmm, sometimes. But it's supposed to be a secret."

Bryce's snort travels loudly across the café. "Not anymore."

"Here you are! If you need anything else, just flag me over, or come up and ring the bell. It's pretty slow in here today," the barista says.

I nod clunkily and take the bag. "Oh, thanks."

"Have a good day!"

My responding smile must look wonky because the barista scrunches her face in confusion before slowly disappearing into the back room. I consider never showing my face in this place again and head back to the table. It's unfortunately not possible to do that. Not when it's the only coffee place within an hour's drive, and coffee made at home never tastes the same, regardless of how many fancy pods I buy for my machine.

"Della! You're back with the goodies," Poppy says once I get close.

Bryce lifts her eyes and flashes me a half-smile. It's as close to a full one as anyone but Daisy will ever get. "Hey."

"Hi, Ms. Delaney. What are you doing here?" Abbie asks, her manners as perfect outside of a classroom as they are inside.

"I was having coffee with your aunt. She's been pretty great company."

"Yeah, you hear that? Make sure you tell your dad exactly that the next time he tries to get out of family dinner," Poppy pokes.

I set the brown bag onto the table and reach inside for the stack of napkins I watched the barista slip inside before taking my seat. Abbie's excited stare follows my movements while I hand out the napkins and finally reach in to pull out the sprinkled donut.

Abbie doesn't reply to Poppy and instead asks, "Is that donut for me?"

"That depends. Do you like sprinkle donuts?"

"Yes! They're my favourite. I get one every Sunday morning with my dad," she explains quickly, the words almost running away from her.

My chest pangs. I relax my grip on the donut in question when I feel my nail dig into it.

"Well, then, this is for you. I love them too."

Did he know he was continuing our tradition with his daughter, or was it subconscious?

It doesn't matter either way. He still did it. Still had me on his mind enough to affect his actions. It's another truth in the claims he's made repeatedly since deciding to seek out contact with me again.

Abbie nearly rips the donut out of my hands and brings it to her mouth. Before her teeth can sink into it, she smiles sheepishly over the rim and says, "Thank you, Ms. Delaney."

"Just Delaney. You don't have to call me Miss unless we're in the classroom."

"Okay! Cool."

"It looks like you cleared them out of pastries," Bryce says, eyeing the larger-than-normal bag.

Poppy takes the bag and looks inside. "I knew it. Della's too sweet to keep you starving, even when you deserve it. Here. Take this and say thank you like a good girl."

"Thank you, Delaney," Bryce sasses.

Poppy hands her best friend the extra turnover before dishing the remaining two out. I ignore mine and watch Abbie set her donut down on the table with one bite missing and start picking the yellow sprinkles off. She sets them into a pile on her napkin, not stopping until they're all off. Then, she pushes aside the napkin and starts eating her donut again.

"She always saves the yellow sprinkles for last," Poppy whispers, following my line of sight.

I blink away from Abbie. "Why?"

"I'm not sure. I imagine it's the same reason we always saved the red Smarties or Skittles for last. Yellow is Abbie's version of that. It's the same for most candy too."

"So, I should try and find a donut with more or less yellow sprinkles on it next time?"

Poppy smirks, glancing at Bryce. "Next time?"

"What's with you and your brother repeating that to me? Yes, next time."

"Touchy, touchy," Bryce teases.

"You know what? Forget I said that at all."

"Oh, no can do. Now, tell me when my brother said that. Was it the other night?" Poppy demands.

Bryce lifts her turnover. "I feel like I missed a discussion that I'm going to want the details on."

"Why are you here, anyway? Get tired of babysitting by yourself?" I ask the self-proclaimed Ice Queen.

Her eyes flare with excitement at my borderline frustrated tone. "Why? Does it bother you?"

"No. I just wasn't expecting you two to be here."

"Bryce is watching Abbie every Saturday afternoon while Darren's at the station this month. The crew is working on one of those fundraisers, and he couldn't get out of it," Poppy explains with an eye roll in Bryce's direction.

I swallow, a weird pang appearing in my side. "He didn't mention that to me."

"Did you two not discuss weekend schedules on your date? Actually, what *did* you discuss? Anything worth sharing?" Bryce asks.

I choke on an exhale and look at Abbie, ensuring she didn't hear the mention of a date. Once I'm satisfied that she's only interested in finishing the last bite of her donut, I turn back to Bryce.

"You know about it too?"

"Of course I did. Did you think he chose a decent outfit on his own?"

"I assumed Poppy did that."

Bryce twists the engagement ring on her finger and winks. "Wrong."

"Well, once my brother's done with the designs for mine and Garrison's new house, I'll be around more often to help with all of his outfits. If he doesn't have someone else to do that by then, of course," Poppy says, her smile sly.

I scoot my chair closer to the table and ask, "Darren's designing your house?"

"Oof, did you even speak on your date?"

"Stop calling it a date, Bryce. You're as bad as he is," I huff.

She tucks her lips together in reply. There's something like smug satisfaction in the blinding blue of her eyes, though. It's impossible to miss.

"Yes, he's designing our place. It's going really good so far too. Have you seen his house at all? It's incredible, and he designed it himself," Poppy says.

Abbie pops her head up. "My house?"

"Yes, your house. It's pretty nice, right?"

"Dad says it's getting too small."

Poppy's brows pinch together. "He did? When?"

"Don't remember. I told him I want a room for all of my dresses if we move, though."

"I'm sure he'd get you a hundred rooms for your dresses, Abs," Poppy murmurs.

Abbie grins and taps Bryce on the shoulder. "Can we make bracelets now?"

I swear I can see Bryce's skin crawl as she digests the question, thinking and thinking . . .

"You don't want to do them later with your dad?"

"Nope. You said we could do them together here if I stopped asking."

Poppy swallows a laugh and cocks her head at Bryce. I take a bite of my turnover and pretend to look out the café window.

"You know, I think Delaney would be interested in bracelet making. Why don't you ask

her?"

Hiding my panic is impossible. Bryce meets my wide-eyed stare with crooked lips.

"Oh, I don't think I even know how," I ramble.

Abbie reaches beneath her chair and suddenly plops a giant pink bag onto the table. "I can teach you. It's easy with practice."

"Oh, you brought your entire collection with you," Poppy jokes.

"I wanted to make lots and give them to Dad's friends at work."

Of course, she's thoughtful too. She's pretty much the perfect daughter.

"Are you really up for teaching me? I might slow you down. I'm sure you're a professional at this point," I say.

Abbie replies by gripping her sack of supplies on both sides and tipping the entire thing upside down. The contents spill all over the table, all neatly organized into clear baggies and neat rolls of clear elastic. A small pair of scissors hits the side of Poppy's empty coffee cup before sliding toward me.

The array of beads is a bit staggering. There's everything

from pearls to sparkles, neon and pastel. Abbie starts sorting through the mess and pushes aside three containers of gems and charms and letters. I'm overwhelmed just from looking at everything.

"How long have you been making bracelets for?" I ask, almost in awe.

"A while. I don't like to colour much. Watching TV is boring."

"That's fair. I'm not much for those things either. Do you like flowers?"

Abbie cocks her head, lips pushing out as she thinks. "I think so."

"I like to take care of mine when I'm bored. Maybe I'll take to bracelet making after today."

"What is your favourite colour?" she asks, already sorting through the bags of colour-coordinated beads.

"I'll go with green."

"Here! I'll show you how to tie the string first."

I nod and wait while she starts unrolling some clear elastic from the first roll on the table. Someone nudges my foot under the table, and I look to my right, catching Poppy's soft expression. I freeze, worry building in my chest before she shakes her head, reading me instantly.

A few simple words from her soothe my anxiety.

"She likes you."

25

Delaney

My arm is weighed down by seven beaded bracelets by the time Bryce interrupts and excuses herself to answer a call. The moment she's gone from the table, Abbie juts her bottom lip out and gazes up at her aunt.

"Can I make one more? Please? Delaney isn't done hers yet!"

Poppy nudges my foot beneath the table before replying, "Alright, but you have to play dumb when Bryce gets back, and don't tattle on me."

"Okay, deal."

I blow out a low laugh and fidget with the unfinished bracelet lined up in front of me. The right side is complete, but there's empty thread where the charms and letters should be. I'm stalling in a very obvious way.

"Do you want me to give you some ideas?" Poppy offers, examining the rows of white letters and numbers in front of me that I've rearranged a thousand times.

"No. I've got it. Just stop watching me while I work."

"While you work? You're suddenly so serious about this, Della. I never took you for a professional bracelet maker."

Abbie giggles while expertly tying the beginning knot on her next bracelet.

I dig the toe of my boots into Poppy's ankle. "Careful, or I'll start using bracelets as my way of blowing off steam. You'll get one in your mailbox with a dirty cuss on it."

"Did you know the way to my heart all this time?" she asks on a gasp.

"At least now I know how Garrison did it."

Of course, Abbie uses now to start paying close attention to what we're saying. Her second giggle is even louder than the first.

"Uncle Garry made you a bracelet with swear words on it?"

"No! He didn't. Delaney is just teasing. Go back to your bracelet. You better finish before Bryce gets back and snatches it away," Poppy rushes out with her narrowed eyes on me.

I smirk while pinching a bead and sliding it onto the string without overthinking it. The bracelet isn't for me, which could be the problem. Making one for Abbie would have been easy. Poppy too.

But no. Of course, I chose the most complicated person to make one for. Darren will understand the odd array of beads and what they mean. I can only hope now that he'll see it as what it is: an offer of friendship.

Working quickly, I listen for Bryce to return. Poppy, I can risk seeing the completed bracelet, but Bryce? Not a chance.

She might not be Darren's sister by blood, but she's the one he's chosen. Poppy's been my friend as much as she has her brother's, and that keeps her tugged in the middle of us more often than not. Bryce is my friend in a loose sense of the word. We're brought together by shared relationships and this town itself. If we'd met in any other circumstances, we wouldn't get along.

That's never been a problem between us, really. I like her, and she likes me—I think. It's just never going to get deeper than that, and because of our lack of a deep relationship, her loyalty is to Darren. She might play everything off as the teasing friend, but she has his interests at heart always when it comes to the two of us. I appreciate that as much as it makes me constantly second-guess myself around her.

Her real feelings about what Darren's doing are unknown to me. She could approve, or she could hate everything about it. I probably won't ever know which one it is. All I can do is try to keep my feelings close to my chest instead of on my sleeve when she's around.

That includes hiding the stupid beads I've strung onto this bracelet.

"Okay, I'm done," I announce a minute later.

The knot I've tied in the elastic is pathetic, but I hide it well as I slip it into the pocket of my jeans.

Abbie glances up from her eighth bracelet and crinkles her face in thought. "Can I see? It looked pretty."

"How about I show you these ones instead?" I ask, lifting my heavy wrist and waving it around.

"I already saw those ones."

I gulp. "The one I just did was bad. Really, really bad. I'm afraid it's so bad that nobody can see it but me. Mm, maybe the next time we make bracelets. If you want to do them with me again. Or we can. Either-or," I ramble, face flushing.

Poppy, apparently having more than enough sympathy for me, jumps in to help. "How about we let it go, Abs? Remember, we're all about respecting boundaries this year. It's what we agreed on when the fireworks went off on New Year's Eve."

"But I want to see it," Abbie argues.

Glancing around, Poppy snaps her fingers and grins, relieved. "Oh, would you look at that. Bryce is back."

"Hi, Bryce," I announce, twisting in my seat to face her.

The tattoos on Bryce's neck and behind her ear catch my eye when she lifts a brow in suspicion at both me and Poppy. "What did you two do?"

"What? Why would we have done anything?" Poppy asks, sounded mockingly offended.

"You're clearly acting weird. What did they do, Abbie?"

"Nothing," Abbie groans.

"Well . . . good. Because I have to go."

"Okay. Can I have a hug before you're gone, Abs?" Poppy's already pushing back out of her chair when Bryce speaks again.

"No, I mean I have to leave alone. I already called Darren to let him know, but Shade needs me at the studio. Something's come up that I can't miss."

Poppy's concerned gaze isn't misplaced. I know Bryce well enough to realize that it isn't normal for her to have to take off so suddenly. The fact that she is should be taken seriously.

"I'm assuming I'm watching Abbie until Darren's off, then?"

"You assume right. He's trying to get out of the station early because I know you have to head home soon."

"Soon as in half an hour soon," Poppy clarifies.

Bryce pushes her empty chair in and offers us a winced smile. "Sorry. I know it's shit timing."

"It's okay, right, Abbie? We'll find something to do. And if your dad can't find a way out of work early, then I guess I'll have to drop you off at the station like a newborn baby, hmm?"

The little girl's eyes bulge. "You wouldn't!"

"Oh, but I could," Poppy sings.

"I'll just go with Delaney, then!" Abbie exclaims.

I freeze up, every muscle in my body locking. "Oh—I don't . . . That wouldn't—Poppy's just teasing."

"Your dad said that was only if he couldn't get off work in time. And if Delaney didn't mind."

There isn't a coherent thought in my head.

"He did?" Poppy asks, not sounding as mind blown by that as I feel.

My mouth has a mind of its own. "You told him I was here? With Abbie?"

Bryce doesn't answer either of us. "I've got to go. Just send Darren a text or call the station. He's doing nothing like always. Bye."

It's blunt and quick, and then she's gone. I'm still trying to reel my thoughts together when Poppy urges to Abbie to clean up her bracelet supplies for real this time. I watch them both work together to rid the table of beads and string without speaking. There are more than enough words in my head that there's no reason to say them out loud.

"Okay, ready to go, Della?"

I slowly follow the line of Poppy's body up to her face. She's standing at the edge of the table watching me, waiting for a reply.

"I'm going to walk home," I tell her, the words forming slow and heavy on my tongue.

She frowns. "What? Why? You don't need to do that. I picked you up, so I can drop you off."

"I have a few things to do today still. You take Abbie to the station. To the *doors*."

"Are you sure? We wouldn't mind the company."

"No, I need to go. It was nice, though. Today. All of us here."

"You won't come with us, Delaney?" Abbie murmurs, immediately sending spikes through my chest.

The guilt from putting that disappointment on her face is sweltering beneath my skin. "I shouldn't."

"Why? You can say hi to my dad!"

"You should come, Della," Poppy urges gently, cautiously.

Run, Delaney. Duck out before you agree to something you shouldn't.

"Okay. Sure. I'll come."

Idiot.

"Yeah, I'll be done in five. You can come inside," Darren says.

His voice is just as strong and commanding when it's coming through the speakers in Poppy's car. It has the hairs on my arms sticking up in anticipation of seeing him and hearing that voice face to face again after a week of being without it. Greedy is what it is.

I went all these years without hearing it, and now that I have again, I can't seem to go on without it. Greedy, *greedy* heart.

"Okie dokie. See you in five," Poppy says before hanging up and pulling into the station parking lot.

I notice Darren's car first and give my head a shake. "Are you sure I shouldn't head home now? It's only a five-minute walk."

She leans over the centre console and twists her mouth to hide an oncoming smile. "As if. What would you do with the bracelet in your hand if you went home before you could give it to him?"

I pull away and glare. Her responding laugh is fully expected.

"Can we just go in now? Dad isn't even working," Abbie grumbles.

Poppy glances over her shoulder into the back seat. "Yeah, let's go in."

Abbie moves frantically, excited to be free of the car after being subjected to the same time-killing drive around town that we suffered through for the last half hour. There are only so many times you can stand seeing the same few businesses on Main Street before you're so bored you want to pull your hair out.

I step out of the car last and keep a step behind the both of them the entire way to the station doors. The engine bay door is open, and the fire engine is sparkling inside, unused once again.

Slipping my hands into my pockets, I loop a finger through the band of the bracelet. I doubt I'll give it to him today. It's not my ideal time or place. The odds of him even being alone here are slim, and with both his daughter and sister with me, I'm sure—

Abbie dives inside the station after Poppy, and before I can lift my arms in time, the open door flies back and smacks me in the face. I cry out at the impact and the searing pain that spiderwebs from my nose outward to my ears and chin. Vision blurring with tears, I spin around and face the street while clutching my nose.

A breeze hits my back, and then shoes scuff the sidewalk. "Jesus Christ, Elle. Are you okay?"

I shake my head and sniff, only to make the liquid now dripping from my nose run faster. It slides down my hand and, without a doubt, onto my clothes as I try to make out the blurry man in front of me.

"You're bleeding. Here."

My vision might be thick with unshed tears, but there's no mistaking the sight of Darren stripping in front of me. Throat drying up, I watch as he tugs his shirt over his head for the second time in only a few weeks and brings it toward my face. I hold my breath as he gently removes my bloodstained hand and eases his shirt to my nose, pressing firmly.

"This is wonderful," I mutter, wincing at the fresh wave of pain.

"Take my hand and come inside."

I don't, but he does it for me. Our fingers glide before interlocking, palms flush and warm. The pain in my nose dulls to a low throb as I blink and blink and try to free my vision of the tears tracking down my cheeks. It doesn't work, and my chest begins to ache.

It's the first real physical contact we've had in years, and I'm completely, embarrassingly weak in the knees. Every step is wobbly and off-centre. I struggle to see where we're going, but that doesn't stop me from moving.

Not when he's the one leading me.

26

Delaney

WHERE IS HE? I'VE BEEN HERE FOR TWO HOURS. ALONE AND waiting for him to come back from wherever it is that he took off to when Poppy left.

Considering I'm only here to spend the weekend with Darren, I'm getting more pissed by the second that he's not here. If it hadn't been the only way that I could guarantee that I'd get time with him tonight, I'd have changed my flight to leave this morning. But of course, I didn't want to leave while we were both still upset about earlier. It didn't occur to him to do the same, I guess.

Whether I'm in my first year of university or the third, my view on the parties is still the same. The only thing I've learned in my time at the few I've been dragged to is that the beer is warm, the chip bowls are infected with every illness known to man, and the boys are unbearably ignorant. This isn't my scene in the slightest, yet here I am—*again*—waiting for the guy who's not my boyfriend but still feels like it the majority of the time to join me.

I blame Poppy for convincing me that I could do this tonight after the fight that transpired in front of her earlier.

Darren's only come to visit me in Vancouver a handful of times, but I've been here to see him in Calgary at least triple that. My course load is lighter, and considering everyone I know and love is back home in Cherry Peak, it's made more sense for me to come here than for him to take the trip alone to Vancouver.

Still, with every flight I take, the more I'm starting to wish he'd make the effort to come see me instead.

We're not supposed to even be doing this at all, though. Not the visiting, at least. It's what we agreed on the day I drove to Vancouver for the first time. *Holiday visits only and a weekly phone call scheduled to keep one another in the loop.*

We've done everything but that.

The last few months have been the hardest, though. After the party in July, things have been weird between us. He's texting less and missing my calls. This is the first time I've been here since then. I could tell that night that things were going to change; I just hoped it wouldn't be so drastically.

Today, the issues I've had with our current relationship blew up into a screaming match, and I embarrassed the both of us in front of someone who shouldn't have been around to see it. His sister drove back to Cherry Peak shortly after.

"It's not too late to just put a pause on this stupid break and stop pretending that it's doing anything but making me miss you so badly I can barely breathe when I'm away! I thought this was what I wanted, but it's not."

"You say that now, but it's not how you felt before. I can't take back the last two years we've put into this! We've already gone on with this for too long. I won't be the one responsible for ruining the plans you laid out years ago."

"Every time I'm here, I feel like I recognize you less. You're ignoring me, Darren. You've never done that before. Did I really ruin everything between us because of one night of honesty? If you didn't

want to keep me in your life, you should have just said that instead of placating me. This isn't what I wanted!"

He swallows, throat straining. "I told you things were getting too complicated. I fucking knew we were going to get like this."

Nausea swirls in my belly at the reminders of our last conversation. It's obvious that I shouldn't be here tonight. Not at this party and not in this city. My money is on Darren knowing that just as well. That would explain his absence.

"He's not here, babe."

The pop can in my hand is heavier than normal when I pull it into my chest and glance up at the guy looming over me. Darren's roommate, Blue, as everyone calls him, drops a hand to the back of their velvet couch and twirls a piece of my hair around his finger.

I sweep my hair over my shoulder and out of his grip. "I can see that."

"He's been gone a while now."

"I'm aware."

"Have you tried calling him?" he asks, the words slurred on his sour breath. "He's always here when you show your pretty face. That reminds me! He hasn't threatened to punch me yet tonight for looking at you too long. Odd."

"Wow, I never thought to try calling him. That's a brilliant idea."

"I sense a bit of sarcasm, Delania. Are you being sarcastic?"

I let the incorrect name go. It's not the first time, and it won't be the last. I'm pretty sure he's just incapable of using the right one at this point.

"You're drunk, Blue. Darren keeps water bottles under his bed— What are you doing?"

With a squeak, I push my body as far back into the couch as possible before Blue falls into my lap. Instead of my thighs, he falls face first into the seat beside me. I crinkle my nose, feeling almost queasy at the thought of what's touching his face.

"I'm tired," he grumbles into the scorched red velvet. His feet kick out, narrowly missing my can before dropping into my lap. "Wanna cuddle me to sleep?"

"No. I'm leaving. If you're not too drunk to remember what I'm going to tell you, make sure to let Darren know when you see him that I went home."

"Don't go yet! What if he comes back? He promised me he'd hold my legs for a keg stand tonight."

"He was probably lying."

"Nah. He did it last weekend, and I won first place in the competition. His biceps are like fucking tree trunks. His fans should be here soon to see him use them again," he mumbles.

My shoulders lock up. "His fans?"

"Just some chicks. Hot ones. I think. . ."

My blood runs cold before I remind myself that he's not my boyfriend. Darren can be ogled as many times as he'd like to be now. I'm not the only one who gets to do that anymore. I chose that.

A groan is Blue's only reaction to me shoving his feet off me and standing. It's too hot in this room anyway. And the music is horrendous. Whoever chose it should have their Bluetooth privileges permanently taken away.

The dorm room is way too small to be packed full of so many people. Darren isn't the party type either. I knew before he told me about the one happening tonight that it wasn't his idea. He still should have been here. *With me.*

Without bothering to speak with anyone else, I focus on my phone and try calling him again. When his voicemail kicks in, I hang up and quicken my stride. Ten minutes later, I've freed myself of the university campus.

Poppy's my next call before I chuck my phone into my car's cup holder. She answers on the first ring, her voice flowing softly while I drive off campus.

"Delaney? Shouldn't you be a bit too busy to call me by now?"

"Do you know where he is?"

She clears her throat, suddenly serious. "Darren?"

"Yes, Darren. Do you know where he is?"

"I thought he was with you."

A tidal wave of worry blasts through me. "No. I haven't seen him since you left . . . he's not answering his phone either. I've been at his place waiting for two hours."

"Do you want me to turn around? I can come back. I'm not that far."

"You're lying. Don't come back. I'll find him."

"I'm turning around," she argues, stubborn like she always is.

"You've got to be nearly home already. I'll find him before you get back. Plus, you hate driving on the highway at night. Don't push yourself."

A slight pause. "What if he's hurt?"

"He's not." I wince at the power in those words and soften my next ones. "He's not, Poppy. Knowing Darren, he's probably sitting somewhere alone, calming down."

"It's unlike him not to tell us where he is first."

I know. "I just left campus. He has to be somewhere around here."

"He seriously left you in his dorm alone? With Blue?"

"Yep. Along with at least forty other people."

"I'm sorry he's being such an idiot," she huffs. "I still don't understand why the two of you agreed to this separation to begin with. You never used to fight before. I knew a breakup wouldn't actually make anything stronger between you. Like, come on, Laney, you're still seeing and calling each other but aren't dating? Is it even really a breakup? I get a migraine just thinking about this."

A pair of bright headlights nearly blinds me as a lifted truck passes in the other lane. I tighten my slick grip on the steering wheel and squint at the small green sign up ahead.

"I know," I say weakly.

"Honestly, you need to just get back together already before it's too late. What if you wait too long and something happens that you can't move on from? The fighting today was just . . . not you. It's never been you."

She's right. Darren and I are different. But this year, we've gone from best friends to strangers in the blink of an eye, and our low-blow attacks and frustrations are making everything worse. Everything's just been miserable. *I've* been miserable.

I blink away the burn in my eyes and focus on keeping my vision clear before I smoke a sleepy deer trying to cross the road. There's a sharp pinch between my ribs as I slow my speed by a few kilometres and let out a tight exhale. There's no mistaking this feeling for anything but dread.

"Do you remember when you told me you weren't my friend solely because I was Darren's girlfriend?" I ask.

"Which time? I've told you that plenty of times, Laney. It's the truth."

"Okay."

"Okay? That's all you're going to say after asking that?" Poppy snaps.

"I believe you, Pops."

"Oh, well whoop-de-fucking-do. I definitely won't worry about a thing, then."

My laugh is garbled and wet as the tears break free. I hastily wipe them as they fall while making the turn into the parking lot of the only place I could think of to check. Darren's car sitting in the third stall surprises me less than I was anticipating.

"I love you, Poppy. I'm really glad I got to get to know you," I declare.

"You're my sister."

Pulling into the stall beside Darren, I say, "I found him."

"Where?"

"He wasn't far."

She scoffs, anger replacing her worry. "He's an asshole."

"I'd have to agree right now."

"Just call me after you're done talking to him, alright? Ream him out and then make up so I can have someone to talk to at Christmas dinner. You're the best part of all our holiday dinners. I'd be subject to Great-Aunt Judy's crochet talk if I was alone."

I let that go, knowing damn well that anything I say would be a lie.

"Thank you for answering the phone."

"I love you like family, Laney."

"I love you too, Pops."

She hangs up, and I sit in silence for a moment, thinking, breathing. Darren's not in the car, and I didn't expect him to be. We were supposed to be a clean break, right? Two years ago, we were supposed to say goodbye and shift our romance into something looser and easier to manage over the next four years that we'd be apart. Instead, we became . . . whatever this is.

A sloppy mess of unclear rules and miserable distance, topped with a sprinkle of insecurity. We should have done everything differently.

I'm yanked from my disastrous thoughts by a light knock on my window. Looking at Darren's closed-off expression as he stares in at me confirms everything I was expecting.

This will be the last time I visit him here.

27

Darren

Her hand is still as small as it was the last time I held it. Maybe even smaller.

I've dreamed of slipping my fingers through hers and feeling the smooth, warm skin during cold, lonely nights. The memories of her never stopped running rampant through my mind, but it was her hands and the way they always held me with love and respect and this . . . outright fucking *ownership* that screwed me up the most.

I never expected today to be the day I'd finally feel her touch again. Or that she'd be pressing my shirt to her nose while wearing a red-splattered one of her own. It's been a weird day, but at least it's the good kind of weird now.

"I need to go home," she attempts to say, her voice nasally and muffled.

"Not until I've checked you out. Your nose could be broken."

"You're not a doctor."

I pull open the door and avoid looking at where I know my sister's standing watching. The shock and worry that morphed into smug satisfaction when I took off running outside has burnt itself into my retinas. At least she took my daughter into the engine bay to check on her chalk drawings before she burst into guilty tears.

"I've passed enough medical courses to know if your nose is broken," I say, clutching her hand a bit tighter when I fear she'll try to slip free of me.

"Where are your credentials?"

"Are you really going to give me a hard time about this? Your nose hasn't clotted yet."

"Maybe it's the shirt I'm using as a wad of tissues. There could be something wrong with the material that's making me bleed worse."

"Yeah, cotton can be a real bitch when it comes to bleeding noses."

"Your sarcasm isn't welcome here."

"Why? Does it make you wanna laugh?"

I can sense her rolling her eyes. "No. It's impossible to laugh when I'm trying not to cry."

"Okay, so it really could be broken, then."

The door to the medical room is open, so I carefully lead her inside and hesitate to shut the door before deciding to go for it. If any of the guys come around and see her in here with me, there won't be any living it down. It's better to keep them trapped outside for as long as possible.

"Can you see the table here?" I ask softly.

"Yes, I can see the table."

"Hop up on it for me."

She blinks quickly, dislodging some of the water lingering in her eyes. Tears soak into my shirt as she uses her free hand to try hoisting herself up. I hover, knowing full well she's probably scoffing internally at me for being so close. It's impossible not to keep a slim distance. She's hurt, and we're alone. *Again.* Only this time, every instinct inside of me is screaming to take care of her and take the pain away that's causing the wrinkle between her brows.

"Keep your claws to yourself for a minute," I whisper.

Then, before she can ask what I'm talking about, I grip both sides of her waist and lift her onto the edge of the table. The soft gasp that escapes her shoots straight down to my groin, and shit, that's the worst place for it. I roll my jaw and focus, ignoring everything but the green eyes piercing into mine.

Delaney rolls her lip between her teeth before saying, "Thank you."

"You're welcome. Now, let me look at your nose. I'll be gentle."

"As opposed to?"

"I could give your nose a pinch and wiggle it around a bit if you want."

She winces, her eyes focusing more now. "I really can't have a broken nose right now."

There's a slight shake to my hand that I hope she can't see when I guide hers away and pull the shirt back. While red and slightly swollen, her nose isn't broken. The blood has slowed to a trickle, which is a good sign as well.

"You'll be okay. Minimal damage," I murmur, using a clean corner of my shirt to pat beneath her nose, wiping some of the blood away.

"Are you sure? I feel like I should still go see a doctor."

I chuckle and tip her chin up with the edge of my knuckle, making a show of examining her nose. "They'll tell you the same thing I am. You might have a bruise in the morning and be a bit sore, but that's it."

"What were your credentials again?"

Lowering the shirt once I know the bleeding's stopped, I stroke my finger from her chin to the edge of her jaw, enamoured with the pink that rises to her cheeks. The silence in this room is harrowing, not awkward. I find the thrill in it and listen for the sound of her breathing, finding it uneven.

"I'm sorry about this," I say, inching into the space she's

unknowingly made for me between her parted legs. "She'll want to apologize to you properly."

Her pupils expand as they fall to my chest. "Who?"

"Abbie."

The jerk of her head is clunky, as if she didn't mean to do it.

"It was their idea for me to come."

"I know."

There's a pause before she asks, "Should I have insisted that I didn't?"

"Absolutely not."

Her gaze flashes up to snare mine, holding it as if she's scared I'll dare look away now. The disbelief that I find so obviously gleaming in her eyes is a jerk to my system. A blatant reminder that I'm the cause of her caution. It's all me. All the things I did and the words I never spoke. Every single unmade call and deleted email I'd written and rewritten for hours hunched over my desk.

My stupid, arrogant decisions that have led us here, unable to get back to what we were and who we should have always been together.

Those reminders are why I'm here, though. They're why I'm pushing past the roadblocks Delaney has put up between us, as if they would ever stop me from getting to her. This woman is my person. She's the one I was always meant to be with, even with the decade of distance that's grown between us. It doesn't matter and never has.

I'll earn back her trust and, eventually, her love because I won't give up until she's mine again. My family, best friend, soulmate. I want it all, no matter what it takes.

"I want to take you out, Elle. On a real date," I declare.

She doesn't pull away from me like I'm half expecting her to. Instead, she lowers her eyes to where our legs have begun to touch. Knee to knee with me, she says, "It's Delaney."

"Fine, Delaney. Let me take you on a date."

"I thought we were supposed to be healing a friendship," she argues, but it's weak, almost like she doesn't have the energy to keep fighting but feels like she needs to.

"We can do both, can't we?"

"I haven't forgiven you."

"And you don't need to have. I'm not done earning that yet."

I suck in a ragged breath when she brings her fingers to my side, the pressure almost too light to feel but still searing. Electricity pounds through me, frying my nervous system as I hold completely still.

The round edges of her nails run across my flesh before the pads of her fingers press down. A shiver rocks me hard enough that I lose my balance and fall forward against her. She leans into my body, whether by accident or intentionally, and I shut my eyes while my fingers curl into a fist on the table.

Her forehead meets my chest, holding there as soft puffs of air blow across my goosebumped skin.

"What are you doing, Delaney?" I ask roughly, my body more alive than it's been since the day she left me.

"I don't know."

"Look at me."

She rolls her head side to side, not removing her forehead from my sternum.

"Please," I croak.

"If I look at you right now, I'll do something I shouldn't."

"Do it anyway."

"I can't—"

Her words die at the first brush of my palms against her cheeks. No others follow as I cup her face and tip her head back until our eyes clash. I stroke my thumbs across the dried tear streaks on her skin and gulp in a breath when the desire to kiss her throttles me.

"It's still here. You feel it. I know you do. Friendship will never be enough. It only works as the foundation beneath something more."

"It has to be enough," she argues weakly.

"Why? Tell me right now that you don't think we can fall in love again."

If we ever fell out of it at all.

Pain ripples through the green in her eyes. "I can't."

"Kiss me."

"I can't."

"Then let me kiss you."

It hangs there between us as both a dare and a plea. I wait, standing frozen with her face in my hands and my heart flopping like a fish out of water on her lap. She hesitates, a million emotions flickering across her face at a pace that terrifies me the longer it takes for her to speak.

"No, Darren. You're not kissing me."

My hands fall to rest at my sides once she pushes free of my hold. I take an off-balanced step back to make room for her to hop off the table and walk straight past me. The silence is suddenly torturous.

"Thank you for making sure my nose was okay," she says, sounding so unlike herself I flinch.

"Don't thank me for taking care of you."

A heavy pause. "I'll see you at the drive-in this week."

"Yeah, you will."

Hesitating with her hand on the door, she taps her foot. I wait for her to say something else, but she leaves without another word. There isn't a damn thing I could say to make her stay, so I keep my mouth shut and groan into the empty room instead.

The chill in the air is obvious to me now that I'm alone. I expect to find my bloodied shirt on the table or even the floor, but it's nowhere to be found. A spark of hope appears in the dark of my mind when I realize Delaney took it with her.

"What happened?" Poppy asks from the doorway.

"I moved too quickly."

"Helpless, lovesick fool."

I can't deny it. "She still cares about me."

"Don't push her, Darren. Even if you don't mean to. You need to be careful if you want a second chance."

"I think I need your help."

Her brows fly up before her mouth splits in a grin. "It's about time you came to me. You should have known better than to rely on Bryce for romance advice."

"She got the go-ahead for the drive-in rebuild."

"And now? Just admit you should have come to me first."

"Only if you agree to help."

She scoffs, coming further into the room. The pointed look she gives my naked chest was to be expected.

"Well, first, I'd suggest not trying to win her over by flashing her your dad bod. You can do that as much as you want after you've got the girl."

"I was helping her with her nose."

"Either way, you need to win her heart first, Darren."

I scrub an antsy hand down my jaw. "I know. I know I pushed too hard and spooked her. She hasn't forgiven me yet."

"No she hasn't, and it will take more than taking care of her bloody nose for you to earn that."

"I'll do whatever it takes. It's always been Delaney for me, Poppy. Always," I rush out.

My sister reaches for me and palms my arm. "I know. And she does too. You just have to help her remember why she fell in love with you in the first place all those years ago. She needs to feel safe with you again because right now, you scare her."

I deflate, collapsing against the table. "She was right here. So close. We were . . ."

"Don't give up yet."

"I couldn't if I tried. I'm not myself anymore. I haven't been in a long time. But when she's with me, I am."

"Hug me, big brother."

I let loose a weak exhale and do exactly that because I know I'll need the borrowed strength for what's coming next.

28

Delaney

"You're not backing out now," Daisy chides, giving another yank on my arm.

"Don't make me do this. I can't believe I ever agreed in the first place."

"Oh, come on. This is actually adorable. Plus, I know Abbie's quite obsessed with the idea."

"Of course she is. To a seven-year-old, I'm sure this is the best idea in the history of good ideas."

I've heard her squeal and brag to her friends more times over the last week than I can count on two hands about the kissing booth her father and I were organizing. It seemed like a fine idea when I was trapped in the passenger seat of Darren's car with a belly full of milkshake and a cheeseburger cooked to perfection. But now?

It's the worst thing I could have ever agreed to do.

Kissing booths are for carnivals or a high school prom fundraiser. They're not meant for something like this. I can already feel the awkwardness that's bound to come when nobody shows up.

Maybe I should have at least offered to help build the booth or even decorate it. At least then I'd have known what kind of image we're going to be giving out to the entire town today. But no. Instead, I let Darren handle it. My only saving grace will be Abbie. If I'm lucky, she'll have snuck away from Sasha long enough to help her dad make the booth look mildly appealing.

"Well, I think it's cute too. It's unique. You could have easily chosen to sell cookies or something instead," Daisy offers.

Her hold on my arm stays tight as I huff and slowly follow her across the field. The drive-in was the obvious place to put the booth, and as we pass the fire truck camped out in front of the first set of full parking stalls, I'm almost relieved we chose this location.

Two food trucks are parked off to the side of the fire truck, along with a huge blow-up castle full to the brim with kids. Folding tables and chairs have been set up in the freshly cut grass, and there's even a small stage with a sound system and a group of little girls in tutus dancing. It's busy too. The entire field is.

It's nothing like I was expecting today.

Daisy giggles, her eyes fixed on my open-mouthed expression. "Before you ask, Bryce and Poppy are already at the booth, triple-checking that Darren hasn't scared all of the people away."

"Who organized all of this?"

"Do you really want to know the answer to that?"

I fidget with the loose material of my overalls, suddenly wishing I'd put a bit more effort into myself today. Darren wasn't supposed to do all of this. It wasn't necessary, nor was it what we'd discussed. He took a simple idea and turned it into this full-out event that drew a crowd that could rival the one at the station's dunking setup.

"I feel underdressed."

"Don't! You look beautiful," Daisy soothes.

"I'm in my housework overalls, Daisy. The same ones I wear when I pull weeds out of the yard."

"You're fine. They look cute on you. Plus, you'll be behind a booth all day. Nobody will care about what you're wearing when you're going to be smacking lips."

"I'm *not* smacking lips with anyone. That's so unhygienic."

Daisy frowns. "Cheek kisses, then?"

"Yes, cheek kisses. Which even then feels gross."

"Oh, you'll be fine. Most of your kisses will probably come from the old folks' home, anyway. I saw the van in the parking lot."

I double blink. "Great. In that case, I can't wait."

"Just think about how much money you could raise for the drive-in today. Your cheeks are so smooth you should be a killer money-maker."

That draws a laugh up my throat. The forever sunny-side-up woman beside me definitely has a way of convincing people that there's a plus side in any bad situation.

"I don't see the booth," I say, squinting to see through the groups of people and the sun that makes me wish I'd worn sunglasses today.

"That's because the line is too long. It's over there."

I follow her finger as she points over the heads of the people crossing in front of us. My stomach cramps as the line she's talking about comes into sight.

"You're joking."

"Nope. It's been like that for the last hour. Darren had to open early. I hope you're okay with taking the second shift."

Shifting to face her, I ask tightly, "Second shift? What are you talking about?"

Daisy presses her lips together nervously, her eyes darting around the field. "Did he tell you *anything*?"

"Clearly not. I wasn't late, was I? I didn't think this started until noon! There weren't supposed to be separate shifts. I thought we were doing this together!"

Oh, I'm going to flip my shit on this guy.

If there's one thing I hate more than anything else, it's being late to an event. Being kept in the dark about something I'm supposed to play a major part in is second on my list. *Talk about a double whammy.*

"What about some lemonade? There's supposed to be a stand around here somewhere. Eliza was in charge, but I know Rory volunteered to help her. And wherever Rory goes, Johnny's sure to follow, so let's go look—"

I cut off Daisy's rambling. "I don't want lemonade right now. What I do want is to go talk to Darren."

"Are you sure? It's super fresh. The lemons are from Eliza's new lemon trees! Who knew a greenhouse would be such a good addition to the ranch?"

With a soft pat on her arm, I shake my head. "No, thanks. But you should grab some. I'll come see you in a bit."

I'm leaving before she has a chance to reply. I don't need lemonade right now, even if it sounds so damn good. I'm starving, but I doubt I'd be able to drink or eat anything with how tight my stomach is currently. I'll treat myself to a handful of lemonades once I'm done with the day.

I slip through a chunk of the crowd before forcing myself to wave at Penny and the group of teachers sitting with her at a table nearby. She tries to call me over, but I smile apologetically.

"Duty calls! I'll come over later!" I offer.

She gives me a thumbs-up and turns back to the group. I breathe out, relieved.

I keep pushing through and wiggle my fingers to try and flick out the tension in them. It doesn't work, so I stop trying. Maybe I should punch Darren right in his mouth so he can't do his part, and he'll have to go home. Ugh, no, that wouldn't work. I'd feel too guilty and wind up holding a bag of frozen peas to his lips until they felt better.

Poppy's red hair catches my eyes before the black hat propped on Bryce's does. Then, I slowly, almost cautiously, bring my eyes to the line of women beside them.

There are at least fifteen of them . . . and is that one using ChapStick right now? My sandals almost catch on a non-existent rock in the grass. Darren's laugh rings out, and I snap my head in his direction.

He's got so much nerve today that it may as well be dripping out of his ears and nose. Considering what happened the last time we saw each other, he's already on thin ice with me. Now? That ice is cracking, and I'm one flirty laugh away from shoving him into the water beneath it.

One moment, he nearly has me kissing him in a medical room with a blood-crusted nose, and the next, he's out here giving a crooked, wicked grin to Sadie Brighton's mom behind a booth that Abbie most certainly painted.

The hearts drawn all over the wooden booth have been painted in shades of pinks and reds, then hit with enough sparkles to blind someone if the sun hit them the right way. Even the Kissing Booth written across the top matches the writing on the worksheets I was grading only last night.

Some of the tightness in my stomach loosens.

"Is it only one kiss per person, or can I bribe you for an extra?"

"Unfortunately, it's one per person, Sarah," Darren answers, his grin unmoving.

Unfortunately? It's unfortunate that he can't kiss her again? And Sarah? He knows her name and everything. I bet they've been chatting for a while now. It would explain the generous line he's collected.

I start toward Bryce and Poppy, needing to not be standing here alone, watching this conversation unfold from afar like a stalker. Both of them are already staring at me, their expressions kept too blank. Like they've been standing here practicing how to appear nonchalant.

"I guess I'll just have to line up again then. Or we could always meet up after you're finished your civil service. We could grab some dinner?" *Sarah* asks, tapping her nails on the edge of the booth.

I scoff. Loudly. Too loudly. So loudly that Bryce coughs a beat after to try and cover it up. There's a lot of heat building in my body right now. The red-hot, I'm-ready-to-scream kind. The sudden spike is concerning. I shouldn't feel like this.

Darren's already looking at me when I risk another glance in his direction. The smug satisfaction stretching across his face is a generous squirt of gasoline on the blaze burning up inside of me. And of course—*of fricking course*—he's wearing that damn hat again. The one that I got him when we were in the eleventh grade as a joke, thinking there was no way he'd actually wear it.

The joke's on me because it seems like he's found a sudden love for the Cherry Peak curling league.

"You look like you're going to smash his face into the booth," Bryce notes, both her and Poppy appearing at my side.

I keep my tone even, unbothered. "If he's going to use this as a speed dating activity, he deserves it."

"Mm, maybe you should go over and smack him around a bit," Poppy agrees.

Bryce palms her hips. "It's been like this for forever now. I'm bored of it."

"I didn't know I should have been here an hour early. Maybe he planned on this the whole time," I grumble.

Poppy cocks her head at her brother and taps her chin. "It's only fair that you took a turn now. I mean, the line is already so long, I'm sure everyone can wait a while for him to return."

"Are you goading me?" I ask, catching on quickly. Darren's still looking in my direction when I roll my eyes and turn to Bryce first. "Are the three of you in cahoots?"

"No! Absolutely not. Does that sound like me?" Poppy asks.

Bryce quirks her lips into a smile as she chuckles. "Yeah, it does, actually."

"We got here early to support Eliza. It was pure luck we chose to check on the kissing booth before it was supposed to open and found Darren waving off a line of old ladies blowing kisses at him." Poppy uses her thumb to point over her shoulder. "Eliza will be my witness."

I cross my arms and fix my glare to the woman still lingering at the booth. "He's probably loving this."

"Shame on him. This is supposed to be a fundraiser. I mean, come on, think of the kids," Poppy says with a cluck of her tongue.

I nod. "That's what I'm saying! Maybe I should go kick him away for a while. The booth is only open for today, and I doubt we've made that much money with all of his flirting clogging the line."

Poppy sets her hands on my shoulders and starts to push me toward the booth. "Go for it, sister!"

My blood pumps quickly as I stop fighting her and walk on my own. The line of women turns to look at me, some of their smiles slipping into frowns the closer I get. It's weird as hell, but I ignore them before I can get too annoyed again.

Darren doesn't appear to be listening to what Sarah's saying because in a blink, I'm held beneath his arrogant stare. He tracks my steps until finally, I reach the booth, stopping so close to him that our shoulders nearly touch.

He can be as smug as he wants right now because in a minute, he's going to be the one in my shoes.

29

Darren

THERE HAVE BEEN SEVERAL TIMES IN MY LIFE WHERE DELANEY'S possessiveness had me shifting uncomfortably to relieve the tightness of my pants, but right now trumps all of those.

I've been hard up since she spotted me. I was watching her from the moment she appeared behind the fire truck in those oversized overalls, welcoming the chance to watch her without her knowing. The only reason I haven't sped my way through the line in front of me yet is exactly because of this. Just so I could see this reaction right now and feel the fire in her eyes as she exposed her jealous side to me for the first time in a near decade.

I worried I wouldn't be able to pull it out of her after this long or that maybe she didn't have it in her at all anymore. It's been a long fucking eight years of being apart, but here she is, damn near vibrating with that same savage glow that she used to have when I'd get stuck in the middle of a conversation with a girl on the sidelines after a football game.

Her perfume is dull, the lily-and-raspberry scent impossible to pick up unless you've become so accustomed to it that you could point it out in a crowd of a thousand people. I take a greedy inhale of it and keep my shoulders down, relaxed even as she tilts into me, ignoring looking up at me.

"Hi, Sarah! It's so great to see you again. Is your daughter here too?" she asks while butting in front of me and discreetly using her elbow to shove me out of the way.

The woman in front of the booth blanches for a moment before straightening and flashing a smile. "Good to see you too, Delaney. Yes, Sadie's off getting a lemonade."

"Oh, that's great. I've heard the lemonade is great. It's Eliza's secret recipe, isn't it?"

"Maybe! That does sound like her," Sarah agrees tensely. "I'll go check on her now, actually."

Delaney doesn't skip a beat in sending her off. "Okay, well, it was great to catch up. Give my best to Sadie."

"Will do. Bye, Darren. If you need my number, I can write it down before I go."

"No need. I've got it in my books from when Sadie was in my class last year. I'll pass it along *if* he's interested. Enjoy the rest of the day," Delaney sings, waving despite their close proximity.

I clear my throat. "Tell Eliza I say hi, Sarah."

Hiding a very obvious frown, the woman stamps her lips together and knocks her knuckles to the booth before leaving. The awkward atmosphere that follows doesn't seem to bother Delaney in the slightest. Actually, I think she's thriving in it. I'm left staring in silent awe as she confidently bends over the booth and reaches up to tap the Open sign that's hanging by a single nail.

"Hi, everyone! I'm sorry to disappoint you, but Darren's actually done for now. I'll be taking over for a while now, so if you want to stay, please do, but if you're only here for a mouthful of mustache, then I recommend coming back in about an hour," she announces.

There's an audible sigh that breaks through the field as the line immediately disperses. It's impossible not to feel the least bit arrogant to have so many single women want to stand in a line for the chance to get a kiss on the cheek, but at the same time, the only one I want in my line is perched in front of me, pissed the hell off.

"Well, I can't say I'm surprised," she mutters under her breath.

My throat pinches, choking off my air supply when she pushes away from the booth and drags the curve of her ass across my groin. Pinpricks of pleasure expand through my muscles as I reach for the edge of the booth and grip it hard enough I half expect it to crack. The sway of her hair across my chest isn't any better, nor is the soft breath she expels before slipping out from in front of me.

"If I'd known you were going to open this thing early, I'd have been here on time," she states, sounding completely unbothered by what just happened.

I don't like that. She should be as untethered as I am right now. How is it so easy for her to pretend that didn't just happen?

"It wasn't the plan. I'd have told you."

"Right. Well, I'm not a fan of surprises like this."

"I know. It just happened."

"Is that your catchphrase or something?" she asks sharply.

"I can't say it is. I'd prefer something a bit less . . . childish for my catchphrase."

She moves around some more, fussing over the lip-shaped money jar and the bag of gum and breath mints Poppy dropped off. When she fishes out the thick stack of movie admission tickets we're really here to hand out with our kisses today, I put an end to the silence.

"Where'd my sister run off to?" I ask.

"Why do you assume I know?"

"You two are never far apart anymore."

Delaney huffs, keeping her body turned away from me as she stares into the field. "She was with Bryce before I came over here. I'm sure that's where she is now."

Frustration licks up my spine the longer she freezes me out.

I'm a patient guy, but there's something about Delaney that makes it damn near impossible to keep my pace slow. Especially after her attitude just five minutes ago. I'm desperate enough for her attention that receiving it has got my pulse tripping over itself and a desperate ache low in my stomach that refuses to settle.

With my hand still gripping the booth, I lean forward and drag the heel of my boot through the grass to settle between her legs. She doesn't react outright. It's subtle. A breath caught between her teeth and a slight shudder that forces her to lean back against my chest.

I give her a moment to slip herself free of my slack hold before dropping my other hand to the booth, trapping her with my body. Her jaw tightens and strains as she keeps staring in front of us, fighting what she couldn't before.

"Are you mad at me, Elle?" I murmur, my chin dropped so the question hits the tip of her ear.

Our height difference is just as staggering as it was back then. If she leaned back completely, she'd feel the bite of what I've kept hidden beneath my shirt since the day I lost her.

"It's Delaney."

"For how much longer?"

Her arm shifts, and then she's gripping my hand. If she meant to push it away from the booth, she's changed her mind. Instead of shoving me, she grips me tighter, her nails pricking into my skin. Head tipping down, she swallows loudly. There's a ghost of a touch over my fourth finger, where my wedding ring once sat.

"Forever," she whispers.

"I'll wait double that."

I hold perfectly still when she starts twisting in my arms. Her lips are parted and the softest shade of pink when her head falls back and those green eyes flick upward. I lean into my grip on the booth to steady myself.

"Nobody would wait that long."

"You underestimate me. There's nothing I want more than you. Not a fucking thing."

It's out before I can chomp down on my tongue hard enough. It's out and there for her to do as she wishes. There's something suddenly fucking terrifying about that, given how my last loose-tongue confession went.

"Hey. Is the booth open?"

I grit my teeth at the sound of the very male voice. Slowly, I peel my gaze from Delaney long enough to glare at the guy standing in front of us. I half expect him to burst into flames when she ducks beneath my arm and into the empty space beside me.

"Yes! Yes, it's open," she rushes out.

The guy, who I can now pinpoint as the one who owns the gas station at the entrance to town, gives her an easy smile and pulls his wallet out of his back pocket—*a stupid spot to keep it.*

"I'm glad to hear that. How much is admission?" he asks, apparently too busy staring at Delaney to read.

I snort. "It's on the sign above my head."

"Right. My bad."

Delaney shoots me a sharp look before nudging me out of the way for the second time today and taking her place in the centre of the booth. I cross my arms and keep the guy pinned beneath my steady glare.

"You can just drop the money into the jar, and then we're good to go. We don't have change. I promise it's awkward for everyone," she says, consoling him as if this isn't her first time either.

He laughs and nods before following her instructions. Once the money falls into the jar, he focuses on her and waits silently.

Delaney instructs him to lean a bit closer before smoothly sweeping in toward him and pressing her lips to his cheek. Before they have a chance to break apart, I'm crouching to fish out a ticket for him and slapping it onto the booth.

"Here you go. Make sure you keep an eye out for opening night at the new drive-in to use your ticket. Thanks."

The guy sends me a confused look while stepping away and taking the ticket. He darts his eyes to Delaney before saying, "Thanks, I guess."

"You're welcome. And thank you! The drive-in appreciates you lending me your cheek," she calls as he's leaving.

I watch him until he's far enough away that I know he won't come rushing back. The lack of a line after him is relieving, but it also means that there's nobody here to witness her scolding my ass any moment now.

"Are you being serious right now, Darren? This kissing booth was your idea. You don't get to be an asshole to the people who actually come and take part in it."

Cocking my head, I reply, "And I suppose you were being a darling with dear Sarah?"

"I was being helpful. You can have her number if you want it that badly."

"Helpful? If that was you being helpful, then I may as well have offered to be giving that guy a step by step on how to receive a kiss on the cheek."

She palms her hips, her eyebrows nearly fastening together. "You don't get to flirt with a line full of single women but be like this when it's my turn."

"Oh, you're planning on flirting with a line of single women?"

There may as well be steam flowing out of her ears by now, while I'm enjoying this all a bit too much.

"Oh, hey, guys! Darren, it's funny seeing you here. I thought this was Delaney's shift."

My sister pops up in front of the booth, all grins and excited eyes. Bryce follows her, an arm slung over Daisy's shoulders and fingers playing loop-de-loop in her hair.

"There aren't shifts," I grunt.

"Oh . . . oops. I thought it was Delaney's turn, and, well,

we've wrangled quite a line for her to get through," Poppy explains pointedly.

I tense up and follow her line of sight to the men slowly moving into a single file line leading right to where Delaney's standing.

"Poppy, you didn't have to do this," Delaney starts.

My sister places a hand to her heart. "Don't worry about a thing. I've vetted them all myself and have already turned away the real weird ones."

"Well, you haven't done a great job of that," I mutter, flicking a look at the guy walking away.

"Good luck, Della. You'll need it," Daisy says.

I clear my throat, drawing my sister's attention. "Is there no limit?"

"A limit on what? Money you should be raising? Come on, Darren. Don't be a buzzkill."

The noise around us grows in a few short seconds. It's the swarm of men surrounding the booth. I scour the line, memorizing the names and faces that I recognize, storing the information for later.

"Come on, D. It's only fair to share the responsibility," Bryce placates me.

I ignore her and reluctantly remove myself from behind the booth. The tether between us pulls in rejection of this idea, but I let it go. I knew what I was doing when I made her jealous earlier, and if she wants to get even, I won't stand in her way.

My chance will come again sooner than she'd like, and this time, I won't give up so easily.

30

Delaney

I PURSE MY LIPS FOR WHAT FEELS LIKE THE TEN MILLIONTH TIME today and press them to another scratchy cheek. The musky, wood-scented cologne belonging to the owner of said cheek sneaks a feel of my bicep and up to my shoulder before Darren clears his throat. The hand drops immediately.

"Groping isn't included in your fee," Darren barks, clapping his hands loudly. "Fuck, my sister vetted you?"

I hide how much I like him stepping in behind a roll of my eyes. Backing away from the man in front of me, I quickly reach beneath the booth for his movie ticket and hand it over. The stack is down by at least half now, meaning there should be way more money in the tip jar than I expected there to be at all, let alone in only half a day.

That's all because of Darren.

"Thank you for participating today and helping rebuild the drive-in. It means a lot to me and the town."

"Anytime, Delaney. Anytime," the guy drawls, a look in his eye that makes my skin ripple and my smile transform into a wince.

Darren walks directly in front of him, blocking off his view of me before using a heavy arm to gesture him away from the line. "Alright, you can leave the line now."

The exasperation in his voice is satisfying as hell. With every man who's come up to buy a kiss and a ticket, it's gotten more obvious. I can't decide if I want to see just how much longer he'll stand by and watch this go on or what he'll do to get it to stop. Both sounds more like it.

"Got it. I didn't know she was taken," the man mutters before following Darren's arm and exiting the line.

I do a double take before shouting out a frantic and pointless "I'm not taken!"

Immediately, I wish I hadn't done that. Darren drops his arm and spins to face me, his stare narrowed. I can't see past him, yet I know there's still a line of guys waiting and watching for their turn at the booth. He doesn't seem to give a flying fuck about them, though. Their presence doesn't stop him from towering over the booth and using the intensity in his eyes to pin me in place, unable to break free.

The muscles in his arms tense beneath the sleeves of his long-sleeve as he grips the booth and uses it to support his weight. Strength and dominance pour from him, and I'm powerless to the desire that begins to swirl in my belly and loosen my muscles because of it. I let my head fall back, and my eyes grow focused on the sheer possessiveness that glows in his.

It's so damn hot.

"Why did you do that?" he asks lowly, almost growly.

I coyly arch a brow, chest starting to rise quicker. "Do what? I was only clarifying."

"He didn't need to know your relationship status. None of these guys do."

"That's not for you to decide."

His tongue slides along his bottom lip as he crooks a dirty grin and drops his chin in an arrogant nod. "Fine. Go ahead, Elle. I've got my entire day open just for being a cockblock."

"It's Delaney, and I'm so happy for you. That's great news."

He takes his hands off the booth and turns away, creating an opening for the line behind him to continue. I shake myself off and refocus, refusing to let him get to me any more than he already has.

The next guy comes, and then another, all without Darren butting in. He stays off to the side, watching with his hands either on his hips or arms folded across his chest. I catch every shift he makes in the corner of my eye despite every effort to pretend he isn't there at all. It's impossible not to notice him, and the cocky asshole knows it.

There's a thread connecting us that I've never been able to make myself cut. We're connected so deeply that there was never a chance of me ignoring him forever. I should have known better.

Nothing good is going to come out of this today. It's only a matter of time before he declares it his turn again and puts on a show that's going to send me into a tailspin. I don't know if I should be ashamed of the fact that I'm still desperately jealous over him or if it's smarter to just accept it. There's no point in denying it now. I've exposed myself already, and there's no taking it back without looking like I'm in denial.

He's won this battle, and I don't know what to do with that yet.

"Hey, Delaney. Fancy seeing you here."

I jerk my head up from the booth to look at Sam. The RCMP officer with the freckles and dimples in both cheeks smiles gently as I correct my slouched posture and return the gesture.

"What a coincidence! Are you by chance here to purchase a movie ticket?"

"Well, that and a kiss from you," he corrects with a wink.

My chest pangs with discomfort. The kind that I feel every single time a guy—a nice one at that—shows any sort of interest in me. It sours my mood, sending it dipping further into a sea of frustration and annoyance.

Over and over again, I've suffered from this outright inability to date. Instead, I've spent most of my nights alone, wishing I could pretend just once that I'm truly open to finding a boyfriend and someone to spend my life with. The whole meet them, see them for a few dates, then cut things off after a bit of kissing hasn't been working.

I'm so tired of being lonely.

"Luckily, I can help you with both of those things," I say.

Sam chuckles while dropping a five-dollar bill into the tip jar. His palm runs down the length of his chest before slipping into the front pocket of his jeans.

"In all honestly, this wasn't how I was planning on getting my first kiss from you," he murmurs, his voice low in an attempt to keep his statement between us.

I know immediately that he didn't manage to pull it off. Looking at Darren to check would be a waste of time.

"That's okay. This is for a good cause," I reply, refusing to take my eyes off him despite my uneasiness.

Sam moves closer to the front of the booth. "You make very good points."

"Which cheek would you prefer?"

"Cheek?"

My laugh sounds ridiculously painful. "Yes. Only cheek kisses from me at this booth."

"Oh! Oh, I thought—I'm sorry. Ignore me, I haven't had my second cup of coffee yet today," he splutters, face turning sunburnt red.

"Oh, it's okay! It's a common mistake. The whole kissing booth thing is a bit deceiving."

He rubs at the back of his neck. "Right. I don't suppose the rules have any bend to them?"

"Hey. Sam, right? Remember me? I was at the drive-in fire," Darren interrupts, joining Sam on the opposite side of the booth.

Sam blinks rapidly when Darren slaps him on the back and steals his hand to shake it. "Uh, no, I don't think so. You were at the fire . . .?"

"I was working to put out the fire while you were, you know, out on the highway helping with traffic. Those U-turns don't always make themselves, right?"

I bite on my tongue and keep my expression flat while staring up at Darren, silently urging him not to be a jackass.

"Oh, maybe I did see you. That was a crazy night," Sam says.

"You're telling me. But anyway. About today, yeah, we aren't doing kisses anywhere but the cheek."

Sam steals my gaze. "There aren't any exceptions?"

"If we give an exception to one person, we'll have to give them to everyone. I'm sure you know how that goes. But by all means, if a cheek doesn't suffice, I'll fish your money out myself," Darren answers, his friendliness leaving a lot to be desired.

"Delaney's cheek will more than suffice. I'm being greedy," Sam relents.

I jump in before Darren can. "You're not being greedy. I'll do both cheeks to help make up for your disappointment."

"That'll be extra," my apparent bodyguard announces.

"No, it won't. I'll throw in an extra cheek for free."

"That's against the rules," Darren states.

"Against what rules? This is our booth."

Darren pushes on as if we don't have watching eyes all around us. "The rules I just made, Elle. We have fifty-fifty ownership of this business, and I'm saying we aren't doing buy-one-get-one-free kisses."

"You're being ridiculous," I snap, my temperature soaring. "And it's Delaney."

He huffs. "I'm just trying to avoid being taken advantage of."

"You're not the one doing the kissing!"

"Not yet. If you want to change the rules, then they count for me too."

I curl my fingers beneath the booth and flick my attention back to Sam. "Come here, Sam."

He jerks forward, and I quickly kiss both of his cheeks.

They're warm from the blush that's still tinting them, and for some reason, that makes me pull away from him as if the heat burnt my lips.

"There. Just please don't tell anyone about the discount," I plead.

His throat bulges as he swallows and then nods in agreement. "I'll see you later."

"Take your movie ticket first. You can't use it yet, but once the drive-in is open, you can redeem it."

I fumble with the stack beneath the booth and shove it out in front of me. He takes it in a smooth, pristine hand.

"Bye, Sam," Darren grits out.

I tap my nails against the booth and offer Sam a weak smile. "Bye."

He's quick to leave, and I don't blame him. Not one bit.

"On that note, you can go take a break," Darren declares.

I almost laugh. "Excuse me?"

"It's my turn."

"Oh, you'd love that, wouldn't you?"

"If you mean because I'm done with watching you do all the kissing, then yes."

I lift my hands in front of me, surrendering. "You know what? Fine. Go for it. I'm sure you'll have one hell of a time."

"Now that you mention it, I'm sure I will."

"I'm going to find the girls, then."

He joins me behind the booth and asks, "What, you're not going to stay?"

"No, thank you."

"Why not?"

"I need to go to the bathroom," I lie.

He doesn't believe me. Of course he doesn't. And apparently, he's done with pandering me as well.

"I'm sure."

I grit my teeth and spin on my heel, prepared to leave.

"Would you mind stopping by the lemonade stand and grabbing me one on your way back? I'm sure I'll feel a little parched after all the kissing I'm about to do."

Glancing over my shoulder, I make sure to smile as sweetly as humanly possible.

"Of course. Would you prefer raspberry syrup or manure from Steele Ranch as your mixer? I'm sure Eliza has both with her."

Darren laughs, deep and raspy, before adjusting the brim of his hat. "How about you surprise me, Elle."

"Manure it is."

31

Darren

A half hour into my shift at the kissing booth, Bryce stops the line for a break and finally says what's been keeping her tense beside me the entire time.

"I hope you know that you're going to get kicked in the ass, D."

"I'll take it," I say.

She joins me behind the booth. With the line dispersing for the time being, she pinches the back of my arm, making me hiss.

"Don't try and be funny."

"I'm not. If Delaney kicks me in the ass, then I'll know she cares enough about me to be bothered."

"That's the dumbest shit I've ever heard."

"Are you saying you'd have an issue with Daisy kicking you in the ass? After all those years of your silent pining?"

Bryce scowls at me, mouth flat. "You're *really* not being funny now."

"Again, I'm not trying to be. It's honesty, B. I'm done with pretending like I wouldn't get donkey kicked in the chest by one of the broncs on the ranch if it meant I'd earned a few uninterrupted hours with Delaney."

"That's . . . pathetic."

I shrug, unbothered by that. "So be it."

"Well, I don't think pissing her off is going to earn you those hours, so if a donkey kick it is . . ."

"Why is she pissed, Bryce? Why did she come over and immediately cut my time short earlier?"

Her eyes dart off to the side before slowly returning. "Your groupies are still hanging around, probably trying to listen to what we're saying. Damn small-town gossips."

"I don't care if they hear or not. I'm done giving a shit about what anyone in this town thinks about me."

Bryce nods, seeming to straighten as her mood tips into one more serious than before. "Alright then. Just don't come running to me complaining when the gossip train pulls into town tomorrow morning."

"I'm sure it's already here. Now, tell me why you think Delaney came over and interrupted what I was doing earlier and why she's made herself scarce now that I'm the kisser?"

"Oh, I know why. You're both jealous fucking idiots. I'm just saying that you're playing a dangerous game here."

"Well, a safe one hasn't done me any good, has it?"

"You could push her too hard."

"I thought I did that already, but she's here again."

"You're playing risky, Darren."

"I'm done with playing it safe. She's my woman, and I want her back."

Her scowl cracks just enough for me to know I've gotten to her. "What exactly happened between you two?"

"What do you mean?"

She lowers her voice, turning to give the line a full view of her back. "Don't get me wrong, I've always known you should have been together. I just feel like I've been kept out of the loop here. I'm getting whiplash."

"I thought I was doing fine, Bryce. A year ago, I made peace with the restlessness that I'd been feeling. I slept for the handful of hours I could get and learned how to live with that bone-deep exhaustion. But then I spoke to her again at your opening at Shade's place, and . . . it hit me."

"Okay, maybe we shouldn't talk about this here," she mutters, eyeing the field in front of the booth.

"I need her. I haven't been myself since she left. There was always something wrong with me. A problem I could never fix."

In a rare moment of softness, Bryce squeezes my wrist. "I know. We know that, D. Whatever you need from me, you've got it."

"The only thing I've needed is your friendship, B. You've given that to me in spades."

"Fuck off, you softy," she says, scoffing lightly.

"I don't want to kiss anyone else."

"But you're going to. Finish what you started so I don't have to feel responsible for talking you out of your plans," she demands.

"Even if it means watching me get kicked in the ass?"

"I'll record the moment for you."

A pointed clearing of a throat has my best friend turning forward. Her eyes immediately narrow into slits.

"What are you doing here?"

"I could ask the same thing."

My ex-wife's voice sours my stomach, making it a struggle to face her. And once I do, I wish I hadn't. Her pursed lips and narrowed eyes are beyond familiar as she leers at me and pulls Abbie in front of her—as a shield, I'd bet.

"Hi, Dad!"

"Hi, sweetheart. I didn't know you were coming, or I would have met you somewhere first. There's lemonade."

Abbie spins to face Sasha and juts her bottom lip. "Can we get some? Please? I've been soooooo good today! I put all my laundry away."

"Of course we can. You don't even have to ask."

I swallow a bitter laugh at her pettiness. "Are you here because you want a kiss, Sasha?"

"No. Abbie just wanted to come see what all the fuss was about over here."

"The booth looks cool, Dad. The hearts shine all the way back there," my daughter says, pointing to the parking lot.

I toss her a wink. "Well, that was all you. Your painting skills are quite top-notch if I do say so myself."

"I thought Abbie was kidding about the kissing booth. It seems she wasn't," Sasha notes.

Bryce ups the venom in her tone, not bothering to hide how little she cares for my ex-wife.

"It's for the drive-in. Everyone's just doing their part. Do you have anything planned?"

"I don't have time. It seems like it's more than handled, anyway. Judging by the line we saw a minute ago, Darren's mouth is quite a hit."

"It's still gross that you're kissing people, Dad."

I choke on a laugh. "They're only cheek kisses, sweetheart. There's no lip action happening around here."

"And it's not just your dad doing all the kissing. Delaney's here too, but she's taking a break too," Bryce explains.

The smoothness of her words is for my daughter's benefit because she stares directly at Sasha as she says them, the devil dancing in her eyes. I sigh and push in before the two of them can get into it here the way they always seem to no matter where we are.

"We're working on this together," I clarify.

Sasha's nostrils flare as she smiles and drops her attention to Abbie. "How about that lemonade?"

"Oh, don't go yet. There's Delaney," Bryce announces.

My heart jolts, feeling like it's flush to my ribs. I spin around and search for her, my pulse loud in my ears. It's an electric feeling, this *excitement*. I could get addicted to it again.

"Can we stay to say hi, Mom? Please?" Abbie asks.

If Sasha answers, I don't hear it. Spotting Delaney, I inhale a lungful of air and adjust my hat despite it already being perfectly in place.

Somehow, she looks even more beautiful now than she did a half hour ago. Her hair is glossier, and the freckles on her face and neck and arms have deepened in the sun, even if it isn't as warm. Even the grassy colour of her eyes is lighter, gleaming with what I hope is excitement.

Well, that is until they flick to Sasha and stay there, frozen. Slowly, I watch the colour drain from her cheeks and a muscle beneath her eye tighten. There's no gloss in her eyes now. Instead, they're dark and unforgiving.

"Hi, Delaney!" Abbie calls excitedly.

My dream woman finally joins us. She keeps a few feet between herself and everyone else while focusing on my daughter.

"Hey, Abbie."

"Is that lemonade?"

Delaney glances down at the two cups in her hands and nods. I examine both of them, trying to figure out if one of them is for me. And if so, whether I'll be drinking manure or not.

"It is," she says.

"Is one for my dad?"

"Yes . . . they accidentally made an extra one. I figured your dad might be thirsty."

Sasha blows out a breath loud enough for everyone to hear, not believing her and making sure she knows it. I strain to keep from saying anything I shouldn't and keep my eyes on Delaney.

"Which one's mine? I'm assuming they're different?"

She rolls her lips, hiding her initial reaction to my questions while handing me the left one.

The corner of my mouth tips up into a teasing smirk as I take it and give it a long look. "Safe to drink?"

"It's safe enough."

"Mm, that's reassuring."

"You should say thank you, Dad," Abbie tells me, nudging me with her shoe.

I let loose a low laugh and ruffle the top of her head. "Thank you for the lemonade, Elle."

"Hi, Delaney," Sasha says under her breath.

"On that note, we should leave to get your lemonade, Abbie. Say goodbye to your dad and his friends," Sasha says.

Abbie frowns for a quick second before stealing a hug from Bryce and then wrapping her arms around my middle. I drop to a crouch to kiss her hair.

"Bye! See you Monday, Delaney."

"Don't forget your library books this week," Delaney reminds her.

"Okay!"

Sasha doesn't give us the same goodbye as our daughter, but I can't say I mind it. I wait for them to get far enough away before taking another look at my lemonade.

It's in a plastic cup with a thick blue straw, but neither of those things means anything to me. What does is the blue syrup floating around inside the cup amongst the slices of lemon and seeds big enough to clog the straw.

"Blue raspberry?" I ask.

Delaney stares at her lemonade, avoiding mine. "It was all they had."

"It's not in your cup."

"Just drink it before I actually do go and poison it," she snaps.

Leaving me standing alone, she goes behind the booth and sets her cup on it. Bryce joins her, glancing between her drink and mine with the same knowledge that's dancing in my mind.

"Did they only have two?" Bryce asks, poking at her.

Delaney doesn't react the way I expected. The tease plops onto the ground and dies.

"Poppy has yours. I didn't have enough hands."

"No worries," Bryce mutters, eyeing me like I'm supposed to know what's wrong.

My stomach drops as I realize it has to have something to do with Sasha.

"Are you going to continue now? Or am I kissing again?" Delaney asks when neither Bryce nor I speak.

I shake my head. "No, I'll continue. Unless you want to go."

"Go for it."

Bryce takes it upon herself to open the line again and invite the lingering women and even a couple of guys back to the booth. I take a long swig of my lemonade and watch Delaney, not caring if she gets pissed off with my hovering. Her good mood from earlier is gone, extinguished with one look at Sasha, and I want it back more than anything.

She takes two steps to the right and stands beside the booth instead of at my side behind it. I don't blame her for keeping her distance.

Going ahead with this doesn't feel right. It's really fucking wrong now, actually. I don't want her jealousy when I'd rather have her smile and ridiculously lame banter.

"Maybe we should call it quits for today. I'm sure we've got more than enough money in the jar," I offer.

Delaney finally looks at me again, hope filling her eyes despite her cheeks still lacking their natural flush. "Are you sure?"

"Positive. This has already been bigger than I—"

"Is the booth still open?"

The familiar voice strikes right through the minuscule amount of progress I've made. Delaney glances at the woman who spoke, and *fuck*. I drop a hand to the booth and watch in awe as her entire demeanour shifts, my lemonade forgotten.

It's not the same as the way she shut down with Sasha, her emotions hidden behind thick walls of steel. No, there's not pain in her eyes this time. It's fire instead. A scorching, wild flame that threatens to burn everything in its path.

"I figured I'd shoot my shot one last time before I took off. What's one more opportunity, right?" the same woman asks.

I'm lost in the wave of possessiveness rippling off Delaney, too stuck to drag my attention to anyone else. She's not even looking at me. Fuck, I wish she would. She could scorch every inch of skin on my body as long as she had her eyes on me.

Someone pokes my arm, a pointy nail pressing into my shirt. "Darren? I hope I'm not interrupting."

Frustration lashes at me when I force myself to look at the woman speaking. It's the same one from earlier in the day. The one Delaney all but shoved away from the booth with a silent *good riddance.*

"Hey," I force out, hoping I don't actually sound *that* breathless.

The woman grins so wide two rows of teeth appear. She shifts her touch to fall fully on my arm, holding me there.

"Hi again. I don't know if you heard me earlier, but I wanted to stop by one last time to try and convince you to take my number. And maybe, see if I could snag another kiss?"

My first instinct is to lurch backward. I don't want to embarrass her, so I stay in place, my arm hanging like a foreign weight at my side.

With a gnawing sensation in my chest, I open my mouth to reply before stamping it closed.

"We're closed."

I'm so high-strung that Delaney's tight voice slips down my spine like a warm, electric touch. My cock stiffens before I shudder, my throat squeezing around a trapped groan.

The woman's gaze grows hot on my face as she feels me move, taking it as a response to her when it isn't. It really isn't.

Her fingers run down my arm to clutch my elbow as she leans fully against the booth. The puffs of perfume hitting me are strong and cloudy, almost enough to turn my stomach.

"There's no touching," Delaney snaps, sounding closer now. "You can drop the hand now."

"What? Are you the security here? Is that a real thing?"

My favourite laugh slashes through the air. "You're lucky I'm not."

The fingers holding me tighten to the point of discomfort. I give my arm a shake.

"I don't see how this has anything to do with you, Delaney."

It's the wrong thing for this woman whose name I can't find in my memory to say. But somehow, she manages to make it worse.

Suddenly, the hand on my arm disappears and finds my neck instead. I flinch back when the woman leans in over the booth and pulls me toward her with strength I wasn't expecting.

Alarms fill my head as I reach out to push her away, needing her to back up before—

Delaney appears in front of me. She shoves the woman away from me and, before I can speak to try and defend myself, brings her hands to my face and pulls me in for our first kiss in a decade.

32

Delaney

I'VE IMAGINED THIS MOMENT.

Of finally feeling the familiar press of Darren's lips against mine again, the same ones that stole my very first kiss all those years ago. I thought the only way I'd be here was in my bed, asleep and caught in the memories of our past. It was never supposed to happen like this. In a fit of anger and hurt and searing jealousy.

Yet here I am, unable to pull myself away like I know I should.

Darren doesn't stay surprised for long. Before I can let what I've just done sink in, he's caging me in his arms and kissing me back with a strength that threatens to sweep my feet out from under me. He'd hold me up if I did, and that certainty—*that trust*—keeps me in place, unable to fight my way free of him.

The noises from the field die to nothing as my brain latches onto our kiss and nothing else. It's cliché, but the world could be burning, and I fear I wouldn't be able to move. Something tells me that the only reason he would is to try and shield me from the flames.

I squeeze my eyes shut when my emotions bubble too high and

tears build behind my eyelids. I release a choked breath against his mouth and push my hands behind his head, his hair soft against my palms. Fingers curling angrily, I inhale sharply and pull with a strength stemming from years of hurt and abandonment.

Darren hisses into my mouth but doesn't pull away. Doesn't tell me to stop or shove my hands free of his hair. He's silent, deadly so, as I only manage to grow angrier. At him, at myself, at Sasha and the entire world for what it's put me through. All of the loss and loneliness and bitterness that's grown like an infestation in my heart.

I dig my teeth into his lip and then let it go at the same time I shove myself away from the booth. The loss of him is instant, burning so hot it's cold in my chest. It's so familiar that for a moment, I feel like I've gone back in time. Only instead of being a naïve twenty-one-year-old with a future stamped with his name, I'm ten years older and jaded.

"Delaney."

His voice makes everything worse. I twirl around and bump into Sarah. She backs up, freeing us from contact before glaring at me, her thoughts obvious in her expression. It's almost laughable that she's still here, watching what I know will be a story told all over town by tonight.

"Sorry," I mumble.

Darren comes toward me, following as the dry grass crunches beneath his boots. "Delaney, don't go. Not yet."

I know better than to look at him. One glance is all it would take for my resolve to disintegrate right now, and the last thing I need is to stay with him after what I've done. I need space. Distance. A chance to get myself together after losing exactly that.

Sarah stays far away from me as I abandon everything I brought and walk away from the booth. The heavy bronze buttons on my overalls clack as I increase my pace and avoid the eyes of everyone I pass. Mortification would be the best word for how I feel when I hit Brody Steele's shoulder and stagger over a step.

"Delaney?" he asks, a cautious hand reaching out to hold my shoulder, steadying me before falling away. The cowboy hat on his head shields his eyes from the sun, casting a shadow over both of us. "Are you okay?"

I'd rather have run into any other member of Darren's friend group. Brody isn't just one of Darren's closest friends, but he's a celebrity inside of Cherry Peak and to the rest of the world. I've never been able to mould the man he is now into the one he was when we were kids, and that's kept me more . . . wary, I guess. He's a stranger to me now.

"I'm fine. I just need to go," I whisper past the ball in my throat.

Brody seems to hear what I don't say. "Do you need a ride? I've got my truck here, or I know Johnny's got his, and all the girls would love an opportunity to drive either one of them if you didn't want us to."

"No. No, I don't need a ride. I'll walk."

"Walk? It's a ten-minute drive back to town. I have no clue how long it would take to walk."

"I've got it," I say shortly, not interested in standing here any longer.

"It's not safe to walk on the highway, Delaney."

"If you're so concerned, you can tell Darren I caught a ride since I know he's who you're going to find the moment I leave," I bite out.

Brody turns away, looking around the field for someone to help him out here, most likely. I use his distraction to my advantage and slip away.

It's terrifying being here again. Not in this place, but rather, this mindset. The sharp tang of regret fills my mouth as I pass the folding tables and food trucks with lines longer than the kissing booth.

The kissing booth . . . what a terrible idea that was. I knew it from the moment Darren brought it up. Agreeing to take part in it was as good as promising that I'd wind up losing my head to the same jealousy that ate me up for years watching him with Sasha.

That same tear through my heart with every hand hold on the street and two seats taken at the diner is back, only this time, there's no ring on his finger.

I'm a mess.

The front pocket of my overalls buzzes at the same time my feet scrape over the fresh gravel in the parking lot. I ignore it and push my hands into the side of my overalls to keep them warm when the wind kicks up.

I push out a long, even breath and slow my pace enough to relax. The more distance I can put between me and Darren, the better right now, even if that means I have to take a very, very long walk. Or at least a few minutes before I call one of the girls to come and get me.

My phone buzzes again, and again, before I fish it out and check the screen. Darren's name is there in thick, bold letters before disappearing, making room for me to read through the texts already collecting.

> Darren: Don't leave like this again.
>
> Darren: At least let me drive you home. It's supposed to start to rain soon.
>
> Anna: Brody told us he saw you leave. I'm sorry he's such a blabbermouth.
>
> Bryce: I told him you'd kick him in the ass. Text me when you need a ride.

I clamp my teeth together to fight more fucking tears and exit the parking lot. The shoulder on this road is non-existent, but the ditch is shallow. It's been that way forever. With how many horses come trotting down this way, the shallow ditch is better on the off chance they misstep. Or at least that's what I've been told. I've only ridden a horse once, and I hated every minute of it.

"You have to hold on to the reins, Delaney! Stop letting go of 'em, or she's goin' to take off on you."

Brody laughs from where he's sitting on the fence, watching me try and fail to ride the horse they supposedly use for training children at Steele Ranch. Yeah, children. Apparently, even six-year-olds have more natural skill than I do at sixteen.

"Why don't you give Darren a hard time? He's even worse than I am!" I call back.

The horse beneath me is gentle, sure. But with how badly my ass is hurting, I can't focus on anything but trying to lean off it. Every time she moves, I wobble like an egg on a post.

"Don't project, Elle. You're going to fall off at this rate," Darren teases.

"You're only doing better than me because Brody let you ride Sky. That's special treatment if I've ever seen it."

Darren laughs. "That's best friend perks, baby. I offered to let you sit on her with me."

Brody hops off the fence and passes Darren with a pat to his personal horse Sky's neck before heading my way. His filthy cowboy boots leave deep grooves in the dirt of the training circle, emphasizing the whole rancher thing he's got going on for him. Well, that plus the hat that hasn't left his head in the time I've known him. Not unless we're having dinner.

"Vera here is a good girl, Delaney. You've just gotta relax a bit," he says.

"It feels like my thighs are going to crack in half."

"They look like it too."

"Don't talk about my girl's thighs, Brody."

The cowboy backs up with his hands in the air and winks at me. "Fine, you possessive fucker."

I adjust my hold on the reins and try to sit properly on the saddle. The helmet on my head is heavy too, which doesn't help. Everything about this is uncomfortable, and I'm not sure I care about the whole muscle-acclimation thing Brody was blabbing about at lunch.

Darren appears in front of me, his smirk so deep it could probably stay sunken into his cheeks forever. "Oh, you're still in the same spot."

"I'm going to punch you."

"You say the hottest things to me, Elle."

Vera, the horse beneath my very sore ass, tries to take a few more steps forward. I squeal, falling against her neck and yanking on the reins. Brody and Darren both bark laughs into the summer air, and I decide I'm never, ever getting on a horse's back again.

I sigh when my phone buzzes again. The name is different than the two previous ones, so I answer it.

"I'm fine, Daisy."

"I knew you'd answer if Daisy called. I'm a bit offended, but I won't get into that right now. How far have you made it from the drive-in?" Poppy asks.

"The whole part of me not telling anyone that I was leaving was so nobody worried."

She laughs coolly. "We're not sixteen anymore, Della. That shit doesn't work anymore."

"You're still not coming to get me right now. The event isn't over, and I'm not going to let it come to an end because I needed to get away."

"Why did you need to leave?"

"As if you haven't already heard. I'm sure half the town has by now."

I stare at the white lines painted on the side of the road, keeping count of each one I pass.

"I want to hear it from you, not some bored gossips."

"So, it is going around, then," I mutter.

"Of course it is. This is Cherry Peak, after all. When I trapped myself in my room for a week crying over Garrison, everyone knew it was because he'd left me. All it took was one person to see his car driving out of town, and the rumours started. That's how it works here."

"That doesn't mean it doesn't still fucking suck, Poppy."

She scoffs. "Let me talk. It's all mindless chatter from people with nothing better to do."

"I only just passed the fruit stand sign," I say, not bothering to read this week's BC selection of fruit. "If you're going to come, it has to just be you."

"I won't let him come."

"I know."

"I'll be right there, and then we're going to go to Peakside and get drunk on their half-off sangrias. Deal?"

I don't even have to think about it.

"Deal, Poppy."

33

TEN YEARS AGO

I STARE OUT AT THE PARK, FEELING SICK TO MY STOMACH.

Nothing about this feels right. Not a single fucking thing.

Knowing that I'm here while Delaney's at my place waiting for me doesn't sit well. I dig my heels into the grass to keep myself from getting back in my car and going right back to her. If I do . . . if I give in, I'll be sleeping beside her tonight, and I'll have done all of this for nothing.

Our fight earlier was the worst we've ever had. The fact that it stemmed from what our relationship has become over the last two years only makes it harder to swallow. The things we said drove me here tonight, but it's what we didn't say that has kept me from going back.

None of this was the plan.

The choices we've been making aren't the right ones. Not for either of us, and not for the future I want to have with her. I've never wanted to take a break, not for one year, and sure as shit not four. But she did.

Since we were sixteen, Delaney's said she wanted this to happen. When I declared my intentions to marry her, she told me I could in four years. She wanted to wait, to test our relationship to see if we were really ready for the commitment I've wanted to give to her so that we never had any regrets. Having her regret this—*us*—would kill me.

That's the only reason I agreed. Because I love her more than life itself, and I'd do just about anything to make sure that it was her beside me at the end. But this . . . this isn't how it was supposed to be. It's all wrong, and it has to be me who puts us on the right track again. I need to do it before I lose her over these hazy lines that we keep crossing. With every wrong step, we're left overthinking and ruining everything good between us in the aftermath.

This is the only right choice, even if I have to risk everything in order to fix us.

Headlights flare out over the road. They're the first set of them to appear in the twenty minutes I've been here. I don't need to look at the car to know it's hers.

She doesn't come out, though. I wait, but soon enough, I lose my patience. I'm on the edge, a change in the breeze nearly threatening to undo me completely. That's why I push myself to go to her door and knock on the window.

Sad, expecting eyes clash against mine through the glass, and my stomach tumbles painfully. Delaney leaves her car running as she steps out and stands close to me, her heat palpable in the night.

"Why didn't you answer your phone?" she asks sharply.

"I was going to."

"When? Once I'd already flown home?"

I choke back my immediate refusal. It's not like I can blame her for thinking that. Not after I've just completely left her alone at my place around people she doesn't know well. I doubt Blue was good for a conversation that would have been intelligent enough for Delaney.

"No, Elle. I was going to call you back once I knew what to say."

She darts her eyes away, looking out at the empty park. "What does that mean?"

"We both know this isn't working."

"That's a bold assumption to make without taking my feelings into actual consideration," she replies, hurt.

I sigh. "Don't do that. The only thing I've been doing these past two years is take your feelings into consideration. I always put them at the forefront of every decision I make."

Delaney blows out a breath. "I have never asked you to put me first. I thought you were okay with this, Darren. That's what you've made me think."

"What was I supposed to do? Tell you not to come to Calgary this time? Send you a text saying that I can't do this fighting anymore? That I can't accept the pieces of who we were two years instead of the real thing?"

"Yes! That's exactly what you say. If you had, maybe we wouldn't be here right now. We could have figured things out and not been like this!" She waves her hand between us. "I want *us* back. You're right. What we're doing isn't working anymore. Fuck this break, Darren."

"Why?" I ask, whipping the word out, needing an answer.

"Why what?"

"Why do you want to put an end to this?"

"Because I miss you. I miss us, and I can't lose you," she admits, the crack in her voice nearly ending me.

I force myself to keep going, the words feeling sticky in my throat. "That's the problem. Can you honestly say that you've learned what you've needed to? Have these last two years proven to you that we're ready for marriage? That you trust our future wholeheartedly? Because those are the reasons behind us taking this break. I won't let you make a decision like this based on emotion."

She looks down, sniffing. "So, that's it, then? You're just going to cut us off?"

I don't want to, baby.

A seed of fear grows roots in my stomach, sprouting leaves of panic that shoot through my veins. "Two more years, Delaney. We're already halfway there."

"Too much can change in that time. I can't—I can't lose you like this. Not . . . Not for real this time." She sucks in a sharp breath as she shakes her head, eyes frantic. "You've always been there. I don't remember what it's like not to have you anymore. *Please* don't."

I'm unable to keep my hands to myself. I take her into my arms and hold her, my lips finding her place on her temple. The shake in her body shoves at my resolve, weakening it.

"You deserve a real chance. No distractions this time. Always having me on the other end of the line won't give you the space you need. We haven't been fair to each other, giving only enough of ourselves to keep us hanging on by a thread. It's all or nothing, Elle. That's the way it's supposed to have been. We can't keep teasing ourselves."

She doesn't speak as she holds me, tears soaking into my shirt. I pull her closer, struggling not to tuck her into my car and bring her home. I'd never let her go again if I did.

"No," she whispers.

Gently, I guide her back until our eyes can meet. "I love you, Delaney Brooks. Give me two years, and I'll make you Delaney Huntsly."

Disapproval is written over every inch of her face. I feel it too. It's like a second pulse. That voice in my head is telling me that I'm making a mistake. Every word I speak tastes sour, and the nausea in my stomach has me swallowing in hopes of keeping it down.

"I love you too." Her broken voice . . .

She knows me better than anyone in the universe. That's how she knows I'm not going to budge. Not now, after all this. I've already made up my mind.

I look away, unable to watch as she lets go of me and starts pulling her ring off. The cool press of it in my palm is bad enough. I curl it into my fist and force myself to stare at her when she steps away from me, needing that last look.

"If you give me an hour, I'll be gone."

My stomach rebels against that. I force myself to jerk my chin in a nod.

"Alright," I choke out, ears starting to buzz.

"Goodbye, Darren."

I can't say anything else. As soon as she gets into her car, I turn away and leave. I pass my car, and then I'm jogging past the cluster of trees and dropping to my knees. The scent of pine needles and wet grass is the last thing I register before I'm emptying my stomach onto the ground.

It's karma for breaking not only Delaney's heart tonight but mine too.

34

Delaney

PRESENT

I'M PAST THE POINT OF FLINCHING AT THE BURN OF VODKA IN MY throat as I toss another shot back. Leaning the entirety of my body weight against Poppy, I rock to the classic country music playing in the bar and smack a kiss to her cheek.

"You're the best, you know?"

She sighs happily. "So are you."

"I could do without the vodka, though."

"No, you couldn't. Oh! I'm still waiting for the juicy deets," she declares, an arm slumping across my shoulders.

"I don't want to talk about him, Pops."

"Either do I! But I wanna talk about you."

"I'm still *me* without Darren."

Her eyes dig into my face as I wave the bartender down again. "That's not what I meant. Of course you are. But together! I'm talking together, Della. It's magic. Fireworks and rainbows."

"You're drunk," I tell her, fully aware that I am too.

My ass feels glued to the bar stool when I lean away from her and drop my elbows to the table. I'm off-balance, but yeah . . . this position is good. Great.

"I'm not just saying it because I'm drunk and Darren's my brother. He's a douche-face sometimes, but he's one of the good ones. He's missed you."

"You don't need to talk him up. I know how great he is. I know it too well."

"He loves you."

I tuck my chin into my chest and shake my head before immediately looking up as the world tips. "He used to love me."

The bartender, a dude named Matty who's lending his services from a bar called the Frosty Mug in a town a couple of hours away, slides two shots and a big ol' glass of water across to me before slipping away.

I frown at the water and take the shots. Poppy takes hers from me and sniffs the vodka.

"Is he putting all of these drinks on Garrison's tab?" I ask.

"Of course," she answers, making it sound obvious. "The only time my man ever looks at his credit card statement is to see if I've spent anything."

"He doesn't want you to?"

Her laugh is loud and wild. "No, babe. He likes me spending his money a bit more than *I* like spending it."

"Oh."

"It sounds backwards, right?"

"I just feel like I don't know him at all. Isn't that wrong? I should have sat him down and grilled him about you at the beginning."

"He'd have pissed you off for sure," she says after taking her shot.

I take mine and tap the empty glass against the bar. The alcohol slides down the hatch like water.

"I heard about him when he got to town and knew that you'd be the only one with the nerve to work his shit out and bring out the good in him."

"And work I did!" she cheers, her head falling back and shaking wildly.

Her hair whips back and forth across her back as she shuts her eyes and taps a beat on the bar. The pink tint to her skin isn't just from the warmth in here. It's a show of her happiness. The kind that goes bone-deep.

I wrap an arm around her body and pull her into me, keeping her locked there. "You're my favourite person in the world."

"Second favourite, but I'll take it, baby cakes." Poppy returns the hug and presses a wet kiss to my cheek. "I love you too."

"I want to love him again," I announce, the vodka cracking open both my head and my heart.

Poppy stiffens in surprise before relaxing again. "Do you think you ever stopped?"

"Maybe or maybe not. I'm not sure. I can't be sure right now. Not without having . . . *more.*"

"Ask him for that, Della. Make him give you more and more and fucking more until you have what you need! How else are you supposed to figure things out?" she asks, slurring heavily.

I can hear the drinks making my words sloppy when I say, "He should have married me."

"He should have."

"And you should have been an aunt to my baby, not Sasha's. She never deserved him."

Oh, my God.

I choke on disbelief, coughing into my wrist as I gawk at the bar. Poppy's hold on me tightens, becoming impossible to slip free of. Her lack of immediate disgust with my comments is more comforting than she knows.

"I've hated her from the moment I met her. Everyone knew she had a crush on Darren all through high school. She wanted him, and once she had him, she broke his soul," Poppy hisses.

I check for traces of venom on the corners of her lips. "He lost himself, didn't he?"

"He did, but there was nothing I or anyone else could do to help him. Not when he was stuck in that marriage—in that house—with her. He designed that house, and she hated everything about it."

"The house he lives in now? How could anyone hate that house?"

"Oh, yeah. He used this custom, stamped tile in the bathroom that she complained about for weeks. It wasn't my style, sure, but it was unique, and he loved it. They're what got him featured in that first magazine, actually. Did you read it?"

I sip a breath between my lips, bewilderment coursing through my veins. "What was stamped on the tiles?"

"They're different mountaintops. All from the Rockies, I think."

"I'll be right back," I whisper, wiggling in her hold.

She lets me go, and I step off the stool, wobbling slightly. Once I've straightened, I give her a thumbs-up and head for the bathroom. I've barely opened the door before I'm pulling out my phone and making a call.

The line only rings once before he answers. "Delaney?"

"You used the tiles in your bathroom. *My* dream tiles."

Silence. Too much silence.

"Say something!" I shout down the line, feeling like with every passing second, I'm losing my hold on myself.

The bathroom is empty. It's so small it's cramped as I stand in front of the sinks and stare at my reflection in the mirror. Beneath the lipstick heart drawn on the corner, my eyes are wide and dark with my expanded pupils but . . . still clear. I see my emotions as starkly as I feel them. They're everywhere.

"Where are you?"

"Why did you use my tiles, Darren? Why would you put them in the same house where you slept beside someone else every night?"

"I didn't sleep beside Sasha in that house. Not once."

My chest expands to make room for my heart to swell. "Don't lie to me."

"I'm not. She slept in the room beside Abbie's. I slept across the hall."

"You hated those tiles," I whisper, spinning to face the stalls when it becomes too much to stare at myself any longer. "They were supposed to be impossible to design around. That's what you said when I brought them up."

"I made it my mission to figure it out. Now, tell me where you are," he murmurs, his voice soft and inviting.

"Would you come if I did?"

"Yes."

I palm my throat, feeling the racing pulse beneath my fingers. "Peakside. I'm with Poppy."

"I'm on my way."

"I haven't changed my mind about us," I ramble, the clarification singeing my stomach like a nasty burn.

"Not yet, Elle. But I told you that I'll be patient, and I meant it. All I need is a chance to try and change your mind."

"You'll need more than one."

"I'm okay with that."

The bathroom door opens, and a woman walks in. She doesn't spare me a look before diving into a stall. I roll my lip between my teeth, thinking.

"I'm drunk."

"I know."

"Be here before I change my mind."

"I'm nearly there already."

"And it's *Delaney*."

I hang up the call and leave the bathroom before I can talk myself out of this. Poppy's still where I left her, but she's moved on to some sort of frozen drink now. There are two tall red slushies waiting on the bar when I slip back onto my stool.

Taking a sip of the drink, I moan at the sweet strawberry flavour. The alcohol is hidden to the point I only catch the tail of it, making it far more dangerous than vodka shots.

"It's nice drinking with someone who doesn't like margaritas. I'm over them," she mumbles.

"This is way better."

"You look . . . less sad," she notes, eyeing me curiously.

I keep my straw in my mouth while saying, "Your brother is coming."

"I know. He was with the guys when you called."

"Garrison told you?" I pout.

Maybe it's the alcohol finally washing away my worries or the whole calling Darren thing, but I'm feeling good now. Free, like if the ceiling floated away, I could grow wings and fly after it. I don't remember the last time I felt like this.

"He's coming too. Not with my brother, but with Brody and Johnny," she says, voice rising and dropping in pitch like she can't choose which tone she wants to use.

"So, everyone is coming?"

Poppy smacks her lips together and swipes a line of dew off the side of her glass. "Not *everyone*. Bryce already has Daisy at home and refuses to give up their alone time. But Anna and Rory are."

"Okay."

The back of her hand smacks my forehead. I flinch and whip my head to the side to glare at her.

"What was that for?"

"Checking for a fever," she says between giggles.

I smack her forehead with the back of my hand. "I don't have a fever. Do you?"

"Maybe. I'll ask Garry to be a sexy nurse for me tonight and check."

"Ew, Pops. I knew that guy was dirty."

"Is he, or am I?"

"Are you a dirty guy?"

She rolls her eyes and tips her head back to lick my hand. "Don't judge me."

"I'm not. Never judged you, Pops. I wish I was half as confident as you are. You see what you want, and you take it. You demand it!"

"You deserve to do the same, Della. Not just from Darren, but the world."

Holding my breath, I rush out, "I haven't had sex in forever. What if I've forgotten how?"

Poppy twists completely on her stool. Her knees smack into mine as she faces me and takes me by the shoulders, shaking twice. There's an unspoken surprise in her expression that I think confuses me more than reassures me.

"How long is forever? Like . . . since my brother forever?"

I'm hot enough to burn through my clothes. "Don't ask it like that!"

"What? I'm just—I just—how?" she gasps.

"I only had one boyfriend! We learned—"

Her hands fly up to cover her ears. "Nope! Don't continue that. I don't think I want to know what you did with my brother."

"Help me, Poppy! I don't remember how to have sex!"

Slowly, she lowers her hands. A sigh falls between us as she pushes forward.

"You have to remember something. Did you have a favourite position?"

The vodka has done its job to relax me, that's for sure. I lean toward Poppy and cage my mouth with two hands before whispering, "I've only done two."

"*Two?*" she shrieks, her eyebrows blending in with her hairline. "Two! No wonder you don't remember. My poor, poor girl."

My cheeks have their own heartbeat as I hide my face in my hands and groan. Her shock is warranted. I'm in my early thirties and haven't had sex with a real penis since I was in my twenties. There are only so many different brands of dildos and vibrators, and I forced myself to stop buying them once I filled a second bin.

Staring down at my drink, I decide to let my mouth run free.

Poppy's never judged me for anything, and from what I know about her very pro-sex-toy stance, she'll probably understand this better than anyone.

"I bought a monster dildo last month. Like, the kind with all the fancy ribbing and everything. I'm too scared to use it. What if it hurts? It's huge too. At least ten inches and as thick as my fist. I can't take that. Wouldn't it hurt?"

Poppy clears her throat pointedly and attempts to straighten her slouched posture. The arm she's leaning against the booth slips, and she giggles for a second before stopping and kicking me beneath the bar.

"Hi, Darren. Fancy seeing you here. Want some daiquiri?"

I jump off the stool in surprise. Poppy reaches to steady me, but Darren's hand is there before hers is. I tip my head back and flutter my lashes, growing lost in his warm, brown gaze.

He hovers so close that I can feel the chill from outside on his clothes. It's a welcome change in temperature, considering my throbbing cheeks and scorching chest.

"I'll pass on the daiquiri. I'm going to need a clear head for tonight, I think."

Yeah, he does, because I surely won't have one.

35

Darren

I STAND BEHIND DELANEY, A HAND GLUED TO THE SMALL OF HER back. It's support for her languid muscles but also for mine. From the moment I heard her talking about ten-inch dildos, I've been harder than one.

Despite the lack of empty glasses on the bar in front of her and my sister, she's had to have drunk more than she's used to. More than I've ever witnessed her drink, at least. It's as interesting as it is worrisome, considering the day we've had. I don't want to be the reason for her pain again.

Spreading my fingers to cover more of her back, I lean as close as I can, glueing us together. She sighs in response before slowly letting her head fall to rest against my chest. I lose the ability to think and keep rooted in place instead.

"Want to dance when Garry gets here?" Poppy asks her.

"You want me to dance with you and your fiancé?"

My sister giggles. "No. You and my brother can dance with us. Rory and Johnny too. Johnny always makes her dance."

"I can't dance," Delaney argues, her voice loose and soft as she rolls her head to the side to stare at Poppy. "Darren can't either."

I stroke her back with my thumb, testing my limits like the

greedy bastard I become around her. The responding twitch of muscle feeds my desire to never let her go.

"I've learned how."

"I don't believe you."

Poppy glances back at me. "Actually, he's gotten better. I think me being a better dancer than him was too much of a punch to the ego."

"Well . . . I don't like to dance," Delaney says, stubborn as hell despite her loosened inhibitions.

My sister turns up the pressure with a killer set of puppy dog eyes. "Just one song, Della. That's all I want."

Selfishly, I want her to say yes. A dance floor isn't the best spot for a conversation, but it's somewhere we can be together. She'll be in my arms, and I'll have her hands on me in a way that I've been dreaming about. I bet I could convince her to give me more than just one song too.

Delaney stares forward again. "I'm not drunk enough."

"Uh, yes, you are. Wait until you stand up again."

"Poppy." She groans, lifting her arms to rest across her chest.

"Delaney."

"Let me get another shot first."

"Fine, but then—Garry!"

Poppy stumbles off her stool and into Garrison's arms. He wraps her in his arms and then stares at me above her head, dragging his eyes to Delaney, his curiosity burning bright. My sister grabs his face in her hands and pulls him down for a kiss, so I take that as my sign to look away.

Brody and Johnny come in next, followed by Rory and Anna, who are pressed together and laughing about something I know better than to ask about. My oldest friend meets me beside Delaney's stool and slaps me on the back.

"It's good to see you back in here," Brody announces.

Johnny joins him, glowing with that same impenetrable happiness that sticks to him like a second skin. His black hair is damp from the rain that was just starting to sprinkle when I arrived, and he shakes it out like a dog, water splattering my arm. It's always odd seeing him without his cowboy hat, but considering Rory's become quite a fan of it, it's only a matter of time before he has to bite the bullet and finally buy another one.

Steele Ranch's favourite ranch hand smirks at me. "You've been hidin' from us, Darren. Both of you."

"Don't start, Johnny. If you miss me that much, you can visit me at my house."

"See, you just want more commitment than I'm up to these days, D-man. I'm a busy man with only so many hours in the day for my groupies."

"You make yourself that busy," Brody corrects.

Johnny hits his shoulder. "You're one to talk. And it's your goddamn grandpa that's keeping me this busy. I blame you for that, by the way."

"You like it. Grandpa's gettin' ready to hand you the ranch, and you damn well know that," Brody says.

"Don't get my hopes up. He's been more of a hard-ass than usual lately."

"You couldn't have expected him to go easy on you now, Johnny."

"Eh, I've got Eliza on my side. She keeps him in check when he gets too growly. And if he doesn't, Rory does."

"Welcome to the Steele life, man," Brody cheers.

"Hey, we'll see you in a bit," I say, picking up on every slight jerk of Delaney's body. It's not necessarily discomfort, but it's close enough to have me urging us away from everyone.

Delaney's been around these people before, but never like this. Overwhelming her right now could be my downfall.

"It's nice havin' you here, Delaney," Johnny says before tugging Brody toward our usual table.

While the owners of Peakside can't stand a single one of us, even they haven't been able to keep the table from becoming as good as ours. Everyone in town knows it belongs to us, and it's going to stay that way until we're all too old to come here on Saturday nights.

"Della, you're here!" Anna cheers, rushing over now that the guys are gone.

"Anna!"

Delaney turns and opens her arms for a hug. Anna hides her surprise well, but still, she doesn't hesitate to accept the affection.

"We don't see enough of each other," Anna murmurs.

"I'm sorry."

"Don't apologize! I just wish we had the chance more often. Maybe I need to start hitching a ride with Poppy every time she goes to see you. The shop can handle a few hours without me every day."

Thistle and Thorn, Anna's hair salon, has boomed over the last couple of years. Appointments book up months in advance, with customers driving hours to see her. Brody's nauseatingly proud of her and the life they've built here in Cherry Peak together. Fuck, I think we all are.

"I've only invited you a million times," Poppy says, coming over with Garrison's hand clutched tight in hers.

Anna stands back and throws Poppy a scowl over her shoulder. "And if I could have, I'd have been there every one of the million."

"You sound too sober, Anna. Do you want a daiquiri, or are you a beer girl now?" my sister asks, already leaning over the bar and flagging the bartender back over.

"Is that a serious question?"

Poppy smacks her lips together. "You're still living on the ranch."

"And? When Garrison was in the guest house, did he start drinking beer? I have my own house! Don't insult me."

The scoffed laugh I let out is completely accidental. Garrison snaps a look at me that I can feel, but it's Delaney's reaction that holds my attention. Her back curves with her own silent giggle as she reaches for the hand I've got pressed to her and pulls on it. The twinkle of laughter I hear next has me disregarding the others and swooping in to use our joint hands to help her off her seat.

Delaney's mouth pops open while her eyes meet mine, questioning what I'm doing. I tilt my lips into a crooked grin and guide her into my side.

"Dance with me."

"I haven't had another drink yet," she whispers, swaying softly.

"You don't need it."

She keeps still for a moment, and I wait with more patience than I thought I possessed. I know everyone's watching us, but they don't matter. They never have when it came to my best friend.

"You better have been telling the truth about the dancing," she says, *finally*.

"You have my word."

"Let's go."

Without another look at our friends, I lead Elle past the empty tables and to the dance floor. With old wood and peeling paint, the bar has seen better days, but that's what makes it Peakside. The scent of stale beer, cigarette smoke sneaking in through the front door and the memories that will follow all of us into the next life.

It was in this bar that we celebrated Delaney's eighteenth birthday with a confetti gun Poppy found at the thrift shop in Oak Point and where Bryce and Darren found me crying at our table a week after Abbie was born. These walls have seen some of my highest highs and lowest lows. I found and lost myself here and everything in between.

And now, it's where I'm holding my Delaney again.

Her overalls hang off her in a way oversized way, making her seem even smaller than she is as she stands across from me on the dancefloor. I stare down at our connected hands and squeeze my fingers. She follows my eyes and takes a step closer. The toes of our shoes touch, and her eyes are waiting for mine when I lift them.

"I'm sorry I called," she blurts out, the words slurred.

"Why?"

"I was the one who ran earlier."

The music drifts around us as I bring our hands up and drop another to hold the curve of her waist. A bit off-kilter, she grabs my shoulder and waits for me to lead. Our friends join us on the dance floor, and I swallow a laugh when Johnny takes Rory's hand and twirls her over and over again, her laugh damn loud. Brody ignores them and focuses on his wife, keeping her close and away from Poppy, who's pouting as Garrison pulls her away from them.

"You make it sound as though I didn't try to chase you or race here tonight to do exactly what we're doing," I say.

"Yeah . . ."

Slowly, I move us into an easy two-step. "You kissed me, Delaney. You kissed me, and I didn't want you to stop."

"It was impulsive," she murmurs, eyes shutting for a moment. When they open again, they're so bright. "I wasn't thinking straight."

"What were you thinking, then?"

Her touch hardens, becoming fierce, maybe even angry. "You hurt me. Bad. But I still couldn't stand there and watch that woman touch you like that in front of me. It's not fair."

"I know, baby."

"Darren," she says on a weak breath. "I'm barely holding on here."

"You can let go."

"I'm too scared to fall."

"I'll catch you. You'll never get hurt again," I swear when she drops her head forward, forehead pressing to my sternum. "I won't make the same mistakes again."

I shiver when her hand falls from my shoulder to my arm

and then curls around my back. Fingers slipping free, she brings her second arm around to hold me with a strength that hits me straight on, like a blast from an explosion only a few feet away. It's a desperate hold, a plea for strength delivered without words.

"I'm never leaving you again," I declare, loud enough only for her to hear.

She rubs her cheek against my chest and curls her fingers into my shirt, clutching me as if she doesn't believe me.

Desperation bubbles my blood, demanding I prove myself to her before I lose her again. I can't. Not before I even get a chance to have her.

"Come with me," I urge.

She blinks up at me, those grassy green eyes unfocused from the alcohol in her system, yet still so vibrant. "Where?"

"Somewhere we can be alone."

THE FOOTBALL FIELD IS DESERTED.

It's cold, and the grass is still damp from the rain that's just stopped. I haven't been back here since my last high school game, and it hasn't changed a bit. There are old, rusty metal bleachers, a score tower with a burnt-out clock, and yard lines in desperate need of a touch-up.

"They could have replaced the bleachers, at least," I note.

Delaney walks ahead of me with her arms slightly extended for balance. "The budget's too tight. They're still wearing the same jerseys you did."

"I can't imagine how they smell, then."

"I've never been close enough to one of the players to take a whiff."

I laugh lowly, following behind her, letting her lead us wherever it is she wants to go.

"It looks different without the snow."

"Just wait a week or so. It's supposed to start soon."

"Already?"

She hums. "It's October."

"Are you cold?"

"Right now?"

"Right now."

The sound of her uneven footsteps in the browning grass is all there is. It's almost eerie how silent it is here. Other than the school, there are only a few houses nearby, none with their lights on. We're completely alone.

"I'm okay," Delaney says.

"It's all the booze."

"Are you going to lecture me about how much I drank? I was waiting to see if you were."

I slide my hands in the back pockets of my jeans, hanging back further. "No. We're not kids anymore."

She stops, standing still. The breeze runs through her hair, making it fly over her shoulders. I force myself to stay where I am when she turns around, eyes guarded as they focus on me.

"You're right. We're not kids anymore. Our decisions aren't . . . fleeting. Every one we make now has a consequence that we can't forget about and move on from. I don't want to make any more mistakes."

"Neither do I. Everything I do now is with a purpose. From the moment I found out about Abbie, I've been making choices for the good of everyone else. First with Abbie, then Sasha. One choice I made led to eight years of decisions that have never felt like mine to make. I lost you, and suddenly, my life was someone else's. You are the only thing I want to decide on right now, and I've already made up my mind. All I need is one chance to prove to you that this is the best decision for both of us."

"What happens if I say yes to you right now, Darren? We just, what? Continue where we left off?" she asks, the doubt in her voice cutting through me.

I take a generous step forward, shrinking the distance between us. She watches me, pinching the top of her ear anxiously.

"No. Too much time has passed. We'd start over."

"It's not possible to start over. Not when we already know so much about each other. Time has passed, but not enough for me to forget you or the way I loved you."

"So, don't forget. There are no rules with this."

"You make it sound easier than it would be," she says, brushing it off.

"What are you most afraid of?"

She blinks rapidly, face blank. "What am I most afraid of? How about everything?"

"Break it down for me."

"What if there's too much history? Or we dive into this only to realize that what we had back then can't be replicated now? We're so different from who we used to be. There's no guarantee that we would be able to do this again."

"Impossible," I declare.

"What is?"

The ball in my throat threatens to choke me completely when I drop to my knees in the wet grass. Her surprised inhale falls between us. I reach for her hands and clutch them like they're the only thing keeping me tethered to the ground.

"All of it. We may be different people now, but I've been in love with you since before I knew what love even was. I know we're meant to be together. It's always been you and me, Elle. No number of years could change that. And if you gave it a chance, you'll be sure of it too. I'll stay here on my knees for weeks begging you if I have to. All you have to do is give me one chance. That's it."

"What about Abbie?" she asks, emotion swelling so fiercely in her eyes that she has to look away, palms growing slick in my hold.

I see her walls crumbling. I'm chipping at the fortress in her mind one brick at a time until finally, the entire thing collapses. Delaney sighs, and I swear I can almost see the weight of it hitting the ground.

"She adores you."

"And Sasha?" she asks, almost too quiet for me to hear.

"She hasn't had a say in my personal life for a long time now."

"She'll always be in your life. You were married, and she's the mother of your daughter."

"And if you say yes, so will you. You'll be everything to me that she never was. I'll give you more than I could have ever given her. Just say yes."

"You make everything sound so easy. So simple. Like there's no risk with a jump this big."

I shake my head, bringing her hands to my mouth and resting them there. "There is a risk. One that scares the shit out of me. What I'm trying to say is that it's worth it. I've had a decade to grow without you, and I didn't like who I saw in the mirror. But then . . . there you were again, and even beneath your anger and blunt words, you were still you. I woke up beneath that fury, Elle, and I've been chasing more of it ever since then.

"We went too long without each other, but that didn't stop me from dreaming of you or the life we had before everything went to shit. I've been chasing a love like ours, and the only thing I've learned is that it's impossible to replicate. A yes doesn't mean everything will go back to how it was. It just means you'll give me a chance to make up for what I've done."

Her throat bulges with the force of her swallow. "And if I decide that I can't do this anymore? That your chance is over? Do you expect me to believe that you'll just walk away as if nothing happened?"

"If that's what you wanted, then yeah, Elle. I'll walk away. For good this time."

"I don't want Abbie to know yet. Not until we know if it's worth telling her. She's my student as well as your daughter."

I push to my feet and eliminate the distance between us until we're so close I can smell her shampoo on the breeze. Her cheek is warm as I cup her chin and guide it back to rub our noses together. My heart is frantic, adrenaline pumping through it now.

"Okay. We don't have to tell anyone yet. Not until you're ready."

Delaney presses two hands to my chest and holds my gaze. "Slow, Darren. We need to take it slow until I know what we're doing."

"You can have anything you want."

And I mean it. She can have absolutely anything because the thought of not giving it to her upsets me more than denying her in the first place. I've recognized it from the moment we met.

Delaney Brooks deserves a king, but she'll have to settle for me, and *fuck*, I've missed having to work hard to keep her.

36

Delaney

SOFT CHATTER FILLS THE LIBRARY, KEEPING ME FROM FALLING ASLEEP reading. It's only noon, but it feels like I've been awake all day already. In reality, I didn't get out of bed until ten.

I missed my morning class *again* after turning my phone off when the alarm wouldn't stop ringing. If I hadn't stayed up so late, I'd have been up far before seven, but over the last six months, long nights have become the norm around here.

At least I'm not sharing a room with anyone this year. Well, I share a bathroom, but considering my first two years here, I was roommates with Brooklyn, I'm grateful for my single room. I'll take a connected bathroom any day.

I blink down at the textbook spread in front of me and sigh. The words are blurring together, and the notes I've been writing are sloppy at best. I'll have to spend more time dissecting each word than I've spent writing them.

Shoving my hands through my hair, I lean back in my seat and stare at the ceiling. Maybe if I look at it long enough, all of the information I've missed from my abandoned classes will appear. It would make it easier to hunt down the information I need, and yeah, I'm going crazy. Is that why I was switched into a single room this year? For the well-being of any potential roommate?

If this were Cherry Peak, I'd have no problem convincing myself of that. Six months isn't anywhere near long enough for the news of Darren and me to blow through that town and be a memory. It's why I didn't go home for Thanksgiving or Christmas this year. He can have the town and the drama that comes with it.

My grandmother is the only one whom I've kept in touch with since . . . the breakup. If you can even call it that.

She flew here for Christmas and even stayed a few extra days afterward to visit the campus and guilt my parents for missing out. I think the lack of nipple-freezing weather here even had her considering moving just to escape the winters back home. For a few minutes, at least. There was no way she'd actually do that, though. Being Albertan is a part of who she is, and no mild winter or beautiful ocean views will change that, even if I wish it could. If things don't go the way I'm hoping after graduation.

My phone vibrates on the table, and I swipe it before the guy at the table across the way can glare at me again.

"Hey."

"Hey? That's all I get? How very college girl of you," Grandma croons.

I cross my legs beneath the table and set an elbow on the table. "What a coincidence, I was just thinking about you. Are you using your juju on me again?"

"Did you feel me prodding around in your brain?"

"Thankfully, no."

"How disappointing. Oh well. Tell me what you're up to."

"I'm rereading the same paragraph I've read three times already in hopes I actually digest something this time."

"Are you tired?"

"I'm always tired, Grams."

Her concern strikes through the phone, feeling just as intense as if I were there beside her. "It's not good for your body to be so drowsy. Maybe you should make an appointment at a clinic."

"I don't need a doctor to tell me what's wrong. I'm just not sleeping well," I explain.

"Still? It's not normal to have such problems sleeping. There could be something wrong."

"My head is overloaded. That's all. I just need to stop thinking so much in bed."

That's a simple way of putting it.

I can't fall asleep because I'm too busy stalking Darren's social media accounts in hopes that he'll post some sappy quote about missing me or that maybe he'll avoid that altogether and just fucking call me.

It's been six months. Six. The longest we'd ever gone without speaking before this was *zero*. It hadn't happened since before we met. From the moment we exchanged names, we became inseparable. Even during our "break," we were in constant contact.

Everything about this has felt wrong in a million different ways. I've had to convince myself too many times to admit not to buy a last-minute plane ticket to Calgary and fly to see him. I thought the risk of him seeing me and telling me to get lost was worth it, until suddenly, it wasn't.

I can't hear him tell me we can't be together again. I just can't.

So instead, I've been here, miserable, alone, and awake until the birds start chirping because I can't get this guy out of my goddamn head.

"I'll send you some of my sleeping pills. They'll have you sleeping right after supper," Grandma declares.

"You're not sending me contraband."

"Oh, it's not illegal to take sleeping pills, Delaney."

"You never know. Campus security is pretty strict. They could be screening our call as we speak," I tease.

"Oh, how I miss you, my girl."

A hollow sensation grows in the pit of my stomach. "I miss you too."

"I know you don't want to come back here, but I would really appreciate if you came to see me. Not just for a day, but a few of them, if you can swing it," she says, suddenly serious despite the easy conversation we were just having.

I straighten in my chair. "What's wrong? Are you okay?"

"I'm okay. I wouldn't ask unless it was important. You know how much I miss you, don't you?"

"Of course I do. I'll come, Grams. Let me just head back to my place so I can check the calendar. Give me like ten minutes."

I'm already up and shoving my shit into the oversized book bag she got me for my birthday by the time she says, "Don't rush on my account. I can wait for a text."

"No, I'll get you an answer while we're already talking."

"Delaney, take a breath," she soothes.

I do that, feeling my lungs suck in the air greedily. "Sorry."

"You make me one hell of a lucky grandmother to have a granddaughter like you."

My throat clogs as I toss my bag over my shoulder and leave the table. Maybe I hit the shoulder of the rude guy from earlier on purpose, or maybe . . . yeah, it was on purpose.

"Are Mom and Dad okay? Grayson?"

She scoffs. "Yes, they're fine. I was serious when I said everything was okay."

"Just triple-checking."

"You know, I saw Poppy the other day. She stopped me and told me about the studio she's wanting to open. You'll never believe it," she says, segueing into another topic I'd rather avoid.

It's spring, but it feels like summer already. Unfortunately for me, the heat doesn't stand a chance against the cold rush coming that follows the sound of Poppy's name.

"Let me guess," I mutter, hurrying down the main path through campus. "A pole studio."

"She told you about it, then? You've started speaking again?"

"No. That was just her plan for a while now. I figured it was only a matter of time before she went for it."

"This is ridiculous. A boy should not get between you, even if it is Darren," Grandma says with a huff.

"He was always going to get between us. They're siblings. I'm just the ex-girlfriend. I knew she wouldn't stay in contact."

"That doesn't sound any less ridiculous."

"Let it go, Grandma."

There isn't anything to do now but hope that when I finally do come back home, I get not only my best girl friend back but her brother too. That was always the plan, even if things have gotten more complicated than expected.

"Fine. But we're talking about it again once you get home."

"In that case, I'm actually busy for the foreseeable future."

Grandma laughs. "We both know you'd miss me too much to stay away much longer."

She's right. I miss Cherry Peak more than I'll ever admit.

Darren

"Get the fuck up, Darren. You're lying on my sweater."

I drape an arm over my eyes and ignore the hand slapping at my back. Exhaustion barks at me, reminding me that it's probably still the middle of the night.

"Get. Up. It's under your stomach."

Rolling onto my side, I expect to fall onto a cool mattress. The immediate jolt of pain in my shoulder as it rolls over hardwood is the opposite of that.

"The hell?" I grunt, my voice sounding like it belongs to someone else.

The backs of my eyes burn when I open them completely and get blinded with the sun. I close them again and manage to lift a numb arm behind me to shove the person bugging me away.

"You look like shit."

"Thanks."

"I mean it. And you stink. Shower and get some breakfast before your sister comes to get you."

"Poppy?"

"Do you have another sister I don't know about?"

"You're an asshole in the morning, B."

"Yeah, I am. And you're an asshole all the time lately. Including last night."

I ignore that, too tired and hungover to dig into it. Instead, I force myself into a sitting position and hiss as my stomach rolls. "Why am I here?"

"You showed up at two in the morning. Drunk, might I add. Again."

"I don't remember that," I admit.

"I doubt you remember much of anything with how drunk you were. Hell, you're still probably drunk. It's only eight."

"In the morning?"

Bryce crouches in front of me and pushes out a breath that smacks me in the face. She shakes her head while pinching my hair between her fingers and tugging.

"You need a haircut. And to shave your face."

"I'll get right on that."

"And cut it out with the sarcasm. It makes you sound like a prick."

I swat her hand away and pull my knees up. "I didn't come here to get chastised. Poppy would have done that for you if I'd gone home."

"You've been avoiding her, and it's making her upset," she says, standing and disappearing into her kitchen.

The property she's renting from her parents is big enough for her and maybe a cat. I'm only lying on the floor, and it feels like the place has shrunk. I don't know how long she plans to live here, but as long as she's happy, what the fuck does what I think matter?

"All Poppy wants to do is ask me about her. If she's so curious, she can text her herself," I snap.

"You can say her name, D."

"I'm good."

"Alright. Or you could just cut this entire thing out and fly to Vancouver to get her back. This is downright pathetic."

I whip out a cold laugh and struggle to my feet. The world tilts and spins as I swallow the throw up trying to find its way to Bryce's floor.

"I'm not talking about this," I manage to say on the way to her bathroom.

Bryce follows. "And what good is that doing? You're not in Calgary at school, and instead, there's a mould of your ass on a stool at Peakside. Everyone's worried about you."

"Let it go, Bryce. I said I didn't want to talk."

The bathroom is hardly big enough for me, let alone the both of us. That doesn't stop Bryce from forcing her way in after me and leaning against the sink to watch me heave over the toilet.

"Is this what you want to do instead? You want to drink yourself to death every night and flunk out of school? A school that you worked hard to get into, by the way. You were almost at the top of your class, and now you're close to flunking out. I know for a fact that Delaney wouldn't want that for you. Nobody does. Not me, or your sister, or Brody either. You need to get yourself together before you do something you regret."

I palm my knees and look up at her with a glare that would have anyone other than her running for the hills. The tightness in my throat garbles my words, but I don't give a shit.

"When I want your input on my terrible life choices, I'll ask for it. Until then, butt out."

Her smile is dark and angry. "Alright, tough guy. If you want to ruin your life, you go ahead and do that. But my door isn't going to be open for you to crash through when you're too scared to go home and deal with the other people who care about you. You can find a park bench to sleep on."

"Fucking fantastic," I spit.

Bryce scoffs a single laugh before leaving, slamming the door behind her. The nausea gets worse following her exit, but when I finally lose the battle and have to heave into the toilet, it isn't the alcohol's fault.

37

Delaney

I DON'T KNOW WHY I EXPECTED THINGS TO BE DRASTICALLY different after this weekend.

Monday morning hasn't brought anything new with it, other than this constant flutter in my stomach every time I get a spare moment to check my phone and see Darren's name. I've been single for so long that I've completely forgotten what dating entails. God, dating. Is that even what we're doing now? The lines are still pretty blurry.

I blame that on all the vodka I consumed.

Sunday was quiet, and I almost felt awkward being alone at my place, behaving as if nothing had happened after Darren walked me home the night before. It wasn't exactly a romantic moonlight stroll, but it was reassuring, and now I guess I just have to wait and see what he's going to do next.

Darren's the one with all of the experience, after all. Even if said experience was a failed marriage where he didn't even share a bed with his wife. That tidbit of information has been repeated a few times in my head since he said it.

My lunch bag is open, the contents splayed out on my desk

as I pick at my wilting salad. It's been almost four hours since I replied to his text, and now it's like a switch has been flipped and I'm anxious, sixteen-year-old Delaney all over again. Lunch is almost over, and the second the bell rings, my classroom will no longer be empty.

I tap my screen and steal another look to see if I've missed his text, but nope. Still nothing. Chewing on my lip, I type in my passcode and open our texts, reading back through them.

Darren: Good morning, Elle.

Me: You're up early.

Me: Good morning.

Darren: I do have a real big boy job, you know?

Me: Oh wow. I thought you just got paid to sit at home and stare out the window.

Darren: That's what you thought I did? Not ran a secret account on Only Fans or something?

Me: You do have nice feet.

Darren: Keep complimenting me and I'll let you see them. Socks off.

Me: Is that what we're doing for our first date? A foot peep show?

Darren: It will be once I change our plans for tonight.

Me: Tonight? What if I had plans already?

Darren: Cancel them.

I didn't reply until I got to school, more for my mental health than as an attempt to keep him waiting, although that was also a bonus. In my mind, the closer I texted to the start of class, the less time I'd have to sit and do nothing but wait for a reply, right? *Not right*. It turns out that my plan backfired worse than an old car in the high school parking lot because now he's making me wait.

> Me: Making demands is brave. Try again.

Ugh, what have I done?

"Can I spend my recess in here with you?"

Abbie's standing in the doorway, holding on to the same bag that she had in the café with both her aunts. The sweet smile on her face is adorable, but it's not the only reason why I wave her close.

"As long as I'm not out on supervision, you can always sit in here during recess."

She beams toward me. I pull a chair up to the other side of the desk for her and sit back in mine.

"What are you having for lunch?" she asks.

The heavy bag in her arms falls to the desk beside my salad container, a few bags of beads rolling out. I take a bit of pride in recognizing what all of the different kinds of strings she pulls out next are for. I'll take any kind of bonus points when it comes to Abbie, and it seems taking part in her bracelet-building sessions earns me the most.

"I made this salad this morning, but it's not great. I'm more of a Greek salad kind of woman, but all I had was plain lettuce and ranch dressing in the fridge," I explain.

Abbie crinkles her nose. "I don't like lettuce."

"I don't blame you."

"Do you have other food?"

"I already ate my chocolate," I admit, almost sheepishly.

"Do you want to share mine?"

"You have chocolate in that bag of yours?"

She giggles and pulls the last of her supplies out before

revealing maybe the most important part of any crafting session —treats.

"Dad always makes sure I have some just in case," she says, shaking the bag of chocolate pretzels.

"He's a pretty good dad, isn't he?"

Her eyes light up as she rips open the bag and sets it between us. "He's the best."

"Well, do we have time to start a couple of new bracelets? There's fifteen minutes left of recess."

"Yep!"

I sit and wait while she gets me the right amount of string and ties the end before offering me my choice of beads. The purple ones grab my attention, so I choose them and get started.

"Did you give my dad the bracelet you made before?" she asks.

I gulp. "No. I didn't get a chance."

"Because I hit you with a door? I'm sorry. It was an accident."

"Oh! It's okay. I know it was. I'm fine, anyway. Good as new," I rush out.

Abbie smiles in reply and slides an L bead onto her string. Watching her concentrate on something she truly loves doing helps settle some of my anxiety about her father. If we were all as unbothered as a seven-year-old, there wouldn't be even a quarter of as many awkward or tense situations as there are.

Sitting in the comfortable silence, I grab another shade of purple beads and start alternating between the two. Abbie doesn't seem to have to think about what she's doing because she just . . . does it. Her fingers move quickly but sure as she starts on the last half of her bracelet. I pick up my pace, casting her curious looks every few seconds.

When there's a knock on the classroom door, she doesn't so much as blink, let alone look toward it. I, on the other hand, do and immediately turn bright red.

"Is now an okay time?"

I stand, my heart trying to leap through my chest. "Yes. Hi. Come in."

"Hey, Elle," Darren drawls, my name rolling perfectly off his tongue. When his eyes flick to the opposite side of my desk, he adds a surprised "Hi, sweetheart."

"Dad? What are you doing here?"

He reaches up to pinch the brim of his hat, almost appearing a bit embarrassed to have been caught here. "Uh, you forgot your pen at home."

"My pen? Which one?"

"The pink one."

Abbie frowns, her lips twisting as she thinks about that answer. I hold back a laugh at her confusion and focus on her father. It's not like I want to jump to conclusions, but it looks a lot like he came just to see me.

"Did you need a bag for her pen?" I ask, the tease coming naturally.

He looks down at the one in his hand, as if he forgot it was there. "Well, that, and something else."

I hum, leaning back in my chair as he starts toward the desk. His outfit is very different than the ones I've seen him in recently. More professional, with a dress shirt and tight-fitting jeans. The hat is still there, though, like it always is. And did he trim the mustache? Because it almost fades into the new scruff on his jaw like he spent a few minutes in front of the bathroom mirror this morning.

He stops a couple of feet away from me and reaches into the bag. First, a bag of Twizzlers appears, and then, a frosty bottle of cherry Coke. Two of my favourite things in the entire world and the reasons behind my occasionally high blood sugar.

I roll my lips together, looking at him and melting. It's not supposed to be this easy, but I'm already doubting that I'll be able to make him work for anything. At this rate, I'll be the one begging him for a chance, and that's totally unacceptable. *We haven't even gone on a date yet, Delaney.*

"Are those for me?" I ask, my tone even as I fight not to give myself away.

His tongue slips across his teeth as he grins and chuckles. "They are. I mean, I had them in my car, so I figured you might like them."

"You keep unopened licorice and cherry Coke in your car?"

"He does! I usually eat the licorice. I'm not allowed to have the Coke, though," Abbie says, focused on tying her bracelet together. "I ate half the bag yesterday."

Surprise flickers through me. He reads my mind, nodding in silent confirmation.

"That's a coincidence," I whisper.

Darren sets everything on my desk, his fingers lingering. "They always find their way into my grocery cart. Almost like I can't help myself."

"I'm not complaining."

"Good."

"Are you leaving now, Dad?"

"Geez, are you in a hurry to get rid of me?" he asks, reaching over to tap the underside of her chin.

"You're distracting Ms. Delaney."

I let out a soft laugh and shrug. "You heard her."

"Oh!" Abbie shouts, making me jump. "His bracelet. Give him his bracelet!"

"What bracelet?" he asks, staring directly at me despite speaking to his daughter.

"The one Ms. Delaney made you at the donut place. Before I hit her in the nose."

My skin burns beneath my heavy blouse. I tuck my hair behind my ear and attempt to play this off with a loose laugh. "Oh, I don't know where I put that."

"You made me a bracelet?" Darren asks, of course not letting it go.

"I was bored."

"And thought of me."

"Don't get ahead of yourself. You were just the topic of conversation, and I wound up making something for you. That's all."

"You're a terrible liar," he taunts.

"And your ego is showing."

"Would you prefer I tucked it away?"

I roll my eyes, rolling my chair until my legs are trapped beneath my desk. "The bell is going to ring any minute."

"I'd better leave, then."

"You should," I reply, immediately wishing he didn't have to.

With Abbie distracted, Darren slides forward and places his hand atop mine, leaving it there while he kisses her forehead. I hold my breath as he squeezes my fingers and then slowly retreats, taking his touch with him.

My skin tingles with the lingering warmth from his hand as I stabilize my breathing and look up at him again, eyes growing lost in the certainty glimmering in his.

"I'll see you later," he promises both of us.

Abbie glances up for a quick moment. "Bye, Dad!"

I can't speak louder than a whisper. "See you."

He's reluctant to leave; I can see it written in every clunky footstep he takes toward the door and the lines between his brows when he looks back at me over his shoulder. I offer him a smile that feels heavy in the moment as that stubborn string between us throws a hissy fit in my chest.

It's not until he's out of view and I watch as my phone lights up at the desk that I release some of the tension that's grown in my limbs.

> Darren: Well? What do you think? Will you please let me take you out tonight?

> Darren: Please say yes. And don't forget my bracelet.

I almost say no but can't get myself to type anything other than a resounding yes.

38

Darren

I SHOULD HAVE PICKED HER UP.

Shit, did I already mess this up? My one chance, and I ruined it already by not fighting her on her decision to meet me at my place instead of being picked up properly. It's not like it would have taken that long. I could have been there and back before the grill got to cooking temperature.

Instead, I'm pacing in my kitchen while the chicken breasts and salad chill in the fridge beside the three bottles of white wine that I couldn't choose between at the store earlier. I haven't seen the house cleaner that it is right now, and that's a bit more embarrassing than it should be.

I reach up to squeeze the brim of my hat, but my hand swipes hair instead. Fuck. My hat is still in my bedroom, abandoned. Both Poppy and Bryce threatened me with no babysitting for the next three years if I wore it tonight. Apparently, there's a time and place for a baseball cap, and a first date with your high school sweetheart isn't one of them.

Sliding open the patio door, I take a deep breath. There won't be many more nights where I'm up to cooking on the deck with the snow approaching. I'm bitter about that, considering I'm a chef who sucks at everything that isn't chucked on a hot grill. If I get the chance to cook for Delaney again, I'll have to try not to reveal my lack of skills in the kitchen.

I keep the door open but venture into the living room. The DVDs on the coffee table are old, with scratched disks and faded artwork, but for tonight, they'll be perfect. Most of them are Delaney's, anyway. After all these years, she needs the option to take them back.

The three knocks on the door are staggered awkwardly and light enough that I nearly don't catch them. In a blink, I'm twisting the doorknob and staring at her through the fogged glass window.

Even the early look can't prepare me for what I see when I open the door. My knees wobble as I tighten my hold on the door and let loose a whispered "fuck."

With her platinum hair twisted and tied at her back, Delaney slowly lifts her eyes from my feet to my awed stare. The corners of her glossy pink lips curl slightly, giving a tease of a smile that only makes me want to try really fucking hard to see the real thing.

I break eye contact just long enough to do a sweep of her, top to bottom and back again. Expectations didn't exist tonight, but even so, she managed to destroy any that I could have ever had. The black tights, burnt-orange dress with the sleeves flowing down to her wrists, and knee-high, heeled boots shouldn't look this good on anyone. Yet, Delaney has a way of making everything she wears look custom-made. The boots make her legs look a million miles long, and the dress is loose yet still clings to the pinch of her waist and curves of her chest. It's the perfect look for her, and fuck me, I'm so screwed tonight.

Swallowing the excess liquid in my mouth, I tighten my grip on the doorknob and find her eyes again, trying my best to make sure she can see just how blown away I am with her before I open my mouth to tell her.

"You look phenomenal. You're gorgeous," I rasp.

Her blush is pink enough to show beneath her makeup.

"Ditto. You look very handsome. And you're not wearing your hat."

I run a hand over my hair. "Yeah, I figured I should prove to you that I haven't balded in the last ten years."

The jump of her brows is followed by a rough, coughed laugh. I join in, too far gone to be embarrassed.

"Thanks. I appreciate that," she says between coughs.

"Anytime. Though maybe I'll save some of these moments for when I'm not trying to impress you. I'm not interested in losing more points tonight."

"What other points have you lost?"

I watch as she bends down and starts unzipping her boots. The sight of calves hasn't really turned me on before, but maybe that's because they weren't hers, and when they were, I wasn't paying this much attention to them. When Delaney was mine, all of her was. Now . . . I'm growing more fascinated by all of the parts of her that I never gave the proper attention to before.

"Not insisting on picking you up, for one. I've always picked you up."

"I'm not sixteen anymore."

"Oh, I'm aware of that," I mutter.

She looks up from her second boot. "What does that mean?"

"Slow, Elle. We're going slow, right?" I ask, pressing a hand to her back to stabilize her when she tugs off her boot and loses her balance.

"Delaney," she corrects me briskly. "And what? Your answer wouldn't follow my rules?"

"Not in the slightest."

"Okay."

She stands, and I keep my hand on her back while guiding us through the entry and into the living room. The gold chain around her neck and cupping the base of her throat makes the one I'm wearing itch. I wait for her to say something about the house, but she stays quiet, her attention floating around the room.

"It's pretty small. The house," I say, needing to fill the silence with something. "I never meant to stay here forever. There aren't enough rooms, especially now that Abbie's started using the guest one for her jewellery making. I'd like a real dining room too. Especially now that my sister's moving closer and we're going to need somewhere in town for holidays. Our parents' house is too small, and Poppy mentioned wanting kids soon—"

"It's beautiful, Darren. This is the house you used to draw in your sketchbook all the time, right?"

I furrow my brows, letting my hand fall when she moves further into the space. "It is. With a few changes. The one I used to draw wasn't exactly affordable for me at the time. I barely got the mortgage for this place."

She wanders to the wall of built-ins and examines the lack of books on the shelves. There are photos of Abbie on nearly every single one instead.

"I'll get more books for them eventually," I say.

Her teasing smile makes my stomach flip. "Maybe a few fake plants instead?"

"That's probably a better idea."

"I never took you for a magazine guy."

The stacks she's talking about are the ones Poppy forced me to keep. Each copy has an article featuring a piece of architecture that I was involved in creating. From this place to Brody and Anna's house on Steele Ranch and a few other apartment buildings in Calgary that I built with the company I work for. I've had a successful career, but it's never meant anything to me more than that.

Not when I've been celebrating my accomplishments alone.

"I'm not usually. But you know how my sister is. She buys five copies of every edition with my name in it and makes sure everyone has a copy," I say.

Delaney chuckles softly, nodding. "Yeah, I know. She sent me clippings of every article in the mail once we started speaking more."

"You've read them?"

"No," she admits, turning back to the stack of magazines. The tips of her fingers run along the bottom edge of the first one. "I couldn't get myself to."

"I don't blame you."

"Can I read them now?"

I pause, frozen in place. "You don't have to. They're pretty useless."

"They're not useless, Darren. Your talent has been noticed in a very public way. That says a lot about how great you are at what you do."

"Alright. Read them," I murmur, letting it go. "I'm going to get the food dished up."

She'll piece together why I didn't want her to read them here the second she opens the first magazine.

"What did you make?" she asks before I get too far.

"Worried I made something you'll hate?"

"No. I'm more worried I'll eat too much and wind up too bloated to sleep tonight."

Pride rushes through me. "Chicken with Greek salad."

"Did Abbie tell on me today?"

"About chicken and salad?" I ask, playing dumb.

Delaney glances away and picks up the magazine before a low, soft laugh escapes her. "Go away now."

"I'll be in the kitchen."

Five minutes later, I'm slicing the last half of my chicken into chunks when the air shifts. Her tight-covered feet help muffle the sound of her footsteps as she joins me at the counter, examining the food I've made. I keep silent, finishing with my plate and pulling hers closer before picking them both up.

"Table or living room?"

Her reply is lagged and wispy. "Living room."

I carry our food out of the kitchen and set both plates on the coffee table. Delaney sits on the couch while I grab the first movie on the stack and get to work. The DVD player sucks in the disk before I switch the TV onto the proper settings and join her.

"Those are all my movies," she states, sitting with her knees touching and hands folded above them.

"You can take them home with you tonight. I've held on to them long enough."

"What if I don't want to take them home?"

It's impossible for me not to read too far into that question. My mind immediately fills with a list of the million reasons as to what she means and the reason behind the question before I blurt out, "Why not?"

She moves. Suddenly, her knees are tucked beneath her, and she's facing me, expression half-broken and half-disbelieving. The clash of emotions is strong, rocking through her to me, even with the distance between us. She sets her arm on the couch back and tips forward enough for her knees to hit the outside of my thigh.

"You had ten years, Darren. Ten years to build me a house that you dreamed of with all of my favourite quirks and additions. Where you'd make me my favourite food, spend a night watching all of my favourite movies on a couch just like this, but beside me. You had every chance in the world to get me back, but you didn't. You waited, and waited, until I became so secluded from my old life that I feared so much as hearing your name in public.

"All this time apart, and you were giving interviews for magazine articles mentioning me and us and a past that used to keep me up at night with tears in my eyes and an ache in my chest. Now, I'm left with knowing that I could have been here sooner. You married someone else, and I thought and hoped that you were happy doing that. At least, enough to stay in that marriage for years longer than you should have. I never said anything to you, or anyone, about it because I assumed you knew what you were doing. But you didn't, did you? Because all this time, you've been wanting me just as badly as I've been wanting you, and I don't know what to do with that!"

She doesn't give me a chance to respond before dropping herself in my lap and taking my shirt in her fists. I swallow, my body coming to life in a way that leaves me breathless, unable to fill my lungs.

"I've been in love with you for half my life, and you didn't fight for me. You told me to go and didn't chase after me. I've been waiting for you to do that for eight years. At every street corner, knock on my door, and my grandma's funeral, I hoped you'd show up, needing me as badly as I needed you. I needed you at the funeral, Darren, and you weren't there."

I slide my hand behind her head and lean forward, bringing our faces an inch apart. Her eyes fall shut as an exhale drifts across my lips.

"I was there," I whisper, blades sinking into every corner of my stomach.

Her lashes flutter as she stares at me. "Where?"

"The funeral. I was there, but I stayed back beside the Steeles. You were grieving, Elle. I didn't think it was the right time to show up beside you. It wouldn't have been fair after everything that happened."

She presses her forehead to mine and shoves me into the couch.

"Kiss me, Darren."

39

Delaney

I DON'T WAIT FOR HIM TO DO IT.

A second is as long as it takes for me to seal our lips, fifteen years of love between us rekindling with a smack. I use my hold on his shirt to keep him anchored down, unable to slip free just yet. It's unnecessary. Darren uses the hand in my hair to drag me with him as he leans his head back against the couch and then takes my hip into his hold.

Moving with him is the most natural thing I've ever done. It's as simple as breathing but as enthralling as sitting at the top of a roller coaster, counting down the seconds until you drop. I don't know where the confidence in my actions is coming from, considering the lack of experience I've had, but maybe that's just how it was supposed to be with him.

He makes everything easy because he's the only one I was ever meant to do this with.

I release his shirt with one hand and slide my fingers through his hair instead. *As fucking if he'd ever go bald.* The hair curling around my fingers is soft and lush, and I have to pull on it to keep from letting it slip free.

We're supposed to be talking tonight.

The movie intro credits have ended, and the pop-up menu

for *Legally Blonde* keeps replaying the same song on the TV speakers. Our dinner is growing cold on the table behind me. Steak and a Greek salad that's heavy on the tomatoes and cheese, just the way I like it. There's an article still open and perched on my dream built-ins with my name printed alongside Darren's, featuring a photo of his bathroom. And he was there. He was at the funeral.

Screw talking. This is the only thing I want tonight.

"Elle." My name is a weak groan on his tongue.

"Only tell me to stop if you mean it."

"I won't be able to let you go after."

I pause, retreating one lonely inch. "It's about time."

He pushes forward, reclaiming my mouth with a demand that creates a blooming pulse between my thighs. I suck in a sharp breath at the pleasure and shiver, my nervous system crashing. His hands abandon my hair and begin to roam with the new approval. From my neck to the curve of my breast and to the flat of my stomach, he touches me softly, like he's nervous to press too hard.

I breathe out against his mouth and keep my hands where they are, unsure in a way that he doesn't seem to be. He remembers where to touch me, and I bite the inside of my cheek to keep from moaning when his fingertip strokes the sensitive underside of my ass.

Surely, it's not supposed to be this hard, but I'm out of practice. So much so that I realize I've stopped kissing him with all of my thinking.

"Did I go too far?" he asks, slightly breathless despite our lack of movement.

"No. No, I'm—" I swallow and drop my eyes, staring at the gap between our bodies. "You heard me. At Peakside."

There's a shift in me as he rolls his jaw, nostrils flaring. "I heard you, Delaney."

"So, you know how out of practice I am."

"You're not taking more inches tonight than my fingers can

offer you, baby. No ridges or rainbows either," he drawls, dipping his head to kiss beneath my jaw.

My throat bulges against his lips and the sear of his tongue. "It's not only that. I'm out of practice with everything."

"Everything?"

"Yes, Darren. Stop making me repeat myself."

His eyes appear when he focuses them on me again, the brown deeper, darker than when I arrived tonight. "Do you think I'm not also out of practice? What you see right now is a guy trying to remember the way you liked to be touched ten years ago and hoping I don't do anything you don't like. You're different now. Even if we hadn't been apart, your body isn't the same it was then. Mine isn't either."

He takes my hand and pushes it down his chest. Wide-eyed, I watch as it moves further and further down until he slides the hem of his shirt under my finger.

"Explore me, and I'll explore you, Elle. Just like the first time we ever touched like this."

My moan is involuntary, but I feel the tensing of his abdomen in response to it. Carefully, I lower myself flat to his lap and sit back to make room to take over for him. I pinch the bottom of his shirt and start to work it up his body, exposing an inch of skin and then another.

He releases a tight exhale when I follow the shirt with my other hand, letting it stroke the bare skin I expose. The muscles he had in high school have changed. Grown thicker and stronger beneath the new trail of hair leading beneath the band of his jeans. There's so much more of him now, and I'm having trouble comparing this new him to the one who took my virginity.

It hits me hard. The rush of heat beneath my skin mixes with the electric thrum in my ears, driving me to move quicker. Suddenly, his shirt is above his pecs, and I'm clawing at it, desperate to be rid of it.

He hesitates to help me get it over his head, but before I can ask him why, he's pulling it off and dropping it on the couch beside us. I jerk forward on his lap and hiss a breath when I feel the outline of him beneath me. That's definitely still the same. I forgot . . .

"What is that?" I blurt out, my gaze snagged on the chain around his neck.

Or more specifically, the ring dangling from it.

Darren loops his finger through the ring and lifts it off his chest. "It's your ring."

"My ring," I repeat softly.

"Your promise ring."

"Why?"

"It's yours," he states bluntly, voice gruff and deep.

A bone-deep shiver moves through me. I hold his shoulder and roll my hips forward, searching for the press of his erection against me. The length of him beneath my middle chases my shock away, replacing it with a pleasure so sharp I lose my ability to breathe.

"When you want it back, I'll hand it over. Until then, it's staying right here," he says tightly. Hands bracket my hips, guiding me back and then forward again.

"Darren," I gasp, spine straight and my head falling forward to watch us move together.

"Not like this, baby. Not after this long. Let me make you come properly." His face scrunches, almost like he's in pain. "Please."

My eyes nearly cross at his plea. "Yes. *Yes*, do that."

He shoots off the couch with me in his arms. I don't even have a chance to hold on to him properly before I'm falling back onto the couch. This time, he's above me, and I'm sinking into the thick cushions at my back.

"I should have made sure you were fed first," he murmurs, staring down at me with this sense of . . . claiming. Like I'm something he's been coveting all this time and finally has in front of him.

I'm starting to believe that's exactly what I am.

"I'm not hungry."

His eyes rove all over me, the muscles in his jaw tight. "I am."

"We can eat first," I murmur, fighting the nerves.

"My appetite doesn't involve anything besides you, Delaney."

I throb between my legs. It's strong and slow, lingering. The tightness in my breasts makes my nipples scrape my bra, heightening the need for relief. I start to close my legs when Darren lurches forward and holds my knees, keeping them spread.

"Has anything changed?" he asks while lowering himself to his knees.

"What do you mean?"

His smirk is criminally filthy. "Do you still like to be touched the same way, or has anything changed with what you need to get off?"

"Isn't that cheating?" I ask between sharp inhales.

Fingers stroke my calves and then behind my knees. Not even the tights can hide the goosebumps on my skin.

"You're right. I'll figure it out for myself."

There's no time to ask him to clarify exactly how he plans to do that before he's lowering himself to his knees once again, this time between my parted legs. I choke on nothing and hold my breath while he glides my dress up my legs. He leaves a hand there, holding the hem of my dress while another sneaks beneath it to rub circles above the band of my tights.

"I only need to know what you're okay with me doing, Delaney. Tell me if there are lines I can't cross with you tonight because I don't trust myself enough not to take things too far once we get started. I need you to give me boundaries."

"I thought you already decided what we could and couldn't do tonight. Nothing longer than a finger."

His head falls forward as he groans and squeezes my lower thigh. "That's my boundary, not yours. Give me something else."

"No."

It's settled.

Darren looks up again, and I shudder all the way down to my toes at the starving look in his eyes. I'm weaker when it comes to him than I originally thought, but right now, I don't see anything wrong with that.

"You can always change your mind," he promises.

"I know."

Watching him hesitate after being given approval, I decide it's up to me to convince him that I really am okay with this. My dress is soft in my hand as I lift my hips and pull it out of the way. His hand is still frozen on the band of my tights, so I take the other side and push them down.

He watches with unbreakable concentration as I tap his fingers and urge them to do the same thing. We both stare at the nylon as it moves down my thighs and my black, lace panties appear.

"Fuck," he mutters, his voice as tight as it is garbled.

I let that word run up my body before the heat of his palms smothers all other sensation. He creeps my tights down to my knees and leans over them, his shoulders pulling taut. The first stroke of his fingertips up my inner thighs yanks a mewled noise up my throat. I pant and let my head rest back against the couch as I sag into the cushion.

"You're still sensitive here," he notes, stroking me again.

The only thing I can do is nod.

My tights move to my ankles next. Darren lifts my right foot and takes the nylon off before moving to the left. Once they've joined his shirt on the floor, he moves between my legs and kisses each thigh. His mustache scrapes at my skin, bringing with it a sensation new to us.

I glance up at the ceiling when he loops my leg around his waist and brings his face to my centre. The puff of his breath across my panties is overwhelming in the best way. I'm not used to the sensation anymore.

"Darren, you don't have to be . . ." I start.

He steals every thought from my mind once he mouths something I don't recognize against my panties. My vision disappears when his mouth closes over my clit and sucks. Leg jerking where he's got it around his side, I let loose a desperate noise that I think encourages the growl-like sound in his throat.

"Don't have to be what?" he asks, digging his teeth into the lace and pulling. The rip that follows is the sexiest sound I've ever heard. Suddenly, I'm bared for him. "On my knees? It's the only place I should be, Elle. The only fucking one."

"I haven't done this in years," I rush out, my lungs constricting around every quick inhale I manage. "I'm not sure I can come like this anymore."

Two fingers slide over my slit before they spread me. Darren grits his teeth and presses the pad of his thumb against my clit, rubbing it softly. "If it works when you do it, it will for me."

"Oh, my God."

"Stop thinking and let me make you come, baby."

I listen. It's too hard to think when he sinks a finger inside of me, anyway. The pressure of his thumb is perfect as he starts flicking his wrist, his finger spearing into me at a slow, consistent pace. My lip burns from how deeply my teeth are buried, but I can't remove them without risking screaming as the zaps of pleasure create a wet mess between my legs.

"You're perfect," he declares, almost like a prayer.

The wet slap of his palm meeting my swollen pussy with every glide of his finger heightens the intensity. I'm holding on to the cushion as I thrust against his hand, my muscles quivering. The ring—my ring—slides back and forth across his chest as he moves, increasing the intimacy of this moment.

"I sound . . ." I whimper, leaning forward on the couch to try and see us better.

It's a desire that I've never had before. The intense need to watch us together, as if that'll make it feel real instead of like a dream. Darren doesn't question what I'm doing. He helps me instead, reaching with his other hand to support my body as I hold myself up and watch him add a second finger.

The sight of us together is enough to make me come, but I shake my head, refusing.

"Nice and slick for me? Yeah, baby. You are. Don't fight it. It's not the only time," he bites out, the gleam in his eyes downright feral as my arousal slips down his wrist. "I have a decade of missed time to make up for, so get me fucking wet and come."

"Not yet!" I cry, digging my nails deep into his shoulder.

"Pull the top of your dress down."

It's hard in this position, but he keeps me in the same upright hold as I stop supporting myself and rip at my dress. I shove it down beneath my breasts before doing the same with my bra, needing that off too. My nipples harden into painful peaks, and I pinch one before I can stop myself.

"Fuck yes," Darren spits, low and dirty. His pupils expand, eating at the remaining brown before his body shakes and his thumb slips from my clit. "Jesus fucking Christ, baby. Come for me."

His desperation is the hottest thing I've ever seen in my life. The pleasure spreading across his face draws out my orgasm like it knew exactly where I'd shoved it away, and I give him what he wants. I don't know if I scream or cry or shout because the world goes black as I reach a release I haven't had in . . . maybe ever.

Falling back into my body, I heave in a lungful of air and slouch into the couch. I'm sensitive with my muscles twitching and even a little sore as I focus my eyes on the man now bent over me, my ring swaying where it hangs.

"I'll be right back," he murmurs, kissing my forehead.

I reach for his hand, stopping him. "Where are you going?"

A bashful smile spreads his lips. "To change my pants."

"Did I . . . get them dirty?"

I've never squirted before, but at one time, I'd spent an entire evening trying to learn how. I was never successful, but Darren can do things with my body that I simply have never been able to. It wouldn't surprise me all that much if he accomplished that tonight.

"No. That was all me."

My eyes bulge as I drop them to his crotch and spot the wet patch. "Oh."

"That's a first for me. I didn't even come in my pants when we were teenagers dry riding in the back seat of my car."

"I'd have remembered if you had."

He chuckles, bending down to kiss my lips this time. "I won't be long. Then, I'll heat up your steak."

"Okay," I agree softly.

There's a very obvious drop in my stomach when he leaves the room, and I know exactly what that means. I miss him already, a.k.a. I'm so screwed.

40

Darren

"Is it your plan to stay in your grandma's house?"

Delaney swallows her sip of wine and brings the bottom of the glass to rest against her knee. The pink tint on her cheeks is still there from earlier, and I'd like to think it's from happiness now rather than lingering arousal. Even if I wouldn't take offense to that either.

I'd just like to believe that she's happy enough here with me that her body's unable to hide it.

"I never planned on living there at all. But it's not like my parents were or have been much help with anything since she passed. I'm still going through all of her things, sorting them into sell piles to keep and give away. She has a storage locker in town, so that's where I've been bringing whatever I decide should be kept. It's just been easier to stay there full-time."

"She always did have a lot of stuff," I muse, stroking my thumb over the bare skin of her ankle.

From the moment I got back from the bathroom, I've been at Delaney's side. It's like I'm afraid to be gone for too long in case she changes her mind and I come back to find her gone. After I came in my pants like a prepubescent, I wouldn't blame her.

I should have seen it coming. She thinks she's inexperienced, but in reality, so am I. I've been celibate since the night Abbie was conceived. However, I don't know if she knows that.

"Was this your master plan after all? To get me relaxed so that I'll be more open to talking about my grandma?" she asks, but there's no anger or defensiveness there.

I may have slipped my shirt back on, but that hasn't stopped her from curling into my side and toying with the ring hidden beneath it. She hasn't left it alone since after we finished eating, and I'm still trying to piece together what that really means.

If she wanted it back, she'd have asked for it. That's what I'm waiting for.

"You know me too well, Elle," I coo, unable to keep my lips to myself and skimming them over her hair. "I want you to talk about her, but only if you feel comfortable doing that."

"She was always trying to get me to come home to see her. The tricks got so good that I'd max my credit card on flights back just to find her sitting at the kitchen table with a deck of cards already shuffled and ready for us."

I grin, resting my chin on her head. "That sounds like her. Blackjack?"

"With nothing to bet besides a few sour green grapes and a tub of cottage cheese."

"Shit."

Delaney takes another swig of her wine, the light in her eyes staying bright. "I miss those moments the most. The thoughtless fun she could always create."

"I remember the time she brought a crib board to one of my games and had a crowd of high school students around her begging to join by the time the third quarter started."

"Oh, she had a big head about that for weeks."

"It was deserved. Everyone loved her and misses her. You're not alone," I say softly.

"I wish I'd have felt like that."

"The entire town let you down."

She shrugs before setting her glass down on the coffee table and tucking her legs beneath her. Leaning into me again, she sighs, cheek rubbing against my shoulder.

"I don't hold it against them. When I left for school, I think there were more than a few people who felt betrayed."

"It wasn't fair. Still isn't. You didn't owe anyone here anything. Vancouver is a part of who you are now, and that isn't going to change."

"Everything is mostly back to how it was before I left. I think I've been almost completely forgiven," she notes.

"I love this town, but the loyalty that's expected from you when you grow up here can be suffocating. It's not fair."

Her head turns as she stares up at me, an expectant expression on her face. "Yet you wouldn't live anywhere else, would you?"

"Not unless you wanted to."

"Oh, don't start. You would not move away from Cherry Peak for anyone."

I pull back and pull all of my focus onto her. "You're wrong. I'd move anywhere for you."

"It will never be that simple. Abbie needs to stay here."

"Not forever."

Her smile is gentle and so beautiful it makes my chest throb. "Where is she tonight?"

"With my parents. They jumped at the chance to watch her when I brought up needing a babysitter."

"I always wondered what their reaction was to you telling them you were having a baby. I'm assuming your mom was a blubbering mess?"

I swallow as those memories try rising to the surface. "She was, but they weren't entirely happy tears."

"I'm sorry."

"I was fresh out of college with a degree in my hand that I didn't know how to use yet and no money to my name. My parents were always going to let me move back in with them until I found a job and saved enough to get my own place, but they weren't expecting me to be bringing anyone with me. Let alone a woman they didn't know who was pregnant with their granddaughter."

I clear my throat, but it doesn't help stop the words from flying out of my mouth. Not now that I've finally let myself talk about this.

"They hid it well, but I know they were disappointed in me, and they had every right to be. I was raised better than the way I acted before and after I found out about the pregnancy, and they didn't know what to do with me or that or anything. Everything just . . . fell apart around me. I was a terrible fucking father for months after Abbie was born. Sasha dealt with more than she deserved from me, but we were married, and I told myself that meant we were together for life, whether we were miserable or not, which we were. Constantly." My laugh is venomous and angry. The years of self-hatred I've worked through left a lingering sting that I'll never be able to get rid of. "Everyone thinks it was me who issued the divorce, but it was her. She had read the interview I gave in the article you saw earlier and slammed it down in front of me one night with the divorce papers already drawn up. After three years of a loveless marriage, she was hoping that I'd have *built a bridge and gotten over her* by now."

"Her, meaning me," Delaney says simply.

"You've always been the 'her' when it came to me and Sasha. I've made too many mistakes, Elle. I did so many things wrong. Too many people were brought into my shit. You, Sasha, Bryce, Poppy, my parents. Everyone who cared about me, I hurt because I was too mad at myself to see a way out of the funk I'd fallen into."

Emotion clogs my throat as I stare ahead at the TV and the second movie we've started tonight. It's been years, but I'm still carrying a lot of baggage. The same baggage that I'm now expecting Delaney to be okay with seeing on my back, like a permanent reminder of everything we've been through.

Gently, two fingers sweep along my jaw before guiding my face back toward her. I hold my breath, waiting for her to tell me that she's changed her mind and what we had is just too complicated to replicate. It would be fair, after everything.

She doesn't look at me like she's considering leaving, though.

"Twenty-two feels old at the time, but it's not. It's naïve, hopeful, and feeling weighed down by the expectations that we feel like we need to meet. We're still learning who we are and who we want to be, Darren. Making mistakes is what we're supposed to be doing, even if that includes hurting those we love. I'll never forget what happened between us, or the way I felt because of it, but I don't have the energy to keep convincing myself that I hate you for the mistakes we made. And you shouldn't either. I'm starting to see the kind of man your mistakes turned you into, and I think they paid off."

I don't know who moves first. All I can think about is how good it feels when she's draped over my body and our lips are touching.

We kiss slowly, with small breaths exchanged between us and hands exploring. She finds my chain and rolls it between her fingers while running her tongue along my bottom lip.

"You didn't drink your wine."

I hum, gliding my tongue over hers. "I don't drink much anymore."

"Why?"

Grabbing her thigh, I tug it up to curl around my hip. "It clouds my judgment. And with you, I'd like to be fully present. I've already missed too much time."

"Mm, alright."

"There's dessert," I whisper.

She drops a hand to the cushion beside my head and pushes herself up, wiggling like she wants to slip out of my arms. "You're just mentioning that now?"

"I was a bit preoccupied."

"What is it?"

"Chocolate cheesecake."

She drops her head and moans into my ear. It's a devilish little maneuver that has the exact effect she was hoping for. My dick stiffens in my second pair of briefs, twitching against her pubic bone.

"It's in the fridge chilling. We can leave it there for a while longer," I muse, running my fingers up the length of her spine.

She arches a brow, pressing herself down on my groin. "And what could you possibly want instead?"

"I'm not picky."

"You're still a hopeless flirt at thirty years old."

"It's been a long decade."

"You never even went on one date? With anyone?"

"Not even one," I admit.

Her tone swoops slightly, revealing a lingering pain when she asks, "Sasha?"

"No."

"How is that possible?"

"When Sasha and I . . ." The flinch on Delaney's face nearly kills me. I ignore the fresh slash of regret and continue. "She was at a party over near Oak Point, out by the campground. I was so drunk I didn't even remember how I got there, but she found me leaning against the shop, drinking my body weight in whiskey. It was the one and only time we slept together, not like that's much of a defense. Once was all it took. But there were no dates. No kissing or hugs. We spoke enough to have dinner together with Abbie or to pretend we weren't at each other's throats all the time while taking her for walks downtown. At home, if there wasn't a crying baby or a toddler throwing a tantrum, it was silent."

"That sounds lonely," she murmurs, blinking away the gleam in her eyes.

"I wasn't the only one of us that was lonely, Elle. At least I was still here. I had my parents and friends. Who did you have?"

"My grandma."

Releasing a heavy breath, I shake my head and bundle her up in my arms again. I drag my hand up and down her back, trying as hard as I can to soothe the hurt that I know she's trying hard to hide.

"I'm sorry."

"You don't have to keep apologizing," she tells me.

"Yes, I do."

"We can't change what happened. It's the story of us, I suppose."

I press my forehead to her temple and hold her a little tighter. "The story of us. I like that."

Her lashes flutter, tickling my throat. Silence creeps in before she pushes it back.

"Please don't break me again."

My heart gives a hard kick. "Breaking you would destroy me, and I can't survive that again."

"You promised not to do it once already."

"I won't make that promise again. I'll prove it to you instead."

Even if it takes me another decade.

41

Darren

My parents' door is unlocked when I give it a yank and then step inside.

Nothing's changed in here since I was a kid and my dad tried his hand at renovations. They ended up having to call in a professional to fix everything he touched, which cost them triple what they thought they were saving by doing it on their own. Now, they've just embraced the out-of-date features and lack of storage space.

Leaving my shoes at the front, I step over Abbie's sneakers and search for where everyone's hiding. It's only seven thirty, but since my mom's up at five every morning, I know she's already gotten Abbie's ready to go by now.

It's been hard to keep my cool all morning after being with Delaney last night. Mom would have lost her mind and run over half-awake in her slippers if I'd actually called her this morning like I'd contemplated doing. It's been a long time since I've been so happy about something to call her about it, and I've been clutching onto that since I woke up.

"You look well rested this morning, sweetheart," she pipes up before jumping out of nowhere and attacking me with a hug.

I steady myself and return the gesture. "I slept good."

"Finally."

"You're telling me. Did my daughter?"

"Of course she did. We went to the playground, and as I suspected, she ran circles around me."

"So, you also slept well?" I ask with a chuckle.

Mom twists to the fridge and pulls out a jug of orange juice. I reach over her head and grab a tall glass, handing it over.

"I always do when my grandbaby is here."

I take the glass of juice when she offers it to me. "Thank you for watching her for me."

"You don't have to thank me! I don't get enough time with her anymore."

"Blame school for that. It's such a time hog," I tease.

Moving around her, I put the juice away and steal a yoghurt to have on my way home. She eyes the container in my hand and huffs.

"Let me make you a real breakfast. You need more than a yoghurt."

I wink while sneaking past her into the hall. "No time, Mom. Where are you hiding my daughter?"

"I'll never tell!"

My laugh fills the quiet hall. Every door is open besides Poppy's old one. Even years after moving out, she refuses to give it up and let Mom turn it into her home gym. Unlike me, who made peace with my room turning into our dad's storage locker.

The soft singing coming from the spare room snatches my attention and makes me smile moments before I see Abbie twirling in front of the bed. She's using the end of her hairbrush as a microphone and singing the lyrics to a song I don't know but can guess Poppy taught her. The curls in her hair flop in the breeze she's creating with her spins, making her laugh.

I step into the room and start to clap. "Encore, encore!"

"Dad!" she squeals before running into my arms and clutching me tight. "You're already here."

Smoothing a hand down the frizzy hairs at the top of her head, I give her a squeeze and then let her go.

"It's seven thirty, you diva. I figured your grandma would make us stay and eat something before school."

"You're taking me today?"

"I am. Your mom will be there to pick you up after. We just had to switch things around a bit, but you'll be with her the rest of the week."

She tosses her brush onto the unmade bed. "Okay. Can we bring something for Delaney?"

"Bring her what?"

"Breakfast. She eats those crunchy bars in the morning. The gross ones."

I swallow a laugh, knowing exactly which bars she's talking about. They're the same ones Sasha keeps trying to put in Abbie's lunchbox despite her smashing them to bits inside the wrapper and bringing them back home.

"You can sure try."

"I like her," she states bluntly.

"Delaney?"

"Yep. She's nice. I teached her how to make my bracelets, and she liked them."

"She's pretty great, sweetie. You should tell her what you told me. I'm sure it would make her happy."

"Grandma likes her too. She said so."

Abbie skips past me out of the room after dropping that bomb, and I follow quickly after her. She makes it to the kitchen mere seconds before I do and starts talking to my mom.

"Grandma, Dad said we can bring Delaney good food," she urges, taking a seat at the table.

"That's not exactly what I said."

My mom spins to face me, an all-knowing grin on her face. "Oh, don't take it back now, Darren."

"Mom," I warn lightly.

"What? I think it's great that your daughter is enjoying her teacher so much. That bond is an important one," she says, eyes twinkling.

I stand in the same spot and stare at her, trying to reveal what I'm thinking without having to say it in front of my daughter. Delaney doesn't want her to know about us yet, and as much as I wish we could tell her already, I know that's the right call. While I'm certain about her, that doesn't mean she won't change her mind, and my daughter can't be a casualty of that. Not when she's still got to sit in the same room with her for the rest of the school year.

"Abbie, how about you go tell your grandpa to leave the shed alone and come inside for breakfast," Mom says.

I nod when Abbie looks to me for confirmation.

"Be right back!" she announces while hopping out of her chair and racing for the back door.

The second it swings shut behind her and we hear Abbie call out for my dad, I take a seat at the table and prepare for the questions.

Mom takes the seat opposite me. "Why didn't you tell me that Delaney was her teacher this year? It's already October."

"Would you have cared who the teacher was if it wasn't her?"

"Probably," she declares before shifting in her seat. "Maybe. If I thought about it, I would have."

"I didn't want to tell you until I knew what exactly I'd be sharing."

"And? You know that now?"

Her enthusiasm is welcome, even if I'm acting like a hard-ass. I've missed seeing her happy while talking about Delaney.

"She came over last night for dinner."

Mom jumps out of her chair and whips open the fridge. She pulls out the same jug of juice she offered me and bypasses a glass, opting to drink right from the spout instead. I laugh under my breath and watch her have a mini-freak-out.

"Sorry, I'm overwhelmed," she announces.

Waving a hand, I say, "Oh, go ahead and let it out. It's just us here."

If my sister were here, then I'd be hauling Abbie out immediately. I can deal with both women separately with things like this, but together? My dad and I run for the hills as soon as we can.

The juice gets slid into the fridge again before Mom spins back to face me and breathes in through her nose.

"How is our sweet girl, Darren? Is she okay? Happy?"

"She's good. More beautiful than ever and just as witty. There are extra freckles on her nose, even with it being fall, so I think they've just multiplied. And— Why do you look like that?"

Mom scoffs, cutting a hand through the air before turning away from me. "I'm not looking at you like anything. I'm listening to you talk about the woman you love. Stop bothering me."

"Are you going to cry? Should I get some tissues?"

"Don't make fun of me, Darren!"

"I'm not, Mom. I'm just asking if you're going to be okay before I say anything that's going to send you over the edge," I explain, teasing just a bit.

She gasps, diving right in. "And do you have something to share of that calibre?"

"It's for real, Mom. I got my chance, and that's that. No wrong turns this time."

"If you're teasing me, I'm going to punch you in the face."

I choke on a laugh. "Pretty sure you're not allowed to say that to your son."

"You can when they're thirty years old. It's an unwritten rule," she argues before huffing and swerving back on topic. "Don't distract me. I need to hear you say all of that one more time."

"The whole 'I have my person back, and I won't let her go again' thing? Do you mean that?"

Despite thinking I was ready for this, her sob takes me aback.

It rattles me, creating a glitch in my brain that leaves an opening for her to attack me with another hug. She kisses the side of my head over and over.

"I've been waiting for this for years. This is the way it was always supposed to be. Our Delaney is back."

"Not officially, Mom. I'm still working on it, but it's looking good. She wants to be careful, and I don't blame her. We're keeping this from Abbie for now."

"Good. Smart. She's too precious." Taking a step back, Mom swipes beneath her eyes. "I was so worried about Delaney. I've been struggling with not forcing my way back into her life."

The stacks of homemade, frozen meals in the garage freezer that I spotted a week after the news of Delaney's grandmother started to spread were gone the next day. Mom never mentioned to me where she took them, but I always knew. She might be my blood, but she's always seen Elle as another daughter. I couldn't bring myself to ask if she'd seen her since she brought the food to her, but even if I did, she wouldn't have told me with the state I was in. If I had to guess, though, I'd say no. Not with Abbie and Sasha being constants in my life.

"I don't think she would have minded you trying, Mom. Not then and not now."

Hope fills her expression. "Really? Is that your approval?"

"It's my approval. But you'll need hers. Just try not to overwhelm her, please."

"Never. Oh, I've been so jealous ever since Poppy started blabbing about all the time they've been spending together. It was torture! Please, let me cook her dinner. Invite her over this week, I'm begging you."

"That might be too soon," I argue, unsure.

"Abbie's with her mother, so she won't have to know. Just at least ask Delaney. If she isn't comfortable with that yet, then I'll wait."

"Alright, I'll ask. But don't get your hopes up just yet, alright?"

She nods, even though I know she's already done that. "You got it."

I crook a half-smile and hold my reply when Abbie comes back inside with my dad in tow. The man who raised me is tall and intimidating as hell but has shown his bleeding heart to me and my sister more than his stern scowl damn near every day. He's kept up the tradition with my daughter.

"Hey, Dad."

"Morning, Darren," he mumbles.

"Breakfast! I'm going to make breakfast!" Mom announces, already setting herself in motion.

Dad checks his watch. "It's quarter to eight."

"I'll be quick. Sit and talk to your son while I cook."

"Yes, dear."

I laugh and keep an eye on them for just long enough to see Dad steal a kiss from Mom before joining me. Abbie takes the seat between us and starts rambling about school while Mom sneaks a look at me and grins.

It's enough to confirm that the moment I leave, she'll have Dad completely up to date on everything we've just talked about. And I'm glad, because it's about time they're allowed to.

42

Delaney

"Why are we at Steele Ranch?" I ask.

Darren taps the steering wheel. "I'll give you two guesses."

I stare out the window as we pass the tall, heavy gate with the Steele Ranch sign and crawl up the gravel road. It's been years since I've been here. Over a decade, at least.

The largest cattle ranch in Alberta is the same as I remember. Open, bright, with rows upon rows of thick trees along the road leading up to the ranch house that seems to expand and expand the closer we get. There's a second stable across the way, settled beside the original but far newer. Beyond them, you can see out for miles and miles, nothing but empty pastures and the towering scape of the Rocky Mountains.

I pat Darren's thigh as he starts to turn us onto the grass in front of the ranch house. "Mm, are we here to pet the donkeys?"

"And risk having my ribs dented when I piss one off? No chance."

"Oh, I know. We're Eliza's special baking testers."

"I'm pretty sure Johnny and Brody have that covered, unfortunately."

I pout and remove my hand. "Well, then I don't know why

we're here. Surely, you didn't bring me here to go horseback riding."

Silence.

"Darren . . ." I start cautiously.

"We deserve a redo. The last time you were on a horse, we were young and too obnoxious to actually try. I want another chance."

"You can't be serious. This isn't a date idea— it's a sure way to piss me off!"

He reaches for my hand, taking it despite my stiffness. Bringing it to his lips, he kisses each one of my knuckles, as if I'm so weak-willed to let him have his way with a few kisses.

"Please, Elle? Don't you want to do something out of the box with me? Live a little to make up for the time we lost?"

My pulse skips at the intensity in his eyes. I groan, scowling at him. "You're such an ass."

"Me? Are you sure?"

"There better be something incredible in it for me after this, or I'm going to be one very, very grumpy girlfriend."

"Girlfriend?" he teases, almost purring at the term.

My scowl grows deeper before I exit the car and close the door *very* pointedly.

"You're not escaping me that easily," he calls, his door closing.

I stand in front of the hood and cross my arms, waiting for him to join me. "Is girlfriend not the correct word for what I am to you?"

"Do you think that's good enough?" He closes in on me and runs his fingers up the length of my arm. "It doesn't feel like it to me. You've been my girlfriend once, and I lost you."

"And you think that it will be different this time because we won't label me as that?"

He cracks a smile, cranking my temper. "Not exactly. I just consider girlfriend the term couples use when they're still on the fence about long-term commitment."

"And you're . . . not on the fence?"

"No, baby. I'm long term or no term with you."

Heat rushes through me from my toes to the tips of my ears. "So, no girlfriend, then."

"No girlfriend. You're just mine. My Elle," he declares, voice low and rasped like it was when he was between my legs last weekend.

The reminder of those hours together sparks the dormant lust that's been driving me crazy for days. I'm not doing well with the lack of time we've been able to spend together this week, but with both of us fully devoted to our careers, things were always going to be different from what they were when we were teenagers. Days are long and nights are short. There are so many hours available to see one another, and unfortunately, we haven't been able to fit each other in much besides sporadic texts and calls.

Today is exactly what I needed, even if we're at the ranch instead of snuggled on the couch again. It's the best way to end a long day of teaching high-intensity children.

"I can live with that," I tell him.

His smile is bashful while I wrap a hand behind his neck and pull him down to kiss me. I sigh against his lips, too happy to hide it.

Darren palms my waist and jerks me toward him. I laugh at the sharp movement, and he does it again, as if he just wanted to hear me laugh again.

"Well, I can't say that this isn't a bit startlin'."

Brody's voice interrupts the moment, but I linger, unable to back away just yet. I steal one more kiss from my not-boyfriend before trailing my hand down his body and linking our fingers.

"You've got amazing timing," Darren grumbles at his friend.

"It's good to see you, Delaney. Too bad you're here with this grumpy guy."

I grin, soaking in the banter. "Oh, he's not always grumpy."

"Only when I've got a buzzkill sniffing around," Darren says.

Brody snorts a laugh. "If you'd prefer, we could skip the refresher lesson, and you could try helpin' Delaney jump on a horse without me."

The deep brown cowboy hat on his head keeps his eyes shielded when the sun flashes in our direction. I squint and lift a hand to try and block it from burning my retinas. It's painfully ineffective.

Darren draws my attention when he slips his hand free and shifts behind me. I open my mouth to ask what's wrong when suddenly, there's a hat on my head. His hat. My pulse skips, contentment drowning out every other feeling inside of me.

The brim of the baseball hat droops down my forehead for all of a second before Darren's tightening the strap at the back. When he removes his fingers and stands in front of me, the hat fits perfectly.

"Better?" he asks, hovering.

I start to ruffle his hair now that it's not covered, and he lets me without complaint. The light in his open eyes exposes how similar he feels to the way I do.

"Perfect," I answer softly.

"It's not the same as a Stetson, but I'm sure the rule still applies," Brody states, humour colouring his tone.

I take a step to the left and stare at him. "Do you still use that rule in your big age, Brody?"

"My big age," he echoes, laughing. "We're the same age."

"Exactly."

"I think she's calling you immature, Pop Star."

"Pop Star?" I ask.

Brody groans, and Darren answers, "He's our resident pop star, Elle. Big and important, this guy. You should hear the drama that comes out of his mouth before a show."

"I'd think Diva would be more appropriate, no?" I tease.

Brody starts toward the road, not giving us a glance back. "You know what? We're goin' to the stables now, and if you keep teasin' me, I'll be trappin' you in there for the day."

"Are you sure you don't wanna change into your fancy boots before we go? Are those ones comfy enough for you?" Darren taunts.

I choke back a laugh and elbow him. "You're going to get us left in the middle of an empty field."

"We both know I'd be the only one left. The girls would come get you the second Brody left."

"It's time you learnt the art of bribery, then."

He drops an arm over my shoulders and tugs me as close as he can without me losing my footing. Ten minutes later, Brody's bossing him around with the adjusting of Sky's saddle while I lean against a pen door and watch.

The horse I'm riding today, Honey, is Poppy's. She was the only reason I ended up agreeing to ride solo instead of with Darren on Sky. It's nothing against Sky. Darren's the one I don't trust on horseback. Not with my life, at least.

I'm pretty sure he'll be pouting about that for days.

"I bet Johnny would have been a bit more patient," Darren says, huffing when Brody slides open the door and guides Sky and Honey outside.

"He would have, but my grandpa gave him the day off, so he's been out riding with Rory. Haven't seen them since breakfast."

Darren nods. "I thought the stable looked a little empty."

"Joker and Frost have been out at his place for a few months now. The construction on his stable finished a bit later than they expected."

"Where's Johnny's place?" I ask.

Following the instructions Brody laid out for us in the stable, Darren pulls himself onto Sky's back and says, "You know the cabin up by the road?"

"With all the trees?"

Brody leaves Darren and comes to me next. Honey's tack is very Poppy, with pinks and even a light sparkle that glistens in the sun. I'd bet Garrison had it custom ordered for her.

"That's the one," Darren says, his voice wavering with a silent laugh.

My blood runs hot. "Oh."

Looking between us, Brody starts to groan and scrunch his face. "You're kidding. Here? On the ranch?"

"Don't fucking say it like that. I know for a fact you had sex in this very stable when you were sixteen," Darren retorts.

"But in the cabin? Does Johnny know that you defiled his home?"

"We didn't defile his home!" I argue, debating fanning my face. "It wasn't his place then."

Darren adds, "And it was *very* respectful sex."

"Alright, that's enough of that. I'm already goin' to have to decline his invites over for a few months, maybe years now," Brody says with a dramatic sigh.

"Give it up, Diva. Help my girl up on her horse so we can go before we scandalize you more."

I meet his stare and shake my head, smirking. He winks at me before I focus on mounting the horse. Brody stands close, but I can almost feel the watchful glare coming from Darren every time he tries to help me. The stool works wonders for me, and finally, I get myself up.

"Alright. I'm goin' to let Johnny know that you'll be on your way, and he'll check on you every few minutes. Keep to the road, and the horses will do all the work for you. Are you sure you don't want me to come with you?"

"It's not my first time on a horse, Brody."

"You've only had a few lessons, though."

"Lessons," I ask, startled. "When did you take horseback lessons?"

Darren shoots daggers where Brody stands.

"A few weeks ago," Brody answers for him.

"Why?"

Reluctantly, Darren lifts his glare and looks to me. The sheepish expression on his face calls to me.

"Just in case."

Instead of asking more questions here, I let it go. Brody's a great guy, but he's not who I came here to spend time with. Especially with all of these revelations appearing.

I lift a hand to the road. "Ready to go?"

"Very."

"Just keep your phones on you, and call if you need anythin'. I'm still sendin' Johnny to check on you," Brody calls when Darren leads Sky into action. "I'll be here when you're done!"

Honey follows Sky without needing me to tell her to, and I swallow my nerves when we get onto the road. Moving side by side, the horses bring us together. I look over at Darren and grip the reins.

"Is there a reason behind why you wanted us to do this ride here that doesn't include going on a date?"

"This place is special to us. It's not the same as the drive-in, but we've made memories here."

"It feels different now," I confess.

"Everyone's older. They're gone doing their own things. Rory and Johnny will always be here, Anna and Brody too, whenever they're not gone touring. Bryce will stay as long as Daisy wants to. But even with Poppy's new house, she'll still be hours away. Her life has expanded far beyond Cherry Peak."

"We always knew she would be the one to leave. Her dreams were too big for this place. There aren't enough possibilities here."

"I know. It's been hard, though."

Nerves swirling, I transfer the reins to one of my hands and use the other to reach across the gap between us. He chuckles and does the same, taking my hand.

"How is the house designing going? You have to be close now, right?"

"We're working on finalizing the plans next week. For a guy who claimed he didn't care much about what the house looked like, Garrison's been the one with all the changes," he says.

"This is their forever house, isn't it?"

"For all this effort, it better be."

I release a light laugh. "A forever house needs to be perfect. Let them be picky."

"Have you thought much about your forever house?"

His thumb draws circles on the back of my hand as our arms sway between the horses. I dart my eyes across the space to find his already there, watching me with a soft certainty that electrifies me.

"It would be here. Plenty of bedrooms so everyone had a place to stay if they drank too much during game nights and a fireplace in the master bedroom. I'd want a mountain view too."

He hums. "What about a yard? How big?"

"A chunk of land would be nice, Somewhere I'd be able to have a garden and a pool in the summertime."

"With plenty of trees," Darren adds, keeping my eyes hostage.

"It would be a beautiful house."

"Come over this weekend and have dinner with my parents," he says, voice soft and low.

My hand almost slips free, but he clutches it. "What?"

"Mom extended the invitation when I picked Abbie up Monday morning. She really wants to see you."

"I don't know. Isn't that too soon?"

"I don't think that exists with us," he argues gently.

My initial response is yes. Spending time with Darren's mother was always a no-brainer for me. At the time our friends were nervous to spend time with the "in-laws," I was excited. They were always like family to me.

But things aren't the same as they once were. Sure, it's not like I'm meeting them again, but so much time has passed.

"Don't talk yourself out of saying yes, Elle. We both know what this is now. We're not dating. This isn't something fleeting."

I can't admit that to myself yet.

"Will your sister be there?"

"No. I wouldn't overstimulate you like that already."

I can't help but laugh at that. "Okay. I'll have dinner."

He answers with a squeeze of my hand and a grin that makes my nipples tighten beneath my sweatshirt. It's a tilt of his lips and a promise all in one.

One that tries like hell to convince me that this time will be different. All I have to do is believe it.

43

Darren

I HAVE TO GIVE MY MOM SOME PROPS FOR NOT RUNNING OUTSIDE like a feral animal the second she heard my car pull up. She opted for the watch-from-the-front-window approach instead. I glue my lips together to keep from laughing when the curtains move around the moment we step onto the porch.

"I'm nervous," Delaney whispers, panic in her eyes.

I cup her face and drop my forehead to hers. "It'll be fine. They adore you."

"They *used* to adore me."

"They still do. Mom's made all of your favourite foods, and I'm not exaggerating. She's never done this for me."

Her nerves break enough for a glimmer of excitement to appear. "Really?"

"Really. She sent me a giant list of things for me to double-check before her grocery trip. I think you'll be very, very happy when we get inside."

"Thank you," she says, voice low and soft.

I reply with a kiss to her crown before opening the door. My mom all but falls out onto the porch.

"Oh! You're here!" she cheers, as if she had no idea. "Daryl, Delaney and Darren are here. Woah, that's a mouthful."

"It's cute that you're pretending you weren't standing with your nose against the door, Mom," I tease.

Delaney curls her arm around my back and stays close while slipping her shoes off. They aren't knee-high boots this time, thank fucking God. I couldn't have handled seeing them tonight without risking a hard-on at my parents' table.

"Leave me alone, Darren. I'm trying to take a look at Delaney," Mom scolds.

Chuckling, I lift a hand and shut my mouth.

Delaney straightens and says, "Hi, Pauline."

"Hi, my darling," Mom rushes out, her voice shaking. "Hug?"

Delaney lets out a breath. "Hug."

I step aside before they launch into one another's open arms. Mom holds her with an unbreakable grip, keeping her locked in her embrace while Delaney sniffles and holds her just as tight. I swallow past the emotion in my throat and glance into the living room at where my dad stands, watching.

He meets my gaze and nods, saying nothing yet everything without needing words. I look back at Delaney and reconfirm what I already know. What's been screaming at me during every silent night I spent alone at home and buzzing in my ears when I should have been focusing on a presentation or speech at work.

This is right. Everything here is the way it was supposed to be. And now, we're finally back on the proper path.

"You're even more beautiful than you were the last time I had a proper look at you," Mom whispers, stroking a hand down Delaney's hair. With a firm hold, she grabs her shoulders and pulls back to smile at her. "And Darren was right about the freckles. There are so, so many more now."

"Darren was talking about my freckles?" Delaney asks, darting her eyes in my direction.

I wink, palming her back and guiding her to my side. "Don't get a big head about it."

"What else did you say about me?"

"Where should we start?" Dad asks, joining us.

He's more cautious than Mom was. While Poppy got her outgoing nature and bubbling personality from our mother, it was Dad who taught me about patience. To spend so much time with both women in one place, we both needed it.

"Welcome home, Delaney," he adds.

There's a fist sailing through my gut. I press my fingers harder into Delaney's back, needing the touch for my suddenly failing balance.

"Thanks, Daryl," she whispers, something heavy passing between them. It feels a lot like appreciation, but I don't know what for.

Mom shakes herself and clears her throat. "Okay, come inside now. We have so much to catch up on. Do you still like chicken parm, love?"

"I haven't had it in forever, but yes, I do."

"I told you, Mom."

Delaney shoots me a curious look. "And how did you know?"

"Good guess," I tease, dropping a hand to swat at her ass when my parents turn away.

She squeals, jumping away from me. I blink innocently and steal a kiss, risking getting bitten in the face. Her blush makes it easy to see through her scowl.

"Have you both checked on the drive-in? I was at the last town council meeting, and it's supposedly at the halfway mark," Mom says, expertly ignoring us.

She's had more than enough practice with that over the years. Poppy and Garrison have ruined her, I fear.

"No, we haven't," I answer.

"Well, you should. Make sure they aren't ruining your place like they did the flowers at the entrance to town."

"You're comparing the drive-in to some flowers?" Dad asks.

"They're not just some flowers, Daryl. They're an outsider's first impression of the town. What impression do two planters of droopy, brown flowers leave, hmm?"

"You could offer to help with the flowers," I suggest as we step into the dining room.

The food is already spread along the table on serving platters, and shit, she's even pulled out the good plates and stored the old, chipped ones she refuses to donate.

"I'm waiting for them to ask for my help, honey."

Dad laughs under his breath and takes his usual seat at the table. Mom sits beside him, and I pull Delaney's out across from her. The hiss dad spits falls over the table before Mom pats his shoulder.

"Pull out my chair next time."

Delaney's cheeks pinch with a subdued smile. She sits, and I join her, sitting a bit too close, probably. The warm press of our thighs is a good reminder that yeah, she's actually here beside me right now.

"Anyway, like I was saying, it might be worth a trip out. I wouldn't be able to stand it if they ruined that place," Mom says.

I grab the bottle of white wine that I know Delaney likes from our dinner date at my house and offer it to her. When she nods, I take her glass and fill it while saying, "I'll ask Bryce tonight and let you know, Mom."

"I'd appreciate that. I'll worry myself sick unless I know."

Handing the full glass back to Elle, I set the bottle down, grab the juice pitcher, and fill my glass. Luckily, it's not the same one Mom drank out of. At least, I hope she only did that once.

Delaney crosses her legs beneath the table, and I stifle a groan, imagining what she's wearing beneath the skirt now pulled taut at her knees. It's a curse being so consumed with these thoughts recently. I'm suddenly a horny teenager again around her, and I still don't know how to shake myself out of it.

She's too goddamn beautiful. Her and those soft legs and perfectly sloped knees that her skirt has been flirting with all night are going to drive me to insanity. I've never given a shit about knees before, yet here I am, fantasizing about their slope and how full they'll fill my palms.

Then, there's her hair. I've become so accustomed to her wearing it back or up, but not tonight. Nope, she has it free and wavy and teasing my hands every time I touch her back. I've caught myself starting to wrap it around my knuckles so many times in the past hour alone that I'm not allowing myself to touch her there anymore.

Fuck, I smacked her ass a foot away from my mother.

"Darren?"

The pinch in my thigh has me jerking in my seat. I look to Delaney and see her staring at me, both of her eyebrows raised.

"Pass your mom the juice," she murmurs, face bright red.

I stare for a moment longer, confused as to why she looks embarrassed. It's not until she pinches my thigh again and draws my gaze to my lap that I rush into motion.

"Here, Mom."

The juice nearly flies into her waiting hand. I gulp and grab a plate of food to try and take my mind off the raging erection I'm hiding beneath the table. The same one Delaney saw and went beet red over.

"Thank you. Is there any update on the Abbie decision?" Mom asks, not mentioning my behaviour.

I fill Delaney's plate on instinct, my dad doing the same with Mom's. "What decision?"

"Are you going to tell her about your relationship?"

Delaney sucks in a breath, and I exchange the plate I'm holding for another. She doesn't answer, so I do.

"Not yet."

"From what I saw the other day, I don't think she'll have an issue with it."

"I know. That's not why we're not telling her."

"Alright, I'll leave it alone."

"Thank you," I mutter, freeing my hands so I can drop one to Delaney's leg.

She lets go of a breath that I know she's been holding.

"You didn't have to make so much food, Pauline. Really, this is incredible. Between you and Darren, I've been very well fed this last week," she says.

Mom glows at the praise. "It's my pleasure. We used to do weekly breakfasts with Darren, Abbie, Poppy, and Garrison, but with Abbie in school full-time now, we've switched to dinner. You're more than welcome to join us from now on."

"Oh, that's really sweet," Delaney starts. Her eyes flash up at me, and I wink, more than okay with that idea. "I'd like that."

Mom claps once. "I can't wait to tell Poppy!"

I lean to the side and drop my head, bringing my mouth close to Elle's ear. "Expect a thousand texts and a call when she does."

Her eye roll explains just how little that scares her.

"What do you usually do when you have the house to yourself like this? I assume that it feels even more empty than it is after you've had Abbie here for a week."

I hum and flick the lights on in the hallway. My bedroom is at the end of the hall, separated from Abbie's and the guest room. Delaney follows me, keeping a pace behind me as she takes in the photos on the wall and the pink sheets I forgot to shove in the laundry room before leaving for my parents' house.

"I'm usually working every night that she's not here. It keeps me busy."

"Ah, so that's why you used to walk around town looking like a zombie."

"That and a few other things that I haven't worried about in about a month now."

I shrug out of my sweatshirt and toss it into the hamper

before sitting on the edge of my bed. Waiting for Delaney to finally step into my room, I take my belt off.

"Are you planning on giving me a striptease?" she asks, eyebrows waggling suggestively when she joins me.

Her steps stop once she crosses into the room. Intrigue fills her expression as her eyes flit around, staring at my desk and the clutter across it before darting to my plain nightstands and then the open closet. I lean back on my hands and watch, waiting for her to come closer.

"Would you like a striptease?"

"It could be fun."

"Say the word, Elle."

Gradually, her eyes make their way to me. She sighs and finally crosses the room.

"Are you sure you didn't want to bring me home?"

I reach for her, filling my hands with her hips. She crawls onto my lap on her own.

"You are home," I murmur, kissing her.

Her lips press firmly against mine, meeting me with the same slow urgency. Her fingers run through my hair, brushing through it as I glide my tongue between her lips.

"Home is with you." A shiver runs down the length of her spine.

I break away long enough to rasp, "Yeah, baby. It is."

"Is it too soon?" she whispers between kisses.

"Is what too soon?"

She bumps my nose with hers and opens her eyes. "To want to . . ."

"Want to what, Elle?"

"To want to have sex . . . to go back to the way things were."

44

Delaney

It all just . . . comes out. The throbbing emotion that's clouded my thoughts distracts me from the fact that yeah, maybe it is too early.

It's only been a few weeks, but I just think I'm ready. I've been ready for a while now, yet I've kept myself away, too scared to fully recommit to the one person who's always held the most power over me. The one who can break my heart with a snap of his fingers or a shrug of a shoulder. Deciding to be with him again is as good as writing my name beside his on a shared gravestone. There won't be any take backs.

Darren's hands have turned to stone on my hips, weighing them down as his silence lingers. The crinkle between his brows is worrisome, as if he's trying to come up with an excuse to not take that step with me. I don't know what I'd do if those words escaped the lips hovering against mine.

"Or maybe it is too soon?" I ask cautiously.

That snaps him out of his thoughts.

His hold on me heats as he runs his hands up my sides. I gasp when he uses that grip to pull me until we're chest to chest, flush together. My stomach flips.

"It's never been too soon. Not with us."

"You're sure?"

"So sure, Elle," he mumbles before his mouth meets my jaw and then its sensitive underside. "Already told you that I'm not letting you go again."

My eyes flutter shut, threatening to roll into my skull as he sucks on my skin, teeth skimming, teasing. "So much lost time, Darren. I don't want to lose any more."

"We won't. Not again."

Letting those words soothe me, I roll my head to the side, offering him more space for his mouth. He takes it, scratching my throat and jaw and chin with his facial hair. I know it will leave marks, and I want it to.

"You'll have to remind me how to do this," I whisper-moan.

Darren nips at my throat before resting a hand at the base of my back and slowly leaning me backward. His lips work their way down my neck while I paw at the back of his, pulling him into me.

"Gotta remind each other, baby."

My stomach jolts. "Yes, please."

I push my knees into the mattress and straighten enough that I can look down at him. He drops his head back to look at me, the devotion blazing so brightly in his eyes I would have given in right now had I not already.

"Love looking up at you," he whispers, pushing my hair back when it drapes between us. "You're so beautiful."

I hold him too tight, like I'm scared he's going to turn into smoke and slip through my fingers. "Make love to me, Darren."

He groans, eyes squeezing shut. When they flash open, I'm being flipped onto my back, gasping.

"You don't know what it does to me when you say things like that."

"So tell me," I plead.

Crawling up the bed, I watch him follow, caging me beneath him. It's a prison I could live with never escaping from.

Grabbing my thigh, Darren lowers his groin to meet mine.

The hard ridge of his erection rolls over my core with a shift of his hips. Stars decorate my vision.

"You can feel what it does, Elle. What *you* do to me."

I bring my other leg to curl around his waist, opening myself up to him. My skirt isn't long, and I know he's been looking at my legs all night. Now, he has all the time in the world to do far more than that.

"Darren," I whisper, my gaze seeking his. Brown eyes focus on me, waiting. "Touch me."

There's a rumble in his chest when he brings his fingers to the pebbled skin beneath my skirt. Each glide of his fingers makes me shake, growing more desperate by the time he strokes the edge of my panties.

My mind shuts down, leaving me with nothing but white noise in my ears.

"I need them off. On the floor and out of my way," he rasps, in warning or as a promise, I'm not sure.

I jerk my head in a nod and keep still as he peels them off me, not noting their dampness until they're bunched in his hands. His throat jumps with a swallow as he drags his thumb over the wet spot in the silk.

"This is for me, Delaney."

"My panties?"

He slips them into his jeans before stepping off the bed. Fingers pulling at the button of his jeans, he says, "Those, but also the sweet pussy they were hiding."

I stop breathing, a deep, all-consuming shudder rolling through me.

He shucks out of his jeans and stands at the edge of the bed in a shirt and very thin, very tight briefs. The full outline of his erection is exposed, thick and proud. I clench between my partially spread legs and lean up on my elbows.

"Keep looking at me like that and I'll have another early exit, baby," he warns lowly.

I can't help it. "You're . . . bigger than you were."

"No, Elle. You've just forgotten."

Fuck. I can't wait any longer to get out of my top, the sensation of my bra digging into my skin too much right now. Darren watches in silence as I pull my top off and work on my bra, my heaving chest snaring his gaze.

Finally, I get it unhooked and let the cups slide, my breasts falling free of them. His jaw tightens, the tension in his muscles growing as he drops a hand to his groin and grabs his cock, massaging it.

"Come back . . ." I whisper.

He grips his erection harder. "Say it again."

"Come back to bed with me, Darren. I want you."

Releasing himself, he whips his shirt off and crawls up the bed. I spread my legs wider, still covered by my skirt but unable to care as he hovers his body over mine and kisses me. The slow pace is gone, replaced by one of fury. Of pain and pleasure and an endless ache that I feel echoed in myself.

I run my hands over his body, up his back and chest, exploring the new areas that I've missed out on touching all these years. The cool burn of his chain against my chest makes me moan, my hips jerking up to where he waits, bare and hard.

"Shit," he hisses, slowing when he slides through my sex, parting me. "So wet, baby. Jesus."

My entire body locks up, pleasure exploding in my belly. "Do that again."

"This?"

The length of him runs over me, between my swollen flesh and over where I'm wet and aching. He hits my clit, and I claw at him, lifting off the bed.

"I need to taste you," he declares.

Before I can reply, he's between my legs, mouth running along my inner thigh. He discards my skirt before getting back in position and pushing my knees up toward my stomach, covering me with his mouth. His tongue finds my clit, lapping at it like he's starving, craving this. I cry out, hands slapping at the mattress as I quiver between my legs, gushing onto his tongue.

"Darren, Darren . . . Darren," I mumble, mindless.

"That's it, Delaney. Remind yourself what my name feels like on your tongue while I stay right here."

I dive a hand between my legs to grapple onto his hair. "Elle. It's *Elle* to you."

Darren's eyes flare hot before he spits onto my pussy and glides a finger inside of me. "My Elle. Only to me. Mine."

My eyes cross. The breach is both familiar and foreign. It's only ever been him, but he's different. A man . . . mine. The thought has me tightening around his finger. He pulls my clit into his mouth and sucks, tongue lashing with a ferocity that sends me toppling.

I buck up, my legs falling and snapping shut around him. He slips his finger free and drags his tongue over my entrance, moaning as he looks up at me, forcing my eyes to focus on him.

"Now, Darren. Please—more," I breathe out.

He wipes his mouth with the back of his hand and moves back up my body. I wait for his kiss, but he waits, his hand moving between our bodies. When something smooth and broad runs over my entrance, he presses his lips to mine. I hold his shoulders as he pushes forward and sinks that first inch inside of me.

"Tell me if—" he starts.

I shake my head, our mouths rubbing. "No. No stopping."

His eyes disappear as he squeezes them shut and jerks his chin. I kiss him again, tasting myself. Darren moves deeper, the stretch biting now after so long since I've so much as used a toy. I gave up on penetration making me orgasm since I stopped being able to make it happen.

"Halfway there," he murmurs.

"It's so much already. I feel too full."

"You can take it. You've taken it before, baby," he soothes, a hand finding my chest and nipple.

Brushing his thumb over the tight peak, he jerks a bit further inside of me, grunting into my mouth. I tighten around him, pleasure sparking inside my core . . . the sensation so unfamiliar I cry out.

"Shit, you feel . . ." His words die when I clench again, on purpose this time.

"Slide the rest inside, Darren."

He pinches my nipple, rolling it firmly before giving in to my demand. Bottoming out, he stays still for a moment, eyes flicking between mine, searching. I bring my hand to his cheek, stroking it. He turns his face into the touch, kissing my palm.

The ring I once wore on my finger drags across my breast when he starts to move, rolling his hips with soft, testing thrusts. Adjusted now, I hold his vibrant gaze and rock with him. My mouth parts on a silent moan that grows in volume with every glide of him inside of me. He's so deep . . . it's like he's found a spot that's been forgotten and lost.

Pleasure coils low in my belly and spiders outward, zapping through my legs and up into my chest. I clutch onto him, feeling the raw strength in his body. Darren holds himself above me, the bulging of his bicep spiking the desire that also pools beneath us, wetting the sheets.

He's so fucking hot that I'm going to find myself beneath him all the goddamn time.

Reading my mind in the way only he knows how to, he smirks, a groaned breath escaping him before he's grinding down, pressing over my clit. I whimper, a buzz rising in volume in my ears again. I'm floating when he does it again, this time thrusting deep and hard at the same time. I scrape my nails down his back and fill my hand with his ass.

"Again," I demand, eyes wide and desperate.

"Again."

He gives me what I need, over and over until I'm mindless, his name a repeated call on my lips.

"Inside or outside, Elle?" he spits, feeling the tightening of my walls as I—

I wind my legs around him, trapping him in place, and keep him buried deep as I come. There's a shatter in my mind as my previous conceptions of sex are broken, memories of Darren replacing themselves with new ones. Old highs fading beneath the light of new ones.

Splashes of warmth fill me. Darren's sexy groans fill the room, intertwining with my cries.

"Fuck," he curses, jerking above and inside of me.

I take a long, deep inhale and nod, releasing my nails from where I've buried them into his ass cheek. Softly, I rub the wounds I've left and smile coyly.

"Did I hurt you?"

He scoffs a laugh before kissing me again, his breathing heavy. "Not a chance."

"Mmm," I hum.

"Give me a minute and I'll roll off of you. My head's all shaken up, baby."

"No rush," I murmur, petting the expanse of his back. "I'm comfortable."

"You're the one woman I've been unprotected with."

The subtle drop of that surprises me. I was aware he didn't use a condom tonight, and I made the decision not to tell him to. I'm grown enough to be careful.

"I guess I just thought with Sasha . . . ?"

"Broken condom."

Slowly, he pulls back and slides free before standing on his knees. His gaze drops to between my legs when I feel myself beginning to leak. There's hunger in his expression, there and gone in a blink.

"Oh." I pause, blinking. "*Oh.*"

He chuckles and steps off the bed. Disappearing into the hall, he comes back a minute later with a cloth in his hand. I try to grab it from him, but he holds it above his head, winking.

"It's my mess to clean, baby."

"If you insist," I drawl.

With a soft, careful touch, he cleans me up before tossing the cloth into his laundry bin. I turn onto my side and rub my cheek against the pillow, watching as he tosses a shirt and boxers on. The second shirt in his hand comes sailing at my face a beat later.

I catch it and give it a once-over. "Did you choose this one on purpose?"

"Why would you think that?"

He pads back to the bed and stretches out behind me, his arms coiling right.

"I'd say the Huntsly on the back of this would be a dead giveaway. God, I can't believe you've kept this. Does it even fit you anymore?"

Nose pressing into my hair, he rubs my belly, melting me. "Nope. Fits you, though."

"Maybe. I'd have to put it on to see, and you're holding me pretty tightly," I tease.

Slowly, he releases me but stays where he is. I slip off the bed and shake out the old Cherry Peak Wranglers football tee. The number seventeen on the front has me cracking a smile while pulling it on.

"Well? Is it everything you wished for when you decided to keep this?" I ask, giving him a twirl.

"Fuck, yeah, it is."

I pull my lip into my mouth and contemplate giving him what I've been carrying with me for a while now. His stare burns into me as I search the room for my purse.

"What are you looking for?"

"My purse."

"In the living room. We didn't bring it to my mom's. I can get it—"

I shake my head quickly, already heading for the door. "Just stay there for a second. Don't move."

"Alright," he says with a laugh. "Consider me glued to the bed."

Too focused to reply, I rush out of the room and to where I left my bag. It's ridiculous how long it's taken me to give this to him, but I guess I was just waiting for the right time. That hasn't been until tonight.

When I get back to the room, Darren's still in the same spot. His brows fly up when he sees me with my fist closed and nothing else.

"Should I be scared?" he asks.

I roll my eyes. "No."

Taking a seat on the bed, I cross my legs in front of him and take a deep breath before opening my hand. The purple bracelet feels like it's made from silver instead of elastic and tiny beads.

"Is that the bracelet Abbie was talking about?"

"It is."

"Can I touch it?"

I almost laugh. "Take it. It's for you, in case you can't read anymore."

"Darebear . . . I haven't heard that in forever."

"That's because it's only for us."

He takes the thin bracelet and slides it onto his wrist. The beads spelling the name I gave him when we first met dig into his skin, but he keeps it on.

"I love it, Elle."

Lying down again, I curl into him and stare at my ring. It stares back, daring me to slide it onto my finger again. Only, I can't. Not yet. Moving forward is what I want, but the ring will have to come later. Once I've finally figured out what it is that's keeping me from taking it back.

45

Delaney

Coming home to Cherry Peak feels different this time.

There's something in the air that unsettles me as I drive into town. It could just be the smell in my car from weeks of unwashed laundry that I'm bringing to my grandma's house. Since flying with all of my things wasn't possible, I packed my car as full as I could so that I didn't have to do this drive more than once. That included dirty laundry and a few boxes of reusable containers with spaghetti sauce stains in them.

I debate turning down the road that leads home instead of following my original plan. I'm exhausted and could use a shower before doing anything else. Or I could just pull my big girl pants on and stop trying to convince myself not to do this.

Tapping the steering wheel, I slow to a turtle crawl. My turn signal ticks as I hesitate to move.

It's getting late . . . maybe he's already asleep. Or his parents are. I already had to ask my grandma for information on whether Darren moved back into his childhood home after graduation, and the last thing I need is to be embarrassed again by showing up and waking his mom.

A loud car horn scares me badly enough that I drop my foot on the gas pedal and jerk forward into motion. I flip the driver behind me the bird, but they can't see it past the piles of stuff blocking my back window.

Turning even slower just to piss off the driver behind me, I take a deep breath and wring the steering wheel. The brown street sign appears, and my stomach twists painfully.

There's a car on the curb in front of his house and two others on the driveway. I pull up behind the one on the road and stay frozen in my seat, terrified to see him again. The sharp ache in my chest is worse than the fear, though, and that's what pushes me to get out of the car.

Over the last two years, I've missed him so much. More than I think any girl in their twenties is supposed to miss a man without being featured on a documentary. It was like losing a piece of my soul when we said goodbye, and what was left of it has flaked away piece by piece with every day we've been apart.

I can't do this separation anymore, and I'm hoping he feels the same. As much as I'd never wish pain on someone I love, I do hope he's been hurting just as badly as I have. I want him to have seen me in the faces of people he's passed on the street and heard my voice in all of our favourite places. That's what I've been dealing with every single day.

Not even seeing my family in the crowd at my graduation was enough to make up for the devastation of searching for him, knowing he wouldn't be there.

Two years, he said. Two years, and everything would be okay again.

I shut the door softly behind me and take slow steps up the sidewalk. The light is on outside now that the sun's begun to set, illuminating the porch steps that look freshly stained. I'd bet Daryl has a list a million pages long of work that Pauline's insisted he gets done this summer. She's always putting him to work on something, and he loves every minute of it.

My hand shakes when I ring the doorbell and gulp. I fidget

as I wait, unable to stand still as nerves feast on my insides. It feels like forever, when in reality, I hardly have a chance to run my fingers through my hair before the door is pulled open.

"Delaney," Darren's mother gasps, her eyes wide.

"Hi, Pauline. I hope I wasn't interrupting anything."

"Oh, no, sweetheart. You're not. We're just—I'm . . . Darren's not here!"

"Oh, he's not? I'm sorry! I should have called first or something. When I saw his car, I just assumed he was here," I ramble apologetically.

Pauline reaches for me when I start to retreat, her touch on my arm soft, familiar. The longing that hits in response is sharp on my tongue.

"Come back tomorrow, honey. After lunch, if you can."

I nod, relaxing slightly at her openness with me. Even after four years away.

"Okay. Tomorrow after lunch, then. I'm staying at my grandma's house, just in case he asks—"

"Mom? Are you trying to hoard your bottles again? It's not a sin to donate them every once in a while."

I freeze, confused. This overwhelming feeling of pure dread swarms me, like a telltale sign that something bad is coming.

Pauline's expression breaks as she looks back into the house, her nerves blaringly obvious. "No. I'll be done in a second. There's no reason for you to come check on me."

"Too bad," Darren grunts.

I'm not ready for the stab of betrayal between my ribs. His mom reaches for me again, but I step back out of reach. When Darren appears, I lose the ability to appear strong and held together.

My knees wobble as I set a hand to the exterior of the house and suck in a tight breath. Pauline moves out of the way, and Darren replaces her. His brown eyes are dull, but the pain in his expression is there . . . so strong I feel the lash of it. The lingering dread grows in intensity, smacking me in the face, warning me.

"Hey," I whisper, unable to move.

"What are you doing here?"

I flinch at the harsh tone. "I just got back."

"Go home, Delaney."

"Is this because I didn't give you a heads-up before coming? If I'm interrupting something, I can come back. I'm back home now, so—"

He lurches toward me, blocking the entire doorway. The change in his height takes me aback. It almost surprises me more than his mess of a beard or the thinning of his muscles. Darren isn't a beard guy. He's a mustache or light stubble one. Concern drives me to move closer and touch his jaw, running my finger over the coarse hair.

His eyes shut, and he leans into my touch, a wavering, pained exhale escaping him. I cup his face in my palm and lean forward, needing to get closer. To feel his warmth and smell his cologne again. Only when I do, it's . . . not the same. There's something wrong with the way he smells. Like maybe he's changed his cologne over the last two years. Only that's not it.

I drop my hand and swallow past the lump of fear in my throat. There's a stillness in the air around us, as if that fog of dread has lifted, the warning of its presence no longer needed.

Darren's eyes flash open, and I watch in slow motion as his lips part around words I don't want to hear.

"Let me explain."

"Are you ready yet? We'll be late for my appointment if we don't leave now!"

It's a woman's voice. A woman who isn't Pauline or Poppy.

Darren winces and steps outside before trying to shut the door behind him. He pulls on it while a head of long, glossy hair appears on the other side, tugging right back.

The woman laughs at him, assuming he's playing some sort of joke on her when the only joke here is me.

"The point is to go to the appointment *together*. How exactly is the doctor supposed to check the baby's heartbeat when the actual pregnant woman isn't there?"

Like a brick through a window, I shatter.

"Give me a minute," Darren barks, eyes on me as I stumble down the stairs and try to breathe.

He follows, giving the woman the opportunity to open the door. I look behind him, getting only a quick look at her before my vision blurs. The small bump on her stomach—

I palm my chest and try not to scream. "It's yours?"

"I haven't seen you in years, Delaney," Sasha says, standing at the top of the stairs with her arms crossed.

Years. Since we were in high school and she was hanging around the sidelines at every football game with a new sign every week with Darren's name on it.

Shaking my head, I ignore her and stare at Darren, willing my tears to hold off just another minute. "Is it yours?"

"Yes."

"The baby or the ring?" Sasha asks proudly.

I choke. The missing weight on my finger is jarring.

Darren speaks again, but I'm already moving. My keys jangle in my hands as I try and use shaky fingers to find the right one. I gasp a sob when I throw my door open and fall inside. The key stabs everywhere but inside the ignition as I blink past the tears. Finally, it slides inside.

His voice follows me, getting louder before I slap a hand down on the lock and put the car in gear. The handle pulls as he thumps a fist to the door. My name comes next, over and over.

I give a warning jolt on my gas pedal before the thumping stops and he falls silent.

A beat later, I risk running over his foot and take off. I only make it around the block before I lose the ability to drive.

Bending over the steering wheel, I scream. My ears ring from how loud I am, the pained noise bouncing off my suitcases and boxes. My nose runs, tears falling as I shake and let my pain transform into anger. Suddenly, I'm whaling my fists into the steering wheel.

The baby or the ring.

The baby or the ring.

The baby or the fucking ring.

I flinch away from the door when the handle pulls again. The figure in the window isn't Darren this time. That's the only reason I unlock the door.

It opens slowly before a familiar, gruff voice says, "Come on, Delaney. Let's get you home. You can't be driving right now."

"Why did he do this?" I whisper, my throat scraped raw.

Daryl Huntsly wraps a heavy arm around me and guides me out of the car. I don't have it in me to be embarrassed. I'm not sure there's much left of me right now at all.

"I'm sorry."

I shake my head, hating those words because I'm the one who's sorry.

I'm sorry that I ever loved Darren in the first place.

46

Darren

"Darren? Are you still sleeping? Darren?"

I crack my eyes open and glance down at the woman sleeping in my arms. Her hair's a mess, but her features are even, at peace. I'm close enough that I could start counting each of her freckles before she woke up.

"Darren!"

Delaney shifts beside me, moaning sleepily. "What's going on?"

"I don't know," I croak.

There's a loud slam that jerks through my sleepy haze. It sounds like the door, but that wouldn't make sense. Nobody has a key to my place but my mom, Poppy, and Bryce, and not a single one of them are early risers. Alarm slaps me right across the face.

There's another key out there.

"I need to get up for a minute, baby," I rumble, trying to keep my voice steady.

Delaney frowns, her lip jutting out in a pout before she reluctantly rolls off me. The comforter is at our hips, and fuck, we didn't put clothes on last night. Not after getting out of the for the third time and growing too tired to slip them on again.

Her chest is bare, breasts exposed and nipples hard from the morning chill in the room. She rolls her head to look at me and smiles softly, the happy daze on her face gnawing at my stomach.

I sit and pull the blankets up to her shoulders. Then, I slip out of bed and throw my discarded clothes on. Every second I'm not beside her feels wrong.

"What's wrong?" she asks, concern eating at that daze.

"There's—"

"Darren, I told you how much I hate when you don't triple-check that she has all of her things in her bag before she comes to my house! How hard is it to remember to pack an iPad? You better be awake by the time I get to your room."

Sasha's booming voice travels through the room, freezing everything in its path. My stomach falls.

"I'll be right back," I say, stealing one more look at Delaney.

In a blink, she's staring down at herself and pulling the comforter up to her chin. I can't wait any longer to leave, even if every bone in my body fights me on moving.

I'm pissed off by the time I make it to the closed door and pull it open. This is my house, and she's storming through it as if she has any right to be here instead of sending a text asking me to bring her whatever she needs. Delaney doesn't need to worry about my ex-wife appearing out of the blue. Especially not after everything.

Slipping out of the room, I catch Sasha only a few feet away. She stares at me, unimpressed.

"Where is Abbie's iPad? This is the third time you've forgotten to pack her with it."

I shut the door behind me. "It's in her room. And you could have texted me and asked for it. You don't get to just show up here and let yourself in whenever you feel like it."

"Oh? Does this new rule have anything to do with the

woman's shoes I nearly tripped over when I got here? Is this woman why you're forgetting to pack our daughter with her things?"

"Are you fucking kidding me right now, Sasha? She hardly even uses that iPad, and you know that as well as I do."

Her brows rise. "Well? You're also still sleeping, and it's past eight. Do you even still have a job?"

"It's Sunday."

"I checked her room already. It wasn't there," she snaps, not enjoying losing a fight.

"Alright, then I'll bring it by later today. You can leave your key on the counter on your way out."

"No, I'll check your room and see if it's there."

"The fuck you will." I place my hand on the door handle before she can and try to keep my temper under control—something I've always struggled with around Sasha. "Back off."

She narrows her eyes. "Who's in there?"

"Don't act like you don't already know. Is that the real reason you're here? To try and piss her off?"

"Oh, please. I don't care about Delaney. It should be you that starts caring a bit less, considering."

My doors aren't soundproof, and my patience grows thinner with every word Elle's forced to her. This morning should have been light and happy. We should have spent all day in bed, eating and cuddling and exploring each other more than we had a chance to before we fell asleep last night. Dealing with Sasha was not on my fucking plan for today.

"Considering what?" I ask, dropping my voice.

"Well, her relationship with our daughter, for one. Are you not worried that anything negative between the two of you will have an impact on her? This is her teacher, Darren! What if other students find out and assume she's getting special treatment or the other teachers don't approve? Are you really willing to risk our daughter's education over her?"

I grit my jaw, letting all of those excuses go in one ear and out the other. I've already thought about every single one.

"And second off, the entire town is watching now! They did this once, and look at what it did to Delaney! She became the poor recluse that everyone was oh so worried about. Nobody cared about you and me, only about the past with you and her. This is going to affect Abbie now. She's not a baby anymore. One wrong move between the two of you and we're all getting dragged into the embarrassment this time."

"Things were different back then. You damn well know that."

She lifts her chin, hands firmly on her hips. "If things go wrong with you two this time, one of you will be leaving this town, and if you want to stay in Abbie's life, it will be Delaney."

"Get out of my house, Sasha. Now," I demand, my patience gone.

"Not without the iPad."

My laugh is short and dark as I turn away and go into the bedroom, making sure to slam the door in her face. The room feels ten times bigger than it is when I see Delaney standing on the opposite side of it, dressed back in her clothes from dinner last night. Purse in her arms, she chews on her lip and avoids my eyes. The shutdown is obvious, and it saws through me.

"She's leaving," I say, softening my voice.

"Yeah, I heard. I'm going to go too."

I take a stunted step forward and plead, "No, Elle. Please don't. Not yet."

She continues to avoid looking at me, keeping her emotions hidden. "I shouldn't have even stayed. This is probably common for her to come. She's—she has a key. Not leaving last night was careless on my part."

"I don't need permission to have a woman stay overnight in my house, Delaney. We weren't careless. Don't let this change anything."

Fuck the iPad, and screw Sasha for doing this too. She's been waiting for the chance to embarrass Delaney for years. Ever since she found that goddamn article.

Head shaking, Delaney moves to the side and eyes the door behind me. "I'm going to go, Darren."

"Baby . . . stay."

"I'll call you later."

I stumble to the side when she moves past me and opens the door. Like a bad smell, Sasha's lingering on the other side of it, her expression less than friendly as she takes a long look at Delaney. The fact that she's in last night's clothes only makes her turn her nose up more.

"Hello, Delaney," she mutters.

My chest constricts to the point of pain when Delaney just pushes past her without a word. Inhaling deeply, I scratch at my jaw. With a look at my ex-wife, I roll my thoughts around until I have something semi-decent to say.

"I've let you get away with a lot of shit, Sasha. Mostly because of how unfair I was to you. I made mistakes in our marriage and before it too, but that's in the past now. If you're searching for another apology, I'll give you a thousand more than I already have, but you'll never speak about or to Delaney like that again. Not to me, to Abbie, or anyone else you come across. You won't approach her and spew your cruel 'what-ifs.' I'm sorry. I'm sorry for hurting you and treating you far worse than I should have. We were both struggling, and I handled myself in the wrong way.

"You deserved better, and so did I. I've never interfered in your engagement, so you need to keep your nose out of my relationship with Delaney. I won't take anything else from you, and I know for a fucking fact nobody in this town will either. Now, feel free to look for the iPad, and then put your key on my kitchen counter and leave. I'm going to try and keep Delaney from leaving my ass again while you do that."

She blinks in silence before I turn and leave her there. The front door closes again, softer this time, and I pick up my pace.

Her car is out front, and I know if she gets in it, she'll be gone, and I'll have lost my chance to fix this today.

I don't bother with shoes. Barefoot, I open the door and step onto the porch. Delaney's already on the street, getting into her car.

I've always known this was fragile. Last night changed a lot between us and put what I want us to be into motion, but she didn't take her ring. Hearing her ask for it back is how I'll know she's completely in it with me, her fear a thing of the past. From the moment she took it off and handed it back to me, I've needed her to have it again. It belongs on her finger, but it's not there yet.

It's still around my fucking neck.

She looks over at me once I step onto the street, crossing to her. The tears in her stop me dead in my tracks. I stare at her, this all-consuming parasite inside of me feasting on every chunk of happiness I've collected.

No, she mouths.

I listen to the silent word this time, forcing myself not to move when she starts her car and drives right past me. The sight of her leaving settles like poison in my stomach. It's wrong. The distance that grows with every house she passes rips at me until I'm sure she's taking all the important parts with her.

Dropping my head back, I stand on the street in nothing but my pyjamas and stare at the sky, hoping that I'll be able to fix this. There's no other option for me. Not this time.

Delaney

AN HOUR into sorting through the piles of shit in my grandma's basement, and I'm no longer in the mood.

To be fair, I wasn't to begin with, but considering what happened this morning, it was either this or slashing Sasha's tires. I've wanted to do that for a looooooong time now. I even dreamed of it once. I stopped searching up what specific types of dreams meant after that.

I kick another one of the plastic tubs of old clothes and yell, letting it punch through the crumbling insulation. My yell turns into a scream and then a broken sob as I bend over my knees and heave. I swipe the tears off my cheeks as they fall and glare at the towering stack of bins I still need to go through.

The ache between my legs when I haul another bin toward me makes my anger swell. I'm sore, tired, and really fucking annoyed. Why is it that Sasha's always there? She does nothing but stab her fingers into all of my wounds, laughing like a hyena the whole time.

I'll never escape her, and this morning only reminded me of that.

My phone buzzes again from wherever I left it earlier, but I already know who it is without needing to look. Darren's called every hour since I left his house, twice at the start. I'm not ready to talk to him yet despite his constant effort.

The bin I chose is overfilled with more clothes, but they don't belong to my grandmother this time. Rounding it, I crouch in front of the single word scrawled across the blue plastic in her writing.

Laney's.

The first thing in the bin is an old sweater that I think used to be purple but is now a washed-out white. I set it on the floor and stare at the next thing. The purple jersey with the number 17 stitched on the arm steals the air from my lungs. I drop to my ass on the dirty concrete and stare at the fabric, my mind running backward as I pull it out of the bin.

"Throw it out! I don't want to see it ever again," I shout.

Grandma shakes her head stubbornly and holds the jersey out of reach. "I'm not throwing this away. You'll regret getting rid of these things, Laney. I promise you that."

"I can't look at them anymore!"

My lungs pinch so tightly I can hardly breathe. The wall I've built around me and my past with Darren is wobbling with every second I stare at his jersey. The burn in my chest is too much right now. Sasha's pregnant belly is branded into the backs of my eyelids, a constant reminder of what I came home to. This is just too much.

"I'm keeping them because one day, you'll wish I had."

"The only thing I wish is that I never met him in the first place." I hold my head, shaking it. "Get rid of it."

She moves, and I look at her again, expecting to see it gone. What she holds up is worse than the jersey.

My tears are instant. The sob that follows leaves me on the floor. Arms wrap around me, holding me up. I try to push her away, but she holds me tighter, pulling me into her chest.

"It's okay, Laney. I've got you. I've got you."

I crack and plead, "Put it away. Please. Take it away from me."

Her arm moves before returning to hold me. "It's gone. I'm sorry, my love. I'm so sorry."

Blinking, I swipe away the tears I didn't feel drip. The jersey smells stale, old. Huntsly is written on the back, the lettering in perfect condition. It feels the same, still thin and cheap with the high school's sports budget.

I rest it in my lap and return my gaze to the bin. The jacket staring back at me steals my breath. My pulse slows, turning thready as I slowly touch the number on the sleeve, then the bronze buttons. I sniff and try to swallow.

She was supposed to get rid of this stuff. All of it. I even watched her throw it in the garbage when I had caught on to the fact that she still hadn't gotten rid of it three years after I came home. Yet here it is.

It's heavy . . . the leather clean and smooth when I lift it and hold it in front of me. I turn it over and stare at his name again. I should have given these things back years ago. They were never mine to keep in the first place. I was holding on to them while we were apart, as if a jersey and bulky jacket would have ever been able to make me feel like he was with me. All it did was remind me that he wasn't.

"What are you doing, Delaney?" I ask myself, sighing as I stand and slip the jacket on.

It weighs me down more than I already am, but God, it feels good. It's a piece of our past that I couldn't seem to rid myself of. My grandma was a stubborn woman, but she loved me. She loved me enough to risk this coming back to haunt our relationship because she was that confident that I'd be grateful one day, and she was right to be.

I clutch the sides of the jacket and pinch my brows together when something pokes my arm. Wiggling, I try to dislodge whatever it is, but it doesn't budge. With a frown, I take the jacket off and give it a shake.

The letter that falls out of the left sleeve makes me laugh. It's a wet laugh, the kind that aches worse than any other.

I unfold the paper and cross my legs before reading.

Dear my Laney,

How mad are you at me right now? Is there steam shooting from your ears, or hot tears splashing and smudging my perfect handwriting?

Whichever it is, I'm just grateful that you're reading this at all. Since you are, that means you've finally found the box of things you thought I got rid of but never could. Honestly, I can't believe you thought that I of all people would have allowed you to discard the things that mean the most to you in the world, but that's not my point.

The point of this letter is this—stop running. From this town, your great love, and the past you've tried to forget about because of them both. Before you sit there and scoff at me, I need you to keep reading. Delaney Marie Brooks has never needed a man. She is strong, proud, and cutthroat when it comes to those she loves. But, my girl, you didn't simply meet _a_ man. You met _the_ man. Your _one_. And I've watched you both find yourself, and lose yourself with and because of him. I've watched you feel every emotion that one can hope to feel in their life. Love, heartache, loneliness, comfort. I've also watched you ache and bleed. You've yearned, and dreamt, and wished for something to change or just one chance to go back in time.

Darren hurt you, sweetheart. But every great love endured heartache. You _deserve_ to live out yours because you've been lucky enough to find it.

If you haven't ripped this into pieces yet and swore my name, please stay for a few more lines. Don't let your story be over. Not yet. You need at least a few more chapters.

I guess, if I had one dying wish, that would be it. For you to offer him a second chance, now that you're both grown up and know who exactly you are, and who you need each other to be.

Maybe it will end in an epilogue, or maybe it will be cut short. I'm just begging you, Laney, at least go see him. Speak to him just once and see for yourself that what I'm saying is true.

I miss you, angel. And I love you no matter what, even if I'm not there to pull you into my arms right now.

Yours,
Grandma

47

Delaney

I'm a firm believer in only using sick days when you're really ill, but for the last two days, I've used mine without being curled in front of a toilet bowl. I've called in to work because I've needed to think, and I can't do that clearly with Abbie sitting in front of me.

My grandma's letter is on my lap. I've read it twenty times, and each time makes me cry harder, her words stabbing deeper into my chest as they sink in. It's like I can hear her voice as I read the words, and I could really, really use her right now. She'd know exactly what to say after what happened.

If her letter is anything to go off, she'd throw me in my car and drag me to Darren's house herself. The old woman always was a romantic. Her romance books remain untouched in the spare room, beckoning me to sort through them nearly every day. I've been dusting them for her, as if she'll come back and haunt me for letting them get dirty.

I glance across the living room at the armchair and the letterman jacket thrown over the back of it. Groaning, I reach for where I chucked my phone when Poppy called. Her voicemail joined the other unanswered ones that I haven't had it in me to listen to yet.

I'm hiding, and everyone can see it. My only saving grace is that unless Darren shared it with the town, nobody knows but us and Sasha. I'm just hoping that he at least warned her off from doing that.

That woman . . . she drives me crazy. First, it was her trying to make herself Darren's partner in every high school class we all shared, then her obnoxious cheering on the sidelines at his games, and for the big hitter, getting pregnant with his baby and getting to call herself his wife.

Sasha's always wanted Darren, but I never considered her a threat. No woman was. Not really. My unwavering belief in a future with him kept me naïve to the people who were judging from the outside. One minute, I was in love, and the next, I was having that love thrown back in my face.

It would be easier to just let this go and call it quits now. Abbie wouldn't be affected in the ways Sasha was right to question, and I can finally use this as motivation to finish with Grandma's house and move on. I could start over somewhere nobody knows me. Maybe in Vancouver or out East. My parents would travel to visit me anywhere just as frequently as they do Cherry Peak, and my friends . . . they'd understand.

I push my hair back behind my shoulders, frustrated when I give myself a mental shove. I'm not leaving. If I was going to, I would have after Grandma's funeral. Maybe I'd managed to convince myself that this house was the only reason I hadn't run off, but that was a lie.

The real reason I came home and why I stayed through every pitiful stare on the street and nervous trip to the grocery store was because I was waiting for this. For him to find his way back to me.

Maybe a part of me always recognized that he wasn't ever hers. One mistake kept us apart, but one decision is all it would take to bring us back together, and this time, the decision hasn't been taken from me.

I get to make it.

I've just got to decide now if I'm prepared for what a life with Darren would look like now. It will never be the life we would have had before. Abbie's involved now, and so is Sasha. Running won't be an option if we go ahead with this, and there isn't another do-over waiting. This is our one and only second chance.

Without thinking twice, I play the first of the voicemails that have collected.

"Elle, I know you don't want to talk to me, but I'm going to keep calling until you do. Not chasing after you has been one of the biggest regrets in my life, so just keep that in mind. We aren't done yet."

I swallow and play the next.

"I drove by your house and saw your car, so I know you got back okay. There's a locksmith on their way over right now, and he's replacing all of my locks. This won't happen again. Have you eaten yet? I know you don't like to eat when you're upset, but you need to. Don't make me send my sister over."

Scrolling through more, I choose one from yesterday.

"Good morning, beautiful. I'm not sure if you've listened to a single one of these, but just in case you're listening to them as they come in just to delete them, I'm calling to remind you that I'm still here, and I'll wait for as long as it takes for you to give me two minutes to talk through this. Have a good day. I miss you."

My heart pinches. I lie on my back and stare at the ceiling before playing the most recent voicemail.

"Hey, Elle. It's me again. Are you sick of hearing my phone voice? If you are, I'll be at home all day, and I've put in an order from the diner just in case you show up. It'll be here at six, and I've made sure to order all of your favourites. No pressure, though. I'll bring it by and drop it on your porch tonight if you choose not to come. Also, your back gate wasn't closing properly, so I fixed it last night. The last thing you need is a coyote disturbing your morning coffee. Okay, well, I hope you're okay . . . I miss you. Bye, baby."

With a glance at the time, I curse. It's quarter after six, and I'm in the same sweatpants I've worn for the last two days, and my hair is a total disaster. Surely, I can't show up like this? Or maybe I can. This is Darren. And if I go to him right now, I may as well be signing off on a companion burial plot.

Fuck it. I'm so done with sitting at home alone, wishing that things could have been different. There's no changing what happened. It's time to create a future out of all the broken pieces of our past.

I STARE DOWN at the time on my dash before getting out of the car and gawking at the unfamiliar van parked in front of me. The voices escaping through Darren's screen door are deep and masculine, ramping up my curiosity.

"Thank you for coming, Jer. If you just send the photos through to my email, I'll take a look at them tonight," Darren says, his voice growing in volume.

"You've got it. We'll touch base tomorrow before the listing goes up."

The door opens, and a guy steps outside, his black suit pressed and shoes so shiny the sun reflects off them. He gives a thumbs-up to the van, and then another man is stepping onto the sidewalk. The bulkier of the two gives me a curious up-and-down look before smiling and pulling a big white sign out of the back seat.

I rest a hand against the side of my car and watch him carry the For Sale sign over to Darren's front yard. The mallet in his other hand is huge as he swings it onto the sign, sending the post deep into the ground.

"Delaney?"

Blinking slowly, I move from my spot and onto the grass. "What's going on?"

"I'm selling the house," Darren announces, as calm as if he'd just said the sky is blue or the sun is hot.

I stare at him as he hops off the porch and starts toward me. He slaps the bigger guy on the shoulder as he passes him, and then the men are getting back into the van.

"Why? This is your house. Where are you going? Are you moving? Is this because I wasn't here at six?" I'm going to be sick. Heat rises to my cheeks. "If I'd known you were going to leave, I'd have decided quicker. I would have been here yesterday."

He ignores my rambling. His eyes are latched onto my upper body, a soul-deep bewilderment glimmering inside of them. "What are you wearing, Elle?"

"Answer me first."

"I can't even think right now with you wearing that."

"Well, try! I'm freaking out right now," I snap.

The sound of his laugh isn't what I was expecting. "You're incredible."

"You won't think that when I kick you in the crotch, Darren. Tell me what's going on."

"I thought that jacket was gone. Assumed you used it for a fire starter or just ran your car over it and left it on some back road," he says, reaching forward to take both sides of it into his hands.

"You can thank my grandmother. She refused to listen to me when I told her to do all of those things. I'm considering trying again right now, though."

His grin is bright, making him appear younger. "How many times did I beg you to wear this jacket at my games?"

"Every time, Darren. You tried every time."

"And you rarely gave in. You chose a jersey instead."

"This jacket is heavy. And it smells like BO."

He tucks a piece of hair behind my ear, letting his touch linger. "I never even wore it."

"Then whoever made it did before they gave it to you, because even now, it still stinks," I grumble.

"Yet, here you are. It looks good on you. Like it was made for you to wear."

My chest pangs as I say, "Tell me why you're selling your house, Darren."

"It's not the right one anymore. I'm not sure it ever was."

"What do you mean? You designed this place."

He nods, eyes holding mine. "Can I take you somewhere? I'll answer all of your questions when we get there."

"All of them, Darren. I mean it."

"Anything you want, Elle."

I let him lead us to his car and keep all of my questions to myself on the drive. He doesn't push, and I don't mind the silence because I'm not alone. We're together.

The drive is longer than I was expecting, though. Once we pass the Cherry Peak sign, I have to bite down on my lip to keep from asking him where we're going. The drive-in grounds come and go before he turns down a dirt road. A moment later, he pulls over beside the ditch.

We're in front of an open field with nothing to see beyond besides the sharp tips of the mountains and a few glowing lights from the town of Oak Point. If I were to turn around, I'd see the drive-in and the wooden structure that's starting to be built to replace the original and, just to the left, the football field would be hovering far into the distance, the goalpost creating a shadow over the freshly worked land.

It's *the* plot of land. Ours from all those years ago.

Stepping outside, I take in a deep breath. "Why are we here?"

"Follow me."

He rounds the hood and takes my hand. We head into the field, and I eye the No Trespassing sign hung on the wire fence.

The opening in the fence kind of ruins the whole privacy thing, but I keep my mouth shut about that.

"I'm afraid to tell you that if you bought me a horse, I'm going to ask you to return it."

Chuckling, he moves around the field as if he's been here a few times and knows where all of the wrong places to step are. I follow him carefully until he stops, turning to face me.

"Why are we here, Darren? Why are you selling your house? Your *home*?" I ask.

"That house has never been a home to me. I tried to make it one, especially for Abbie, but something was always missing."

"Stop being cryptic," I demand, my breath turning shallow.

Taking my other hand into his, he holds them both firmly. "I tried to fit you into that house, Elle. I bought your tiles, and I designed my entire bathroom around them because I thought that if I'd just nail those tiles, there would be that piece of you in the foundation of my house that couldn't be scrubbed away. The built-ins in the living room and the panelling in the master bedroom were more failed attempts to build you into my life when you were no longer there. It didn't matter how many things I did to that place because it was never right. It never was going to be right because you weren't actually there.

"I've been in love with you for so long that everything I did had a little piece of you in it. A memory or a drifting thought. And now . . . Now, I'm done with trying to make a piece of you work. I want all of you, Delaney. I want your laugh and your touch because it's the only one that can make me feel every emotion under the fucking sun. I want to see you in our room every morning and watch as you unpack your things beside mine. And I want to see you with my daughter. I want you to spend hours making bracelets together and giggling about the things I've done that day that the two of you can't believe. I'm not okay with anything less than that anymore. So, I bought this land, and I've spent the last two days doing this."

He lets go of my hand and reaches into the back pocket of his jeans. A thick piece of folded parchment settles between us, and then he starts to peel it open. God, he's even left the bracelet I made him on his wrist.

"It's not finished yet. I just wanted something to show you that this land is going to *be* something. A place for us and our future. It's time, Delaney. We've waited long enough, don't you think?"

I bite down on my lip and focus on the charcoal sketches on the paper. The two-storey house with the wraparound porch and garden. Four bedrooms, a large dining room, and fireplace in the living room. He's even drawn a pool in the yard beneath a rough sketch of a sun wearing a pair of sunglasses.

"You don't know how long I've dreamed of you saying that to me," I whisper.

He moves in close, the strong wall of his body shielding me from the wind as it rips by, the air turning crisp. "I'm sorry it took me so long."

"We needed to wait. It wasn't the right time."

"I love you," he declares, the certainty in his voice echoing what I feel.

"Give me my ring back, Darren."

Without a second of hesitation, he reaches up beneath his hoodie and rips the chain clean off. I extend my hand and wait for him to drop the ring into his and then glide it back into place onto my finger.

"Should I take that as an I love you too?" he teases softly, twisting the ring.

I roll my eyes and yank him into me by the pocket of his hoodie. "Take that as an obviously. I'm choosing you, Darren. I'm choosing forever with you because of how much I love you."

The first snowflake of the year hits my nose, and then he's kissing me, cementing my belief that this is where we've always supposed to have wound up. Together, right now, right here.

EPILOGUE

"Do we really have to do this today? There are a million other things I'd prefer instead."

Delaney touches my thigh, her fingers creeping closer to my dick as I bark a laugh. Taking her hand, I pull it away and ignore the pout she gives me.

"It's time, Elle. We've already organized the storage locker, and now we need to fill it. You can't keep living in this house. Not with it in this shape."

"Are you sure this just isn't your way of making more room for your things?"

I smirk, pulling her toward the tower of boxes in front of us. "It's a bit of both. I know we're waiting a bit longer, so at least give me this. If we're both going to stay here once the house closes, it needs to be more liveable."

"You're right. Just don't let it get to your head."

"Too late."

She sits on the ground and pats the ground in front of her. "Let's start, then."

"I promise to reward you, baby," I tease.

"Oh? How?"

"Let's get through a few boxes first."

"Jerk," she grumbles, watching as I lower the first box in front of her.

Looking over the stack, I can't help but feel a bit overwhelmed. It's a miracle that Delaney's been able to stand living in this house for so long without tossing everything out on the lawn. There's no room for her things, and I know that's started to take its toll.

It wasn't until Abbie came over with me for the first time and had her favourite beads roll behind the boxes and get lost that she decided enough was enough. Delaney ordered her multiples of those same beads that night, but it was the experience itself that shoved this into motion.

Moving another box to the ground, I open the flaps and start pulling all of the old CDs out. I snicker when I find the first-ever Brody Steele one tucked between a few I don't recognize.

Delaney looks at my hands. "Oh! Brody would have a hell of a time with that. Should we put it on? There's a stereo in the guest room."

"He hates this album cover."

"Why? He looks adorable."

I snort. "He looks like a grumpy teenager. Garrison still teases him about how pissy he was during the photoshoot."

"I still can't believe Garrison's his boss. Or that they didn't get along at first. They seem pretty close to me."

"It's also been like four years since Brody came back home. Time changes everything."

She hums, leaning her cheek against my knee for a second before getting back to work. It's only been a month since I brought her to our new plot of land, but it's like we've hit fast-forward on life. One minute, I was listing my house for sale, and the next, it was selling, and we were breaking ground on a forever home. The place we'll grow old together.

Abbie's probably the most excited out of everyone. She's already demanded exactly what she wants in her new room, from the size of the closet to the colours of paint on the walls. If there was any doubt that she would be happy about my decision to sell our old house and build a new one for us, she proved them all wrong. Her love for Delaney was instant, and I've watched it grow tenfold. As if I had any worries about that.

"Should we just start a pile of donation things?" Elle asks.

"That's probably the easiest way to do this. I'm sure Poppy can take it all with her to Calgary and drop everything where you want her to."

"I'll call her tonight—"

The doorbell rings four times, and Delaney starts pushing herself off the ground before I drop a hand to her cheek and say, "I'll get it."

She nods, settling again.

The first face I see when I open the door is Johnny's. He's flashing me that shit-eating grin he always wears as he shakes a brown takeout bag in front of him.

"The cavalry has arrived," he announces, strolling inside as if he's been here a million times before. "And we have food."

Rory rolls her eyes at him and pats my arm. "Hi, Darren. I hope we aren't interrupting."

"As if. Not unless they were plannin' on getting busy on dusty boxes," Brody says.

He steps inside and immediately takes his boots off, leaving them beside Johnny's before passing me with a slap on the back.

Anna follows, her hand tucked into his. Then, my sister comes in carrying a tray of drinks. Garrison's glued to her back, holding another.

"What are you doing here?" I ask, looking between everyone who passes and the Rustic Ridge haul they've brought with them.

Poppy grins at me as she steps over the collection of shoes beside the door. "We figured you guys could use some help."

Shutting the door, I watch as my closest friends greet my girl, immediately setting their things down and grabbing boxes and getting to work.

"You didn't have to do that."

"Well, the faster you get this place organized and cleaned out, the faster I can have Delaney's attention while we get the details sorted for my wedding. We're only six months away now."

"Don't you have a wedding planner?"

Poppy huffs at me. "It's not the same thing."

"Right."

"When you get married, you'll understand what I mean."

"I had a wedding before, Poppy," I say, wincing at the reminder.

She scowls. "That didn't count. A quick trip to the courthouse is not the same."

I let it go, knowing I won't win here. With a glance at everyone piled in the cramped living room, I ask, "Where are Bryce and Daisy?"

"Ice had something to do before she came. They'll be here soon."

"Alright. Come on, I'll show you what I found in one of the boxes."

"Oooh, I do love hidden treasures."

Anna's sitting on Brody's lap on the armchair as they sort through one of the smaller boxes. I smirk when I pass, my hand running over the back of Delaney's head.

She looks up at me, her eyes so full of light they're almost blinding. "Did you call them over?"

Crouching beside her, I grab the CD album and shake my head. "No, baby. They came all on their own."

The immediate warmth that spreads across her face . . . Yeah, I'm pretty lucky. Lucky to have her in my life but also all of these people here in this room.

"What do you have there?" Johnny asks, leaning over my shoulder.

With a smirk, I lift the CD into the air and wave it around. It's

Garrison who recognizes it first, his deep laugh drawing Brody's attention.

"Risky move, Darren," Garrison says.

I shrug. "It's such a beautiful photo, it would be a waste not to show it off again. Remind everyone about it."

Brody finally catches on to what I've got and pounces. With his wife on his lap, he can't get close enough to grab it from me, especially not when Johnny takes it and cracks into a fit of rumbled laughter.

"How come I don't think I've ever seen this?"

"We changed it after the first run sold out," Garrison says.

"Oh, precious Brody," Poppy coos.

Anna pats Brody's chest and tries to soothe him. "You look handsome."

"It's a collector's piece. Elle's grandma was holding on to it for us," I tease.

Delaney runs a hand down my arm, grinning. "She probably knew we would do this."

"It's no wonder she and Eliza got along so well," Poppy says while pulling all of the Styrofoam cups from the holders she and Garrison hauled in.

She hands Delaney hers, and Rory reads the flavour scribbled on the side of it.

"Banana pudding?"

"Careful there, Rory. Delaney takes her milkshake flavour very seriously," I warn teasingly.

Johnny rolls his lips while Brody chuckles. Delaney looks at them both, growing suspicious.

"Why do you look like that?" she asks.

Garrison stops looking through the box he grabbed. "I've never seen that on the flavour list before."

Poppy smirks, glancing at me as if to warn me before saying, "That's because they stopped offering that kind, what? Seven years ago now, Darren?"

"So, how come I've been ordering it for twice that long, then?" Delaney asks, assuming they're lying to her.

I take a seat on the floor beside her and watch every slight twitch in her expression as everyone continues talking.

"Darren told them to keep sellin' it to you. Wouldn't let them get rid of it completely," Brody explains.

First, there's confusion and then a flush of pink. Delaney's lips curl at the corners in a delicate smile that I want to feel against my skin. She sighs, the sound light and easy, before her hand is on my cheek, holding me steady. Our kiss is full of everything she won't say in front of everyone, and I soak it all in.

"You're a tattletale," I hear Anna scold Brody.

His twanged voice filters through the room, but I ignore it. When Delaney pulls back, I immediately want her close again. I'm positive that's how it will always be.

The sound of the front door opening and closing draws her attention from me. There's a slight stiffening of her muscles that urges me to follow her gaze.

"Sorry we're late. I made a couple stops along the way," Bryce says, releasing Daisy's hand.

Her fiancée joins us in the living room with a soft smile and a cheery hello while she stays in place. Abbie beams from beside her, a box of donuts in her arms. And behind her—

"Sasha," Delaney mutters.

My immediate reaction is to be angry with Bryce for bringing her here. But as my ex-wife shuffles in place, clearly uncomfortable, it slips to frustration.

"I'm not staying," she clarifies, letting go of Abbie's shoulder. The way she's staring right at Delaney seems odd. I've never seen her look at her like that. "Can I talk to you?"

"Uh, yeah, sure."

Delaney pushes onto her feet and chews on her lip before leaving my side. She stops in front of my daughter before anything, giving her a genuine smile and a rub on the arm.

"Hi, Abbie. Are those donuts?"

"Yep! Yellow sprinkles only, like the ones you get for me on Sundays."

My throat clogs. Suddenly, all of our friends are looking at me, and I glare at every single one of them until they get back to work.

"That was really thoughtful," Elle says.

"How about you hand them to your dad so everyone can have one?" Sasha suggests.

"Okay!"

Abbie rushes toward me, and I reluctantly let the two women out of my sight. Once they step outside, I lose the ability to hear them too.

Poppy pinches the back of my arm when I stay silent for a moment too long, and I quickly snap into motion. Delaney can take care of herself . . . even if having to do so with my ex-wife won't ever sit right with me.

Delaney

"You didn't have to bring her here," I blurt out the moment I step outside with Sasha. "I know it's your week."

Sasha tongues her cheek, antsy gaze far away. "I'm sorry."

"What?"

"I'm sorry. For what happened back then. I was cruel to you."

I pause, running that back in my head. It still sounds as unbelievable the fourth time as it did the first.

"Did Bryce force you to say that? Because I didn't tell her to get involved here."

"No. Bryce can't force me to do anything. All she did was

remind me that I was a bitch to you and that Abbie doesn't need to pick up on that energy. Not now."

"Did something happen?"

She fidgets, still avoiding my gaze. "I'm pregnant."

"Oh. Well, congratulations," I offer, beyond awkward. "Does Darren know?"

"Not yet. I didn't come to share that, anyway. I'd just like to not bring another baby into an environment so hostile. Abbie's old enough to pick up on these things now, and with a new sibling, I worry she'll already be upset with all of the changes coming."

"So, you want a truce or something?"

Her laugh is short, almost disbelieving. "A truce would work, yeah. You're not a threat to me, Delaney. What Darren and I had, or didn't have, I guess, doesn't matter anymore. I'm assuming you're not going anywhere. That's why he sold the house."

"Yeah, it is."

"Okay. Well, I just wanted to clear the air."

I can't say that I'd consider it cleared entirely, but at least I'm not choking on her pollution anymore. This has to be better than before. We'll never be friends, and that's perfectly okay with me. All I need is some room to try and be a part of her daughter's life without feeling like I'm being judged for everything I do.

"Thank you," I say.

"Abbie wanted to stay for a while. If you're okay with that, I'll come back in a few hours to get her."

My brows jump, a fleck of hope floating in my chest. "Of course that's okay. She's always welcome."

"She chose those donuts especially for you."

"You've done a great job with her, Sasha. Both of you have," I say.

The small smile on her lips is genuine. "Thanks."

"I'll let Darren know the plan."

She nods and starts down the sidewalk, heading for the SUV

that's still running. I watch her get inside before going back inside.

The moment I shut the door behind me, everyone turns to me, their curiosity obvious. Bryce sits on the arm of the couch, staring as if she's trying to speak mind to mind. I know her well enough by now not to need to hear the question she's asking.

The appreciation in my gaze answers her.

Darren snares my eyes once I join him and Abbie on the floor. He takes my hand, stroking my fingers and the ring I never take off.

I nod at him and lean into his body. His arms bracket me, and Abbie hands me a donut. Our friends start to chatter again, seeing that I'm okay, and I swallow the emotions trying to escape.

This moment is perfect. A sneak peek into the rest of forever.

EXTENDED EPILOGUE

SIX MONTHS LATER

There's something to be said about soulmates.

I don't mean the type you read about in fantasy novels, but the real ones. The non-fiction type that you don't hear about as often. Not romantic partners, but best friends. I've been lucky enough in my life to have both, and while I love Darren, we were always written in the stars. Chalking up what we've been through as just something that was always meant to be negates what we overcame to be together.

Best friends, on the other hand, yeah, I'll take soulmates. Poppy's that to me. She's someone who I found through Darren, but who never truly was just my boyfriend's little sister. Instead, she became my family. A sister who I hadn't found because of blood, but by fate.

I couldn't have ever thought that by falling in love with Darren, I'd get Poppy too. It wasn't a coincidence that the guy who I'd recognize as my forever would have a sister who I would connect with so deeply to the point we became best friends. That was all fate.

Standing beside her at the altar today, watching as she

marries a man who would get on his hands and knees and pave the ground she walks on . . . it's surreal. Looking past her at where her brother stands with his daughter as he watches me with such raw, open love might be even more so.

I've spent the last few weeks helping Poppy perfect this day, and I'd be lying if I hadn't found myself daydreaming a few times about what marrying Darren would be like. The draw for that experience nearly sent me home once or twice in tears. It's too intense for me to think about often.

Marrying Darren is my childhood, teenage, and adult dream.

"I understand that you've both prepared your own vows," the minister announces.

I swallow, forcing myself to look away from Darren. Focusing on Poppy and Garrison, I find myself at a loss for words once again. The soon-to-be husband and wife are simply stunning together.

Poppy's let her hair go to her natural brown for today and chose a classic low bun. The veil tucked inside of it is long, draping past her dress and onto the custom stage set up on their property, a gorgeous new home hovering in the distance. We all knew she needed a classic look to allow her dress to hold the full attention of everyone here today. And that it did.

The off-shoulder dress hangs off her arms and drapes down her body with an elegance that stole my breath the first time I saw her in it at the bridal shop. It's non-traditional in the sense that instead of white, it's silver, and covered top to bottom in shimmer, making her look less like a bride and more like a goddess.

Garrison wasn't the only one crying as he watched her walk down the aisle. I don't think a single one of us up here could help it. Even Bryce's tears fell to join ours on stage before Daisy swiped them away.

I swallow the ball in my throat when Garrison clears his and adjusts his grip on Poppy's hands.

"I've spent hours on this, Poppy, but I've still only managed to come up with a few lines that I feel do justice to describe the way I feel about you. It's impossible to take everything you make me feel and somehow fit them into words. Insulting is what it is. You're beyond words.

"There isn't a single piece of you that I haven't seen and loved. Your spirit, the bravery you have in spades, your honesty, and the openness you have to learn what you don't know. Not only about yourself or the world, but others around you. Before I met you, I didn't know people could be like that. So viscerally sincere with a positive outlook in any situation. You've taken me by the shoulders and shaken me so hard that you've rattled all of these new pieces of myself free that I didn't know existed before you. I think that's what I love most about you. The way you are the only person I've ever met who's known that those pieces were there. And ever since you became my person, I haven't been the same. I won't be that man from the past ever again. Fuck, I won't even be the same man I am today, tomorrow. That's what you do to me, honey. And I'm looking forward to being ever-changing with you for the rest of my life. As husband and wife."

The burn in my eyes must pale in comparison to the one in his. The rough sniff that follows his words cuts through the awed silence, and then Poppy's leaning into him and thumbing away the tears dripping down his cheeks. I look away, knowing I'm one second from ruining this moment with a sob.

Instead, I find Darren. He's already watching me, his eyes glistening. I try to smile, but I know it's weak. He rubs his chest and holds my gaze for a few moments longer, until we're pulled away by Poppy's voice.

There's a smack on my hand, and I look over to see Bryce staring straight ahead at the bride but taking my hand into hers. The squeeze she gives me is tight, and I know she's doing the same with Daisy's without having to look and confirm.

"I knew I should have gone first," Poppy scolds half-heartedly. Wet laughter follows, reminding me that everyone here loves these two as much as they deserve. "Garrison—my Sir Douchealot—I've never had too much trouble with putting my feelings into words before, but as I wrote these, I struggled so badly that I considered bribing you so that I didn't have to. Obviously, I didn't give up the way I thought I was going to. How could I, when you were lying in bed beside me as I tapped my pen to this paper? One look down at you with your laptop open on your lap and a wrinkle between your brows, and I knew I had to figure it out.

"I know that when you look at me, you see this invincible woman with an endless supply of confidence and wit. But I'm here to tell you today that you're wrong. Before I met you, I had half of everything I do now."

Poppy cuts herself off, sniffling as the paper in her hand shakes. The man in front of her slides his hold to her wrists, keeping her hold steady.

"I didn't need you to teach me how to love myself, so you showed me how to allow someone else to love me instead. That was a lesson that I'd skipped, assuming that if I'd had enough confidence in myself, I'd never need anyone else. There would be no heartbreak or disappointment, because I'd never let myself down the way someone else could. Only, I hadn't known how much I'd like sharing some of that responsibility. And you, Garrison, have not only shared that responsibility, but you've taken it over as your own. You love me so fiercely, so openly, that sometimes, I can just . . . *live*, because I know you're there. I'm sure I'll never be able to truly thank you enough for the strength you've offered me, but I hope this is a start. I have the rest of forever to finish."

With a sticky throat, I watch as they ignore the rest of us and the order of the ceremony and kiss, sealing their declarations with the first of their marriage.

And for the rest of the ceremony, there's nothing the rest of us can do but watch as they promise to spend the rest of their lives together. Forever and always.

The happy couple dances on the grass, beneath the lights of the drive-in screen and to the music being projected through the field. I watch in silence, my heart full and aching with the love I've seen today. From the ceremony, the first dance beneath the setting sun, and the laughter booming from the bed of Brody's truck as he drove us all from the ranch, to the drive-in hours after all the guests went home.

It would have been easiest for us to stay at the Becketts' new home for the night, but the newlyweds demanded we come back to Cherry Peak despite the drive and the time. By two in the morning, we were here, at the drive-in. Darren broke into the newly completed projection room and turned it into a DJ booth, and we've been dancing, drinking, and singing together ever since.

A warm chest meets my back before arms curl around me. "Are you happy, Elle?"

I dab away a rogue tear and nod, leaning into Darren's hold. He sways us, his cheek rubbing my temple.

"I'm so happy," I whisper.

"Where do you want to get married?"

Turning in his arms, I lift my eyes, holding his. "Here."

"At the drive-in?"

"It's fitting. It's our place."

He tucks my hair behind my ear and nods. Lowering his head, he presses our foreheads together and slowly leads me into a slow dance. I press my hands against his back and smile.

"Here it is. All that's left is for you to tell me when," he rasps.

I laugh softly. "I don't think that's how it's supposed to work."

"Why not? We're already engaged."

"We are? Since when?"

He reaches behind his back, and suddenly, my promise ring

is being pulled off my finger. I watch his expression closely, but he gives nothing away. Not until another ring is being slid back into place, this one heavier, thicker even.

My laugh is weak, stunted when I pull my hand from behind him and lift it into the space between us. The huge, square-shaped diamond has my head shaking, tears I can't afford to lose pooling in my eyes.

"You're supposed to ask," I croak.

"Would you like me to get on my knees again, Delaney?"

My answer is instant as I lift my hands to hold his face. "No. I'll marry you, Darren. I've been dreaming of marrying you for fifteen years."

"Next week."

"What?"

"Marry me next week. I can't wait any longer."

There's no point in arguing. We've been ready to be husband and wife for far too long already. Why delay the inevitable?

"Next week," I confirm, a giddy smile cutting through my cheeks.

He steals a kiss, lips hovering when he says, "I can't wait to start forever with you, Mrs. Delaney Huntsly."

"It's about time."

Nothing has ever sounded so right.

Thank you for reading Choosing Forever! If you enjoyed it, please leave a review on Amazon and Goodreads.

The Cherry Peak series is finished, but this is not the last time you will see some of these characters. Next, we take a trip to Oak Point, the home of Into The Shade, Alberta's most popular tattoo studio.
Book 1 in the Oak Point series is coming in October, with Shade's book. (Runaway bride, spicy lessons)

While you're waiting for more of these characters, jump into my backlist! Want to learn a bit more about Garrison before he met Poppy? Or meet Anna before she came to Cherry Peak? Jump into my Greatest Love series.

To be kept up to date on all my releases, check out my website!
www.hannahcowanauthor.com
Subscribe to my newsletter now!

Acknowledgements

Cherry Peak will always feel like home to me. Not only because it's really set only a few hours from where I grew up, but because these characters feel like family. The Steeles, Becketts, Mitchells, and Huntslys are four families which mean so much to me and to all of you.

When I first wrote Strung Along, I had no idea how much these characters would demand their own stories. It was supposed to be just one book. A standalone in a new genre that I had never written before. Instead, it came to life and took control of my brain. Now, we're at the end of the fifth book and I feel very, very overwhelmed about that.

I want to say thank you to all of you for being here and for encouraging me to write these stories. I'm not sure where I would be if I had never written Anna's journey to Cherry Peak, Poppy's confidence and fearlessness, Johnny's open heart, Bryce's take-no-shit attitude, or Delaney's heartbreak. So, thank you. I wrote these characters for all of us.

Now, before I start to cry, here are my other thank yous.

As always, I owe a very big thank you to the women in my life who are my girl gang. Nicole and Becci, you have all of my love. The person I am now has you to thank.

To Sierra, I love you endlessly. Thank you for being only a text away and for being here on this journey with me.

To Lauren-Brooke, thank you for being the constant voice in

my head reminding me about something that I should have done four days ago. I love you.

To my team of creative masterminds, Sandra, Julie, Mary, Andra, Silver, and Cassie. Thank you for the thousands of things you do for me. These beautiful book covers, designs, and social posts are all because of you.

To everyone who has helped share this series and bring them into the world, thank you. This last book is for you.